JAMES FENIMORE COOPER

THE SPY

A TALE OF THE NEUTRAL GROUND

Elibron Classics
www.elibron.com

Elibron Classics series.

ISBN 0-543-89950-0 (paperback)
ISBN 0-543-89949-7 (hardcover)

This Elibron Classics book contains the complete text of the
edition published in 1864 by Routledge, Warne, and Routledge, London.

AUTHOR'S INTRODUCTION

The Author has often been asked if there were any foundation in real life for the delineation of the principal character in this book. He can give no clearer answer to the question than by laying before his readers a simple statement of the facts connected with its original publication.

Many years since, the writer of this volume was at the residence of an illustrious man, who had been employed in various situations of high trust during the darkest days of the American Revolution. The discourse turned upon the effects which great political excitement produces on character, and the purifying consequences of a love of country, when that sentiment is powerfully and generally awakened in a people. He who, from his years, his services, and his knowledge of men, was best qualified to take the lead in such a conversation, was the principal speaker. After dwelling on the marked manner in which the great struggle of the nation, during the war of 1775, had given a new and honorable direction to the thoughts and practices of multitudes whose time had formerly been engrossed by the most vulgar concerns of life, he illustrated his opinions by relating an anecdote, the truth of which he could attest as a personal witness.

The dispute between England and the United States of America, though not strictly a family quarrel, had many of the features of a civil war. The people of the latter were never properly and constitutionally subject to the people of the former, but the inhabitants of both countries owed allegiance to a common king. The Americans, as a nation, disavowed this allegiance, and thc English choosing to support their sovereign in the attempt to regain his power, most of the feelings of an internal struggle were involved in the conflict. A large proportion of the emigrants from Europe, then established in the colonies, took part with the crown; and there were many districts in which their influence, united to that of the Americans who refused to lay aside their allegiance, gave a decided preponderance to the royal cause. America was then too young, and too much in need of every heart and hand, to regard these partial divisions, small as they were in actual amount, with indifference. The evil was greatly increased by the activity of the English in profiting by these internal dissensions; and it became doubly serious when it was found that attempts were made to raise various corps of provincial troops, who were to be banded with those from Europe, to reduce the young republic to subjection. Congress named an especial and a secret committee, therefore, for the express purpose of defeating this object. Of this committee Mr.—, the narrator of the anecdote, was chairman.

In the discharge of the novel duties which now devolved on him, Mr.— had occasion to employ an agent whose services differed but little from those of a common spy. This man, as will easily be understood, belonged to a condition in life which rendered him the least reluctant to appear in so equivocal a character. He was poor, ignorant, so far as the usual instruction was concerned; but cool, shrewd, and fearless by nature. It was his office to learn in what part of the country the agents of the crown were making their efforts to embody men, to repair to the place, enlist, appear zealous in the cause he affected to serve, and otherwise to get possession of as many of the secrets of the enemy as possible. The last he of course communicated to his employers, who took all the means in their power to counteract the plans of the English, and frequently with success.

It will readily be conceived that a service like this was attended with great personal hazard. In addition to the danger of discovery, there was the daily risk of falling into the hands of the Americans themselves, who invariably visited sins of this nature more severely on the natives of the country than on the Europeans who fell into their hands. In fact, the agent of Mr.— was several times arrested by the local authorities; and, in one instance, he was actually condemned by his exasperated countrymen to the gallows. Speedy and private orders to the jailer alone saved him from an ignominious death. He was permitted to escape; and this seeming and indeed actual peril was of great aid in supporting his assumed character among the English. By the Americans, in his little sphere, he was denounced as a bold and inveterate Tory. In this manner he continued to serve his country in secret during the early years of the struggle, hourly environed by danger, and the constant subject of unmerited opprobrium.

In the year—, Mr.— was named to a high and honorable employment at a European court. Before vacating his seat in

Congress, he reported to that body an outline of the circumstances related, necessarily suppressing the name of his agent, and demanding an appropriation in behalf of a man who had been of so much use, at so great risk. A suitable sum was voted; and its delivery was confided to the chairman of the secret committee.

Mr.— took the necessary means to summon his agent to a personal interview. They met in a wood at midnight. Here Mr.— complimented his companion on his fidelity and adroitness; explained the necessity of their communications being closed; and finally tendered the money. The other drew back, and declined receiving it. "The country has need of all its means," he said; "as for myself, I can work, or gain a livelihood in various ways." Persuasion was useless, for patriotism was uppermost in the heart of this remarkable individual; and Mr.— departed, bearing with him the gold he had brought, and a deep respect for the man who had so long hazarded his life, unrequited, for the cause they served in common.

The writer is under an impression that, at a later day, the agent of Mr.— consented to receive a remuneration for what he had done; but it was not until his country was entirely in a condition to bestow it.

It is scarcely necessary to add, that an anecdote like this, simply but forcibly told by one of its principal actors, made a deep impression on all who heard it. Many years later, circumstances, which it is unnecessary to relate, and of an entirely adventitious nature, induced the writer to publish a novel, which proved to be, what he little foresaw at the time, the first of a tolerably long series. The same adventitious causes which gave birth to the book determined its scene and its general character. The former was laid in a foreign country; and the latter embraced a crude effort to describe foreign manners. When this tale was published, it became matter of reproach among the author's friends, that he, an American in heart as in birth, should give to the world a work which aided perhaps, in some slight degree, to feed the imaginations of the young and unpracticed among his own countrymen, by pictures drawn from a state of society so different from that to which he belonged. The writer, while he knew how much of what he had done was purely accidental, felt the reproach to be one that, in a measure, was just. As the only atonement in his power, he determined to inflict a second book, whose Subject should admit of no cavil, not only on the world, but on himself. He chose patriotism for his theme: and to those who read this introduction and the book itself, it is scarcely necessary to add, that he took the hero of the anecdote just related as the best illustration of his subject.

Since the original publication of The Spy, there have appeared several accounts of different persons who are supposed to have been in the author's mind while writing the book. As Mr.— did not mention the name of his agent, the writer never knew any more of his identity with this or that individual, than has been here explained. Both Washington and Sir Henry Clinton had an unusual number of secret emissaries; in a war that partook so much of a domestic character, and in which the contending parties were people of the same blood and language, it could scarcely be otherwise.

The style of the book has been revised by the author in this edition. In this respect, he has endeavored to make it more worthy of the favor with which it has been received; though he is compelled to admit there are faults so interwoven with the structure of the tale that, as in the case of a decayed edifice, it would cost perhaps less to reconstruct than to repair. Five-and-twenty years have been as ages with most things connected with America. Among other advantages, that of her literature has not been the least. So little was expected from the publication of an original work of this description, at the time it was written, that the first volume of The Spy was actually printed several months, before the author felt a sufficient inducement to write a line of the second. The efforts expended on a hopeless task are rarely worthy of him who makes them, however low it may be necessary to rate the standard of his general merit.

One other anecdote connected with the history of this book may give the reader some idea of the hopes of an American author, in the first quarter of the present century. As the second volume was slowly printing, from manuscript that was barely dry when it went into the compositor's hands, the publisher intimated that the work might grow to a length that would consume the profits. To set his mind at rest, the last chapter was actually written, printed, and paged, several weeks before the chapters which precede it were even thought of. This circumstance, while it cannot excuse, may serve to explain the manner in which the actors are hurried off the scene.

A great change has come over the country since this book was originally written. The nation is passing from the gristle into the bone, and the common mind is beginning to keep even pace with the growth of the body politic. The march from Vera Cruz to Mexico was made under the orders of that gallant soldier who, a quarter of a century before, was mentioned with honor, in the last chapter of this very book. Glorious as was that march, and brilliant as were its results in a military point of view, a stride was then made by the nation, in a moral sense, that has hastened it by an age, in its progress toward real independence and high political influence. The guns that filled the valley of the Aztecs with their thunder, have been heard in echoes on the other side of the Atlantic, producing equally hope or apprehension.

There is now no enemy to fear, but the one that resides within. By accustoming ourselves to regard even the people as erring beings, and by using the restraints that wisdom has adduced from experience, there is much reason to hope that the same Providence which has so well aided us in our infancy, may continue to smile on our manhood.

Coopers town, March 29, 1849.

CHAPTER I

And though amidst the calm of thought entire,
Some high and haughty features might betray
A soul impetuous once—'twas earthly fire
That fled composure's intellectual ray.
As Etna's fires grow dim before the rising day.

— Gertrude of Wyoming.

It was near the close of the year 1780 that a solitary traveler was seen pursuing his way through one of the numerous little valleys of Westchester[1]. The easterly wind, with its dulling dampness and increasing violence, gave unerring notice of the approach of a storm, which, as usual, might be expected to continue for several days; and the experienced eye of the traveler was turned in vain, through the darkness of the evening, in quest of some convenient shelter, in which, for the term of his confinement by the rain that already began to mix the atmosphere in a thick mist, he might obtain such accomodations as his purposes required. Nothing whatever offered but the small and inconvenient tenements of the lower order of the inhabitants, with whom, in that immediate neighborhood, he did not think it either safe or politic to trust himself.

The county of Westchester, after the British had obtained possession of thc island of Ncw York,[2] bccamc common ground, in which both parties continued to act for the remainder of the

---

[1] As cach statc of thc Amcrican Union has its own countics, it often happens that there are several which bear the same name. The scene of this tale is in New York, whose county of Westchester is the nearest adjoining to the city.

[2] The city of New York is situated on an island called Manhattan: but it is at one point separated from the county of Westchester by a creek of only a few feet in width. The bridge at this spot is called King's Bridge. It was the scene of many skirmishes during the war, and is alluded to in this tale. Every Manhattanese knows the difference between "Manhattan Island" and the "island of Manhattan." The first is applied to a small district in the vicinity of Corlaer's Hook, while the last embraces the whole island; or the city and county of New York as it is termed in the laws.

war of the Revolution. A large proportion of its inhabitants, either restrained by their attachments, or influenced by their fears, affected a neutrality they did not feel. The lower towns were, of course, more particularly under the dominion of the crown, while the upper, finding a security from the vicinity of the continental troops, were bold in asserting their revolutionary opinions, and their right to govern themselves. Great numbers, however, wore masks, which even to this day have not been thrown aside; and many an individual has gone down to the tomb, stigmatized as a foe to the right of his countrymen, while, in secret, he has been the useful agent of the leaders of the Revolution; and, on the other hand, could the hidden repositories of divers flaming patriots have been opened to the light of day, royal protections would have been discovered concealed under piles of British gold.

At the sound of the tread of the noble horse ridden by the traveler, the mistress of the farmhouse he was passing at the time might be seen cautiously opening the door of the building to examine the stranger; and perhaps, with an averted face communicating the result of her observations to her husband, who, in the rear of the building, was prepared to seek, if necessary, his ordinary place of concealment in the adjacent woods. The valley was situated about midway in the length of the county, and was sufficiently near to both armies to make the restitution of stolen goods no uncommon occurrence in that vicinity. It is true, the same articles were not always regained; but a summary substitute was generally resorted to, in the absence of legal justice, which restored to the loser the amount of his loss, and frequently with no inconsiderable addition for the temporary use of his property. In short, the law was momentarily extinct in that particular district, and justice was administered subject to the bias of personal interests and the passions of the strongest.

The passage of a stranger, with an appearance of somewhat doubtful character, and mounted on an animal which, although unfurnished, with any of the ordinary trappings of war partook largely of the bold and upright carriage that distinguished his rider, gave rise to many surmises among the gazing inmates of the different habitations; and in some instances, where conscience was more than ordinarily awake, to no little alarm.

Tired with the exercise of a day of unusual fatigue, and anxious to obtain a speedy shelter from the increasing violence of the storm, that now began to change its character to large drops of driving rain, the traveler determined, as a matter of necessity, to make an application for admission to the next dwelling that offered. An opportunity was not long wanting: and riding through a pair of neglected bars, he knocked loudly at the outer door of a building of a very humble exterior, without quitting the saddle. A female of middle age, with an outward hearing but little more prepossessing than that of her dwelling, appeared to answer the summons. The startled woman half closed her door again in affright, as she saw, by the glare of a large wood fire, a mounted man so unexpectedly near its threshold; and an expression of terror mingled with her natural curiosity, as she required his pleasure.

Although the door was too nearly closed to admit of a minute scrutiny of the accommodations within, enough had been seen to cause the horseman to endeavor, once more, to penetrate the gloom, with longing eyes, in search of a more promising roof, before, with an ill-concealed reluctance, he stated his necessities and wishes. His request was listened to with evident unwillingness, and, while yet unfinished, it was eagerly interrupted by the reply:

"I can't say I like to give lodgings to a stranger in these ticklish times," said the female, in a pert, sharp key. "I'm nothing but a forlorn lone body; or, what's the same thing, there's nobody but the old gentleman at home; but a half mile farther up the road is a house you can get entertainment, and that for nothing. I am sure 'twill be much convenienter to them, and more agreeable to me—because, and I said before, Harvey is away; I wish he'd take advice, and leave off wandering; he's well to do in the world by this time; and he ought to leave off his uncertain courses, and settle himself, handsomely, in life, like other men of his years and property. But Harvey Birch will have his own way, and die vagabond after all!"

The horseman did not wait to hear more than the advice to pursue his course up the road; but he had slowly turned his horse towards the bars and was gathering the folds of an ample cloak around his manly form, preparatory to facing the storm again, when something in the speech of the female suddenly arrested the movement.

"Is this, then, the dwelling of Harvey Birch?" he inquired, in an involuntary manner, apparently checking himself, as he was about to utter more.

"Why, one can hardly say it is his dwelling," replied the other, drawing a hurried breath, like one eager to answer; "he is never in it, or so seldom, that I hardly remember his face, when he does think it worth his while to show it to his poor old father and me. But it matters little to me, I'm sure, if he ever comes back again, or not;—turn in the first gate on your left;—no, I care but little, for my part, whether Harvey ever shows his face again or not—not I"—and she closed the door abruptly on the horseman, who gladly extended his ride a half mile farther, to obtain lodgings which promised both more comfort and greater security.

Sufficient light yet remained to enable the traveler to distinguish the improvements[3] which had been made in the cultivation, and in the general appearance of the grounds around the building to which he was no approaching. The house was of stone, long, low, and with a small wing at each extremity. A piazza, extending along the front, with neatly turned pillars of wood, together with the good order and preservation of the fences and outbuildings, gave the place an air altogether superior to the common farmhouses of the country. After leading his horse behind an angle of the wall, where it was in some degree protected from the wind and rain, the traveler threw his valise, over his arm, and knocked loudly at the entrance of the building for admission. An aged black soon appeared; and without seeming to think it necessary, under the circumstances, to consult his superiors,—first taking one prying look at the applicant, by the light of the candle in his hand,—he acceded to the request for accommodations. The traveler was shown into an extremely neat parlor, where a fire had been lighted to cheer the dullness of an easterly storm and an October evening. After giving the valise into the keeping of his civil attendant, and politely repeating his request to the old gentleman, who arose to receive him, and paying his compliments to the three ladies who were seated at work with their nee-

---

[3] Improvements is used by the Americans to express every degree of change in converting land from its state of wilderness to that of cultivation. In this meaning of the word, it is an improvement to fell the trees; and it is valued precisely by the supposed amount of the cost.

dles, the stranger commenced laying aside some of the outer garments which he had worn in his ride.

On taking an extra handkerchief from his neck, and removing a cloak of blue cloth, with a surtout of the same material, he exhibited to the scrutiny of the observant family party, a tall and extremely graceful person, of apparently fifty years of age. His countenance evinced a settled composure and dignity; his nose was straight, and approaching to Grecian; his eye, of a gray color, was quiet, thoughtful, and rather melancholy; the mouth and lower part of his face being expressive of decision and much character. His dress, being suited to the road, was simple and plain, but such as was worn by the higher class of his countrymen; he wore his own hair, dressed in a manner that gave a military air to his appearance, and which was rather heightened by his erect and conspicuously graceful carriage. His whole appearance was so impressive and so decidedly that of a gentleman, that as he finished laying aside the garments, the ladies arose from their seats, and, together with the master of the house, they received anew, and returned the complimentary greetings which were again offered.

The host was by several years the senior of the traveler, and by his manner, dress, and everything around him, showed he had seen much of life and the best society. The ladies were, a maiden of forty, and two much younger, who did not seem, indeed, to have reached half those years. The bloom of the elder of these ladies had vanished, but her eyes and fine hair gave an extremely agreeable expression to her countenance; and there was a softness and an affability in her deportment, that added a charm many more juvenile faces do not possess. The sisters, for such the resemblance between the younger females denoted them to be, were in all the pride of youth, and the roses, so eminently the property of the Westchester fair, glowed on their cheeks, and lighted their deep blue eyes with that luster which gives so much pleasure to the beholder, and which indicated so much internal innocence and peace. There was much of that feminine delicacy in the appearance of the three, which distinguishes the sex in this country; and, like the gentleman, their demeanor proved them to be women of the higher order of life.

After handing a glass of excellent Madeira to his guest, Mr. Wharton, for so was the owner of this retired estate called, resumed his seat by the fire, with another in his own hand. For a moment he paused, as if debating with his politeness, but at length threw an inquiring glance on the stranger, as he inquired,—

"To whose health am I to have the honor of drinking?"

The traveler had also seated himself, and he sat unconsciously gazing on the fire, while Mr. Wharton spoke; turning his eyes slowly on his host with a look of close observation, he replied, while a faint tinge gathered on his features,—

"Mr. Harper."

"Mr. Harper," resumed the other, with the formal precision of that day, "I have the honor to drink your health, and to hope you will sustain no injury from the rain to which you have been exposed."

Mr. Harper bowed in silence to the compliment, and he soon resumed the meditations from which he had been interrupted, and for which the long ride he had that day made, in the wind, might seem a very natural apology.

The young ladies had again taken their seats beside the work-stand, while their aunt, Miss Jeanette Peyton, withdrew to superintend the preparations necessary to appease the hunger of their unexpected visitor. A short silence prevailed, during .which Mr. Harper was apparently enjoying the change in his situation, when Mr. Wharton again broke it, by inquiring whether smoke was disagreeable to his companion; to which, receiving an answer in the negative, he immediately resumed the pipe which had been laid aside at the entrance of the traveler.

There was an evident desire on the part of the host to enter into conversation, but either from an apprehension of treading on dangerous ground, or an unwillingness to intrude upon the rather studied taciturnity of his guest, he several times hesitated, before he could venture to make any further remark. At length, a movement from Mr. Harper, as he raised his eyes to the party in the room, encouraged him to proceed.

"I find it very difficult," said Mr. Wharton, cautiously avoiding at first, such subjects as he wished to introduce, "to procure that quality of tobacco for my evenings' amusement to which I have been accustomed."

"I should think the shops in New York might furnish the best in the country," calmly rejoined the other.

"Why—yes," returned the host in rather a hesitating manner, lifting his eyes to the face of Harper, and lowering them quickly under his steady look, "there must be plenty in town; but the war has made communication with the city, however innocent, too dangerous to be risked for so trifling an article as tobacco."

The box from which Mr. Wharton had just taken a supply for his pipe was lying open, within a few inches of the elbow of Harper, who took a small quantity from its contents, and applied it to his tongue, in a manner perfectly natural, but one that filled his companion with alarm. Without, however, observing that the quality was of the most approved kind, the traveler relieved his host by relapsing again into his meditations. Mr. Wharton now felt unwilling to lose the advantage he had gained, and, making an effort of more than usual vigor, he continued,—

"I wish from the bottom of my heart, this unnatural struggle was over, that we might again meet our friends and relatives in peace and love."

"It is much to be desired," said Harper, emphatically, again raising his eyes to the countenance of his host.

"I hear of no movement of consequence, since the arrival of our new allies," said Mr. Wharton, shaking the ashes from his pipe, and turning his back to the other under the pretense of receiving a coal from his youngest daughter.

"None have yet reached the public, I believe."

"Is it thought any important steps are about to be taken?" continued Mr. Wharton, still occupied with his daughter, yet suspending his employment, in expectation of a reply.

"Is it intimated any are in agitation?"

"Oh! nothing in particular; but it is natural to expect some new enterprise from so powerful a force as that under Rochambeau."

Harper made an assenting inclination with his head, but no other reply, to this remark; while Mr. Wharton, after lighting his pipe, resumed the subject.

"They appear more active in the south; Gates and Cornwallis seem willing to bring the war to an issue there."

The brow of Harper contracted, and a deeper shade of melancholy crossed his features; his eye kindled with a transient beam of fire, that spoke a latent source of deep feeling. The admiring gaze of the younger of the sisters had barely time to read its expression, before it passed away, leaving in its room the acquired composure which marked the countenance of the stranger, and that impressive dignity which so conspicuously denotes the empire of reason.

The elder sister made one or two movements in her chair, before she ventured to say, in a tone which partook in no small measure of triumph,—

"General Gates has been less fortunate with the earl, than with General Burgoyne."

"But General Gates is an Englishman, Sarah," cried the younger lady, with quickness; then, coloring to the eyes at her own boldness, she employed herself in tumbling over the contents of her work basket, silently hoping the remark would be unnoticed.

The traveler had turned his face from one sister to the other, as they had spoken in succession, and an almost imperceptible movement of the muscles of his mouth betrayed a new emotion, as he playfully inquired of the younger,—

"'May I venture to ask what inference you would draw from that fact?"

Frances blushed yet deeper at this direct appeal to her opinions upon a subject on which she had incautiously spoken in the presence of a stranger; but finding an answer necessary, after some little hesitation, and with a good deal of stammering in her manner, she replied,—

"Only—only—sir—my sister and myself sometimes differ in our opinions of the prowess of the British." A smile of much meaning played on a face of infantile innocency, as she concluded.

"On what particular points of their prowess do you differ?" continued Harper, meeting her look of animation with a smile of almost paternal softness.

"Sarah thinks the British are never beaten, while I do not put so much faith in their invincibility."

The traveler listened to her with that pleased indulgence, with which virtuous age loves to contemplate the ardor of youthful innocence; but making no reply, he turned to the fire, and continued for some time gazing on its embers, in silence.

Mr. Wharton had in vain endeavored to pierce the disguise of his guest's political feelings; but, while there was nothing forbidding in his countenance, there was nothing communicative; on the contrary it was strikingly reserved; and the master of the house arose, in profound ignorance of what, in those days, was the most material point in the character of his guest, to lead the way into another room, and to the supper table. Mr. Harper offered his hand to Sarah Wharton, and they entered the room together; while Frances followed, greatly at a loss to know whether she had not wounded the feelings of her father's inmate.

The storm began to rage with great violence without; and the dashing rain on the sides of the building awakened that silent sense of enjoyment, which is excited by such sounds in a room of quiet comfort and warmth, when a loud summons at the outer door again called the faithful black to the portal. In a minute the servant returned, and informed his master that another traveler, overtaken by the storm, desired to be admitted to the house for a shelter through the night.

At the first sounds of the impatient summons of this new applicant, Mr. Wharton had risen from his seat in evident uneasiness; and with eyes glancing with quickness from his guest to the door of the room, he seemed to be expecting something to proceed from this second interruption, connected with the stranger who had occasioned the first. He scarcely had time to bid the black, with a faint voice, to show this second corner in, before the door was thrown hastily open, and the stranger himself entered the apartment. He paused a moment, as the person of Harper met his view, and then, in a more formal manner, repeated the request he had before made through the servant. Mr. Wharton and his family disliked the appearance of this new visitor excessively; but the inclemency of the weather, and the uncertainty of the consequences, if he were refused the desired lodgings, compelled the old gentleman to give a reluctant acquiescence.

Some of the dishes were replaced by the orders of Miss Peyton, and the weather-beaten intruder was invited to partake of the remains of the repast, from which the party had just risen. Throwing aside a rough greatcoat, he very composedly took the offered chair, and unceremoniously proceeded to allay the cravings of an appetite which appeared by no means delicate. But at every mouthful he would turn an unquiet eye on Harper, who studied his appearance with a closeness of investigation that was very embarrassing to its subject. At length, pouring out a glass of wine, the newcomer nodded significantly to his examiner, previously to swallowing the liquor, and said, with something of bitterness in his manner,—

"I drink to our better acquaintance, sir; I believe this is the first time we have met, though your attention would seem to say otherwise."

The quality of the wine seemed greatly to his fancy, for, on replacing the glass upon the table, he gave his lips a smack, that resounded through the room; and, taking up the bottle, he held it between himself and the light, for a moment, in silent contemplation of its clear and brilliant color.

"I think we have never met before, sir," replied Harper with a slight smile on his features, as he observed the movements of the other; but appearing satisfied with his scrutiny, he turned to Sarah Wharton, who sat next him, and carelessly remarked,—

"You doubtless find your present abode solitary, after being accustomed to the gayeties of the city."

"Oh! excessively so," said Sarah hastily. "I do wish, with my father, that this cruel war was at an end, that we might return to our friends once more."

"And you, Miss Frances, do you long as ardently for peace as your sister?"'

"On many accounts I certainly do," returned the other, venturing to steal a timid glance at her interrogator; and, meeting the same benevolent expression of feeling as before, she continued, as her own face lighted into one of its animated and bright smiles of intelligence, "but not at the expense of the rights of my countrymen."

"Rights!" repeated her sister, impatiently; "whose rights can be stronger than those of a sovereign: and what duty is clearer, than to obey those who have a natural right to command?"

"None, certainly," said Frances, laughing with great pleasantry; and, taking the hand of her sister affectionately within both of her own, she added, with a smile directed towards Harper,—

"I gave you to understand that my sister and myself differed in our political opinions; but we have an impartial umpire in my father, who loves his own countrymen, and he loves the British,— so he takes sides with neither."

"Yes," said Mr. Wharton, in a little alarm, eying first one guest, and then the other; "I have near friends in both armies, and I dread a victory by either, as a source of certain private misfortune."

"I take it, you have little reason to apprehend much from the Yankees, in that way," interrupted the guest at the table, coolly helping himself to another glass, from the bottle he had admired.

"His majesty may have more experienced troops than the continentals,"* answered the host fearfully, "but the Americans have met with distinguished success."

Harper disregarded the observations of both; and, rising, he desired to be shown to his place of rest. A small boy was directed to guide him to his room; and wishing a courteous good-night to the whole party, the traveler withdrew. The knife and fork fell from the hands of the unwelcome intruder, as the door closed on the retiring figure of Harper; he arose slowly from his seat; listening attentively, he approached the door of the room—opened it—seemed to attend to the retreating footsteps of the other—and, amidst the panic and astonishment of his companions, he closed it again. In an instant, the red wig which concealed his black locks, the large patch which hid half his face from observation, the stoop that had made him appear fifty years of age, disappeared.

"My father!—my dear father!"— cried the handsome young man; "and you, my dearest sisters and aunt!—have I at last met you again?"

"Heaven bless you, my Henry, my son!" exclaimed the astonished but delighted parent; while his sisters sank on his shoulders, dissolved in tears.

The faithful old black, who had been reared from infancy in the house of his master, and who, as if in mockery of his degraded state, had been complimented with the name of Cæsar, was the only other witness of this unexpected discovery of the son of Mr. Wharton. After receiving the extended hand of his young master, and imprinting on it a fervent kiss, Cæsar withdrew. The boy did not re-enter the room; and the black himself, after some time, returned, just as the young British captain was exclaiming,—

"But who is this Mr. Harper?— is he likely to betray me?"

"No, no, no, Massa Harry," cried the negro, shaking his gray head confidently; "I been to see—Massa Harper on he knee—pray to God—no gemman who pray to God tell of good son, come to see old fader—Skinner do that — no Christian!"

This poor opinion of the Skinners was not confined to Mr. Cæsar Thompson, as he called himself—but Cæsar Wharton, as he was styled by the little world to which he was known. The convenience, and perhaps the necessities, of the leaders of the American arms, in the neighborhood of New York, had induced them to employ certain subordinate agents, of extremely irregular habits, in executing their lesser plans of annoying the enemy. It was not a moment for fastidious inquiries into abuses of any description, and oppression and injustice were the natural consequences of the possession of a military power that was uncurbed by the restraints of civil authority. In time, a distinct order of the community was formed, whose sole occupation appears to have been that of relieving their fellow citizens from any little excess of temporal prosperity they might be thought to enjoy, under the pretense of patriotism and the love of liberty.

Occasionally, the aid of military authority was not wanting, in enforcing these arbitrary distributions of worldly goods; and a petty holder of a commission in the state militia was to be seen giving the sanction of something like legality to acts of the most unlicensed robbery, and, not infrequently, of bloodshed.

On the part of the British, the stimulus of loyalty was by no means suffered to sleep, where so fruitful a field offered on which it might be expended. But their freebooters were enrolled, and their efforts more systematized. Long experience had taught their leaders the efficacy of concentrated force; and, unless tradition does great injustice to their exploits, the result did no little credit to their foresight. The corps—we presume, from their known affection to that useful animal—had received the quaint appellation of "Cowboys."

Cæsar was, however, far too loyal to associate men who held the commission of George III, with the irregular warriors whose excesses he had so often witnessed, and from whose rapacity, neither his poverty nor his bondage had suffered even him to escape uninjured. The Cowboys, therefore, did not receive their proper portion of the black's censure, when he said, no Christian, nothing but a "Skinner," could betray a pious child, while honoring his father with a visit so full of peril.

CHAPTER II

And many a halcyon day he lived to see
Unbroken, but by one misfortune dire,
When fate had reft his mutual heart—but she
Was gone—and Gertrude climbed a widowed father's knee.
— Gertrude of Wyoming.

The father of Mr. Wharton was a native of England, and of a family whose parliamentary interest had enabled them to provide for a younger son in the colony of New York. The young man, like hundreds of others in this situation, had settled permanently in the country. He married; and the sole issue of his connection had been sent early in life to receive the benefits of the English schools. After taking his degrees at one of the universities of the mother country, the youth had been suffered to acquire a knowledge of life with the advantages of European society. But the death of his father recalled him, after passing two years in this manner, to the possession of an honorable name, and a very ample estate.

It was much the fashion of that day to place the youth of certain families in the army and navy of England, as the regular stepping-stones to preferment. Most of the higher offices in the colonies were filled by men who had made arms their profession; and it was even no uncommon sight to see a veteran warrior laying aside the sword to assume the ermine on the benches of the highest judicial authority.

In conformity with this system, the senior Mr. Wharton had intended his son for a soldier; but a natural imbecility of character in his child interfered with his wishes.

A twelvemonth had been spent by the young man in weighing the comparative advantages of the different classes of troops, when the death of his father occurred. The ease of his situation, and the attentions lavished upon a youth in the actual enjoyment of one of the largest estates in the colonies, interfered greatly with his ambitious projects. Love decided the matter; and Mr. Wharton, in becoming a husband, ceased to think of becoming a soldier. For many years he continued happy in his family, and sufficiently respected by his countrymen, as a man of integrity and consequence, when all his enjoyments vanished, as it were, at a blow. His only son, the youth introduced in the preceding chapter, had entered the army, and had arrived in his native country, but a short time before the commencement of hostilities, with the re-enforcements the ministry had thought it prudent to throw into the disaffected parts of North America. His daughters were just growing into life, and their education required all the advantages the city could afford. His wife had been for some years in declining health, and had barely time to fold her son to her bosom, and rejoice in the reunion of her family, before the Revolution burst forth, in a continued blaze, from Georgia to Massachusetts. The shock was too much for the feeble condition of the mother, who saw her child called to the field to combat against the members of her own family in the South, and she sank under the blow.

There was no part of the continent where the manners of England and its aristocratical notions of blood and alliances, prevailed with more force than in a certain circle immediately around the metropolis of New York. The customs of the early Dutch inhabitants had, indeed, blended in some measures, with the English manners; but still the latter prevailed. This attachment to Great Britain was increased by the frequent intermarriages of the officers of the mother country with the wealthier and most powerful families of the vicinity, until, at the commencement of hostilities, their united influence had very nearly thrown the colony into the scale on the side of the crown. A few, however, of the leading families espoused the cause of the people; and a sufficient stand was made against the efforts of the ministerial party, to organize, and, aided by the army of the confederation, to maintain an independent republican form of government.

The city of New York and the adjacent territory were alone exempted from the rule of the new commonwealth; while the royal authority extended no further than its dignity could be supported by the presence of an army. In this condition of things, the loyalists of influence adopted such measures as best accorded with their different characters and situations. Many bore arms in support of the crown, and, by their bravery and exertions, endeavored to secure what they deemed to be the rights of their prince, and their own estates from the effects of the law of attainder. Others left the country; seeking in that place they emphatically called home, an asylum, as they fondly hoped, for a season only, against the confusion and dangers of war. A third, and a more wary portion, remained in the place of their nativity, with a prudent regard to their ample possessions, and, perhaps, influenced by their attachments to the scenes of their youth. Mr. Wharton was of this description. After making a provision against future contingencies, by secretly transmitting the whole of his money to the British funds, this gentleman determined to continue in the theater of strife, and to maintain so strict a neutrality as to insure the safety of his large estate, whichever party succeeded. He was apparently engrossed in the education of his daughters, when a relation, high in office in the new state, intimated that a residence in what was now a British camp differed but little, in the eyes of his countrymen, from a residence in the British capital. Mr. Wharton soon saw this was an unpardonable offense in the existing state of things, and he instantly determined to remove the difficulty, by retiring to the country. He possessed a residence in the county of Westchester; and having been for many years in the habit of withdrawing thither during the heats of the summer months, it was kept furnished and ready for his accommodations. His eldest daughter was already admitted into the society of women; but Frances, the younger, required a year or two more of the usual cultivation, to appear with proper éclat; at least so thought Miss Jeanette Peyton; and as this lady, a younger sister of their deceased mother, had left her paternal home, in the colony of Virginia, with the devotedness and affection peculiar to her sex, to superintend the welfare of her orphan nieces, Mr. Wharton felt that her opinions were entitled to respect. In conformity to her advice, therefore, the feelings of the parent were made to yield to the welfare of his children.

Mr. Wharton withdrew to the Locusts, with a heart rent with the pain of separating from all that was left him of a wife he had adored, but in obedience to a constitutional prudence that pleaded loudly in behalf of his worldly goods. His handsome town residence was inhabited, in the meanwhile, by his daughters and their aunt. The regiment to which Captain Wharton belonged formed a part of the permanent garrison of the city; and the knowledge of the presence of his son was no little relief to the father, in his unceasing meditations on his absent daughters.

But Captain Wharton was a young man and a soldier; his estimate of character was not always the wisest; and his propensities led him to imagine that a red coat never concealed a dishonorable heart.

The house of Mr. Wharton became a fashionable lounge to the officers of the royal army, as did that of every other family that was thought worthy of their notice. The consequences of this association were, to some few of the visited, fortunate; to more, injurious, by exciting expectations which were never to be realized, and, unhappily, to no small number ruinous. The known wealth of the father and, possibly, the presence of a high-spirited brother, forbade any apprehension of the latter danger to the young ladies: but it was impossible that all the admiration bestowed on the fine figure and lovely face of Sarah Wharton should be thrown away. Her person was formed with the early maturity of the climate, and a strict cultivation of the graces had made her decidedly the belle of the city. No one promised to dispute with her this female sovereignty, unless it might be her younger sister. Frances, however, wanted some months to the charmed age of sixteen; and the idea of competition was far from the minds of either of the affectionate girls. Indeed, next to the conversation of Colonel Wellmere, the greatest pleasure of Sarah was in contemplating the budding beauties of the little Hebe, who played around her with all the innocency of youth, with all the enthusiasm of her ardent temper, and with no little of the archness of her native humor. Whether or not it was owing to the fact that Frances received none of the compliments which fell to the lot of her elder sister, in the often repeated discussions on the merits of the war, between the military beaux who frequented the house, it is certain their effects on the sisters were exactly opposite. It was much the fashion then for the British officers to speak slightingly of their enemies; and Sarah took all the idle vaporing of her danglers to be truths. The first political opinions which reached the ears of Frances were coupled with sneers on the conduct of her countrymen. At first she believed them; but there was occasionally a general, who was obliged to do justice to his enemy in order to obtain justice for himself; and Frances became somewhat skeptical on the subject of the inefficiency of her countrymen. Colonel Wellmere was among those who delighted most in expending his wit on the unfortunate Americans; and, in time, Frances began to listen to his eloquence with great suspicion, and sometimes with resentment.

It was on a hot, sultry day that the three were in the parlor of Mr. Wharton's house, the colonel and Sarah seated on a sofa, engaged in a combat of the eyes, aided by the usual flow of small talk, and Frances was occupied at her tambouring frame in an opposite corner of the room, when the gentleman suddenly exclaimed,—

"How gay the arrival of the army under General Burgoyne will make the city, Miss Wharton!"

"Oh! how pleasant it must be," said the thoughtless Sarah, in reply; "I am told there are many charming women with that army; as you say, it will make us all life and gayety."

Frances shook back the abundance of her golden hair, and raised her eyes, dancing with the ardor of national feeling; then laughing, with a concealed humor, she asked,—

"Is it so certain that General Burgoyne will 'be permitted to reach the city?"

"Permitted!" echoed the colonel. "Who is there to prevent it, my pretty Miss Fanny?"

Frances was precisely at that age when young people are most jealous of their station in society; neither quite a woman, nor yet a child. The "pretty Miss Fanny" was too familiar to be relished, and she dropped her eyes on her work again with cheeks that glowed like crimson.

"General Stark took the Germans into custody," she answered, compressing her lip; "may not General Gates think the British too dangerous to go at large?"

"Oh! they were Germans, as you say," cried the colonel, excessively vexed at the necessity of explaining at all; "mere mercenary troops; but when the really British regiments come in question, you will see a very different result."

"Of that there is no doubt," cried Sarah, without in the least partaking of the resentment of the colonel to her sister, but hailing already in her heart the triumph of the British.

"Pray, Colonel Wellmere," said Frances, recovering her good humor, and raising her joyous eyes once more to the face of the gentleman, "was the Lord Percy of Lexington a kinsman of him who fought at Chevy Chase?"

"Why, Miss Fanny, you are becoming a rebel," said the

colonel, endeavoring to laugh away the anger he felt; "what you are pleased to insinuate was a chase at Lexington, was nothing more than a judicious retreat—a—kind of—"

"Running fight," interrupted the good-humored girl, laying a great emphasis on the first word.

"Positively, young lady"—Colonel Wellmere was interrupted by a laugh from a person who had hitherto been unnoticed.

There was a small family apartment adjoining the room occupied by the trio, and the air had blown open the door communicating between the two. A fine young man was now seen sitting near the entrance, who, by his smiling countenance, was evidently a pleased listener to the conversation. He rose instantly, and coming through the door, with his hat in his hand, appeared a tall, graceful youth, of dark complexion, and sparkling eyes of black, from which the mirth had not entirely vanished, as he made his bow to the ladies.

"Mr. Dunwoodie!" cried Sarah, in surprise; "I was ignorant of your being in the house; you will find a cooler seat in this room."

"I thank you," replied the young man, "but I must go and seek your brother, who placed me there in ambuscade, as he called it, with a promise of returning an hour ago." Without making any further explanation, the youth bowed politely to 'the young women, distantly and with hauteur to the gentleman, and withdrew. Frances followed him into the hall, and blushing richly, inquired, in a hurried voice,—

"But why—why do you leave us, Mr. Dunwoodie? Henry must soon return."

The gentleman caught one of her hands in his own, and the stern expression of his countenance gave place to a look of admiration as he replied,—

"You managed him famously, my dear little kinswoman; never—no, never, forget the land of your birth; remember, if you are the granddaughter of an Englishman, you are, also, the granddaughter of a Peyton."

"Oh!" returned the laughing girl, "it would be difficult to forget that, with the constant lectures on genealogy before us, with which we are favored by Aunt Jeanette; but why do you go?"

"I am on the wing for Virginia, and have much to do." He pressed her hand as he spoke, and looking back, while in the act of closing the door, exclaimed, "Be true to your country—be American." The ardent girl kissed her hand to him as he retired, and then instantly applying it with its beautiful fellow to her burning cheeks, ran into her own apartment to hide her confusion.

Between the open sarcasm of Frances, and the ill-concealed disdain of the young man. Colonel Wellmere had felt himself placed in an awkward predicament; but ashamed to resent such trifles in the presence of his mistress, he satisfied himself with observing, superciliously, as Dunwoodie left the room,—

"Quite a liberty for a youth in his situation; a shop boy with a bundle, I fancy."

The idea of picturing the graceful Peyton Dunwoodie as a shop boy could never enter the mind of Sarah, and she looked around her in surprise, when the colonel continued,—

"This Mr. Dun—Dun—"

"Dunwoodie! Oh,no—he is a relation of my aunt," cried the young lady, "and an intimate friend of my brother; they were at school together, and only separated in England, when one went into the army, and the other to a French military academy."

"His money appears to have been thrown away," observed the colonel, betraying the spleen he was unsuccessfully striving to conceal.

"We ought to hope so," added Sarah, with a smile, "for it is said he intends joining the rebel army. He was brought in here in a French ship, and has just been exchanged; you may soon meet him in arms."

"Well, let him—I wish Washington plenty of such heroes;" and he turned to a more pleasant subject, by changing the discourse to themselves.

A few weeks after this scene occurred, the army of Burgoyne laid down their arms. Mr. Wharton, beginning to think the result of the contest doubtful, resolved to conciliate his countrymen, and gratify himself, by calling his daughters into his own abode. Miss Peyton consented to be their companion; and from that time, until the period at which we commenced our narrative, they had formed one family.

Whenever the main army made any movements, Captain

Wharton had, of course, accompanied it; and once or twice, under the protection of strong parties, acting in the neighborhood of the Locusts, he had enjoyed rapid and stolen interviews with his friends. A twelvemonth had, however, passed without his seeing them, and the impatient Henry had adopted the disguise we have mentioned, and unfortunately arrived on the very evening that an unknown and rather suspicious guest was an inmate of the house, which seldom contained any other than its regular inhabitants.

"But do you think he suspects me?" asked the captain, with anxiety, after pausing to listen to Cæsar's opinion of the" Skinners.

"How should he?" cried Sarah, "when your sisters and father could not penetrate your disguise."

"There is something mysterious in his manner; his looks are too prying for an indifferent observer," continued young Wharton thoughtfully, "and his face seems familiar to me. The recent fate of Andre has created much irritation on both sides. Sir Henry threatens retaliation for his death; and Washington is as firm as if half the world were at his command. The rebels would think me a fit subject for their plans just now, should I be so unlucky as to fall into their hands."

"But my son," cried his father, in great alarm, "you are not a spy; you are not within the rebel—that is, the American lines; there is nothing here to spy."

"That might be disputed," rejoined the young man, musing. "Their pickets were as low as the White Plains when I passed through in disguise. It is true my purposes are innocent; but how is it to appear? My. visit to you would seem a cloak to other designs. Remember, sir, the treatment you received not a year since, for sending me a supply of fruit for the winter."

"That proceeded from the misrepresentations of my kind neighbors," said Mr. Wharton, "who hoped, by getting my estate confiscated, to purchase good farms at low prices. Peyton Dunwoodie, however, soon obtained our discharge; we were detained but a month."

"We!" repeated the son, in amazement; "did they take my sisters, also? Fanny, you wrote me nothing of this."

"I believe," said Frances, coloring highly, "I mentioned the kind treatment we received from your old friend. Major Dunwoodie; and that he procured my father's release."

"True; but were you with him in the rebel camp?"

"Yes," said the father, kindly; "Fanny would not suffer me to go alone. Jeanette and Sarah took charge of the Locusts, and this little girl was my companion, in captivity."

"And Fanny returned from such a scene a greater rebel than ever," cried Sarah, indignantly; "one would think the hardships her father suffered would have cured her of such whims."

"What say you to the charge, my pretty sister?" cried the captain gayly; "did Peyton strive to make you hate your king, more than he does himself?"

"Peyton Dunwoodie hates no one," said Frances, quickly; then, blushing at her own ardor, she added immediately, "he loves you, Henry, I know; for he has told me so again and again."

Young Wharton tapped his sister on the cheek, with a smile, as he asked her, in an affected whisper, "Did he tell you also that he loved my little sister Fanny?"

"Nonsense!" said Frances; and the remnants of the supper-table soon disappeared under her superintendence.

CHAPTER III

'Twas when the fields were swept of Autumn's store,
And growing winds the fading foliage tore
Behind the Lowmon hill, the short-lived light,
Descending slowly, ushered in the night;
When from the noisy town, with mournful look,
His lonely way the meager peddler took.

—Wilson

A storm below the highlands of the Hudson, if it be introduced with an easterly wind, seldom lasts less than two days. Accordingly, as the inmates of the Locusts assembled, on the following morning, around their early breakfast, the driving rain was seen to strike in nearly horizontal lines against the windows of the building, and forbade the idea of exposing either man or beast to the tempest. Harper was the last to appear; after taking a view of the state of the weather, he apologized to Mr. Wharton for the necessity that existed for his trespassing on his goodness for a longer time. To appearances, the reply was as courteous as the excuse; yet Harper wore a resignation in his deportment that was widely different from the uneasy manner of the father. Henry Wharton had resumed his disguise with a reluctance amounting to disgust, but in obedience to the commands of his parent. No communications passed between him and the stranger, after the first salutations of the morning had been paid by Harper to him, in common with the rest of the family. Frances had, indeed, thought there was something like a smile passing over the features of the traveler, when, on entering the room, he first confronted her brother; but it was confined to the eyes, seeming to want power to affect the muscles of the face, and was soon lost in the settled and benevolent expression which reigned in his countenance, with a sway but seldom interrupted. The eyes of the affectionate sister were turned in anxiety, for a moment, on her brother, and glancing again on their unknown guest, met his look, as he offered her, with marked attention, one of the little civilities of the table; and the heart of the girl, which had begun to throb with violence, regained a pulsation as tempered as youth, health, and buoyant spirits could allow. While yet seated at the table, Cæsar entered, and laying a small parcel in silence by the side of his master, modestly retired behind his chair, where, placing one hand on its back, he continued in an attitude half familiar, half respectful, a listener.

"What is this, Cæsar?" inquired Mr. Wharton, turning the bundle over to examine its envelope, and eying it rather suspiciously.

"The 'baccy, sir; Harvey Birch, he got home, and he bring you a little good 'baccy from York."

"Harvey Birch.'" rejoined the master with great deliberation, stealing a look at his guest. "I do not remember desiring him to purchase any tobacco for me; but as he has brought it, he must be paid for his trouble."

For an instant only, as the negro spoke, did Harper suspend his silent meal; his eye moved slowly from the servant to the master, and again all remained in impenetrable reserve.

To Sarah Wharton, this intelligence gave unexpected pleasure; rising from her seat with impatience, she bade the black show Birch into the apartment; when, suddenly recollecting herself, she turned to the traveler with an apologizing look, and added, "If Mr. Harper will excuse the presence of a peddler."

The indulgent benevolence expressed in the countenance of the stranger, as he bowed a silent acquiescence, spoke more eloquently than the nicest framed period, and the young lady repeated her order, with a confidence in its truth that removed all embarrassment.

In the deep recesses of the windows of the cottage were seats of paneled work; and the rich damask curtains, that had ornamented the parlor in Queen Street,[4] had been transferred to the Locusts, and gave to the room that indescribable air of comfort, which so gratefully announces the approach of a domestic winter. Into one of these recesses Captain Wharton now threw

---

[4] The Americans changed the names of many towns and streets at the Revolution, as has since been done in France. Thus, in the city of New York, Crown Street has become Liberty Street; King Street, Pine Street; and Queen Street, then one of the most fashionable quarters of the town, Pearl Street. Pearl Street is now chiefly occupied by the auction dealers, and the wholesale drygoods merchants, for warehouses and counting-rooms.

himself, drawing the curtain before him in such a manner as to conceal most of his person from observation; while his younger sister, losing her natural frankness of manner, in an air of artificial constraint, silently took possession of the other.

Harvey Birch had been a peddler from his youth; at least so he frequently asserted, and his skill in the occupation went far to prove the truth of the declaration. He was a native of one of the eastern colonies; and, from something of superior intelligence which belonged to his father, it was thought they had known better fortune in the land of their nativity. Harvey possessed, however, the common manners of the country, and was in no way distinguished from men of his class, but by his acuteness, and the mystery which enveloped his movements. Ten years before, they had arrived together in the vale, and, purchasing the humble dwelling at which Harper had made his unsuccessful application, continued ever since peaceful inhabitants, but little noticed and but little known. Until age and infirmities had prevented, the father devoted himself to the cultivation of the small spot of ground belonging to his purchase, while the son pursued with avidity his humble barter. Their orderly quietude had soon given them so much consideration in the neighborhood, as to induce a maiden of five-and-thirty to forget the punctilio of her sex, and to accept the office of presiding over their domestic comforts. The roses had long before vanished from the cheeks of Katy Haynes, and she had seen in succession, both her male and female acquaintances forming the union so desirable to her sex, with but little or no hope left for herself, when, with views of her own, she entered the family of the Birches. Necessity is a hard master, and, for the want of a better companion, the father and son were induced to accept her services; but still Katy was not wanting in some qualities which made her a very tolerable housekeeper. On the one hand, she was neat, industrious, honest, and a good manager. On the other, she was talkative, selfish, superstitious, and inquisitive. By dint of using the latter quality with consummate industry, she had not lived in the family five years when she triumphantly declared that she had heard, or rather overheard, sufficient to enable her to say what had been the former fate of her associates. Could Katy have possessed enough of divination to pronounce upon their future lot, her task would have been accomplished. From the private conversations of the parent and child, she learned that a fire had reduced them from competence to poverty, and at the same time diminished the number of their family to two. There was a tremulousness in the voice of the father, as he touched lightly on the event, which affected even the heart of Katy; but no barrier is sufficient to repel vulgar curiosity. She persevered, until a very direct intimation from Harvey, by threatening to supply her place with a female a few years younger than herself, gave her awful warning that there were bounds beyond which she was not to pass. From that period the curiosity of the housekeeper had been held in such salutary restraint, that, although no opportunity of listening was ever neglected, she had been able to add but little to her stock of knowledge. There was, however, one piece of intelligence, and that of no little interest to herself, which she had succeeded in obtaining; and from the moment of its acquisition, she directed her energies to the accomplishment of one object, aided by the double stimulus of love and avarice.

Harvey was in the frequent habit of paying mysterious visits in the depth of the night, to the fireplace of the apartment that served for both kitchen and parlor. Here he was observed by Katy; and availing herself of his absence and the occupations of the father, by removing one of the hearthstones, she discovered an iron pot, glittering with a metal that seldom fails to soften the hardest heart. Katy succeeded in replacing the stone without discovery, and never dared to trust herself with another visit. From that moment, however, the heart of the virgin lost its obduracy, and nothing interposed between Harvey and his happiness, but his own want of observation.

The war did not interfere with the traffic of the peddler, who seized on the golden opportunity which the interruption of the regular trade afforded, and appeared absorbed in the one grand object of amassing money. For a year or two his employment was uninterrupted, and his success proportionate; but, at length, dark and threatening hints began to throw suspicion around his movements, and the civil authority thought it incumbent on them to examine narrowly into his mode of life. His imprisonments, though frequent, were not long; and his escapes from the guardians of the law easy, compared to what he endured from the persecution of the military. Still Birch survived, and still he continued his trade, though compelled to be very guarded in-his movements, especially whenever he approached the northern boundaries of the country; or in other words, the neighborhood of the American lines. His visits to the Locusts had become less frequent, and his appearance at his own abode so seldom, as to draw forth from the disappointed Katy, in the fullness of her heart, the complaint we have related, in her reply to Harper. Nothing, however, seemed to interfere with the pursuits of this indefatigable trader, who, with a view to dispose of certain articles for which he could only find purchasers in the very wealthiest families of the county, had now braved the fury of the tempest, and ventured to cross the half mile between his own residence and the house of Mr. Wharton.

In a few minutes after receiving the commands of his young mistress, Cæsar reappeared, ushering into the apartment the subject of the foregoing digression. In person, the peddler was a man above the middle height, spare, but full of bone and muscle. At first sight, his strength seemed unequal to manage the unwieldy burden of his pack; yet he threw it on and off with great dexterity, and with as much apparent ease as if it had been filled with feathers. His eyes were gray, sunken, restless, and, for the flitting moments that they dwelt on the countenance of those with whom he conversed, they seemed to read the very soul. They possessed, however, two distinct expressions, which, in a great measure, characterized the whole man. When engaged in traffic, the intelligence of his face appeared lively, active, and flexible, though uncommonly acute; if the conversation turned on the ordinary transactions of life, his air became abstracted and restless; but if, by chance, the Revolution and the country were the topic, his whole system seemed altered—all his faculties were concentrated: he would listen for a great length of time, without speaking, and then would break silence by some light and jocular remark, that was too much at variance with his former manner, not to be affectation. But of the war, and of his father, he seldom spoke, and always from some very obvious necessity.

To a superficial observer, avarice would seem his ruling passion—and, all things considered, he was as unfit a subject for the plans of Katy Haynes as can be readily imagined. On entering the room, the peddler relieved himself from his burden, which, as it stood on the floor, reached nearly to his shoulders, and saluted the family with modest civility. To Harper he made a silent bow, without lifting his eyes from the carpet; but the curtain prevented any notice of the presence of Captain Wharton. Sarah gave but little time for the usual salutations, before she commenced her survey of the contents of the pack; and, for several minutes, the two were engaged in bringing to light the various articles it contained. The tables, chairs, and floor were soon covered with silks, crapes, gloves, muslins, and all the stock of an itinerant trader. Cæsar was employed to hold open the mouth of the pack, as its hoards were discharged, and occasionally he aided his young lady, by directing her admiration to some article of finery, which, from its deeper contrast in colors, he thought more worthy of her notice. At length, Sarah, having selected several articles, and satisfactorily arranged the prices, observed in a cheerful voice,—

"But, Harvey, you have told us no news. Has Lord Cornwallis beaten the rebels again?"

The question could not have been heard; for the peddler, burying his body in the pack, brought forth a quantity of lace of exquisite fineness, and, holding it up to view, he required the admiration of the young lady. Miss Peyton dropped the cup she was engaged in washing, from her hand; and Frances exhibited the whole of that lovely face, which had hitherto only suffered one of its joyous eyes to be seen, beaming with a color that shamed the damask which enviously concealed her figure.

The aunt quitted her employment; and Birch soon disposed of a large portion of his valuable article. The praises of the ladies had drawn the whole person of the younger sister into view; and Frances was slowly rising from the window, as Sarah repeated her question, with an exultation in her voice, that proceeded more from pleasure in her purchase, than her political feelings. The younger sister resumed her seat, apparently examining the state of the clouds, while the peddler, finding a reply was expected, answered,—

"There is some talk, below, about Tarleton having defeated General Sumter, on the Tiger River."

Captain Wharton now involuntarily thrust his head between the opening of the curtains into the room; and Frances, turning her ear in breathless silence, noticed the quiet eyes of Harper looking at the peddler, over the book he was affecting to read, with an expression that denoted him to be a listener, of no ordinary interest.

"Indeed!" cried the exulting Sarah; "Sumter—Sumter—who is he? I'll not buy even a pin, until you tell me all the news," she continued, laughing and throwing down a muslin she had been examining.

For a moment the peddler hesitated; his eye glanced towards Harper, who was yet gazing at him with settled meaning, and the whole manner of Birch was altered. Approaching the fire, he took from his mouth a large allowance of the Virginian weed, and depositing it, with the superabundance of its juices, without mercy to Miss Peyton's shining andirons, he returned to his goods.

"He lives somewhere among the niggers to the south," answered the peddler, abruptly.

"No more nigger than be yourself, Mister Birch," interrupted Cæsar tartly, dropping at the same time the covering of the goods in high displeasure.

"Hush Cæsar—hush; never mind it now," said Sarah Wharton soothingly, impatient to hear further.

"A black man so good as white, Miss Sally," continued the offended negro, "so long as he behave heself."

"And frequently he is much better," rejoined his mistress. "But, Harvey, who is this Mr. Sumter?"

A slight indication of humor showed itself on the face of the peddler, but it disappeared, and he continued as if the discourse had met with no interruption from the sensitiveness of the domestic.

"As I was saying, he lives among the colored people in the south"—Cæsar resumed his occupation—"and he has lately had a scrimmage with this Colonel Tarleton—"

"Who defeated him, of course?" said Sarah, with confidence.

"So say the troops at Morrisania."

"But what do you say?" Mr. Wharton ventured to inquire, yet speaking in a low tone.

"I repeat but what I hear," said Birch, offering a piece of cloth to the inspection of Sarah, who rejected it in silence, evidently determined to hear more before she made another purchase.

"They say, however, at the Plains," the peddler continued, first throwing his eyes again around the room, and letting them rest for an instant on Harper, "that Sumter and one or two more were all that were hurt, and that the rig'lars were all cut to pieces, for the militia were fixed snugly in a log barn."

"Not very probable," said Sarah, contemptuously, "though I make no doubt the rebels got behind the logs."

"I think," said the peddler coolly, again offering the silk, "it's quite ingenious to get a log between one and a gun, instead of getting between a gun and a log."

The eyes of Harper dropped quietly on the pages of the volume in his hand, while Frances, rising, came forward with. a smile in her face, as she inquired, in a tone of affability that the peddler had never witnessed from her,—

"Have you more of the lace, Mr. Birch?"

The desired article was immediately produced, and Frances became a purchaser also. By her order a glass of liquor was offered to the trader, who took it with thanks, and having paid his compliments to the master of the house and the ladies, drank the beverage.

"So, it is thought that Colonel Tarleton has worsted General Sumter?" said Mr. Wharton, affecting to be employed in mending the cup that was broken by the eagerness of his sister-in-law.

"I believe they think so at Morrisania," said Birch, dryly.

"Have you any other news, friend?" asked Captain Wharton, venturing to thrust his face without the curtains.

"Have you heard that Major Andre has been hanged?"

Captain Wharton started, and for a moment glances of great significance were exchanged between him and the trader, when he observed, with affected indifference, "That must have been some weeks ago."

"Does his execution make much noise?" asked the father, striving to make the broken china unite.

"People will talk, you know, 'squire."

"Is there any probability of movements below, my friend, that will make traveling dangerous?" asked Harper, looking steadily at the other, in expectation of his reply.

Some bunches of ribbons fell from the hands of Birch; his countenance changed instantly, losing its keen expression in intent meaning, as he answered slowly, "It is some time since the rig'lar cavalry were out, and I saw some of De Lancey's men cleaning their arms, as I passed their quarters; it would be no wonder if they took the scent soon, for the Virginia horse are low in the county."

"Are they in much force?" asked Mr. Wharton, suspending all employment in anxiety.

"I did not count them.",

Frances was the only observer of the change in the manner of Birch, and, on turning to Harper, he had resumed his book in silence. She took some of the ribbons in her hand—laid them down again—and, bending over goods, so that her hair, falling in rich curls, shaded her face, she observed, blushing with a color that suffused her neck,—

"I thought the Southern horse had marched towards the Delaware."

"It may be so," said Birch; "I passed the troops at a distance." Cæsar had now selected a piece of calico, in which the gaudy colors of yellow and red were contrasted on a white ground, and, after admiring it for several minutes, he laid it down with a sigh, as he exclaimed, "Berry pretty calico."

"That," said Sarah; "yes, that would make a proper gown for your wife, Cæsar."

"Yes, Miss Sally," cried the delighted black, "it make old Dinah heart leap for joy—so berry genteel."

"Yes," added the peddler, quaintly, "that is only wanting to make Dinah look like a rainbow."

Cæsar eyed his young mistress eagerly, until she inquired of Harvey the price of the article.

"Why, much as I light of chaps," said the peddler.

"How much?" demanded Sarah in surprise.

"According to my luck in finding purchasers; for my friend Dinah, you may have it at four shillings."

"It is too much," said Sarah, turning to some goods for herself. "Monstrous price for coarse calico, Mister Birch," grumbled Cæsar, dropping the opening of the pack again.

"We will say three, then," added the peddler, "if you like that better."

"Be sure he like 'em better," said Cæsar, smiling good-humoredly, and reopening the pack; "Miss Sally like a free shilling when she give, and a four shilling when she take."

The bargain was immediately concluded; but in measuring, the cloth wanted a little of the well-known ten yards required by the dimensions of Dinah. By dint of a strong arm, however, it grew to the desired length, under the experienced eye of the peddler, who conscientiously added a ribbon of corresponding brilliancy with the calico; and Cæsar hastily withdrew, to communicate the joyful intelligence to his aged partner.

During the movements created by the conclusion of the purchase, Captain Wharton had ventured to draw aside the curtain, so as to admit a view of his person, and he now inquired of the peddler, who had begun to collect the scattered goods, at what time he had left the city.

"At early twilight," was the answer.

"So lately!" cried the other in surprise: then correcting his manner, by assuming a more guarded air, he continued, "Could you pass the pickets at so late an hour?"

"I did," was the laconic reply.

"You must be well known by this time, Harvey, to the officers of the British army," cried Sarah, smiling knowingly on the peddler.

"I know some of them by sight," said Birch, glancing his eyes round the apartment, taking in their course Captain Wharton, and resting for an instant on the countenance of Harper.

Mr. Wharton had listened intently to each speaker, in succession, and had so far lost the affectation of indifference, as to be crushing in his hand the pieces of china on which he had expended so much labor in endeavoring to mend it; when, observing the peddler tying the last knot in his pack, he asked abruptly,—

"Are we about to be disturbed again with the enemy?"

"Who do you call the enemy?" said the peddler, raising himself erect, and giving the other a look, before which the eyes of Mr. Wharton sank in instant confusion.

"All are enemies who disturb our peace," said Miss Peyton, observing that her brother was unable to speak. "But are the royal troops out from below?"

" 'Tis quite likely they soon may be," returned Birch, raising his pack from the floor, and preparing to leave the room.

"And the continentals," continued Miss. Peyton mildly, "are the continentals in the county?"

Harvey was about to utter something in reply, when the door opened, and Cæsar made his appearance, attended by his delighted spouse.

The race of blacks of which Cæsar was a favorable specimen is becoming very rare. The old family servant who, born and reared in the dwelling of his master, identified himself with the welfare of those whom it was his lot to serve, is giving place in every direction to that vagrant class which has sprung up within the last thirty years, and whose members roam through the country unfettered by principles, and uninfluenced by attachments. For it is one of the curses of slavery that its victims become incompetent to the attributes of a freeman. The short curly hair of Cæsar had acquired from age a coloring of gray, that added greatly to the venerable cast of his appearance. Long and indefatigable applications of the comb had straightened the close curls of his forehead, until they stood erect in a stiff and formal brush, that gave at least two inches to his stature. The shining black of his youth had lost its glistening hue, and it had been succeeded by a dingy brown. His eyes, which stood at a most formidable distance from each other, were small, and characterized by an expression of good feeling, occasionally interrupted by the petulance of an indulged servant; they, however, now danced with inward delight. His nose possessed, in an eminent manner, all the requisites for smelling, but with the most modest unobtrusiveness; the nostrils being abundantly capacious, without thrusting themselves in the way of their neighbors. His mouth was capacious to a fault, and was only tolerated on account of the double row of pearls it contained. In person Cæsar was short, and we should say square, had not all the angles and curves of his figure bid defiance to anything like mathematical symmetry. His arms were long and muscular, and terminated by two bony hands, that exhibited on one side a coloring of blackish gray, and on the other, a faded pink. But it was in his legs that nature had indulged her most capricious humor. There was an abundance of material injudiciously used. The calves were neither before nor behind, but rather on the outer side of the limb, inclining forward, and so close to the knee as to render the free use of that joint a subject of doubt. In the foot, considering it as a base on which the body was to rest, Csar had no cause of complaint, unless, indeed, it might be that the leg was placed so near the center, as to make it sometimes a matter of dispute, whether he was not walking backwards. But whatever might be the faults a statuary could discover in his person, the heart of Cæsar Thompson was in the right place, and, we doubt not, of very just dimensions.

Accompanied by his ancient companion, Cæsar now advanced, and paid his tribute of gratitude in words. Sarah received them with great complacency, and made a few compliments to the taste of the husband, and the probable appearance of the wife. Frances, with a face beaming with a look of pleasure that corresponded to the smiling countenances of the blacks, offered the service of her needle in fitting the admired calico to its future uses. The offer was humbly and gratefully accepted.

As Cæsar followed his wife and the peddler from the apartment, and was in the act of closing the door, he indulged himself in a grateful soliloquy, by saying aloud,—

"Good little lady—Miss Fanny—take care of he fader—love to make a gown for old Dinah, too." What else his feeling might have induced him to utter is unknown, but the sound of his voice was heard some time after the distance rendered his words indistinct.

Harper had dropped his book, and he sat an admiring witness of the scene; and Frances enjoyed a double satisfaction, she received an approving smile from a face which concealed, under the traces of deep thought and engrossing care, the benevolent expression which characterizes all the best feelings of the human heart.

CHAPTER IV

"It is the form, the eye, the word,
The bearing of that stranger lord,
His stature, manly, bold, and tall,
Built like a castle's battled wall,
Yet molded in such just degrees
His giant strength seems lightsome ease.
Weather and war their rougher trace
Have left on that majestic face;
But 'tis his dignity of eye!
There, if a suppliant, would I fly,
Secure, 'mid danger, wrongs, and grief,
Of sympathy, redress, relief—
That glance, if guilty, would I dread
More than the doom that spoke me dead."
"Enough, enough!" the princess cried,
'Tis Scotland's hope, her joy, her pride!"
—Walter Scott.

The party sat in silence for many minutes after the peddler had withdrawn. Mr. Wharton had heard enough to increase his uneasiness, without in the least removing his apprehensions on behalf of his son. The captain was impatiently wishing Harper in any other place than the one he occupied with such apparent composure, while Miss Peyton completed the disposal of her breakfast equipage, with the mild complacency of her nature, aided a little by an inward satisfaction at possessing so large a portion of the trader's lace; Sarah was busily occupied in arranging her purchases, and Frances was kindly assisting in the occupation, disregarding her own neglected bargains, when the stranger suddenly broke the silence by saying,—

"If any apprehensions of me induce Captain Wharton to maintain his disguise, I wish him to be undeceived; had I motives for betraying him, they could not operate under present circumstances."

The younger sister sank into her seat colorless and astonished. Miss Peyton dropped the tea tray she was lifting from the table, and Sarah sat with her purchases unheeded in her lap, in speechless surprise. Mr. Wharton was stupefied; but the captain, hesitating a moment from astonishment, sprang into the middle of the room, and exclaimed, as he tore off the instruments of his disguise,—

"I believe you from my soul, and this tiresome imposition shall continue no longer. Yet I am at a loss to conceive in what manner you should know me."

"You really look so much better in your proper person, Captain Wharton," said Harper, with a slight smile, "I would advise you never to conceal it in future. There is enough to betray you, if other sources of detection were wanting." As he spoke, he pointed to a picture suspended over the mantel piece, which exhibited the British officer in his regimentals.

"I had flattered myself," cried young Wharton, with a laugh, "that I looked better on the canvas than in a masquerade. You must be a close observer, sir."

"Necessity has made me one," said Harper, rising from his seat.

Frances met him as he was about to withdraw, and, taking his hand between both her own, said with eamestness, her cheeks mantling with their/idlest vermilion, "You cannot—you will not betray my brother."

For an instant Harper paused in silent admiration of the lovely pleader, and then, folding her hands on his breast, he replied solemnly, "I cannot, and I will not." He released her hands, and laying his own on her head gently, continued, "If the blessing of a stranger can profit you, receive it." He turned, and, bowing low, retired, with a delicacy that was duly appreciated by th 'se he quitted, to his own apartment.

The whole party were deeply impressed with the ingenuous and solemn manner of the traveler, and all but the father found immediate relief in his declaration. Some of the castoff clothes of the captain, which had been removed with the goods from the city, were produced; and young Wharton, released from the uneasiness of his disguise, began at last to enjoy a visit which had been undertaken at so much personal risk to himself. Mr. Wharton retiring to his apartment, in pursuance of his regular engagements, the ladies, with the young man, were left to an uninterrupted communication on such subjects as were most agreeable. Even Miss Peyton was affected with the spirits of her young relatives; and they sat for an hour enjoying, in heedless confidence, the pleasures of an unrestrained conversation, without reflecting on any danger which might be impending over them. The city and their acquaintances were not long neglected; for Miss Peyton, who had never forgotten the many agreeable hours of her residence within its boundaries,, soon inquired, among others, after their old acquaintance, Colonel Wellmere.

"Oh!" cried the captain, gayly, "he yet continues there, as handsome and as gallant as ever."

Although a woman be not actually in love, she seldom hears without a blush the name of a man whom she might love, and who has been connected with herself by idle gossips, in the amatory rumor of the day. Such had been the case with Sarah, and she dropped her eyes on the carpet with a smile, that, aided by the blush which suffused her cheek, in no degree detracted from her native charms.

Captain Wharton, without heeding this display of interest in his sister, immediately continued, "At times he is melancholy—we tell him it must be love." Sarah raised her eyes to the face of her brother, and was consciously turning them on the rest of the party, when she met those of her sister laughing with good humor and high spirits, as she cried, "Poor man! does he despair?"

"Why, no—one would think he could not; the eldest son of a man of wealth, so handsome, and a colonel."

"Strong reasons, indeed, why he should prevail," said Sarah, endeavoring to laugh; "more particularly the latter."

"Let me tell you," replied the captain, gravely, "a lieutenant colonelcy in the Guards is a very pretty thing."

"And Colonel Wellmere a very pretty man," added Frances.

"Nay, Frances," returned her sister, "Colonel Wellmere was never a favorite of yours; he is too loyal to his king to be agreeable to your taste."

Frances quickly answered, "And is not Henry loyal to his king?"

"Come, come," said Miss Peyton, "no difference of opinion about the colonel—he is a favorite of mine."

"Fanny likes majors better," cried the brother, pulling her upon his knee.

"Nonsense!" said the blushing girl, as she endeavored to extricate herself from the grasp of her laughing brother.

"It surprises me," continued the captain, "that Peyton, when he procured the release of my father, did not endeavor to detain my sister in the rebel camp."

"That might have endangered his own liberty," said the smiling girl, resuming her seat. "You know it is liberty for which Major Dunwoodie is fighting."

"Liberty!" exclaimed Sarah; "very pretty liberty which exchanges one master for fifty."

"The privilege of changing masters at all is a liberty."

"And one you ladies would sometimes be glad to exercise," cried the captain.

"We like, I believe, to have the liberty of choosing who they shall be in the first place," said the laughing girl. "Don't we, Aunt Jeanette?"

"Me!" cried Miss Peyton, starting; "what do I know of such things, child? You must ask someone else, if you wish to learn such matters."

"Ah! you would have us think you were never young! But what am I to believe of all the tales I have heard about the handsome Miss Jeanette Peyton?"

"Nonsense, my dear, nonsense," said the aunt, endeavoring to suppress a smile; "it is very silly to believe all you hear."

"Nonsense, do you call it?" cried the captain, gayly. "To this hour General Montrose toasts Miss Peyton; I heard him within the week, at Sir Henry's table."

"Why, Henry, you are as saucy as your sister; and to break in upon your folly, I must take you to see my new home-made manufactures which I will be bold enough to put in contrast with the finery of Birch."

The young people rose to follow their aunt, in perfect good humor with each other and the world. On ascending the stairs to the place of deposit for Miss Peyton's articles of domestic economy, she availed herself, however, of an opportunity to inquire of her nephew, whether General Montrose suffered as much from the gout as he had done when she knew him.

It is a painful discovery we make, as we advance in life, that even those we most love are not exempt from its frailties. When the heart is fresh, and the view of the future unsullied by the blemishes which have been gathered from the experience of the past, out feelings are most holy: we love to identify with the persons of our natural friends all those qualities to which we ourselves aspire, and all those virtues we have been taught to revere. The confidence with which we esteem seems a part of our nature; and there is a purity thrown around the affections which tie us to our kindred that after life can seldom hope to see uninjured. The family of Mr. Wharton continued to enjoy, for the remainder of the day, a happiness to which they had long been strangers; and one that sprang, in its younger members, from the delights of the most confident affection, and the exchange of the most disinterested endearments.

Harper appeared only at the dinner table, and he retired with the cloth, under the pretense of some engagement in his own room. Notwithstanding the confidence created by his manner, the family felt his absence a relief; for the visit of Captain Wharton was necessarily to be confined to a very few days, both from the limitation of his leave of absence, and the danger of a discovery.

All dread of consequences, however, was lost in the pleasure of the meeting. Once or twice during the day, Mr. Wharton had suggested a doubt as to the character of his unknown guest, and the possibility of the detection of his son proceeding in some manner from his information; but the idea was earnestly opposed by all his children; even Sarah uniting with her brother and sister in pleading warmly in favor of the sincerity expressed in the outward appearance of the traveler.

"Such appearances, my children," replied the desponding parent, "are but too often deceitful; when men like Major Andre lend themselves to the purposes of fraud, it is idle to reason from qualities, much less externals."

"Fraud!" cried his son quickly. "Surely, sir, you forget that Major Andre was serving his king, and that the usages of war justified the measure."

"And did not the usages of war justify his death, Henry?" inquired Frances, speaking in a low voice, unwilling to abandon what she thought the cause of her country, and yet unable to suppress her feelings for the man.

"Never!" exclaimed the young man, springing from his seat, and pacing the floor rapidly. "Frances, you shock me; suppose it should be my fate, even now, to fall into the power of the rebels; you would vindicate my execution—perhaps exult in the cruelty of Washington."

"Henry!" said Frances, solemnly, quivering with emotion, and with a face pale as death, "you little know my heart."

"Pardon me, my sister—my little Fanny," cried the repentant youth, pressing her to his bosom, and kissing off the tears which had burst, spite of her resolution, from her eyes.

"It is very foolish to regard your hasty words, I know," said Frances, extricating herself from his arms, and raising her yet humid eyes to his face with a smile; "but reproach from those we love is most severe, Henry; particularly—where we—we think—we know"—her paleness gradually gave place to the color of the rose, as she concluded in a low voice, with her eyes directed to the carpet, "we arc undeserving of it."

Miss Peyton moved from her own seat to the one next her niece, and, kindly taking her hand, observed, "You should not suffer the impetuosity of your brother to affect you so much; boys, you know, are proverbially ungovernable."

"And, from my conduct, you might add cruel," said the captain, seating himself on the other side of his sister. "But on the subject of the death of Andre we are all of us uncommonly sensitive. You did not know him: he was all that was brave—that was accomplished—that was estimable." Frances smiled faintly, and shook her head, but made no reply. Her brother, observing the marks of incredulity in her countenance, continued, "You doubt it, and justify his death?"

"I do not doubt his worth," replied the maid, mildly, "nor his being deserving of a more happy fate; but I cannot doubt the propriety of Washington's conduct, I know but little of the customs of war, and wish to know less; but with what hopes of success could the Americans contend, if they yielded all the principles which long usage had established, to the exclusive purposes of the British?"

"Why contend at all?" cried Sarah, impatiently. "Besides, being rebels, all their acts are illegal."

"Women are but mirrors, which reflect the images before them," cried the captain, good-naturedly. "In Frances I see the picture of Major Dunwoodie, and in Sarah—"

"Colonel Wellmere," interrupted the younger sister, laughing, and blushing crimson. "I must confess I am indebted to the major for my reasoning—am I not, Aunt Jeanette?"

"I believe it is something like his logic, indeed, child."

"I plead guilty; and you, Sarah, have not forgotten the learned. discussions of Colonel Wellmere."

"I trust I never forget the right," said Sarah, emulating her sister in color, and rising, under the pretense of avoiding the heat of the fire.

Nothing occurred of any moment during the rest of the day; but in the evening Cæsar reported that he had overheard voices in the room of Harper, conversing in a low tone. The apartment occupied by the traveler was the wing at the extremity of the building, opposite to the parlor in which the family ordinarily assembled; and it seems that Cæsar had established a regular system of espionage, with a view to the safety of his young master. This intelligence gave some uneasiness to all the members of the family; but the entrance of Harper himself, with the air of benevolence and sincerity which shone through his reserve, soon removed the doubts from the breast of all but Mr. Wharton. His children and sister believed Cæsar to have been mistaken, and the evening passed off without any additional alarm.

On the afternoon of the succeeding day, the party were assembled in the parlor around the tea table of Miss Peyton, when a change in the weather occurred. The thin scud, that apparently floated but a short distance above the tops of the hills, began to drive from the west towards the east in astonishing rapidity. The rain yet continued to beat against the eastern windows of the house with fury; in that direction the heavens were dark and gloomy. Frances was gazing at the scene with the desire of youth to escape from the tedium of confinement, when, as if by magic, all was still. The rushing winds had ceased, the pelting of the storm was over, and, springing to the . window, with delight pictured in her face, she saw a glorious ray of sunshine lighting the opposite wood. The foliage glittered with the checkered beauties of the October leaf, reflecting back from the moistened boughs the richest luster of an American autumn. In an instant, the piazza, which opened to the south, was thronged with the inmates of the cottage. The air was mild, balmy, and refreshing; in the east, clouds, which might be likened to the retreating masses of a discomfited army, hung around the horizon in awful and increasing darkness. At a little elevation above the cottage, the thin vapor was still rushing towards the east with amazing velocity; while in the west the sun had broken forth and shed his parting radiance on the scene below, aided by the fullest richness of a clear atmosphere and a freshened herbage. Such moments belong only to the climate of America, and are enjoyed in a degree proportioned to the suddenness of the contrast, and the pleasure we experience in escaping from the turbulence of the elements to the quiet of a peaceful evening, and an air still as the softest mornings in June.

"What a magnificent scene!" said Harper, in a low tone. "How grand! how awfully sublime!—may such a quiet speedily await the struggle in which my country is engaged, and such a glorious evening follow the day of her adversity!"

Frances, who stood next to him, alone heard the voice. Turning in amazement from the view to the speaker, she saw him standing bareheaded, erect, and with his eyes lifted to heaven. There was no longer the quiet which had seemed their characteristic, but they were lighted into something like enthusiasm, and a slight flush passed over his features.

There can be no danger apprehended from such a man, thought Frances; such feelings belong only to the virtuous.

The musings of the party were now interrupted by the sudden appearance of the peddler. He had taken advantage of the first gleam of sunshine to hasten to the cottage. Heedless of wet or dry as it lay in his path, with arms swinging to and fro, and with his head bent forward of his body several inches, Harvey Birch approached the piazza, with a gait peculiarly his own. It was the quick, lengthened pace of an itinerant vender of goods.

"Fine evening," said the peddler, saluting the party, without raising his eyes; "quite warm and agreeable for the season."

Mr. Wharton assented to the remark, and inquired kindly after the health of his father. Harvey heard him, and continued standing for some time in moody silence; but the question being repeated, he answered with a slight tremor in his voice,—

"He fails fast; old age and hardships will do their work." The peddler turned his face from the view of most of the family; but Frances noticed his glistening eyes and quivering lip, and, for the second time, Harvey rose in her estimation.

The valley in which the residence of Mr. Wharton stood ran in a direction from northwest to southeast, and the house was placed on the side of a hill which terminated its length in the former direction. A small opening, occasioned by the receding of the opposite hill, and the fall of land to the level of the tide water, afforded a view of the Sound[5] over the tops of the distant woods on its margin. The surface of the water which had so lately been lashing the shores with boisterous fury, was already losing its ruffled darkness in the long and regular undulations that succeeded a tempest, while the light air from the southwest was gently touching their summits, lending its feeble aid in stilling the waters. Some dark spots were now to be distinguished, occasionally rising into view, and again sinking behind the lengthened waves which interposed themselves to the sight. They were unnoticed by all but the peddler. He had seated himself on the piazza, at a distance from Harper, and appeared to have forgotten the object of his visit. His roving eye, however, soon caught a glimpse of these new objects in the view, and he sprang up with alacrity, gazing intently towards the water. He changed his place, glanced his eye with marked uneasiness on Harper, and then said with great emphasis,—

"The rig'lars must be out from below."

"Why do you think so?" inquired Captain Wharton, eagerly. "God send it may be true; I want their escort in again."

"Them ten whaleboats would not move so fast unless they were better manned than common."

"Perhaps," cried Mr. Wharton in alarm, "they are—they are continentials returning from the island."

"They look like rig'lars," said the peddler, with meaning.

"Look!"—repeated the captain, "there is nothing but spots to be seen."

Harvey disregarded his observation, but seemed to be soliloquizing, as he said in an undertone, "They came out before the gale—have laid on the islands these two days—horse are on the road—there will soon be fighting near us." During this speech, Birch several times glanced his eye towards Harper, with evident uneasiness, but no corresponding emotion betrayed any

---

[5] An island more than forty leagues in length lies opposite the coasts of New York and Connecticut. The arm of the sea which separates it from the main is technically called a sound, and in that part of the country *par excellence, the* Sound. This sheet of water varies in its breadth from five to thirty miles.

interest of that gentleman in the scene. He stood in silent contemplation of the view, and seemed enjoying the change in the air. As Birch concluded, however, Harper turned to his host, and mentioned that his business would not admit of unnecessary delay; he would, therefore, avail himself of the fine evening to ride a few miles on his journey. Mr. Wharton made many professions of regret at losing so agreeable an inmate; but was too mindful of his duty not to speed the parting guest, and orders were instantly given to that effect.

The uneasiness of the peddler increased in a manner for which nothing apparent could account; his eye was constantly wandering towards the lower end of the vale as if in expectation of some interruption from that quarter. At length Cæsar appeared, leading the noble beast which was to bear the weight of the traveler. The peddler officiously assisted to tighten the girths, and fasten the blue cloak and valise to the mailstraps.

Every precaution being completed, Harper proceeded to take his leave. To Sarah and her aunt he paid his compliments with ease and kindness; but when he came to Frances, he paused a moment, while his face assumed an expression of more than ordinary benignity. His eye repeated the blessing which had before fallen from his lips, and the girl felt her cheeks glow, and her heart beat with a quicker pulsation, as he spoke his adieus. There was a mutual exchange of polite courtesy between the host and his parting guest; but as Harper frankly offered his hand to Captain Wharton, he remarked, in a manner of great solemnity—

"The step you have undertaken is one of much danger, and disagreeable consequences to yourself may result from it; in such a case, I may have it in my power to prove the gratitude I owe your family for its kindness."

"Surely, sir," cried the father, losing sight of delicacy in apprehension for his child, "you will keep secret the discovery which your being in my house has enabled you to make?"

Harper turned quickly to the speaker, and then, losing the sternness which had begun to gather on his countenance, he answered mildly, "I have learned nothing in your family, sir, of which I was ignorant before; but your son is safer from my knowledge of his visit than he would be without it."

He bowed to the whole party, and without taking any notice of the peddler, other than by simply thanking him for his attentions, mounted his horse, and, riding steadily and gracefully through the little gate, was soon lost behind the hill which sheltered the valley to the northward.

The eyes of the peddler followed the retiring figure of the horseman so long as it continued within view, and as it disappeared from his sight, he drew a long and heavy" sigh, as if relieved from a load of apprehension. The Whartons had meditated in silence on the character and visit of their unknown guest for the same period, when the father approached Birch and observed,—

"I am yet your debtor, Harvey, for the tobacco you were so kind as to bring me from the city."

"If it should not prove so good as the first," replied the peddler, fixing a last and lingering look in the direction of Harper's route, "it is owing to the scarcity of the article."

"I like it much," continued the other; "but you have forgotten to name the price."

The countenance of the trader changed, and, losing its expression of deep care in a natural acuteness, he answered,—

"It is hard to say what ought to be the price; I believe I must leave it to your own generosity."

Mr. Wharton had taken a hand well filled with the images of Carolus III from his pocket, and now extended it towards Birch with three of the pieces between his finger and thumb. Harvey's eyes twinkled as he contemplated the reward; and rolling over in his mouth a large quantity of the article in question, coolly stretched forth his hand, into which the dollars fell with a most agreeable sound: but not satisfied with the transient music of their fall, the peddler gave each piece in succession a ring on the stepping-stone of the piazza, before he consigned it to the safe-keeping of a huge deerskin purse, which vanished from the sight of the spectators so dexterously, that not one of them could have told about what part of his person it was secreted.

This very material point in his business so satisfactorily completed, the peddler rose from his seat on the floor of the piazza, and approached to where Captain Wharton stood, supporting his sisters on either arm, as they listened with the lively interest of affection to his conversation.

The agitation of the preceding incidents had caused such an expenditure of the juices which had become necessary to the mouth of the peddler, that a new supply of the weed was required before he could turn his attention to business of lesser moment. This done, he asked abruptly,—

"Captain Wharton, do you go in to-night?"

"No!" said captain, laconically, and looking at his lovely .burdens with great affection. "Mr. Birch, would you have me leave such company so soon, when I may never enjoy it again?"

"Brother!" said Frances, "jesting on such a subject is cruel."

"I rather guess," continued the peddler, coolly, "now the storm is over, the Skinners may be moving; you had better shorten your visit, Captain Wharton."

"Oh!" cried the British officer, "a few guineas will buy off those rascals at any time, should I meet them. No, no, Mr. Birch, here I stay until morning."

"Money could not liberate Major Andre," said the peddler, dryly.

Both the sisters now turned to the captain in alarm, and the elder observed,—

"You had better take the advice of Harvey; rest assured, his opinion in such matters ought not to be disregarded."

"Yes," added the younger, "if, as I suspect, Mr. Birch assisted you to come here, your safety, our happiness, dear Henry, requires you to listen to him now."

"I brought myself out, and can take myself in," said the captain positively. "Our bargain went no further than to procure my disguise, and to let me know when the coast was clear; and in the latter particular, you were mistaken, Mr. Birch."

"I was," said the peddler, with some interest, "and the greater is the reason why you should get back to-night; the pass I gave you will serve but once."

"Cannot you forge another?"

The pale cheek of the trader showed an unusual color, but he continued silent, with his eyes fixed on the ground, until the young man added, with great positiveness, "Here I stay this night, come what will."

"Captain Wharton," said the peddler, with great deliberation and marked emphasis, "beware a tall Virginian, with huge whiskers; he is below you, to my knowledge; the devil can't deceive him; I never could but once."

"Let him beware of me," said Wharton, haughtily. "But, Mr.

Birch, I exonerate you from further responsibility."

"Will you give me that ,in writing?" asked the cautious Birch.

"Oh; cheerfully," cried the captain, with a laugh. "Cæsar! pen, ink, and paper, while I write a discharge for my trusty attendant, Harvey Birch, peddler, etc., etc."

The implements for writing were produced, and the captain, with great gayety, wrote the desired acknowledgment in language of his own; which the peddler took, and carefully depositing it by the side of the image of his Catholic Majesty, made a sweeping bow to the whole family, and departed as he had approached. He was soon seen at a distance, stealing into the door of his own humble dwelling.

The father and sisters of the captain were too much rejoiced in retaining the young man to express, or even entertain, the apprehensions his situation might reasonably excite; but on retiring to their evening repast, a cooler reflection induced the captain to think of changing his mind. Unwilling to trust himself out of the protection of his father's domains, the young man dispatched Cæsar to desire another interview with Harvey. The black soon returned with the unwelcome intelligence that it was now too late. Katy had told him that Harvey must be miles on his road to the northward, "having left home at early candlelight with his pack." Nothing now remained to the captain but patience, until the morning should afford further opportunity of deciding on the best course for him to pursue.

"This Harvey Birch, with his knowing looks and portentous warnings, gives me more uneasiness than I am willing to own," said Captain Wharton, rousing himself from a fit of musing in which the danger of his situation made no small part of his meditations.

"How is it that he is able to travel to and fro in these difficult times, without molestation?" inquired Miss Peyton.

"Why the rebels suffer him to escape so easily, is more than I can answer," returned the other; "but Sir Henry would not permit a hair of his head to be injured."

"Indeed!" cried Frances, with interest. "Is he then known to Sir Henry Clinton?"

"At least he ought to be."

"Do you think, my son," asked Mr. Wharton, "there is no

danger of his betraying you?"

"Why—no; I reflected on that before I trusted myself to his power," said the captain, thoughtfully. "He seems to be faithful in matters of business. The danger to himself, should he return to the city, would prevent such an act of villainy."

"I think," said Frances, adopting the manner of her brother, "Harvey Birch is not without good feelings; at least he has the appearance of them at times."

"Oh!" cried his sister, exulting, "he has loyalty, and that with me is a cardinal virtue."

"I am afraid," said her brother, laughing, "love of money is a stronger passion than love of his king."

"Then," said the father, "you cannot be safe while in his power—-for no love will withstand the temptations of money, when offered to avarice."

"Surely, sir," cried the youth, recovering his gayety, "there must be one love that can resist anything—is there not. Fanny?"

"Here is your candle; you keep your father up beyond his usual hour."

CHAPTER V

Through Solway sands, through Taross moss,
Blindfold, he knew the paths to cross:
By wily turns, by desperate bounds,
Had baffled Percy's best bloodhounds.
In Eske, or Liddel, fords were none,
But he would ride them, one by one;
Alike to him was time or tide,
December's snow or July's pride;
Alike to him was tide or time,
Moonless midnight or matin prime.

—Walter Scott

All the members of the Wharton family laid their heads on their pillows that night, with a foreboding of some interruption to their ordinary quiet. Uneasiness kept the sisters from enjoying their usual repose, and they rose from their beds, on the following morning, unrefreshed, and almost without having closed their eyes.

On taking an eager and hasty survey of the valley from the windows of their room, nothing, however, but its usual serenity was to be seen. It was glittering with the opening brilliancy of one of those lovely, mild days, which occur about the time of the falling of the leaf; and which, by their frequency, class the American autumn with the most delightful seasons of other countries. We have no spring; vegetation seems to leap into existence, instead of creeping, as in the same latitudes of the Old World; but how gracefully it retires! September, October, even November and December, compose the season for enjoyment in the open air; they have their storms, but they are distinct, and not of long continuance, leaving a clear atmosphere and a cloudless sky.

As nothing could be seen likely to interrupt the enjoyments and harmony of such a day, the sisters descended to the parlor, with a returning confidence in their brother's security, and their own happiness.

The family were early in assembling around the breakfast

table; and Miss Peyton, with a little of that minute, precision which creeps into the habits of single life, had pleasantly insisted that the absence of her nephew should in no manner interfere with the regular hours she had established; consequently, the party were already seated when the captain made his appearance; though the untasted coffee sufficiently proved that by none of his relatives was his absence disregarded.

"I think I did much better," he cried, taking a chair between his sisters, and receiving their offered salutes, "to secure a good bed and such a plentiful breakfast, instead of trusting to the hospitality of that renowned corps, the Cowboys."

"If you could sleep," said Sarah, "you were more fortunate than Frances and myself; every murmur of the night air sounded to me like the approach of the rebel army."

"Why," said the captain, laughing, "I do acknowledge a little inquietude myself—but how was it with you?" turning to his younger and evidently favorite sister, and tapping her cheek. "Did you see banners in the clouds, and mistake Miss Peyton's Æolian harp for rebellious music?"

"Nay, Henry," rejoined the maid, looking at him affectionately, "much as I love my own country, the approach of her troops just now would give me great pain."

The brother made no reply; but returning the fondness expressed in her eye by a look of fraternal tenderness, he gently pressed her hand in silence; when Cæsar, who had participated largely in the anxiety of the family, and who had risen with the dawn, and kept a vigilant watch on the surrounding objects, as he stood gazing from one of the windows, exclaimed with a face that approached to something like the hues of a white man,—

"Run—Massa Harry—run—if he love old Cæsar, run—here come a rebel horse."

"Run!" repeated the British officer, gathering himself up in military pride. "No, Mr. Cæsar, running is not my trade." While speaking, he walked deliberately to the window, where the family were already collected in the greatest consternation.

At the distance of more than a mile, about fifty dragoons were to be seen, winding down one of the lateral entrances of the valley. In advance, with an officer, was a man attired in the dress of a countryman, who pointed in the direction of the cottage. A small party now left the main body, and moved rapidly towards the object of their destination.

On reaching the road which led through the bottom of the valley, they turned their horses' heads to the north.

The Whartons continued chained in breathless silence to the spot, watching their movements, when the party, having reached the dwelling of Birch, made a rapid circle around his grounds, and in an instant his house was surrounded by a dozen sentinels.

Two or three of the dragoons now dismounted and disappeared; in a few minutes, however, they returned to the yard, followed by Katy, from whose violent gesticulations, it was evident that matters of no trifling concern were on the carpet. A short communication with the loquacious housekeeper followed the arrival of the main body of the troop, and the advance party remounting, the whole moved towards the Locusts with great speed.

As yet none of the family had sufficient presence of mind to devise any means of security for Captain Wharton; but the danger now became too pressing to admit of longer delay, and various means of secreting him were hastily proposed; but they were all haughtily rejected by the young man, as unworthy of his character. It was too late to retreat to the woods in the rear of the cottage, for he would unavoidably be seen, and, followed by a troop of horse, as inevitably taken.

At length his sisters, with trembling hands, replaced his original disguise, the instruments of which had been carefully kept at hand by Cæsar, in expectation of some sudden emergency.

This arrangement was hastily and imperfectly completed, as the dragoons entered the lawn and orchard of the Locusts, riding with the rapidity of the wind; and in their turn the Whartons were surrounded.

Nothing remained now, but to meet the impending examination with as much indifference as the family could assume. The leader of the horse dismounted, and, followed by a couple of his men, he approached the outer door of the building, which was slowly and reluctantly opened for his admission by Cæsar. The heavy tread of the trooper, as he followed the black to the door of the parlor, rang in the ears of the females as it approached nearer and nearer, and drove the blood from their faces to their hearts, with a chill that nearly annihilated feeling.

A man, whose colossal stature manifested the possession of vast strength, entered the room, and removing his cap, he saluted the family with a mildness his appearance did not indicate as belonging to his nature. His dark hair hung around his brow in profusion, though stained with powder which was worn at that day, and his face was nearly hid in the whiskers by which it was disfigured. Still, the expression of his eye, though piercing, was not bad, and his voice, though deep and powerful, was far from unpleasant. Frances ventured to throw a timid glance at his figure as he entered, and saw at once the man from whose scrutiny Harvey Birch had warned them there was so much to be apprehended.

"You have no cause for alarm, ladies," said the officer, pausing a moment, and contemplating the pale faces around him. "My business will be confined to a few questions, which, if freely answered, will instantly remove us from your dwelling."

"And what may they be, sir?" stammered Mr. Wharton, rising from his chair and waiting anxiously for the reply.

"Has there been a strange gentleman staying with you during the storm?" continued the dragoon, speaking with interest, and in some degree sharing in the evident anxiety of the father.

"This gentleman—here—favored us with his company during the rain, and has not yet departed."

"This gentleman!" repeated the other, turning to Captain Wharton, and contemplating his figure for a moment until the anxiety of his countenance gave place to a lurking smile. He approached the youth with an air of comic gravity, and with a low bow, continued, "I am sorry for the severe cold you have in your head, sir."

"I!" exclaimed the captain, in surprise; "I have no cold in my head."

"I fancied it then, from seeing you had covered such handsome black locks with that ugly old wig. It was my mistake; you will please to pardon it."

Mr. Wharton groaned aloud; but the ladies, ignorant of the extent of their visitor's knowledge, remained in trembling yet rigid silence. The captain himself moved his hand involuntarily to his head, and discovered that the trepidation of his sisters had left some of his natural hair exposed. The dragoon watched the movement with a continued smile, when, seeming to recollect himself, turning to the father, he proceeded,—

"Then, sir, I am to understand there has not been a Mr. Harper here, within the week?"

"Mr. Harper," echoed the other, feeling a load removed from his heart, "yes, I had forgotten; but he is gone; and if there be anything wrong in his character, we are in entire ignorance of it; to me he was a total stranger."

"You have but little to apprehend from his character," answered the dragoon dryly. "But he is gone—how—when—and whither?"

"He departed as he arrived," said Mr. Wharton, gathering renewed confidence from the manner of the trooper; "on horseback, last evening, and he took the northern road."

The officer listened to him with intense interest, his countenance gradually lighting into a smile of pleasure, and the instant Mr. Wharton concluded his laconic reply he turned on his heel and left the apartment. The Whartons, judging from his manner, thought he was about to proceed in quest of the object of his inquiries. They observed the dragoon, on gaining the lawn, in earnest and apparently pleased conversation with his two subalterns. In a few moments orders were given to some of the troops, and horsemen left the valley, at full speed, by its various roads.

The suspense of the party within, who were all highly interested witnesses of this scene, was shortly terminated; for the heavy tread of the dragoon soon announced his second approach. He bowed again politely as he re-entered the room, and walking up to Captain Wharton, said, with comic gravity,—

"Now, sir, my principal business being done, may I beg to examine the quality of that wig?"

The British officer imitated the manner of the other, as he deliberately uncovered his head, and handing him the wig, observed, "I hope, sir, it is to your liking."

"I cannot, without violating the truth, say it is," returned the dragoon. "I prefer your ebony hair, from which you seem to have combed the powder with great industry. But that must have been a sad hurt you have received under this enormous black patch."

"You appear so close an observer of things, I should like your opinion of it, sir," said Henry, removing the silk, and exhibiting the cheek free from blemish.

"Upon my word, you improve most rapidly in externals,"

added the trooper, preserving his muscles in inflexible gravity. "If I could but persuade you to exchange this old surtout for that handsome blue coat by your side, I think I never could witness a more agreeable metamorphosis, since I was changed myself from a lieutenant to a captain."

Young Wharton very composedly did as was required and stood an extremely handsome, well-dressed young man. The dragoon looked at him for a minute with the drollery that characterized his manner, and then continued,—

"This is a newcomer in the scene; it is usual, you know, for strangers to be introduced; I am Captain Lawton, of the Virginia horse."

"And I, sir, am Captain Wharton, of his Majesty's 60th regiment of foot," returned Henry, bowing stiffly, and recovering his natural manner.

The countenance of Lawton changed instantly, and his assumed quaintness vanished. He viewed the figure of Captain Wharton, as he stood proudly swelling with a pride that disdained further concealment, and exclaimed with great earnestness,—

"Captain Wharton, from my soul I pity you!"

"Oh! then," cried the father in agony, "if you pity him, dear sir, why molest him? He is not a spy; nothing but a desire to see his friends prompted him to venture so far from the regular army in disguise. Leave him with us; there is no reward, no sum, which I will not cheerfully pay."

"Sir, your anxiety for your friend excuses your language," said Lawton, haughtily; "but you forget I am a Virginian, and a gentleman." Turning to the young man, he continued, "Were you ignorant, Captain Wharton, that our pickets have been below you for several days?"

"I did not know it until I reached them, and it was then too late to retreat," said Wharton sullenly. "I came out, as my father has mentioned, to see my friends, understanding your parties to be at Peekskill, and near the Highlands, or surely I would not have ventured."

"All this may be true; but the affair of Andre has made us on the alert. When treason reaches the grade of general officers, Captain Wharton, it behooves the friends of liberty to be vigilant."

Henry bowed to this remark in distant silence, but Sarah ventured to urge something in behalf of her brother. The dragoon heard her politely, and apparently with commiseration; but willing to avoid useless and embarrassing petitions, he answered mildly,—

"I am not the commander of the party, madam; Major Dunwoodie will decide what must be done with your brother; at all events he will receive nothing but kind and gentle treatment."

"Dunwoodie!" exclaimed Frances, with a face in which the roses contended for the mastery with the paleness of apprehension. "Thank God! then Henry is safe!"

Lawton regarded her with a mingled expression of pity and admiration; then shaking his head doubtfully, he continued,—

"I hope so; and with your permission, we will leave the matter for his decision."

The color of Frances changed from the paleness of fear to the glow of hope. Her dread on behalf of her brother was certainly greatly diminished; yet her form shook, her breathing became short and irregular, and her whole frame gave tokens of extraordinary agitation. Her eyes rose from the floor to the dragoon, and were again fixed immovably on the carpet—she evidently wished to utter something but was unequal to the effort. Miss Peyton was a close observer of these movements of her niece, and advancing with an air of feminine dignity, inquired,—

"Then, sir, we may expect the pleasure of Major Dunwoodie's company shortly?"

"Immediately, madam," answered the dragoon, withdrawing his admiring gaze from the person of Frances. "Expresses are already on the road to announce to him our situation, and the intelligence will speedily bring him to this valley; unless, indeed, some private reasons may exist to make a visit particularly unpleasant."

"We shall always be happy to see Major Dunwoodie."

"Oh! doubtless; he is a general favorite. May I presume on it so far as to ask leave to dismount and refresh my men, who compose a part of his squadron?"

There was a manner about the trooper that would have made the omission of such a request easily forgiven by Mr. Wharton, but he was fairly entrapped by his own eagerness to conciliate, and it was useless to withhold a consent which he thought would probably be extorted; he therefore made the most of necessity, and gave such orders as would facilitate the wishes of Captain Lawton.

The officers were invited to take their morning's repast at the family breakfast table, and having made their arrangements without, the invitation was frankly accepted. None of the watch-ful-ness, which was so necessary to their situation, was neglected by the wary partisan.* Patrols were seen on the distant hills, taking their protecting circuit around their comrades, who were enjoying, in the midst of danger, a security that can only spring from the watchfulness of discipline and the indifference of habit.

The addition to the party at Mr. Wharton's table was only three, and they were all of them men who, under the rough exterior induced by actual and arduous service, concealed the manners of gentlemen. Consequently, the interruption to the domestic privacy of the family was marked by the observance of strict decorum. The ladies left the table to their guests, who proceeded, without much superfluous diffidence, to do proper honors to the hospitality of Mr. Wharton.

At length Captain Lawton suspended for a moment his violent attacks on the buckwheat cakes, to inquire of the master of the house, if there was not a peddler of the name of Birch who lived in the valley at times.

"At times only, I believe, sir," replied Mr. Wharton, cautiously. "He is seldom here; I may say I never see him."

"That is strange, too," said the trooper, looking at the disconcerted host intently, "considering he is your next neighbor; he must be quite domestic, sir; and to the ladies it must be somewhat inconvenient. I doubt not that that muslin in the window seat cost twice as much as he would have asked them for it."

Mr. Wharton turned in consternation, and saw some of the recent purchases scattered about the room.

The two subalterns struggled to conceal their smiles; but the captain resumed his breakfast with an eagerness that created a doubt, whether he ever expected to enjoy another. The necessity of a supply from the dominion of Dinah soon, however, afforded another respite, of which Lawton availed himself.

"I had a wish to break this Mr. Birch of his unsocial habits, and gave him a call this morning," he said. "Had I found him within, I should have placed him where he would enjoy life in the midst of society, for a short time at least."

"And where might that be, sir?" asked Mr. Wharton, conceiving it necessary to say something.

"The guardroom," said the trooper, dryly.

"What is the offense of poor Birch?" asked Miss Peyton, handing the dragoon a fourth dish of coffee.

"Poor!" cried the captain. "If he is poor, King George is a bad paymaster."

"Yes,, indeed," said one of the subalterns, "his Majesty owes him a dukedom."

"And congress a halter," continued the commanding officer commencing anew on a fresh supply of the cakes.

"I am sorry," said Mr. Wharton, "that any neighbor of mine should incur the displeasure of our rulers."

"If I catch him," cried the dragoon, while buttering another cake, "he will dangle from the limbs of one of his namesakes."

"He would make no bad ornament, suspended from one of those locusts before his own door," added the lieutenant.

"Never mind," continued the captain; "I will have him yet before I'm a major."

As the language of the officers appeared to be sincere, and such as disappointed men in their rough occupations are but too apt to use, the Whartons thought it prudent to discontinue the subject. It was no new intelligence to any of the family, that Harvey Birch was distrusted and greatly harassed by the American army. His escapes from their hands, no less than his imprisonments, had been the conversation of the country in too many instances, and under circumstances of too great mystery, to be easily forgotten. In fact, no small part of the bitterness expressed by Captain Lawton against the peddler, arose from the unaccountable disappearance of the latter, when intrusted to the custody of two of his most faithful dragoons.

A twelvemonth had not vet elapsed, since Birch had been seen lingering near the headquarters of the commander in chief, and at a time when important movements were expected hourly to occur. So soon as the information of this fact was communicated to the officer whose duty it was to guard the avenues of the American camp, he dispatched Captain Lawton in pursuit of the peddler.

Acquainted with all the passes of the hills, and indefatigable in the discharge of his duty, the trooper had, with much trouble and toil, succeeded in effecting his object. The party had halted at a farmhouse for the purposes of refreshment, and the prisoner was placed in a room by himself, but under the keeping of the two men before mentioned; all that was known subsequently is, that a woman was seen busily engaged in the employments of the household near the sentinels, and was particularly attentive to the wants of the captain, until he was deeply engaged in the employments of the supper table.

Afterwards, neither woman nor peddler was to be found. The pack, indeed, was discovered open, and nearly empty, and a small door, communicating with a room adjoining to the one in which the peddler had been secured, was ajar.

Captain Lawton never could forgive the deception; his antipathies to his enemies were not very moderate, but this was adding an insult to his penetration that rankled deeply. He sat in . portentous silence, brooding over the exploit of his prisoner, yet mechanically pursuing the business before him, until, after sufficient time had passed to make a very comfortable meal, a trumpet suddenly broke on the ears of the party, sending its martial tones up the valley, in startling melody. The trooper rose instantly from the table, exclaiming,—

"Quick, gentlemen, to your horses; there comes Dunwoodie," and, followed by his officers, he precipitately left the room.

With the exception of the sentinels left to guard Captain Wharton, the dragoons mounted, and marched out to meet their comrades.

None of the watchfulness necessary in a war, in which similarity of language, appearance, and customs rendered prudence doubly necessary, was omitted by the cautious leader. On getting sufficiently near, however, to a body of horse of more than double his own number, to distinguish countenances, Lawton plunged his rowels into his charger, and in a moment he was by the side of his commander.

The ground in front of the cottage was again occupied by the horse; and observing the same precautions as before, the newly arrived troops hastened to participate in the cheer prepared for their comrades.

CHAPTER VI

And let conquerors boast
Their fields of fame—he who in virtue arms
A young warm spirit against beauty's charms,
Who feels her brightness, yet defies her thrall,
Is the best, bravest conqueror of them all.

—Moore.

The ladies of the Wharton family had collected about a window, deeply interested in the scene we have related.

Sarah viewed the approach of her countrymen with a smile of contemptuous indifference; for she even undervalued the personal appearance of men whom she thought arrayed in the unholy cause of rebellion. Miss Peyton looked on the gallant show with an exulting pride, which arose in the reflection that the warriors before her were the chosen troops of her native colony; while Frances gazed with a singleness of interest that absorbed all other considerations.

The two parties had not yet joined, before her quick eye distinguished one horseman in particular from those around him. To her it appeared that even the steed of this youthful soldier seemed to be conscious that he sustained the weight of no common man: his hoofs but lightly touched the earth, and his airy tread was the curbed motion of a blooded charger.

The dragoon sat in the saddle, with a firmness and ease that showed him master of himself and horse,— his figure uniting the just proportions of strength and activity, being tall, round, and muscular. To this officer Lawton made his report, and, side by side, they rode into the field opposite to the cottage.

The heart of Frances beat with a pulsation nearly stifling, as he paused for a moment, and took a survey of the building, with an eye whose dark and sparkling glance could be seen, notwithstanding the distance. Her color changed, and for an instant, as she saw the youth throw himself from the saddle, she was compelled to seek relief for her trembling limbs in a chair.

The officer gave a few hasty orders to his second in command, walked rapidly into the lawn, and approached the cottage.

Frances rose from her seat, and vanished from the apartment. The dragoon ascended the steps of the piazza, and had barely time to touch the outer door, when it opened to his admission.

The youth of Frances, when she left the city, had prevented her sacrificing, in conformity to the customs of that day, all her native beauties on the altar of fashion. Her hair, which was of a golden richness of color, was left, untortured, to fall in the natural ringlets of infancy, and it shaded a face which was glowing with the united charms of health, youth, and artlessness; her eyes spoke volumes, but her tongue was silent; her hands were interlocked before her, and, aided by her taper form, bending forward in an attitude of expectation, gave a loveliness and an interest to her appearance, that for a moment chained her lover in silence to the spot.

Frances silently led the way into a vacant parlor, opposite to the one in which the family were assembled, and turning to the soldier frankly, placing both her hands in his own, exclaimed,—

"Ah, Dunwoodie! how happy, on many accounts, I am to see you! I have brought you in here to prepare you to meet an unexpected friend in the opposite room."

"To whatever cause it may be owing," cried the youth, pressing her hands to his lips, "I, too, am happy in being able to see you alone. Frances, the probation you have decreed is cruel; war and distance may separate us forever."

"We must submit to the necessity which governs us. But it is not love speeches I would hear now; I have other and more important matter for your attention."

"What can be of more importance than to make you mine by a tie that will be indissoluble! Frances, you are cold to me—me—from whose mind, days of service and nights of alarm have never been able to banish your image for a single moment."

"Dear Dunwoodie," said Frances, softening nearly to tears, and again extending her hand to him, as the richness of her color gradually returned, "you know my sentiments—this war once ended, and you may take that hand forever—but I can never consent to tie myself to you by any closer union than already exists, so long as you are arrayed in arms against my only brother. Even now, that brother is awaiting your decision to restore him to liberty, or to conduct him to a probable death."

"Your brother!!" cried Dunwoodie, starting and turning

pale; "your brother! explain yourself—what dreadful meaning is concealed in your words?"

"Has not Captain Lawton told you of the arrest of Henry by himself this very morning?" continued Frances, in a voice barely audible, and fixing on her lover a look of the deepest concern.

"He told me of arresting a captain of the 60th in disguise, but without mentioning where or whom," replied the major in a similar tone; and dropping his head between his hands, he endeavored to conceal his feelings from his companion.

"Dunwoodie! Dunwoodie!" exclaimed Frances, losing all her former confidence in the most fearful apprehensions, "what means this agitation?" As the major slowly raised his face, in which was pictured the most expressive concern, she continued, "Surely, surely, you will not betray your friend—my brother—your brother—to an ignominious death."

"Frances!" exclaimed the young man in agony, "what can I do?"

"Do!" she repeated, gazing at him wildly. "Would Major Dunwoodie yield his friend to his enemies—the brother of his betrothed wife?"

"Oh, speak not so unkindly to me, dearest Miss Wharton—my own Frances. I would this moment die for you—for Henry—but I cannot forget my duty—cannot forfeit my honor; you yourself would be the first to despise me if I did."

"Peyton Dunwoodie!" said Frances, solemnly, and with a face of ashy paleness, "you have told me, you have sworn, that you love me—"

"I do," interrupted the soldier, with fervor; but motioning for silence she continued, in a voice that trembled with her fears,—

"Do you think I can throw myself into the arms of a man whose hands are stained with the blood of my only brother?"

"Frances, you wring my very heart!" Then pausing, to struggle with his feelings, he endeavored to force a smile, as he added, "But, after all, we may be torturing ourselves with unnecessary fears, and Henry, when I know the circumstances, may be nothing more than a prisoner of war; in which case, I can liberate him on parole."

There is no more delusive passion than hope; and it seems to be the happy privilege of youth to cull all the pleasures that can be gathered from its indulgence. It is when we are most worthy of confidence ourselves, that we are least apt to distrust others; and what we think ought to be, we are prone to think will be.

The half-formed expectations of the young soldier were communicated to the desponding sister, more by the eye than the voice, and the blood rushed again to her cheeks, as she cried,—

"Oh, there can be no just grounds to doubt it. I know—I knew—Dunwoodie, you would never desert us in the hour of our greatest need!" The violence of her feelings prevailed, and the agitated girl found relief in a flood of tears.

The office of consoling those we love is one of the dearest prerogatives of affection; and Major Dunwoodie, although but little encouraged by his own momentary suggestion of relief, could not undeceive the lovely girl, who leaned on his shoulder, as he wiped the traces of her feeling from her face, with a trembling, but reviving confidence in the safety of her brother, and the protection of her lover.

Frances, having sufficiently recovered her recollection to command herself, now eagerly led the way to the opposite room, to communicate to her family the pleasing intelligence which she already conceived so certain.

Dunwoodie followed her reluctantly, and with forebodings of the result; but a few moments brought him into the presence of his relatives, and he summoned all his resolution to meet the trial with firmness.

The salutations of the young men were cordial and frank, and, on the part of Henry Wharton, as collected as if nothing had occurred to disturb his self-possession.

The abhorrence of being, in any manner, auxiliary to the arrest of his friend; the danger to the life of Captain Wharton; and the heart-breaking declarations of Frances, had, however, created an uneasiness in the bosom of Major Dunwoodie, which all his efforts could not conceal. His reception by the rest of the family was kind and sincere, both from old regard, and a remembrance of former obligations, heightened by the anticipations they could not fail to read in the expressive eyes of the blushing girl by his side. After exchanging greetings with every member of the family, Major Dunwoodie beckoned to the sentinel, whom the wary prudence of Captain Lawton had left in charge of the prisoner, to leave the room. Turning to Captain Wharton, he inquired mildly,—

"Tell me, Henry, the circumstances of this disguise, in which Captain Lawton reports you to have found, and remember—remember—Captain Wharton—your answers are entirely voluntary."

"The disguise was used by me. Major Dunwoodie," replied the English officer, gravely, "to enable me to visit my friends, without incurring the danger of becoming a prisoner of war."

"But you did not wear it, until you saw the troop of Lawton approaching?"

"Oh, no," interrupted Frances, eagerly, forgetting all the circumstances in her anxiety for her brother. "Sarah and myself placed them on him when the dragoons appeared; and it was our awkwardness that has led to the discovery."

The countenance of Dunwoodie brightened, as turning his eyes in fondness on the speaker, he listened to her explanation.

"Probably some articles of your own," he continued, "which were at hand, and were used on the spur of the moment."

"No," said Wharton, with dignity, "the clothes were worn by me from the city; they were procured for the purpose to which they were applied, and I intended to use them in my return this very day."

The appalled Frances shrank back from between her brother and lover, where her ardent feelings had carried her, as the whole truth glanced over her mind, and she sank into a seat, gazing wildly on the young men.

"But the pickets—the party at the Plains?" added Dunwoodie, turning pale.

"I passed them, too, in disguise. I made use of this pass, for which I paid; and, as it bears the name of Washington, I presume it is forged."

Dunwoodie caught the paper from his hand, eagerly, and stood gazing on the signature for some time in silence, during which the soldier gradually prevailed over the man; when he turned to the prisoner, with a searching look, as he asked,—

"Captain Wharton, whence did you procure this paper?"

"This is a question, I conceive, Major Dunwoodie has no right to ask."

"Your pardon, sir; my feelings may have led me into an impropriety."

Mr. Wharton, who had been a deeply interested auditor, now so far conquered his feelings as to say, "Surely, Major Dunwoodie, the paper cannot be material; such artifices are used daily in war."

"This name is no counterfeit," said the dragoon, studying the characters, and speaking in a low voice; "is treason yet among us undiscovered? The confidence of Washington has been abused, for the fictitious name is in a different hand from the pass. Captain Wharton, my duty will not suffer me to grant you a parole; you must accompany me to the Highlands."

"I did not expect otherwise, Major Dunwoodie."

Dunwoodie turned slowly towards the sisters, when the figure of Frances once more arrested his gaze. She had risen from her seat, and stood again with her hands clasped before him in an attitude of petition; feeling himself unable to contend longer with his feelings, he made a hurried excuse for a temporary absence, and left the room. Frances followed him, and, obedient to the direction of her eye, the soldier re-entered the apartment in which had been their first interview.

"Major Dunwoodie," said Frances, in a voice barely audible, as she beckoned to him to be seated; her cheek, which had been of a chilling whiteness, was flushed with a suffusion that crimsoned her whole countenance. She struggled with herself for a moment, and continued, "I have already acknowledged to you my esteem; even now, when you most painfully distress me, I wish not to conceal it. Believe me, Henry is innocent of everything but imprudence. Our country can sustain no wrong." Again she paused, and almost gasped for breath; her color changed rapidly from red to white, until the blood rushed into her face, covering her features with the brightest vermilion; and she added hastily, in an undertone, "I have promised, Dunwoodie, when peace shall be restored to our country, to become your wife. Give to my brother his liberty on parole, and I will this day go with you to the altar, follow you to the camp, and, in becoming a soldier's bride, learn to endure a soldier's privations."

Dunwoodie seized the hand which the blushing girl, in her ardor, had extended towards him, and pressed it for a moment to his bosom; then rising from his seat, he paced the room in excessive agitation.

"Frances, say no more, I conjure you, unless you wish to break my heart."

"You then reject my offered hand?" she said, rising with dignity, though her pale cheek and quivering lip plainly showed the conflicting passions within.

"Reject it! Have I not sought it with entreaties—with tears? Has it not been the goal of all my earthly wishes? But to take it under such conditions would be to dishonor both. We will hope for better things. Henry must be acquitted; perhaps not tried. No intercession of mine shall be wanting, you must well know; and believe me, Frances, I am not without favor with Washington."

"That very paper, that abuse of his confidence, to which you alluded, will steel him to my brother's case. If threats or entreaties could move his stern sense of justice, would Andre have suffered?" As Frances uttered these words she fled from the room in despair.

Dunwoodie remained for a minute nearly stupefied; and then he followed with a view to vindicate himself, and to relieve her apprehensions. On entering the hall that divided the two parlors, he was met by a small ragged boy, who looked one moment at his dress, and placing a piece of paper in his hands, immediately vanished through the outer door of the building. The bewildered state of his mind, and the suddenness of the occurrence, gave the major barely time to observe the messenger to be a country lad, meanly attired, and that he held in his hand one of those toys which are to be bought in cities, and which he now apparently contemplated with the consious pleasure of having fairly purchased, by the performance of the service required. The soldier turned his eyes to the subject of the note. It was written on a piece of torn and soiled paper, and in a hand barely legible; but after some little labor, he was able to make out as follows:—

"The rig'lars are at hand, horse and foot."[6]

---

[6] There died a few years since, in Bedford, Westchester, a yeoman named Elisha H—. This person was employed by Washington as one of his most confidential spies. By the conditions of their bargain, H— was never to be required to deal with third parties, since his risks were too imminent. He was allowed to enter also into the service of Sir Henry Clinton; and so much confidence had Washington in his love of country and discretion, that he was often intrusted with the minor military movements, in order that he might enhance his value with the English

Dunwoodie started; and, forgetting everything but the duties of a soldier, he precipitately left the house. While walking rapidly towards the troops, he noticed on a distant hill a vidette riding with speed. Several pistols were fired in quick succession; and the next instant the trumpets of the corps rang in his ears

---

general, by communicating them. In this manner H— had continued to serve for a long period, when chance brought him into the city (then held by the British) at a moment when an expedition was about to quit it, to go against a small post established at Bedford, his native village, where the Americans had a depot of provisions. H— easily ascertained the force and destination of the detachment ordered on this service, but he was at a loss in what manner to communicate his information to the officer in command at Bedford, without betraying his own true character to a third person. There was not time to reach Washington, and under the circumstances, he finally resolved to hazard a short note to the American commandant, stating the danger, and naming the time when the attack might be expected. To this note he even ventured to affix his own initials, E. H., though he had disguised the hand, under a belief that, as he knew himself to be suspected by his countrymen, it might serve to give more weight to his warning. His family being at Bedford, the note was transmitted with facility and arrived in good season, H— himself remaining in New York.The American commandant did what every sensible officer, in a similar case, would have done. He sent a courier with the note to Washington, demanding orders, while he prepared his little party to make the best defense in his power.The headquarters of the American army were, at that time, in the Highlands. Fortunately, the express met Washington, on a tour of observation, near their entrance. The note was given to him, and he read it in the saddle; adding, in pencil, "Believe all that E. H. tells you. George Washington." He returned it to the courier, with an injunction to ride for life or death.The courier reached Bedford after the British had made their attack. The commandant read the reply, and put it in his pocket. The Americans were defeated, and their leader killed. The note of H—, with the line written on it by Washington, was found on his person.The following day H— was summoned to the presence of Sir Henry Clinton. After the latter had put several general questions, he suddenly gave the note to the spy, and asked if he knew the handwriting, and demanded who the E. H. was. "It is Elijah Hadden, the spy you hanged yesterday at Powles Hook." The readiness of this answer, connected with the fact that a spy having the same initials had been executed the day before, and the coolness of H—, saved him. Sir Henry Clinton allowed him to quit his presence, and he never saw him afterwards.

with the enlivening strain of "To arms!" By the time he had reached the ground occupied by his squadron, the major saw that every man was in active motion. Lawton was already in the saddle, eying the opposite extremity of the valley with the eagerness of expectation, and crying to the musicians, in tones but little lower than their own,—

"Sound away, my lads, and let these Englishmen know that the Virginia horse are between them and the end of their journey."

The videttes and patrols now came pouring in, each making in succession his hasty report to the commanding officer, who gave his orders coolly, and with a promptitude that made obedience certain. Once only, as he wheeled his horse to ride over the ground in front, did Dunwoodie trust himself with a look at the cottage, and his heart beat with unusual rapidity as he saw a female figure standing, with clasped hands, at a window of the room in which he had met Frances. The distance was too great to distinguish her features, but the soldier could not doubt that it was his mistress. The paleness of his cheek and the languor of his eye endured but for a moment longer. As he rode towards the intended battle ground, a flush of ardor began to show itself on his sunburst features; and his dragoons, who studied the face of their leader, as the best index to their own fate, saw again the wonted flashing of the eyes, and the cheerful animation, which they had so often witnessed on the eve of battle. By the additions of the videttes and parties that had been out, and which now had all joined, the whole number of the horse was increased to nearly two hundred. There was also a small body of men, whose ordinary duties were those of guides, but who, in case of emergency, were embodied and did duty as foot soldiers; these were dismounted, and proceeded, by the order of Dunwoodie, to level the few fences which might interfere with the intended movements of the cavalry. The neglect of husbandry, which had been occasioned by the war, left this task comparatively easy. Those long lines of heavy and durable walls, which now sweep through every part of the country, forty years ago were unknown. The slight and tottering fences of stone were then used more to clear the land for the purposes of cultivation than as permanent barriers, and required the constant attention of the husbandman, to preserve them against the fury of the tempests and the frosts of winter. Some few of them had been built with more care immediately around the dwelling of Mr. Wharton; but those which had intersected the vale below were now generally a pile of ruins, over which the horses of the Virginians would bound with the fleetness of the wind. Occasionally a short line yet preserved its erect appearance; but as none of those crossed the ground on which Dunwoodie intended to act, there remained only the slighter fences of rails to be thrown down. Their duty was hastily but effectually performed; and the guides withdrew to the post assigned to them for the approaching fight.

Major Dunwoodie had received from his scouts all the intelligence concerning his foe, which was necessary to enable him to make his arrangements. The bottom of the valley was an even plain, that fell with a slight inclination from the foot of the hills on either side, to the level of a natural meadow that wound through the country on the banks of a small stream, by whose waters it was often inundated and fertilized. This brook was easily forded in any part of its course; and the only impediment it offered to the movements of the horse, was in a place where it changed its bed from the western to the eastern side of the valley, and where its banks were more steep and difficult of access than common. Here the highway crossed it by a rough wooden bridge, as it did again at the distance of half a mile above the Locusts.

The hills on the eastern side of the valley were abrupt, and frequently obtruded themselves in rocky prominences into its bosom, lessening the width to half the usual dimensions. One of these projections was but a short distance in the rear of the squadron of dragoons, and Dunwoodie directed Captain Lawton to withdraw, with two troops, behind its cover. The officer obeyed with a kind of surly reluctance, that was, however, somewhat lessened by the anticipations of the effect his sudden appearance would make on the enemy. Dunwoodie knew his man and had selected the captain for this service, both because he feared his precipitation in the field, and knew, when needed, his support would never fail to appear. It was only in front of the enemy that Captain Lawton was hasty; at all other times his discernment and self-possession were consummately preserved; but he sometimes forgot them in his eagerness to engage. On the left of the ground on which Dunwoodie intended to meet his foe, was a close wood, which skirted that side of the valley for the distance of a mile. Into this, the guides retired, and took their station near its edge, in such a manner as would enable them to maintain a scattering, but effectual fire, on the advancing column of the enemy.

It cannot be supposed that all these preparations were made unheeded by the inmates of the cottage; on the contrary, every feeling which can agitate the human breast, in witnessing such a scene, was actively alive. Mr. Wharton alone saw no hopes to himself in the termination of the conflict. If the British should prevail, his son would be liberated; but what would then be his own fate! He had hitherto preserved his neutral character in the midst of trying circumstances. The fact of his having a son in the royal, or, as it was called, the regular army, had very nearly brought his estates to the hammer. Nothing had obviated this result, but the powerful interest of the relation who held a high political rank in the state, and his own vigilant prudence. In his heart, he was a devoted loyalist; and when the blushing Frances had communicated to him the wishes of her lover, on their return from the American camp the preceding spring, the consent he had given, to her future union with a rebel, was as much extracted by the increasing necessity which existed for his obtaining republican support, as by any considerations for the happiness of his child. Should his son now be rescued, he would, in the public mind, be united with as a plotter against the freedom of the States; and should he remain a captive and undergo the impending trial, the consequences might be still more dreadful. Much as he loved his wealth, Mr. Wharton loved his children better; and he sat gazing on the movements without, with a listless vacancy in his countenance, that fully denoted his imbecility of character.

Far different were the feelings of the son. Captain Wharton had been left in the keeping of two dragoons, one of whom marched to and fro on the piazza with a measured tread, and the other had been directed to continue in the same apartment with his prisoner. The young man had witnessed all the movements of Dunwoodie with admiration mingled with fearful anticipations of the consequences to friends. He particularly disliked the ambush of the detachment under Lawton, who could be distinctly seen from the windows of the cottage, cooling his impatience, by pacing on foot the ground in front of his men. Henry Wharton threw several hasty and inquiring glances around, to see if no means of liberation would offer, but invariably found the eyes of his sentinel fixed on him with the watchfulness of an Argus. He longed, with the ardor of youth, to join in the glorious fray, but was compelled to remain a dissatisfied spectator of a scene in which he would so cheerfully have been an actor. Miss Peyton and Sarah continued gazing on the preparations with varied emotions, in which concern for the fate of the captain formed the most prominent feeling, until the moment of shedding blood seemed approaching, when, with the timidity of their sex, they sought the retirement of an inner room. Not so Frances; she returned to the apartment where she had left Dunwoodie, and, from one of its windows, had been a deeply interested spectator of all his movements. The wheelings of the troops, the deadly preparations, had all been unnoticed; she saw her lover only, and with mingled emotions of admiration and dread that nearly chilled her. At one moment the blood rushed to her heart, as she saw the young warrior riding through his ranks, giving life and courage to all whom he addressed; and the next, it curdled with the thought that the very gallantry she so much valued might prove the means of placing the grave between her and the object of her regard. Frances gazed until she could look no longer.

In a field on the left of the cottage, and at a short distance in the rear of the troops, was a small group, whose occupation seemed to differ from that of all around them. They were in number only three, being two men and a mulatto boy. The principal personage of this party was a man, whose leanness made his really tall stature appear excessive. He wore spectacles —was unarmed, had dismounted, and seemed to be dividing his attention between a cigar, a book, and the incidents of the field before him. To this party Frances determined to send a note, directed to Dunwoodie. She wrote hastily, with a pencil, "Come to me, Peyton, if it be but for a moment"; and Cæsar emerged from the cellar kitchen, taking the precaution to go by the rear of the building, to avoid the sentinel on the piazza, who had very cavalierly ordered all the family to remain housed. The black delivered the note to the gentleman, with a request that it might be forwarded to Major Dunwoodie. It was the surgeon of the horse to whom Cæsar addressed himself; and the teeth of the African chattered, as he saw displayed upon the ground the several instruments which were in preparation for the anticipated operations. The doctor himself seemed to view the arrangement with great satisfaction, as he deliberately raised his eyes from his book to order the boy to convey the note to his commanding officer, and then dropping them quietly on the page he continued his occupation. Cæsar was slowly retiring, as the third personage, who by his dress might be an inferior assistant of the surgical department, coolly inquired "if he would have a leg taken off?" This question seemed to remind the black of the existence of those limbs, for he made such use of them as to reach the piazza at the same instant that Major Dunwoodie rode up, at half speed. The brawny sentinel squared himself, and poised his sword with military precision as he stood on his post, while his officer passed; but no sooner had the door closed, then, turning to the negro, he said, sharply,—

"Harkee, blackee, if you quit the house again without my knowledge, I shall turn barber, and shave off one of those ebony ears with this razor."

Thus assailed in another member, Cæsar hastily retreated into his kitchen, muttering something, in which the words "Skinner," and "rebel rascal," formed a principal part of speech.

"Major Dunwoodie," said Frances to her lover as he entered, "I may have done you injustice; if I have appeared harsh —"

The emotions of the agitated girl prevailed, and she burst into tears.

"Frances," cried the soldier with warmth, "you are never harsh, never unjust, but when you doubt my love."

"Ah! Dunwoodie," added the sobbing girl, "you are about to risk your life in battle; remember that there is one heart whose happiness is built on your safety; brave I know you are: be prudent —"

"For your sake?" inquired the delighted youth.

"For my sake," replied Frances, in a voice barely audible, and drooping on his bosom.

Dunwoodie folded her to his heart, and was about to speak, as a trumpet sounded in the southern end of the vale. Imprinting one long kiss of affection on her unresisting lips, the soldier tore himself from his mistress, and hastened to the scene of strife.

Frances threw herself on a sofa, buried her head under its cushion, and with her shawl drawn over her face, to exclude as much of sound as possible, continued there until the shouts of the combatants, the rattling of the firearms, and the thundering tread of the horses had ceased.

CHAPTER VII

The game's afoot;
Follow your spirit.
—Shakespeare.

The rough and unimproved face of the country, the frequency of covers, together with the great distance from their own country, and the facilities afforded them for rapid movements to the different points of the war, by the undisputed command of the ocean, had united to deter the English from employing a heavy force in cavalry, in their early efforts to subdue the revolted colonies.

Only one regiment of regular horse was sent from the mother country, during the struggle. But legions and independent corps were formed in different places, as it best accorded with the views of the royal commanders, or suited the exigency of the times. These were not unfrequently composed of men raised in the colonies, and at other times drafts were had from the regiments of the line, and the soldiers were made to lay aside the musket and bayonet, and taught to wield the saber and carabine. One particular body of the subsidiary troops was included in this arrangement, and the Hessian yagers were transformed into a corps of heavy and inactive horse.

Opposed to them were the hardiest spirits of America. Most of the cavalry regiments of the continental army were led and officered by gentlemen from the South. The high and haughty courage of the commanders had communicated itself to the privates, who were men selected with care and great attention to the service they were intended to perform.

While the British were confined to their empty conquests in the possession of a few of the larger towns, or marched through counties that were swept of everything like military supplies, the light troops of their enemies had the range of the whole interior.

The sufferings of the line of the American army were great beyond example; but possessing the power, and feeling themselves engaged in a cause which justified severity, the cavalry officers were vigilant in providing for their wants, and the horse were well mounted, well fed, and consequently eminently effective. Perhaps the world could not furnish more brave, enterprising, and resistless corps of light cavalry, than a few that were in the continental service at the time of which we write.

Dunwoodie's men had often tried their prowess against the enemy, and they now sat panting to be led once more against foes whom they seldom charged in vain. Their wishes were soon to be gratified; for their commander had scarcely time to regain his seat in the saddle, before a body of the enemy came sweeping round the base of the hill, which intersected the view to the south. A few minutes enabled the major to distinguish their character. In one troop he saw the green coats of the Cowboys, and in the other the leathern helmets and wooden saddles of the yagers. Their numbers were about equal to the body under his immediate orders.

On reaching the open space near the cottage of Harvey Birch, the enemy halted and drew up his men in line, evidently making preparations for a charge. At this moment a column of foot appeared in the vale, and pressed forward to the bank of the brook we have already mentioned.

Major Dunwoodie was not less distinguished by coolness and judgment, than, where occasion offered, by his dauntless intrepidity. He at once saw his advantage, and determined to profit by it. The column he led began slowly to retire from the field, when the youthful German, who commanded the enemy's horse, fearful of missing an easy conquest, gave the word to charge. Few troops were more hardy than the Cowboys; they sprang eagerly forward in the pursuit, with a confidence created by the retiring foe and the column in their rear; the Hessians followed more slowly, but in better order. The trumpets of the Virginians now sounded long and lively; they were answered by a strain from the party in ambush that went to the hearts of their enemies. The column of Dunwoodie wheeled in perfect order, opened, and, as the word to charge was given, the troops of Lawton emerged from their cover, with their leader in advance, waving his saber over his head, and shouting, in a voice that was heard above the clangor of the martial music.

The charge threatened too much for the refugee troop. They scattered in every direction, flying from the field as fast as their horses, the chosen beasts of Westchester, could carry them. Only a few were hurt; but such as did meet the arms of their avenging countrymen never survived the blow, to tell who struck it. It was upon the poor vassals of the German tyrant that the shock fell. Disciplined to the most exact obedience, these ill-fated men met the charge bravely, but they were swept before the mettled horses and nervous arms of their antagonists like chaff before the wind. Many of them were literally ridden down, and Dunwoodie soon saw the field without an opposing foe. The proximity of the infantry prevented pursuit, and behind its column the few Hessian who escaped unhurt sought protection.

The more cunning refugees dispersed in small bands, taking various and devious routes back to their old station in front of Harlem. Many was the sufferer, in cattle, furniture, and person, that was created by this rout; for the dispersion of a troop of Cowboys was only the extension of an evil.

Such a scene could not be expected to be acted so near them, and the inmates of the cottage take no interest in the result. In truth, the feelings it excited pervaded every bosom, from the kitchen to the parlor. Terror and horror had prevented the ladies from being spectators, but they did not feel the less. Frances continued lying in the posture we have mentioned, offering up fervent and incoherent petitions for the safety of her countrymen, although in her inmost heart she had personified her nation by the graceful image of Peyton Dunwoodie. Her aunt and sister were less exclusive in their devotions; but Sarah began to feel, as the horrors of war were thus brought home to her senses, less pleasure in her anticipated triumphs.

The inmates of Mr. Wharton's kitchen were four, namely, Cæsar and his spouse, their granddaughter, a jet-black damsel of twenty, and the boy before alluded to. The blacks were the remnants of a race of negroes which had been entailed on his estate from Mr. Wharton's maternal ancestors, who were descended from the early Dutch colonists. Time, depravity, and death had reduced them to this small number; and the boy, who was white, had been added by Miss Peyton to the establishment, as an assistant, to perform the ordinary services of a footman.

Cæsar, after first using the precaution to place himself under the cover of an angle in the wall, for a screen against any roving bullet which might be traversing the air, became an amused spectator of the skirmish. The sentinel on the piazza was at the distance of but a few feet from him, and he entered into the spirit of the chase with all the ardor of a tried bloodhound. He noticed the approach of the black, and his judicious position, with a smile of contempt, as he squared himself towards the enemy, offering his unprotected breast to any dangers which might come.

After considering the arrangement of Cæsar, for a moment, with ineffable disdain, the dragoon said, with great coolness,—

"You seem very careful of that beautiful person of yours, Mr. Blueskin."

"A bullet hurt a colored man as much as a white," muttered the black, surlily, casting a glance of much satisfaction at his rampart.

"Suppose I make the experiment," returned the sentinel. As he spoke, he deliberately drew a pistol from his belt, and leveled it at the black. Cæsar's teeth chattered at the appearance of the dragoon, although he believed nothing serious was intended. At this moment the column of Dunwoodie began to retire, and the royal cavalry commenced their charge.

"There, Mister Light-Horseman," said Cæsar eagerly, who believed the Americans were retiring in earnest; "why you rebels don't fight—see—see how King George's men make Major Dunwoodie run! Good gentleman, too, but he don't like to fight a rig'lar."

"Damn your regulars," cried the other, fiercely. "Wait a minute, blackey, and you'll see Captain Jack Lawton come out from behind yonder hill, and scatter these Cowboys like wild geese who've lost their leader."

Cæsar supposed the party under Lawton to have sought the shelter of the hill from motives similar to that which had induced him to place the wall between himself and the battle ground; but the fact soon verified the trooper's prophecy, and the black witnessed with consternation the total rout of the royal horse.

The sentinel manifested his exultation at the success of his comrades with loud shouts, which soon brought his companion, who had been left in the more immediate charge of Henry Wharton, to the open window of the parlor.

"See, Tom, see," cried the delighted trooper, "how Captain Lawton makes that Hessian's leather cap fly; and now the major has killed the officer's horse—zounds, why didn't he kill the Dutchman and save the horse?"

A few pistols were discharged at the flying Cowboys, and a spent bullet broke a pane of glass within a few feet of Cæsar. Imitating the posture of the great tempter of our race, the black sought the protection of the inside of the building, and immediately ascended to the parlor.

The lawn in front of the Locusts was hidden from the view of the road by a close line of shrubbery, and the horses of the two dragoons had been left, linked together, under its shelter, to await the movements of their masters.

At this moment two Cowboys, who had been cut off from retreat to their own party, rode furiously through the gate, with an intention of escaping to the open wood in the rear of the cottage.

The victorious Americans pressed the retreating Germans until they had driven them under the protection of the fire of the infantry; and feeling themselves, in the privacy of the lawn, relieved from any immediate danger, the predatory warriors yielded to a temptation that few of the corps were ever known to resist—opportunity and horseflesh. With a hardihood and presence of mind that could only exist from long practice in similar scenes, they made towards their intended prizes, by an almost spontaneous movement. They were busily engaged in separating the fastenings of the horses, when the trooper on the piazza discharged his pistols, and rushed, sword in hand, to the rescue.

The entrance of Cæsar into the parlor had induced the wary dragoon within to turn his attention more closely on his prisoner; but this new interruption drew him again to the window. He threw his body out of the building, and with dreadful imprecations endeavored, by his threats and appearance, to frighten the marauders from their prey. The moment was enticing. Three hundred of his comrades were within a mile of the cottage; unridden horses were running at large in every direction, and Henry Wharton seized the unconscious sentinel by his legs, and threw him headlong into the lawn. Cæsar vanished from the room, and drew a bolt of the outer door.

The fall of the soldier was not great, and recovering his feet, he turned his fury for a moment on his prisoner. To scale the window in the face of such an enemy, was, however, impossible, and on trial he found the main entrance barred.

His comrade now called loudly upon him for aid, and forgetful of everything else, the discomfited trooper rushed to his assistance. One horse was instantly liberated, but the other was already fastened to the saddle of a Cowboy, and the four retired behind the building, cutting furiously at each other with their sabers, and making the air resound with their imprecations. Cæsar threw the outer door open, and pointing to the remaining horse, that was quietly biting the faded herbage of the lawn, he exclaimed,—

"Run—now—run—Massa Harry, run."

"Yes," cried the youth as he vaulted into the saddle; "now, indeed, my honest fellow, is the time to run." He beckoned hastily to his father, who stood at the window in speechless anxiety, with his hands extended towards his child in the attitude of benediction, and adding "God bless you, Cæsar, salute the girls," he dashed through the gate with the rapidity of lightning.

The African watched him with anxiety as he gained the highway, saw him incline to the right, and riding furiously under the brow of some rocks, which on that side rose perpendicularly, disappear behind a projection, which soon hid him from view.

The delighted Cæsar closed the door, pushing bolt after bolt, and turning the key until it would turn no more, soliloquizing the whole time on the happy escape of his young master.

"How well he ride—teach him good deal myself—salute a young lady—Miss Fanny wouldn't let old colored man kiss a red cheek."

When the fortune of the day was decided, and the time arrived for the burial of the dead, two Cowboys and a Virginian were found in the rear of the Locusts, to be included in the number.

Happily for Henry Wharton, the searching eyes of his captors were examining, through a pocket glass, the column of infantry that still held its position on the bank of the stream, while the remnants of the Hessian yagers were seeking its friendly protection. His horse was of the best blood of Virginia, and carried him with the swiftness of the wind along the valley; and the heart of the youth was already beating tumultuously with pleasure at his deliverance, when a well-known voice reached his startled ear, crying aloud,—

"Bravely done, captain! Don't spare the whip, and turn to your left before you cross the brook."

Wharton turned his head in surprise, and saw, sitting on the point of a jutting rock that commanded a bird's-eye view of the valley, his former guide, Harvey Birch. His pack, much diminished in size, lay at the feet of the peddler, who waved his hat to the youth, exultingly, as the latter flew by him. The English captain took the advice of this mysterious being, and finding a good road, which led to the highway, that intersected the valley, turned down its direction, and was soon opposite to his friends. The next minute he crossed the bridge, and stopped his charger before his old acquaintance, Colonel Wellmere.

"Captain Wharton!" exclaimed the astonished commander of the English troops, "dressed in mohair, and mounted on a rebel dragoon horse! Are you from the clouds in this attire, and in such a style?"

"Thank God!" cried the youth, recovering his breath, "I am safe, and I have escaped from the hands of my enemies; but five minutes since and I was a prisoner, and threatened with the gallows."

"The gallows, Captain Wharton! surely those traitors to the king would never dare to commit another murder in cold blood; is it not enough that they took the life of Andre? Wherefore did they threaten you with a similar fate?"

"Under the pretense of a similar offense," said the captain, briefly explaining to the group of listeners the manner of his capture, the grounds of his personal apprehensions, and the method of his escape. By the time he had concluded his narration, the fugitive Germans were collected in the rear of the column of infantry, and Colonel Wellmere cried aloud,—

"From my soul I congratulate you, my brave friend; mercy is a quality with which these traitors arc unacquainted, and you are doubly fortunate in escaping from their hands uninjured. Preparc yourself to grant me your assistance, and I will soon afford you a noble revenge."

"I do not think there was danger of personal outrage to any man, Colonel Wellmere, from a party that Major Dunwoodie commands," returned young Wharton, with a slight glow on his face. "His character is above the imputation of such an offense; neither do I think it altogether prudent to cross this brook into the open plain, in the face of those Virginian horse, flushed as they must be with the success they have just obtained."

"Do you call the rout of those irregulars and these sluggish Hessians a deed to boast of?" said the other with a contemptuous smile. "You speak of the affair, Captain Wharton, as if your boasted Mr. Dunwoodie, for major he is none, had discomfited the bodyguards of your king."

"And I must be allowed to say, Colonel Wellmere, that if the bodyguards of my king were in yon field, they would meet a foe that would be dangerous to despise. Sir, my boasted Mr. Dunwoodie is the pride of Washington's army as a cavalry officer," cried Henry with warmth.

"Dunwoodie, Dunwoodie!" repeated the colonel slowly, "surely I have met the gentleman before."

"I have been told you once saw him for a moment, at the town residence of my sisters," replied Wharton, with a lurking smile.

"Ah! I do remember me of such a youth; and does the most potent congress of these rebellious colonies intrust their soldiers to the leading of such a warrior!!"

"Ask the commander of yon Hessian horse, whether he thinks Major Dunwoodie worthy of the confidence."

Colonel Wellmere was far from wanting that kind of pride which makes a man bear himself bravely in the presence of his enemies. He had served in America a long time, without ever meeting with any but new raised levies, or the militia of the country. These would sometimes fight, and that fearlessly, but they as often chose to run away without pulling a trigger. He was too apt to judge from externals, and thought it impossible for men whose gaiters were so clean, whose tread so regular, and who wheeled with so much accuracy, to be beaten. In addition to all these, they were Englishmen, and their success was certain. Colonel Wellmere had never been kept much in the field, or these notions, which he had brought with him from home, and which had been greatly increased by the vaporing of a garrisoned town, would have long since vanished. He listened to the warm reply of Captain Wharton with a supercilious smile, and then inquired,—

"You would not have us retire, sir, before these boasted horsemen, without doing something that may deprive them of part of the glory which you appear to think they have gained!"

"I would have you advised. Colonel Wellmere, of the danger you are about to encounter."

"Danger is but an unseemly word for a soldier," continued the British commander with a sneer.

"And one as little dreaded by the 60th, as any corps who wear the royal livery," cried Henry Wharton, fiercely. "Give but the word to charge, and let our actions speak."

"Now again I know my young friend," cried Wellmere, soothingly; "but if you have anything to say before we fight, that can in any manner help us in our attack, we'll listen. You know the force of the rebels; are there more of them in ambush?"

"Yes," replied the youth, chafing still under the other's sneers, "in the skirt of this wood on our right are a small party of foot; their horse are all before you."

"Where they will not continue long," cried Wellmere, turning to the few officers around him. "Gentlemen, we will cross the stream in column, and deploy on the plain beyond, or else we shall not be able to entice these valiant Yankees within the reach of our muskets. Captain Wharton, I claim your assistance as an aide-de-camp."

The youth shook his head in disapprobation of a movement which his good sense taught him was rash, but prepared with alacrity to perform his duty in the impending trial.

During this conversation, which was held at a small distance in advance of the British column, and in full view of the Americans, Dunwoodie had been collecting his scattered troops, securing his few prisoners, and retiring to the ground where he had been posted at the first appearance of his enemy. Satisfied with the success he had already obtained, and believing the English too wary to give him an opportunity of harassing them further, he was about to withdraw the guides; and, leaving a strong party on the ground to watch the movements of the regulars, to fall back a few miles, to a favorable place for taking up his quarters for the night. Captain Lawton was reluctantly listening to the reasoning of his commander, and had brought out his favorite glass, to see if no opening could be found for an advantageous attack, when he suddenly exclaimed,—

"How's this! a bluecoat among those scarlet gentry? As I hope to live to see old Virginia, it is my masquerading friend of the 60th, the handsome Captain Wharton, escaped from two of my best men!"

He had not done speaking when the survivor of these heroes joined his troop, bringing with him his own horse and those of the Cowboys; he reported the death of his comrade, and the escape of his prisoner. As the. deceased was the immediate sentinel over the person of young Wharton, and the other was not to be blamed for defending the horses, which were more particularly under his care, his captain heard him with uneasiness but without anger.

This intelligence made an entire change in the views of Major Dunwoodie. He saw at once that his own reputation was involved in the escape of his prisoner. The order to recall the guides was countermanded, and he now joined his second in command, watching as eagerly as the impetuous Lawton himself, for some opening to assail his foe to advantage.

But two hours before, and Dunwoodie had felt the chance which made Henry Wharton his captive, as the severest blow he had ever sustained. Now he panted for an opportunity in which, by risking his own life, he might recapture his friend. All other considerations were lost in the goadings of a wounded spirit, and he might have soon emulated Lawton in hardihood, had not Wellmere and his troops at this moment crossed the brook into the open plain.

"There," cried the delighted captain, as he pointed out the movement with his finger, "there comes John Bull into the mousetrap, and with eyes wide open."

"Surely," said Dunwoodie eagerly, "he will not deploy his column on that flat. Wharton must tell him of the ambush. But if he does—"

"We will not leave him a dozen sound skins in his battalion," interrupted the other, springing into his saddle.

The truth was soon apparent; for the English column, after advancing for a short distance on the level land, deployed with an accuracy that would have done them honor on a field day in their own Hyde Park.

"Prepare to mount—mount!" cried Dunwoodie; the last word being repeated by Lawton in a tone that rang in the ears of Cæsar, who stood at the open window of the cottage. The black recoiled in dismay, having lost all his confidence in Captain Lawton's timidity; for he thought he yet saw him emerging from his cover and waving his sword on high.

As the British line advanced slowly and in exact order, the guides opened a galling fire. It began to annoy that part of the royal troops which was nearest to them. Wellmere listened to the advice of the veteran, who was next to him in rank, and ordered two companies to dislodge the American foot from their hiding place. The movement created a slight confusion; and Dunwoodie siezed the opportunity to charge. No ground could be more favorable for the maneuvers of horse, and the attack of the Virginians was irresistible. It was aimed chiefly at the bank opposite to the wood, in order to clear the Americans from the fire of their friends who were concealed; and it was completely successful. Wellmere, who was on the left of his line, was overthrown by the impetuous fury of his assailants. Dunwoodie was in time to save him from the impending blow of one of his men, and raised him from the ground, had him placed on a horse, and delivered to the custody of his orderly. The officer who had suggested the attack upon the guides had been intrusted with its execution, but the menace was sufficient for these irregulars. In fact, their duty was performed, and they retired along the skirt of the wood, with intent to regain their horses, which had been left under a guard at the upper end of the valley.

The left of the British line was outflanked by the Americans, who doubled in their rear, and thus made the rout in that quarter total. But the second in command, perceiving how the battle went, promptly wheeled his party, and threw in a heavy fire on the dragoons, as they passed him to the charge; with this party was Henry Wharton, who had volunteered to assist in dispersing the guides. A ball struck his bridle arm, and compelled him to change hands. As the dragoons dashed by them, rending the air with their shouts, and with trumpets sounding a lively strain, the charger ridden by the youth became ungovernable—he plunged, reared, and his rider being unable with his wounded arm, to manage the impatient animal, Henry Wharton found himself, in less than a minute, unwillingly riding by the side of Captain Lawton. The dragoon comprehended at a glance the ludicrous situation of his new comrade, but had only time to cry aloud, before they plunged into the English line,—

"The horse knows the righteous cause better than his rider. Captain Wharton, you are welcome to the ranks of freedom."

No time was lost, however, by Lawton, after the charge was

completed, in securing his prisoner again; and perceiving him to be hurt, he directed him to be conveyed to the rear.

The Virginian troopers dealt out their favors, with no gentle hands, on that part of the royal foot who were thus left in a great measure at their mercy. Dunwoodie, observing that the remnant of the Hessians had again ventured on the plain, led on in pursuit, and easily overtaking their light and half-fed horses, soon destroyed the remainder of the detachment.

In the meanwhile, great numbers of the English, taking advantage of the smoke and confusion in the field, were enabled to get in the rear of the body of their countrymen, which still preserved its order in a line parallel to the wood, but which had been obliged to hold its fire, from the fear of injuring friends as well as foes. The fugitives were directed to form a second line within the wood itself, and under cover of the trees. This arrangement was not yet completed, when Captain Lawton called to a youth, who commanded the other troop left with that part of the force which remained on the ground, and proposed charging the unbroken line of the British. The proposal was as promtly accepted as it had been made, and the troops were arrayed for the purpose. The eagerness of their leader prevented the preparations necessary to insure success, and the horse, receiving a destructive fire as they advanced, were thrown into additional confusion. Both Lawton and his more juvenile comrade fell at this discharge. Fortunately for the credit of the Virginians, Major Dunwoodie re-entered the field at this critical instant; he saw his troops in disorder; at his feet lay weltering in blood George Singleton, a youth endeared to him by numberless virtues, and Lawton was unhorsed and stretched on the plain. The eye of the youthful warrior flashed fire. Riding between this squadron and the enemy, in a voice that reached the hearts of his dragoons, he recalled them to their duty. His presence and word acted like magic. The clamor of voices ceased; the line was formed promptly and with exactitude; the charge sounded; and, led on by their commander, the Virginians swept across the plain with an impetuosity that nothing could withstand, and the field was instantly cleared of the enemy; those who were not destroyed sought a shelter in the woods. Dunwoodie slowly withdrew from the fire of the English who were covered by the trees, and commenced the painful duty of collecting his dead and wounded.

The sergeant charged with conducting Henry Wharton to a place where he might procure surgical aid, set about performing his duty with alacrity, in order to return as soon as possible to the scene of strife. They had not reached the middle of the plain, before the captain noticed a man whose appearance and occupation forcibly arrested his attention. His head was bald and bare, but a well-powdered wig was to be seen, half-concealed, in the pocket of his breeches. His coat was off, and his arms were naked to the elbow; blood had disfigured much of his dress, and his hands, and even face, bore this mark of his profession; in his mouth was a cigar; in his right hand some instruments of strange formation, and in his left the remnants of an apple, with which he occasionally relieved the duty of the before-mentioned cigar. He was standing, lost in the contemplation of a Hessian, who lay breathless before him. At a little distance were three or four of the guides, leaning on their muskets, and straining their eyes in the direction of the combatants and at his elbow stood a man who, from the implements in his hand, seemed an assistant.

"There, sir, is the doctor," said the attendant of Henry very coolly. "He will patch up your arm in the twinkling of an eye"; and beckoning to the guides to approach, he whispered and pointed to his prisoner, and then galloped furiously towards his comrades.

Wharton advanced to the side of this strange figure, and observing himself to be unnoticed, was about to request his assistance, when the other broke silence in a soliloquy:—

"Now, I know this man to have been killed by Captain Lawton, as well as if I had seen him strike the blow. How often have I strove to teach him the manner in which he can disable his adversary, without destroying life! It is cruel thus unnecessarily to cut off the human race, and furthermore, such blows as these render professional assistance unnecessary; it is in a measure treating the lights of science with disrespect."

"If, sir, your leisure will admit," said Henry Wharton, "I must beg your attention to a slight hurt."

"Ah!" cried the other, starting, and examining him from head to foot, "you are from the field below. Is there much business there, sir?"

"Indeed," answered Henry, accepting the offer of the surgeon to assist in removing his coat, " 'tis a stirring time."

"Stirring!" repeated the surgeon, busily employed with his dressings; "you give me great pleasure, sir; for so long as they can stir there must be life; and while there is life, you know, there is hope; but here my art is of no use. I did put in the brains of one patient, but I rather think the man must have been dead before I saw him. It is a curious case, sir; I will take you to see it—only across the fence there, where you may perceive so many bodies together. Ah! the ball has glanced around the bone without shattering it; you are fortunate in falling into the hands of an old practitioner, or you might have lost this limb."

"Indeed!" said Henry, with a slight uneasiness. "I did not apprehend the injury to be so serious."

"Oh, the hurt is not bad, but you have such a pretty arm for an operation; the pleasure of the thing might have tempted a novice."

"The devil!" cried the captain. "Can there be any pleasure in multilating a fellow creature?"

"Sir," said the surgeon, with gravity, "a scientific amputation is a very pretty operation, and doubtless might tempt a younger man, in the hurry of business, to overlook all the particulars of the case."

Further conversation was interrupted by the appearance of the dragoons, slowly marching towards their former halting place, and new applications from the slightly wounded soldiers, who now came riding in", making hasty demands on the skill of the doctor.

The guides took charge of Wharton, and, with a heavy heart, the young man retraced his steps to his father's cottage.

The English had lost in the several charges about one third of their foot, but the remainder were rallied in the wood; and Dunwoodie, perceiving them to be too strongly posted to assail, had left a strong party with Captain Lawton, with orders to watch their motions, and to seize every opportunity to harass them before they re-embarked.

Intelligence had reached the major of another party being out, by the way of the Hudson, and his duty required that he should hold himself in readiness to defeat the intentions of these also. Captain Lawton received his orders with strong injunctions to make no assault on the foe, unless a favorable chance should offer.

The injury received by this officer was in the head, being stunned by a glancing bullet; and parting with a laughing declaration from the major, that if he again forgot himself, they should all think him more materially hurt, each took his own course.

The British were a light party without baggage, that had been sent out to destroy certain stores, understood to be collecting for the use of the American army. They now retired through the woods to the heights, and, keeping the route along their summits, in places unassailable by cavalry, commerced a retreat to their boats.

CHAPTER VIII

With fire and sword the country round
Was wasted far and wide;
And many a childing mother then,
And new-born infant, died;
But things like these, you know, must be
At every famous victory.
—Southey.

The last sounds of the combat died on the ears of the anxious listeners in the cottage, and were succeeded by the stillness of suspense. Frances had continued by herself, striving to exclude the uproar, and vainly endeavoring to summon resolution to meet the dreaded result. The ground where the charge on the foot had taken place was but a short mile from the Locusts, and, in the intervals of the musketry, the cries of the soldiers had even reached the ears of its inhabitants. After witnessing the escape of his son, Mr. Wharton had joined his sister and eldest daughter in their retreat, and the three continued fearfully waiting for the news from the field. Unable longer to remain under the painful uncertainty of her situation, Frances soon added herself to the uneasy group, and Cæsar was directed to examine into the state of things without, and report on whose banners victory had alighted. The father now briefly related to his astonished children the circumstance and manner of their brother's escape. They were yet in the freshness of their surprise, when the door opened, and Captain Wharton, attended by a couple of the guides, and followed by the black, stood before them.

"Henry—my son, my son," cried the agitated parent, stretching out his arms, yet unable to rise from his seat; "what is it I see; are you again a captive, and in danger of your life?"

"The better fortune of these rebels has prevailed," said the youth, endeavoring to force a cheerful smile, and taking a hand of each of his distressed sisters. "I strove nobly for my liberty; but the perverse spirit of rebellion has even lighted on their horses. The steed I mounted carried me, greatly against my will, I acknowledge, into the very center of Dunwoodie's men."

"And you were again captured," continued the father, casting a fearful glance on the armed attendants who had entered the room.

"That, sir, you may safely say; this Mr. Lawton, who sees so far, had me in custody again immediately."

"Why you no hold 'em in, Massa Henry?" cried Cæsar, pettishly.

"That," said Wharton, smiling, "was a thing easier said than done, Mr. Cæsar, especially as these gentlemen" (glancing his eyes at the guides) "had seen proper to deprive me of the use of my better arm."

"Wounded!" exclaimed both sisters in a breath.

"A mere scratch, but disabling me at a most critical moment," continued the brother, kindly, and stretching out the injured limb to manifest the truth of his declaration. Cæsar threw a look of bitter animosity on the irregular warriors who were thought to have had an agency in the deed, and left the room. A few more words sufficed to explain all that Captain Wharton knew relative to the fortune of the day. The result he thought yet doubtful, for when he left the ground, the Virginians were retiring from the field of battle.

"They had treed the squirrel," said one of the sentinels abruptly, "and didn't quit the ground without leaving a good hound for the chase when he comes down."

"Aye," added his comrade dryly, "I'm thinking Captain Law-ton will count the noses of what are left before they see their whaleboats."

Frances had stood supporting herself, by the back of a chair, during this dialogue, catching, in breathless anxiety, every syllable as it was uttered; her color changed rapidly; her limbs shook under her; until, with desperate resolution, she inquired,—

"Is any officer hurt on—the—on either side?"

"Yes," answered the man, cavalierly, "these Southern youths are so full of mettle, that it's seldom we fight but one or two gets knocked over; one of the wounded, who came up before the troops, told me that Captain Singleton was killed, and Major Dunwoodie—"

Frances heard no more, but fell lifeless in the chair behind her. The attention of her friends soon revived her when the captain, turning to the man, said fearfully,—

"Surely Major Dunwoodie is unhurt?"

"Never fear him," added the guide, disregarding the agitation of the family. "They say a man who is born to be hanged will never be drowned; if a bullet could kill the major, he would have been dead long ago. I was going to say, that the major is in a sad taking because of the captain's being killed; but had I know how much store the lady set by him, I wouldn't have been so plain-spoken."

Frances now rose quickly from her seat, with cheeks glowing with confusion, and, leaning on her aunt, was about to retire, when Dunwoodie himself appeared. The first emotion of the agitated girl was unalloyed happiness; in the next instant she shrank back appalled from the unusual expression that reigned in his countenance. The sternness of battle yet sat on his brow; his eye was fixed and severe. The smile of affection that used to lighten his dark features on meeting his mistress, was supplanted by the lowering look of care; his whole soul seemed to be absorbed in one engrossing emotion, and he proceeded at once to his object.

"Mr. Wharton," he earnestly began, "in times like these, we need not stand on idle ceremony: one of my officers, I am afraid, is hurt mortally; and, presuming on your hospitality, I have brought him to your door."

"I am happy, sir, that you have done so," said Mr. Wharton, at once perceiving the importance of conciliating the American troops. "The necessitous are always welcome, and doubly so, in being the friend of Major Dunwoodie."

"Sir, I thank you for myself, and in behalf of him who is unable to render you his thanks," returned the other, hastily. "If you please, we will have him conducted where the surgeon may see and report upon his case without delay." To this there could be no objection; and Frances felt a chill at her heart, as her lover withdrew, without casting a solitary look on herself.

There is a devotedness in female love that admits of no rivalry. All the tenderness of the heart, all the powers of the imagination, are enlisted in behalf of the tyrant passion; and where all is given, much is looked for in return. Frances had spent hours of anguish, of torture, on account of Dunwoodie, and he now met her without a smile, and left her without a greeting. The ardor of her feelings was unabated, but the elasticity of her hopes was weakened. As the supporters of the nearly lifeless body of Dunwoodie's friend passed her, in their way to the apartment prepared for his reception, she caught a view of this seeming rival.

His pale and ghastly countenance, sunken eye, and difficult breathing, gave her a glimpse of death in its most fearful form. Dunwoodie was by his side and held his hand, giving frequent and stern injunctions to the men to proceed with care, and, in short, manifesting all the solicitude that the most tender friendship could, on such an occasion, inspire. Frances moved lightly before them, and, with an averted face, she held open the door for their passage to the bed; it was only as the major touched her garments, on entering the room, that she ventured to raise her mild blue eyes to his face. But the glance was unreturned, and Frances unconsciously sighed as she sought the solitude of her own apartment.

Captain Wharton voluntarily gave a pledge to his keepers not to attempt again escaping, and then proceeded to execute those duties on behalf of his father, which were thought necessary in a host. On entering the passage for that purpose, he met the operator who had so dexterously dressed his arm, advancing to the room of the wounded officer.

"Ah!" cried the disciple of Æsculapius, "I see you are doing well; but stop; have you a pin? No! here, I have one; you must keep the cold air from your hurt, or some of the youngsters will be at work at you yet."

"God forbid," muttered the captain, in an undertone, attentively adjusting the bandages, when Dunwoodie appeared at the door, impatiently crying aloud,—

"Hasten Sitgreaves, hasten; or George Singleton will die from loss of blood."

"What! Singleton! God forbid! Bless me—is it George—poor little George?" exclaimed the surgeon, as he quickened his pace with evident concern, and hastened to the side of the bed. "He is alive, though, and while there is life there is hope. This is the first serious case I have had to-day, where the patient was not already dead. Captain Lawton teaches his men to strike with so little discretion—poor George—bless me, it is a musket bullet."

The youthful sufferer turned his eyes on the man of science, and with a faint smile endeavored to stretch forth his hand. There was an appeal in the look and action that touched the heart of the operator. The surgeon removed his spectacles to wipe an unusual moisture from his eyes, and proceeded carefully to the discharge of his duty. While the previous arrangements were, however, making, he gave vent in some measure to his feelings, by saying,—

"When it is only a bullet, I have always some hopes; there is a chance that it hits nothing vital. But, bless me, Captain Lawton's men cut so at random—generally sever the jugular or the carotid artery, or let out the brains, and all are so difficult to remedy—the patient mostly dying before one can get at him. I never had success but once in replacing a man's brains, although I have tried three this very day. It is easy to tell where Lawton's troops charge in a battle, they cut so at random."

The group around the bed of Captain Singleton were too much accustomed to the manner of their surgeon to regard or to reply to his soliloquy; but they quietly awaited the moment when he was to commence his examination. This now took place, and Dunwoodie stood looking the operator in the face, with an expression that seemed to read his soul. The patient shrank from the application of the probe, and a smile stole over the features of the surgeon, as he muttered,—

"There has been nothing before it in that quarter." He now applied himself in earnest to his work, took off his spectacles, and threw aside his wig. All this time Dunwoodie stood in feverish silence, holding one of the hands of the sufferer in both his own, watching the countenance of Doctor Sitgreaves. Al length Singleton gave a slight groan, and the surgeon rose with alacrity, and said aloud,—

"Ah! there is some pleasure in following a bullet; it may be said to meander through the human body, injuring nothing vital; but as for Captain Lawton's men—"

"Speak," interrupted Dunwoodie; "is there hope?—can you find the ball?"

"It's no difficult matter to find that which one has in his hand, Major Dunwoodie," replied the surgeon, coolly, preparing his dressings. "It took what that literal fellow, Captain Lawton, calls a circumbendibus, a route never taken by the swords of his men, notwithstanding the multiplied pains I have been at to teach him how to cut scientifically. Now, I saw a horse this day with his head half severed from his body."

"That," said Dunwoodie, as the blood rushed to his cheeks again, and his dark eyes sparkled with the rays of hope, "was some of my handiwork; I killed that horse myself."

"You!" exclaimed the surgeon, dropping his dressings in surprise, "you! But you knew it was a horse!"

"I had such suspicions, I own," said the major, smiling, and holding a beverage to the lips of his friend.

"Such blows alighting on the human frame are fatal," continued the doctor, pursuing his business. "They set at naught the benefits which flow from the lights of science; they are useless in a battle, for disabling your foe is all that is required. I have sat, Major Dunwoodie, many a cold hour, while Captain Lawton has been engaged, and after all my expectation, not a single case worth recording has occurred—all scratches or death wounds. Ah, the saber is a sad weapon in unskillful hands! Yes, Major Dunwoodie, many are the hours I have thrown away in endeavoring to impress this truth on Captain John Lawton."

The impatient major pointed silently to his friend, and the surgeon quickened his movements.

"Ah! poor George, it is a narrow chance; but"—he was interrupted by a messenger requiring the presence of the commanding officer in the field. Dunwoodie pressed the hand of his friend, and beckoned the doctor to follow him, as he withdrew.

"What think you?" he whispered, on reaching the passage. "Will he live?"

"He will."

"Thank God!" cried the youth, hastening below.

Dunwoodie for a moment joined the family, who were now collecting in the ordinary parlor. His face was no longer wanting in smiles, and his salutations, though hasty, were cordial. He took no notice of the escape and recapture of Henry Wharton, but seemed to think the young man had continued where he had left him before the encounter. On the ground they had not met. The English officer withdrew in haughty silence to a window, leaving the major uninterrupted to make his communications.

The excitement produced by the events of the day in the youthful feelings of the sisters, had been succeeded by a languor that kept them both silent, and Dunwoodie held his discourse with Miss Peyton.

"Is there any hope, my cousin, that your friend can survive

his wound?" said the lady, advancing towards her kinsman, with a smile of benevolent regard.

"Everything, my dear madam, everything," answered the soldier cheerfully. "Sitgreaves says he will live, and he has never deceived me."

"Your pleasure is not much greater than my own at this intelligence. One so dear to Major Dunwoodie cannot fail to excite an interest in the bosom of his friends."

"Say one so deservedly dear, madam," returned the major, with warmth. "He is the beneficent spirit of the corps, equally beloved by us all; so mild, so equal, so just, so generous, with the meekness of a lamb and the fondness of a dove—it is only in the hour of battle that Singleton is a lion."

"You speak of him as if he were your mistress, Major Dunwoodie," observed the smiling spinster, glancing her eye at her niece, who sat pale and listening, in a corner of the room.

"I love him as one," cried the excited youth. "But he requires care and nursing; all now depends on the attention he receives."

"Trust me, sir, he will want for nothing under this roof."

"Pardon me, dear madam; you are all that is benevolent, but Singleton requires a care which many men would feel to be irksome. It is at moments like these, and in sufferings like this, that the soldier most finds the want of female tenderness." As he spoke, he turned his eyes on Frances with an expression that again thrilled to the heart of his mistress; she rose from her seat with burning cheeks, and said,—

"All the attention that can with propriety be given to a stranger, will be cheerfully bestowed on your friend."

"Ah!" cried the major, shaking his head, "that cold word propriety will kill him; he must be fostered, cherished, soothed."

"These are offices for a sister or a wife."

"A sister!" repeated the soldier, the blood rushing to his own face tumultuously; "a sister! He has a sister; and one that might be here with to-morrow's sun." He paused, mused in silence, glanced his eyes uneasily at Frances, and muttered in an undertone, "Singleton requires it, and it must be done."

The ladies had watched his varying countenance in some surprise, and Miss Peyton now observed that,—

"If there were a sister of Captain Singleton near them, her

presence would be gladly requested both by herself and nieces."

"It must be, madam; it cannot well be otherwise," replied Dunwoodie, with a hesitation that but ill agreed with his former declarations. "She shall be sent for express this very night." And then, as if willing to change the subject, he approached Captain Wharton, and continued, mildly,—

"Henry Wharton, to me honor is dearer than life; but in your hands I know it can safely be confided. Remain here unwatched until we leave the county, which will not be for some days."

The distance in the manner of the English officer vanished, and taking the offered hand of the other, he replied with warmth, "Your generous confidence, Peyton, will not be abused, even though the gibbet on which your Washington hung Andre be ready for my own execution."

"Henry, Henry Wharton," said Dunwoodie reproachfully, "you little know the man who leads our armies, or you would have spared him that reproach; but duty calls me without. I leave you where I could wish to stay myself, and where you cannot be wholly unhappy."

In passing Frances, she received another of those smiling looks of affection she so much prized, and for a season the impression made by his appearance after the battle was forgotten.

Among the veterans that had been impelled by the times to abandon the quiet of age for the service of their country, was Colonel Singleton. He was a native of Georgia, and had been for the earlier years of his life a soldier by profession. When the struggle for liberty commenced, he offered his services to his country, and from respect to his character they had been accepted. His years and health had, however, prevented his discharging the active duties of the field, and he had been kept in command of different posts of trust, where his country might receive the benefits of his vigilance and fidelity without inconvenience to himself. For the last year he had been intrusted with the passes into the Highlands, and was now quartered, with his daughter, but a short day's march above the valley where Dunwoodie had met the enemy. His only other child was the wounded officer we have mentioned. Thither, then, the major prepared to dispatch a messenger with the unhappy news of the captain's situation, and charged with such an invitation from the ladies as he did not doubt would speedily bring the sister to the couch of her brother. This duty performed, though with an unwillingness that only could make his former anxiety more perplexing, Dunwoodie proceeded to the field where his troops had halted. The remnant of the English were already to be seen, over the tops of the trees, marching along the heights towards their boats, in compact order and with great watchfulness. The detachment of the dragoons under Lawton were a short distance on their flank, eagerly awaiting a favorable moment to strike a blow. In this manner both parties were soon lost to view.

A short distance above the Locusts was a small hamlet where several roads intersected each other, and from which, consequently, access to the surrounding country was easy. It was a favorite halting place of the horse, and frequently held by the light parties of the American army during their excursions below. Dunwoodie had been the first to discover its advantages, and as it was necessary for him to remain in the county until further orders from above, it cannot be supposed he overlooked them now. To this place the troops were directed to retire, carrying with them their wounded; parties were already employed in the sad duty of interring-the dead. In making these arrangements, a new object of embarrassment presented itself to our young soldier. In moving through the field, he was struck with the appearance of Colonel Wellmere, seated by himself, brooding over his misfortunes, uninterrupted by anything but the passing civilities of the American officers. His anxiety on behalf of Singleton had hitherto banished the recollection of his captive from the mind of Dunwoodie, and he now approached him with apologies for his neglect. The Englishman received his courtesies with coolness, and complained of being injured by what he affected to think was the accidental stumbling of his horse. Dunwoodie, who had seen one of his own men ride him down, and that with very little ceremony, slightly smiled, as he offered him surgical assistance. This could only be procured at the cottage, and thither they both proceeded.

"Colonel Wellmere!" cried young Wharton in astonishment as they entered, "has the fortune of war been thus cruel to you also? But you are welcome to the house of my father, although I could wish the introduction to have taken place under more happy circumstances."

Mr. Wharton received this new guest with the guarded caution that distinguished his manner, and Dunwoodie left the room to seek the bedside of his friend. Everything here looked propitious, and he acquainted the surgeon that another patient waited his skill in the room below. The sound of the word was enough to set the doctor in motion, and seizing his implements of office, he went in quest of this new applicant. At the door of the parlor he was met by the ladies, who were retiring. Miss Peyton detained him for a moment, to inquire into the welfare of Captain Singleton. Frances smiled with something of natural archness of manner, as she contemplated the grotesque appearance of the bald-headed practitioner; but Sarah was too much agitated, with the surprise of the unexpected interview with the British colonel, to observe him. It has already been intimated that Colonel Wellmere was an old acquaintance of the family. Sarah had been so long absent from the city, that she had in some measure been banished from the remembrance of the gentleman; but the recollections of Sarah were more vivid. There is a period in the life of every woman when she may be said to be predisposed to love; it is at the happy age when infancy is lost in opening maturity—when the guileless heart heats with those anticipations of life which the truth can never realize—and when the imagination forms images of perfection that are copied after its own unsullied visions. At this happy age Sarah left the city, and she had brought with her a picture of futurity, faintly impressed, it is true, but which gained durability from her solitude, and in which Wellmere had been placed in the foreground. The surprise of the meeting had in some measure overpowered her, and after receiving the salutations of the colonel, she had risen, in compliance with a signal from her observant aunt, to withdraw.

"Then, sir," observed Miss Peyton, after listening to the surgeon's account of his young patient, "we may be flattered with the expectation that he will recover."

" 'Tis certain, madam," returned the doctor, endeavoring, out of respect to the ladies, to replace his wig; " 'tis certain, with care and good nursing."

"In those he shall not be wanting," said the spinster, mildly. "Everything we have he can command, and Major Dunwoodie has dispatched an express for his sister."

"His sister!" echoed the practitioner, with a meaning look. "If the major has sent for her, she will come."

"Her brother's danger would induce her, one would imagine."

"No doubt, madam," continued the doctor, laconically, bowing low, and giving room to the ladies to pass. The words and the manner were not lost on the younger sister, in whose presence the name of Dunwoodie was never mentioned unheeded.

"Sir," cried Dr. Sitgreaves, on entering the parlor, addressing 'himself to the only coat of scarlet in the room, "I am advised you are in want of my aid. God send 'tis not Captain Lawton with whom you came in contact, in which case I may be too late."

"There must be some mistake, sir," said Wellmere, haughtily. "It was a surgeon that Major Dunwoodie was to send me, and not an old woman."

" 'Tis Dr. Sitgreaves," said Henry Wharton, quickly, though with difficulty suppressing a laugh. "The multitude of his engagements, to-day, has prevented his usual attention to his attire."

"Your pardon, sir," added Wellmere, very ungraciously proceeding to lay aside his coat, and exhibit what he called a wounded arm.

"If, sir," said the surgeon dryly, "the degrees of Edinburgh— walking your London hospitals—amputating some hundreds of limbs—operating on the human frame in every shape that is warranted by the lights of science, a clear conscience, and the commission of the Continental Congress, can make a surgeon, I am one."

"Your pardon, sir," repeated the colonel stiffly. "Captain Wharton has accounted for my error."

"For which I thank Captain Wharton," said the surgeon, proceeding coolly to arrange his amputating instruments, with a formality that made the colonel's blood run cold. "Where are you hurt, sir? What! is it then this scratch in your shoulder? In what manner might you have received this wound, sir?"

"From the sword of a rebel dragoon," said the colonel, with emphasis.

"Never. Even the gentle George Singleton would not have breathed on you so harmlessly." He took a piece of sticking plaster from his pocket, and applied it to the part. "There, sir; that will answer your purpose, and I am certain it is all that is required of me."

"What do you take to be my purpose, then, sir?"

"To report yourself wounded in your dispatches," replied the doctor, with great steadiness; "and you may say that an old woman dressed your hurts—for if one did not, one easily might!"

"Very extraordinary language," muttered the Englishman.

Here Captain Wharton interfered; and, by explaining the mistake of Colonel Wellmere to proceed from his irritated mind and pain of body, he in part succeeded in mollifying the insulted practitioner, who consented to look further into the hurts of the other. They were chiefly bruises from his fall, to which Sitgreaves made some hasty applications, and withdrew.

The horse, having taken their required refreshment, prepared to fall back to their intended position, and it became incumbent on Dunwoodie to arrange the disposal of his prisoners. Sitgreaves he determined to leave in the cottage of Mr. Wharton, in attendance on Captain Singleton. Henry came to him with a request that Colonel Wellmere might also be left behind, under his parole, until the troops marched higher into the country. To this the major cheerfully assented; and as all the rest of the prisoners were of the vulgar herd, they were speedily collected, and, under the care of a strong guard, ordered to the interior. The dragoons soon after marched; and the guides, separating in small parties, accompanied by patrols from the horse, spread themselves across the country, in such a manner as to make a chain of sentinels from the waters of the Sound to those of the Hudson.[7]

Dunwoodie had lingered in front of the cottage, after he paid his parting compliments, with an unwillingness to return, that he thought proceeded from his solicitude for his wounded friends. The heart which has not become callous, soon sickens with the glory that has been purchased with a waste of human life. Peyton Dunwoodie, left to himself, and no longer excited by the visions which youthful ardor had kept before him throughout the day, began to feel there were other ties than those which bound the soldier within the rigid rules of honor. He did not waver in his duty, yet he felt how strong was the temptation. His blood had ceased to flow with the impulse created by the battle.

---

[7] The scene of this tale is between these two waters, which are but a few miles from each other.

The stem expression of his eye gradually gave place to a look of softness; and his reflections on the victory brought with them no satisfaction that compensated for the sacrifices by which it had been purchased. While turning his last lingering gaze on the Locusts, he remembered only that it contained all that he most valued. The friend of his youth was a prisoner, under circumstances that endangered both life and honor. The gentle companion of his toils, who could throw around the rude enjoyments of a soldier the graceful mildness of peace, lay a bleeding victim to his success. The image of the maid who had held, during the day, a disputed sovereignty in his bosom, again rose to his view with a loveliness that banished her rival, glory, from his mind.

The last lagging trooper of the corps had already disappeared behind the northern hill, and the major unwillingly turned his horse in the same direction. Frances, impelled by a restless inquietude, now timidly ventured on the piazza of the cottage. The day had been mild and clear, and the sun was shining brightly in a cloudless sky. The tumult, which so lately disturbed the valley, was succeeded by the stillness of death, and the fair scene before her looked as if it had never been marred by the passions of men. One solitary cloud, the collected smoke of the contest, hung over the field; and this was gradually dispersing, leaving no vestige of the conflict above the peaceful graves of its victims. All the conflicting feelings, all the tumultuous circumstances of the eventful day, appeared like the deceptions of a troubled vision. Frances turned, and caught a glimpse of the retreating figure of him who had been so conspicuous an actor in the scene, and the illusion vanished. She recognized her lover, and, with the truth, came other recollections that drove her to the room, with a heart as sad as that which Dunwoodie himself bore from the valley.

CHAPTER IX

A moment gazed adown the dale,
A moment snuffed the tainted gale,
A moment listened to the cry,
That thickened as the chase drew nigh;
Then, as the headmost foe appeared,
With one brave bound the copse he cleared
And, stretching forward free and far,
Sought the wild heaths of Uam- Var.
—Lady of the Lake. "

The party under Captain Lawton had watched the retiring foe to his boats with the most unremitting vigilance, without finding any fit opening for a charge. The experienced successor of Colonel Wellmere knew too well the power of his enemy to leave the uneven surface of the heights, until compelled to descend to the level of the water. Before he attempted this hazardous movement, he threw his men into a compact square, with its outer edges bristling with bayonets. In this position, the impatient trooper well understood that brave men could never be assailed by cavalry with success, and he was reluctantly obliged to hover near them, without seeing any opportunity of stopping their slow but steady march to the beach. A small schooner, which had been their convoy from the city, lay with her guns bearing on the place of embarkation. Against this combination of force and discipline, Lawton had sufficient prudence to see it would be folly to contend, and the English were suffered to embark without molestation. The dragoons lingered on the shore till the last moment, and then they reluctantly commenced their own retreat back to the main body of the corps.

The gathering mists of the evening had begun to darken the valley, as the detachment of Lawton made its reappearance, at its southern extremity. The march of the troops was slow, and their line extended for the benefit of ease. In the front rode the captain, side by side with his senior subaltern, apparently engaged in close conference, while the rear was brought up by a young cornet, humming an air, and thinking of the sweets of a straw bed after the fatigues of a hard day's duty.

"Then it struck you too?" said the captain. "The instant I placed my eyes on her I remembered the face; it is one not easily forgotten. By my faith, Tom, the girl does no discredit to the major's taste."

"She would do honor to the corps," replied the lieutenant, with some warmth. "Those blue eyes might easily win a man to gentler employments than this trade of ours. In sober truth, I can easily imagine such a girl might tempt even me to quit the broadsword and saddle, for a darning-needle and pillion."

"Mutiny, sir, mutiny," cried the other, laughing. "What, you, Tom Mason, dare to rival the gay, admired, and withal rich, Major Dunwoodie in his love! You, a lieutenant of cavalry, with but one horse, and he none of the best! whose captain is as tough as a pepperidge log, and has as many lives as a cat!"

"Faith," said the subaltern, smiling in his turn, "the log may yet be split, and grimalkin lose his lives, if you often charge as madly as you did this morning. What think you of many raps from such a beetle as laid you on your back to-day?"

"Ah! don't mention it, my good Tom; the thought makes my head ache," replied the other, shrugging up his shoulders. "It is what I call forestalling night."

"The night of death?"

"No, sir, the night that follows day. I saw myriads of stars, things which should hide their faces in the presence of the lordly sun. I do think nothing but this thick cap saved me for your comfort a little longer, mauger the cat's lives."

"I have much reason to be obliged to the cap," said Mason dryly. "That or the skull must have had a reasonable portion of thickness, I admit."

"Come, come, Tom, you are a licensed joker, so I'll not feign anger with you," returned the captain, good-humoredly. "But Singleton's lieutenant, I am fearful, will fare better than yourself for the day's service."

"I believe both of us will be spared the pain of receiving promotion purchased by the death of a comrade and friend," observed Mason kindly. "It was reported that Sitgreaves said he would live."

"From my soul I hope so," exclaimed Lawton. "For a beardless face, that boy carries the stoutest heart I have ever met with. It surprises me, however, that as we both fell at the same instant, the men behaved so well."

"For the compliment, I might thank you," cried the lieutenant with a laugh; "but modesty forbids. I did my best to stop them, but without success."

"Stop them!" roared the captain. "Would you stop men in the middle of a charge?"

"I thought they were going the wrong way," answered the subaltern.

"Ah! our fall drove them to the right about?"

"It was either your fall, or apprehensions of their own; until the major rallied us, we were in admirable disorder."

"Dunwoodie! the major was on the crupper of the Dutchman."

"Ah! but he managed to get off the crupper of the Dutchman. He came in, at half speed, with the other two troops, and riding between us and the enemy, with that imperative way he has when roused, brought us in line in the twinkling of an eye. Then it was," added the lieutenant, with animation, "that we sent Johh Bull to the bushes. Oh! it was a sweet charge — heads and tails, until we were upon them."

"The devil! What a sight I missed!"

"You slept through it all."

"Yes," returned the other, with a sigh; "it was all lost to me and poor George Singleton. But, Tom, what will George's sister say to this fair-haired maiden, in yonder white building?"

"Hang herself in her garters," said the subaltern. "I owe a proper respect to my superiors, but two such angels are more than justly falls to the share of one man, unless he be a Turk or a Hindoo."

"Yes, yes," said the captain, quickly, "the major is ever preaching morality to the youngsters, but he is a sly fellow in the main. Do you observe how fond he is of the cross roads above this valley? Now, if I were to halt the troops twice in the same place, you would all swear there was a petticoat in the wind."

"You are well known to the corps."

"Well, Tom, a slanderous propensity is incurable—but," stretching forward his body in the direction he was gazing, as if to aid him in distinguishing objects through the darkness, "what animal is moving through the field on our right?"

" 'Tis a man," said Mason, looking intently at the suspicious object.

"By his hump 'tis a dromedary!" added the captain, eying it keenly. Wheeling his horse suddenly from the highway he exclaimed, "Harvey Birch! — take him, dead or alive!"

Mason and a few of the leading dragoons only understood the sudden cry, but it was heard throughout the line". A dozen of the men, with the lieutenant at their head, followed the impetuous Lawton, and their speed threatened the pursued with a sudden termination of the race.

Birch prudently kept his position on the rock, where he had been seen by the passing glance of Henry Wharton, until evening had begun to shroud the surrounding objects in darkness. From this height he had seen all the events of the day, as they occurred. He had watched with a beating heart the departure of the troops under Dunwoodie, and with difficulty had curbed his impatience until the obscurity of night should render his moving free from danger. He had not, however, completed a fourth of his way to his own residence, when his quick ear distinguished the tread of the approaching horse. Trusting to the increasing darkness, he determined to persevere. By crouching and moving quickly along the surface of the ground, he hoped yet to escape unseen. Captain Lawton was too much engrossed with the foregoing conversation to suffer his eyes to indulge in their usual wandering; and the peddler, perceiving by the voices that the enemy he most feared had passed, yielded to his impatience, and stood erect, in order to make greater progress. The moment his body arose above the shadow of the ground, it was seen, and the chase commenced. For a single instant, Birch was helpless, his blood curdling in his veins at the imminence of the danger, and his legs refusing their natural and necessary office. But it was only for a moment. Casting his pack where he stood, and instinctively tightening the belt he wore, the peddler betook himself to flight. He knew that by bringing himself in a line with his pursuers and the wood, his form would be lost to sight. This he soon effected, and he was straining every nerve to gain the wood itself, when several horsemen rode by him but a short distance on his left, and cut him off from this place of refuge. The peddler threw himself on the ground as they came near him, and was passed unseen. But the delay now became too dangerous for him to remain in that position. He accordingly rose, and still keeping in the shadow of the wood, along the skirts of which he heard voices crying to each other to be watchful, he ran with incredible speed in a parallel line, but in an opposite direction, to the march of the dragoons.

The confusion of the chase had been heard by the whole of the men, though none. distinctly understood the order of Lawton but those who followed. The remainder were lost in doubt as to the duty that was required of them; and the aforesaid cornet was making eager inquiries of the trooper near him on the subject, when a man, at a short distance in his rear, crossed the road at a single bound. At the same instant, the stentorian voice of Lawton rang through the valley, shouting,—

"Harvey Birch—take him, dead or alive!"

Fifty pistols lighted the scene, and the bullets whistled in every direction round the head of the devoted peddler. A feeling of despair seized his heart, and in the bitterness of that moment he exclaimed, —

"Hunted like a beast of the forest!"

He felt life and its accompaniments to be a burden, and was about to yield himself to his enemies. Nature, however, prevailed. If taken, there was great reason to apprehend that he would not be honored with the forms of a trial, but that most probably the morning sun would witness his ignominious execution; for he had already been condemned to death, and had only escaped that fate by stratagem. These considerations, with the approaching footsteps of his pursuers, roused him to new exertions. He again fled before them. A fragment of a wall, that had withstood the ravages made by war in the adjoining fences of wood, fortunately crossed his path. He hardly had time to throw his exhausted limbs over this barrier, before twenty of his enemies reached its opposite side. Their horses refused to take the leap in the dark, and amid the confusion of the rearing chargers, and the execrations of their riders, Birch was enabled to gain a sight of the base of the hill, on whose summit was a place of perfect security. The heart of the peddler now beat high with hope, when the voice of Captain Lawton again rang in his ears, shouting to his men to make room. The order was obeyed, and the fearless trooper rode at the wall at the top of his horse's speed, plunged the rowels in his charger, and flew over the obstacle in safety. The triumphant hurrahs of the men, and the thundering tread of the horse, too plainly assured the peddler of the emergency of his danger. He was nearly exhausted, and his fate no longer seemed doubtful.

"Stop, or die!" was uttered above his head, and in fearful proximity to his ears.

Harvey stole a glance over his shoulder, and saw, within a bound of him, the man he most dreaded. By the light of the stars he beheld the uplifted arm and the threatening saber. Fear, exhaustion, and despair seized his heart, and the intended victim fell at the feet of the dragoon. The horse of Lawton struck the prostrate peddler, and both steed and rider came violently to the earth.

As quick as thought. Birch was on his feet. again, with the sword of the discomfited dragoon in his hand. Vengeance seems but too natural to human passions. There are few who have not felt the seductive pleasure of making our injuries recoil on their authors; and yet there are some who know how much sweeter it is to return good for evil.

All the wrongs of the peddler shone on his brain with a dazzling brightness. For a moment the demon within him prevailed, and Birch brandished the powerful weapon in the air; in the next, it fell harmless on the reviving but helpless trooper. The peddler vanished up the side of the friendly rock.

"Help Captain Lawton, there!" cried Mason, as he rode up, followed by a dozen of his men; "and some of you dismount with me, and search these rocks; the villain lies here concealed."

"Hold!" roared the discomfited captain, raising himself with difficulty on his feet. "If one of you dismount, he dies. Tom, my good fellow, you will help me to straddle Roanoke again."

The astonished subaltern complied in silence, while the wondering dragoons remained as fixed in their saddles, as if they composed part of the animals they rode.

"You are much hurt, I fear," said Mason, with something of condolence in his manner, as they re-entered the highway, biting off the end of a cigar for the want of a better quality of tobacco.

"Something so, I do believe," replied the captain, catching his breath, and speaking with difficulty. "I wish our bonesetter was at hand, to examine into the state of my ribs."

"Sitgreaves is left in attendance on Captain Singleton, at the house of Mr. Wharton."

"Then there I halt for the night, Tom. These rude times must abridge ceremony; besides, you may remember the old gentleman professed a kinsman's regard for the corps. I can never think of passing so good a friend without a halt."

"And I will lead the troop to the Four Comers; if we all halt there, we shall breed a famine in the land."

"A condition I never desire to be placed in. The idea of that graceful spinster's cakes is no bad solace for twenty-four hours in the hospital."

"Oh! you won't die if you can think of eating," said Mason, with a laugh.

"I should surely die if I could not," observed the captain, gravely.

"Captain Lawton," said the orderly of his troop, riding to the side of his commanding officer, "we are now passing the house of the peddler spy; is it your pleasure that we bum it?"

"No!" roared the captain, in a voice that startled the disappointed sergeant. "Are you an incendiary? Would you bum a house in cold blood? Let but a spark approach, and the hand that carries it will never light another."

"Zounds!" muttered the sleepy cornet in the rear, as he was nodding on his horse, "there is life in the captain, notwithstanding his tumble."

Lawton and Mason rode on in 'silence, the latter ruminating on the wonderful change produced in his commander by his fall, when they arrived opposite to the gate before the residence of Mr. Wharton. The troop continued its march; but the captain and his lieutenant dismounted, and, followed by the servant of the former, they proceeded slowly to the door of the cottage.

Colonel Wellmere had already sought a retreat in his own room; Mr. Wharton and his son were closeted by themselves; and the ladies were administering the refreshments of the tea table to the surgeon of the dragoons, who had seen one of his patients in his bed, and the other happily enjoying the comforts of a sweet sleep. A few natural inquiries from Miss Peyton had opened the soul of the doctor, who knew every individual of her extensive family connection in Virginia, and who even thought it possible that he had seen the lady herself. The amiable spinster smiled as she felt it to be improbable that she should ever have met her new acquaintance before, and not remember his singularities. It however greatly relieved the embarrassment of their situation, and something like a discourse was maintained between them; the nieces were only listeners, nor could the aunt be said to be much more.

"As I was observing, Miss Peyton, it was merely the noxious vapors of the lowlands that rendered the plantation of your brother an unfit residence for man; but quadrupeds were—"

"Bless me, what's that?" said Miss Peyton, turning pale at the report of the pistols fired at Birch.

"It sounds prodigiously like the concussion on the atmosphere made by the explosion of firearms." said the surgeon, sipping his tea with great indifference. "I should imagine it to be the troop of Captain Lawton returning, did I know the captain never uses the pistol, and that he dreadfully abuses the saber."

"Merciful providence!" exclaimed the agitated maiden, "he would not injure one with it, certainly."

"Injure!" repeated the other quickly. "It is certain death, madam; the most random blows imaginable; all that I can say to him will have no effect."

"But Captain Lawton is the officer we saw this morning, and is surely your friend," said Frances, hastily, observing her aunt to be seriously alarmed.

"I find no fault with his want of friendship; the man is well enough if he would learn to cut scientifically. All trades, madam, ought to be allowed to live; but what is to become of a surgeon, if his patients are dead before he sees them!"

The doctor continued haranguing on the probability and improbability of its being the returning troop, until a loud knock at the door gave new alarm to the ladies. Instinctively laying his hand on a small saw, that had been his companion for the whole day, in the vain expectation of an amputation, the surgeon, coolly assuring the ladies that he would stand between them and danger, proceeded in person to answer the summons.

"Captain Lawton," exclaimed the surgeon, as he beheld the trooper leaning on the arm of his subaltern, and with difficulty crossing the threshold.

"Ah! my dear bonesetter, is it you? You are here very fortunately to inspect my carcass; but do lay aside that rascally saw!"

A few words from Mason explained the nature and manner of his captain's hurts, and Miss Peyton cheerfully accorded the required accommodations. While the room intended for the trooper was getting ready, and the doctor was giving certain portentous orders, the captain was invited to rest himself in the parlor. On the table was a dish of more substantial food than ordinarily adorned the afternoon's repast, and it soon caught the attention of the dragoons. Miss Peyton, recollecting that they had probably made their only meal that day at her own table, kindly invited them to close it with another. The offer required no pressing, and in a few minutes the two were comfortably seated, and engaged in an employment that was only interrupted by an occasional wry face from the captain, who moved his body in evident pain. These interruptions, however, interfered but little with the principal business in hand; and the captain had got happily through with this important duty, before the surgeon returned to announce all things ready for his accommodation in the room above stairs.

"Eating!" cried the astonished physician. "Captain Lawton, do you wish to die?"

"I have no particular ambition that way," said the trooper, rising, and bowing good night to the ladies, "and, therefore, have been providing materials necessary to preserve life."

The surgeon muttered his dissatisfaction, while he followed Mason and the captain from the apartment.

Every house in America had, at that day, what was emphatically called its best room, and this had been allotted, by the unseen influence of Sarah, to Colonel Wellmere. The down counterpane, which a clear frosty night would render extremely grateful over bruised limbs, decked the English officer's bed. A massive silver tankard, richly embossed with the Wharton arms, held the beverage he was to drink during the night; while beautiful vessels of china performed the same office for the two American captains. Sarah was certainly unconscious of the silent preference she had been giving to the English officer; and it is equally certain, that but for his hurts, bed, tankard, and everything but the beverage would have been matters of indifference to Captain Lawton, half of whose nights were spent in his clothes, and not a few of them in the saddle. After taking possession, however, of a small but very comfortable room, Doctor Sitgreaves proceeded to inquire into the state of his injuries. He had begun to pass his hand over the body of his patient, when the latter cried impatiently,—

"Sitgreaves, do me the favor to lay that rascally saw aside, or I shall have recourse to my saber in self-defense; the sight of it makes my blood cold."

"Captain Lawton, for a man who has so often exposed life and limb, you are unaccountably afraid of a very useful instrument."

"Heaven keep me from its use," said the trooper, with a shrug.

"You would not despise the lights of science, nor refuse surgical aid, because this saw might be necessary?"

"I would."

"You would!"

"Yes; you shall never joint me like a quarter of beef, while I have life to defend myself," cried the resolute dragoon. "But I grow sleepy; are any of my ribs broken?"

"No."

"Any of my bones?"

"No."

"Tom, I'll thank you for that pitcher." As he ended his draft, he very deliberately turned his back on his companions, and good-naturedly cried, "Good night. Mason; good night, Galen."

Captain Lawton entertained a profound respect for the surgical abilities of his comrade, but he was very skeptical on the subject of administering internally for the ailings of the human frame. With a full stomach, a stout heart, and a clear conscience, he often maintained that a man might bid defiance to the worlds and its vicissitudes. Nature provided him with the second, and, to say the truth, he strove manfully himself to keep up the other two requisites in his creed. It was a favorite maxim with him, that the last thing death assailed was the eyes, and next to the last, the jaws. This he interpreted to be a clear expression of the intention of nature, that every man might regulate, by his own volition, whatever was to be admitted into the sanctuary of his mouth; consequently, if the guest proved unpalatable, he had no one to blame but himself. The surgeon, who was well acquainted with these views of his patient, beheld him, as he cavalierly turned his back on Mason and himself, with a commiserating contempt, replaced in their leathern repository the phials he had exhibited, with a species of care that was allied to veneration, gave the saw, as he concluded, a whirl of triumph, and departed, without condescending to notice the compliment of the trooper. Mason, finding, by the breathing of the captain, that his own good night would be unheard, hastened to pay his respects to the ladies—after which he mounted and followed the troop at the top of his horse's speed.

CHAPTER X

On some fond breast the parting soul relies,
Some pious drops the closing eye requires,
E'en from the tomb the voice of nature cries,
E'en in our ashes live their wonted fires.
-Gray.

The possessions of Mr. Wharton extended to some distance on each side of the house in which he dwelt, and most of his land was unoccupied. A few scattered dwellings were to be seen in different parts of his domains, but they were fast falling to decay, and were untenanted. The proximity of the country to the contending armies had nearly banished the pursuits of agriculture from the land. It was useless for the husbandman to devote his time and the labor of his hands, to obtain overflowing garners, that the first foraging party would empty. None tilled the earth with any other view than to provide the scanty means of subsistence, except those who were placed so near to one of the adverse parties as to be safe from the inroads of the light troops of the other. To these the war offered a golden harvest, more especially to such as enjoyed the benefits of an access to the royal army. Mr. Wharton did not require the use of his lands for the purposes of subsistence; and he willingly adopted the guarded practice of the day, limiting his attention to such articles as were soon to be consumed within his own walls, or could be easily secreted from the prying eyes of the foragers. In consequence, the ground on which the action was fought had not a single inhabited building, besides the one belonging to the father of Harvey Birch. This house stood between the place where the cavalry had met, and that where the charge had been made on the party of Wellmere.

To Katy Haynes it had been a day fruitful of incidents. The prudent housekeeper had kept her political feelings in a state of rigid neutrality; her own friends had espoused the cause of the country, but the maiden herself never lost sight of that important moment, when, like females of more illustrious hopes, she might be required to sacrifice her love of country on the altar of domestic harmony. And yet, notwithstanding all her sagacity, there were moments when the good woman had grievous doubts into which scale she ought to throw the weight of her eloquence, in order to be certain of supporting the cause favored by the peddler. There was so much that was equivocal in his movements and manner, that often, when, in the privacy of their household, she was about to offer a philippic on Washington and his followers, discretion sealed her mouth, and distrust beset her mind. In short, the whole conduct of the mysterious being she studied was of a character to distract the opinions of one who took a more enlarged view of men and life than came within the competency of his housekeeper.

The battle of the Plains had taught the cautious Washington the advantages his enemy possessed in organization, arms, and discipline. These were difficulties to be mastered by his own vigilance and care. Drawing off his troops to the heights, in the northern part of the county, he had bidden defiance to the attacks of the royal army, and Sir William Howe fell back to the enjoyment of his barren conquest—a deserted city. Never afterwards did the opposing armies make the trial of strength within the limits of Westchester; yet hardly a day passed, that the partisans did not make their inroads; or a sun rise, that the inhabitants were spared the relation of excesses which the preceding darkness had served to conceal. Most of the movements of the peddler were made at the hours which others allotted to repose. The evening sun would frequently leave him at one extremity of the county, and the morning find him at the other. His pack was his never-failing companion; and there were those who closely studied him, in his moments of traffic, and thought his only purpose was the accumulation of gold. He would be often seen near the Highlands, with a body bending under its load; and again near the Harlem River, traveling with lighter steps, with his face toward the setting sun. But these glances at him were uncertain and fleeting.. The intermediate time no eye could penetrate. For months he disappeared, and no traces of his course were ever known.

Strong parties held the heights of Harlem, and the northern end of Manhattan Island was bristling with the bayonets of the English sentinels, yet the peddler glided among them unnoticed and uninjured. His approaches to the American lines were also frequent; but generally so conducted as to baffle pursuit. Many a sentinel, placed in the gorges of the mountains, spoke of a strange figure that had been seen gliding by them in the mists of the evening. These stories reached the ears of the officers, and, as we have related, in two instances the trader had fallen into the hands of the Americans. The first time he had escaped from Lawton, shortly after his arrest; but the second he was condemned to die. On the morning of his intended execution, the cage was opened, but the bird had flown. This extraordinary escape had been made from the custody of a favorite officer of Washington, and sentinels who had been thought worthy to guard the person of the commander in chief. Bribery and treason could not be imputed to men so well esteemed, and the opinion gained ground among the common soldiery, that the peddler had dealings with the dark one. Katy, however, always repelled this opinion with indignation; for within the recesses of her own bosom, the housekeeper, in ruminating on the events, concluded that the evil spirit did not pay in gold. Nor, continued the wary spinster in her cogitations, does Washington; paper and promises were all that leader of the American troops could dispense to his servants. After the alliance with France, when silver became more abundant in the country, although the scmtinizing eyes of Katy never let any opportunity of examining into the deerskin purse pass unimproved, she was never able to detect the image of Louis intruding into the presence of the well-known countenance of George III. In short, the secret board of Harvey sufficiently showed in its contents that all its contributions had been received from the British.

The house of Birch had been watched at different times by the Americans, with a view to his arrest, but never with success; the reputed spy possessing a secret means of intelligence, that invariably defeated their schemes. Once, when a strong body of the continental army held the Four Corners for a whole summer, orders had been received from Washington himself, never to leave the door of Harvey Birch unwatched. The command was rigidly obeyed, and during this long period the peddler was unseen; the detachment was withdrawn, and the following night Birch re-entered his dwelling. The father of Harvey had been greatly molested, in consequence of the suspicious character of the son. But, notwithstanding the most minute scrutiny into the conduct of the old man, no fact could be substantiated against him to his injury, and his property was too small, to keep alive the zeal of patriots by profession. Its confiscation and purchase would not have rewarded their trouble. Age and sorrow were now about to spare him further molestation, for the lamp of life had been drained of its oil. The recent separation of the father and son had been painful, but they had submitted in obedience to what both thought a duty. The old man had kept his dying situation a secret from the neighborhood, in the hope that he might still have the company of his child in his last moments. The confusion of the day, and his increasing dread that Harvey might be too late, helped to hasten the event he would fain arrest for a little while. As night set in, his illness increased to such a degree, that the dismayed housekeeper sent a truant boy, who had shut up himself with them during the combat, to the Locusts, in quest of a companion to cheer her solitude. Cæsar, alone, could be spared, and, loaded with eatables and cordials by the kind-hearted Miss Peyton, the black had been dispatched on his duty. The dying man was past the use of medicines and his chief anxiety seemed to center in a meeting with his child.

The noise of the chase had been heard by the group in the house, but its cause was not understood; and as both the black and Katy were apprised of the detachment of American horse being below them, they supposed it to proceed from the return of that party. They heard the dragoons, as they moved slowly by the building; but in compliance with the prudent injunction of the black, the housekeeper forbore to indulge her curiosity. The old man had closed his eyes, and his attendants believed him to be asleep. The house contained two large rooms and as many small ones. One of the former served for kitchen and sitting room; in the other lay the father of Birch; of the latter, one was the sanctuary of the vestal, and the other contained the stock of provisions. A huge chimney of stone rose in the center, serving, of itself, for a partition between the larger rooms; and fireplaces of corresponding dimensions were in each apartment. A bright flame was burning in that of the common room, and within the very jambs of its monstrous jaws sat Cæsar and Katy, at the time of which we write. The African was impressing his caution on the housekeeper, and commenting on the general danger of indulging an idle curiosity.

"Best nebber tempt a Satan," said Cæsar, rolling up his eyes till the whites glistened by the glare of the fire. "I berry like he-self to lose an ear for carrying a little bit of a letter; dere much mischief come of curiosity. If dere had nebber been a man curious to see Africa, dere would be no color people out of dere own country; but I wish Harvey get back."

"It is very disregardful in him to be away at such a time," said Katy, imposingly. "Suppose now his father wanted to make his last will in the testament, who is there to do so solemn and awful an act for him? Harvey is a very wasteful and very disregardful man!"

"Perhaps he make him afore?"

"It would not be a wonderment if he had," returned the housekeeper; "he is whole days looking into the Bible."

"Then he read a berry good book," said the black solemnly. "Miss Fanny read in him to Dinah now and den."

"You are right, Cæsar. The Bible is the best of books, and one that reads it as often as Harvey's father should have the best of reasons for so doing. This is no more than common sense."

She rose from her seat, and stealing softly to a chest of drawers in the room of the sick man, she took from it a large Bible, heavily bound, and secured with strong clasps of brass, with which she returned to the negro. The volume was eagerly opened, and they proceeded instantly to examine its pages. Katy was far from an expert scholar, and to Cæsar the characters were absolutely strangers. For some time the housekeeper was occupied in finding out the word Matthew, in which she had no sooner succeeded than she pointed out the word, with great complacency, to the attentive Cæsar.

"Berry well, now look him t'rough," said the black, peeping over the housekeeper's shoulder, as he held a long lank candle of yellow tallow, in such a manner as to throw its feeble light on the volume.

"Yes, but I must begin with the very beginning of the book," replied the other, turning the leaves carefully back, until moving two at once, she lighted upon a page covered with writing. "Here," said the housekeeper, shaking with the eagerness of expectation, "here are the very words themselves; now I would give the world itself to know whom he has left the big silver shoe buckles to."

"Read 'em," said Cæsar, laconically.

"And the black walnut drawers; for Harvey could never want furniture of that quality, as long as he is a bachelor!"

"Why he no want 'em as well as he fader?"

"And the six silver tablespoons; Harvey always uses the iron!"

"P'r'ap he say, without so much talk," returned the sententious black, pointing one of his crooked and dingy fingers at the open volume.

Thus repeatedly advised, and impelled by her own curiosity, Katy began to read. Anxious to come to the part which most interested herself, she dipped at once into the center of the subject.

"Chester Birch, born September 1st, 1755,"—read the spinster with a deliberation that did no great honor to her scholarship.

"Well, what he gib him?"

"Abigail Birch, born July 12th, 1757," continued the housekeeper, in the same tone.

"I t'ink he ought to gib her 'e spoon."

"June 1st, 1760. On this awful day, the judgment of an offended God lighted on my house." A heavy groan from the adjoining room made the spinster instinctively close the volume, and Cæsar, for a moment, shook with fear. Neither possessed sufficient resolution to go and examine the condition of the sufferer, but his heavy breathing continued as usual. Katy dared not, however, reopen the Bible, and carefully securing its clasps, it was laid on the table in silence. Cæsar took his chair again, and after looking timidly round the room, remarked,—

"I t'ought he time war' come!"

"No," said Katy, solemnly, "he will live till the tide is out, or the first cock crows in the morning."

"Poor man!" continued the black, nestling still farther into the chimney corner, "I hope he lay quiet after he die."

" 'Twould be no astonishment to me if he didn't; for they say an unquiet life makes an uneasy grave."

"Johnny Birch a berry good man in he way. All mankind can't be a minister; for if he do, who would be a congregation?"

"Ah! Cæsar, he is good only who does good. Can you tell me why honestly gotten gold should be hidden in the bowels of the earth?"

"Grach!—I t'ink it must be to keep t'e Skinner from findin' him; if he know where he be, why don't he dig him up?"

"There may be reasons not comprehensible to you," said Katy, moving her chair so that her clothes covered the charmed stone, underneath which lay the secret treasures of the peddler, unable to refrain from speaking of what she would have been very unwilling to reveal; "but a rough outside often holds a smooth inside." Cæsar stared around the building, unable to fathom the hidden meaning of his companion, when his roving eyes suddenly became fixed, and his teeth chattered with affright. The change in the countenance of the black was instantly perceived by Katy, and turning her face, she saw the peddler himself, standing within the door of the room.

"Is he alive?" asked Birch, tremulously, and seemingly afraid to receive the answer.

"Surely," said Katy, rising hastily, and officiously offering her chair. "He must live till day, or till the tide is down."

Disregarding all but the fact that his father still lived, the peddler stole gently into the room of his dying parent. The tie which bound the father and son was of no ordinary kind. In the wide world they were all to each other. Had Katy but read a few lines further in the record, she would have seen the sad tale of their misfortunes. At one blow competence and kindred had been swept from them, and from that day to the present hour, persecution and distress had followed their wandering steps. Approaching the bedside, Harvey leaned his body forward, and in a voice nearly choked by his feelings, he whispered near the ear of the sick,—

"Father, do you know me?"

The parent slowly opened his eyes, and a smile of satisfaction passed over his pallid features, leaving behind it the impression of death, more awful by the contrast. The peddler gave a restorative he had brought with him to the parched lips of the sick man, and for a few minutes new vigor seemed imparted to his frame. He spoke, but slowly, and with difficulty. Curiosity kept Katy silent; awe had the same effect on Cæsar; and Harvey seemed hardly to breathe, as he listened to the language of the departing spirit.

"My son," said the father in a hollow voice, "God is as merciful as He is just; if I threw the cup of salvation from my lips when a youth, He graciously offers it to me in mine age. He has chastised to purify, and I go to join the spirits of our lost family.

In a little while, my child, you will be alone. I know you too well not to foresee you will be a pilgrim through life. The bruised reed may endure, but it will never rise. You have that within you, Harvey, that will guide you aright; persevere as you have begun, for the duties of life are never to be neglected and"—a noise in the adjoining room interrupted the dying man, and the impatient peddler hastened to learn the cause, followed by Katy and the black. The first glance of his eye on the figure in the doorway told the trader but too well his errand, and the fate that probably awaited himself. The intruder was a man still young in years, but his lineaments bespoke a mind long agitated by evil passions. His dress was of the meanest materials, and so ragged and unseemly, as to give him the appearance of studied poverty. His hair was prematurely whitened, and his sunken, lowering eye avoided the bold, forward look of innocence. There was a restlessness in his movements, and an agitation in his manner, that proceeded from the workings of the foul spirit within him, and which was not less offensive to others than distressing to himself. This man was a well-known leader of one of those gangs of marauders who infested the county with a semblance of patriotism, and who were guilty of every grade of offense, from simple theft up to murder. Behind him stood several other figures clad in a similar manner, but whose countenances expressed nothing more than the indifference of brutal insensibility. They were well armed with muskets and bayonets, and provided with the usual implements of foot soldiers. Harvey knew resistance to be vain, and quietly submitted to their directions. In the twinkling of an eye both he and Cæsar were stripped of their decent garments, and made to exchange clothes with two of the filthiest of the band. They were then placed in separate corners of the room, and, under the muzzles of the muskets, required faithfully to answer such interrogatories as were put to them.

"Where is your pack?" was the first question to the peddler.

"Hear me," said Birch, trembling with agitation; "in the next room is my father, now in the agonies of death. Let me go to him, receive his blessing, and close his eyes, and you shall have all—aye, all."

"Answer me as I put the questions, or this musket shall send you to keep the old driveler company: where is your pack?"

"I will tell you nothing, unless you let me go to my father," said the peddler, resolutely.

His persecutor raised his arm with a malicious sneer, and was about to execute his threat, when one of his companions checked him.

"What would you do?" he said. "You surely forget the reward. Tell us where are your goods, and you shall go to your father."

Birch complied instantly, and a man was dispatched in quest of the booty; he soon returned, throwing the bundle on the floor, swearing it was as light as feathers.

"Aye," cried the leader, "there must be gold somewhere for what it did contain. Give us your gold, Mr. Birch; we know you have it; you will not take continental, not you."

"You break your faith," said Harvey.

"Give us your gold," exclaimed the other, furiously, pricking the peddler with his bayonet until the blood followed his pushes in streams. At this instance a slight movement was heard in the adjoining room, and Harvey cried,—

"Let me—let me go to my father, and you shall have all."

"I swear you shall go then," said the Skinner.

"Here, take the trash," cried Birch, as he threw aside the purse, which he had contrived to conceal, notwithstanding the change in his garments.

The robber raised it from the floor with a hellish laugh.

"Aye, but it shall be to your father in heaven."

"Monster! have you no feeling, no faith, no honesty?"

"To hear him, one would think there was not a rope around his neck already," said the other, laughing. "There is no necessity for your being uneasy, Mr. Birch; if the old man gets a few hours the start of you in the journey, you will be sure to follow him before noon to-morrow."

This unfeeling communication had no effect on the peddler, who listened with gasping breath to every sound from the room of his parent until he heard his own name spoken in the hollow, sepulchral tones of death. Birch could endure no more, but shrieking out,—

"Father! hush—father! I come—I come!" he darted by his keeper, and was the next moment pinned to the wall by the bayonet of another of the band. Fortunately, his quick motion had caused him to escape a thrust aimed at his life, and it was by his clothes only that he was confined.

"No, Mr. Birch," said the Skinner, "we know you too well to trust you out of sight—your gold, your gold!"

"You have it," said the peddler, writhing with agony.

"Aye, we have the purse, but you have more purses. King George is a prompt paymaster, and you have done him many a piece of good service. Where is your hoard? Without it you will never see your father."

"Remove the stone underneath the woman," cried the peddler, eagerly—"remove the stone."

"He raves! he raves!" said Katy, instinctively moving her position to a different stone from the one on which she had been standing. In a moment it was torn from its bed, and nothing but earth was seen beneath.

"He raves! You have driven him from his right mind," continued the trembling spinster. "Would any man in his senses keep gold under a hearth?"

"Peace, babbling fool!" cried Harvey. "Lift the corner stone, and you will find that which will make you rich, and me a beggar."

"And then you will be despisable," said the housekeeper bitterly. "A peddler without goods and without money is sure to be despisable."

"There will be enough left to pay for his halter," cried the Skinner, who was not slow to follow the instructions of Harvey, soon lighting upon a store of English guineas. The money was quickly transferred to a bag, notwithstanding the declarations of the spinster, that her dues were unsatisfied, and that, of right, ten of the guineas were her property.

Delighted with a prize that greatly exceeded their expectations, the band prepared to depart, intending to take the peddler with them, in order to give him up to the American troops above, and to claim the reward offered for his apprehension. Everything was ready, and they were about to lift Birch in their arms, for he resolutely refused to move an inch, when a form appeared in their midst, which appalled the stoutest heart among them. The father had arisen from his bed, and he tottered forth at the cries of his son. Around his body was thrown the sheet of the bed, and his fixed eye and haggard face gave him the appearance of a being from another world. Even Katy and Cæsar thought it was the spirit of the elder Birch, and they fled the house, followed by the alarmed Skinners in a body.

The excitement which had given the sick man strength, soon vanished, and the peddler, lifting him in his arms, reconveyed him to his bed. The reaction of the system which followed hastened to close the scene.

The glazed eye of the father was fixed upon the son; his lips moved, but his voice was unheard. Harvey bent down, and, with the parting breath of his parent, received his dying benediction. A life of privation, and of wrongs, embittered most of the future hours of the peddler. But under no sufferings, in no misfortunes, the subject of poverty and obloquy, the remembrance of that blessing never left him; it constantly gleamed over the images of the past, shedding a holly radiance around his saddest hours of despondency; it cheered the prospect of. the future with the prayers of a pious spirit; and it brought the sweet assurance of having faithfully discharged the scared offices of filial love.

The retreat of Cæsar and the spinster had been too precipitate to admit of much calculation; yet they themselves instinctively separated from the Skinners. After fleeing a short distance they paused, and the maiden commenced in a solemn voice,—

"Oh! Cæsar, was it not dreadful to walk before he had been laid in his grave! It must have been the money that disturbed him; they say Captain Kidd walks near the spot where he buried gold in the old war."

"I never t'ink Johnny Birch hab such a big eye!" said the African, his teeth yet chattering with the fright.

"I'm sure 'twould be a botherment to a living soul to lose so much money. Harvey will be nothing but an utterly despisable, poverty-stricken wretch. I wonder who he thinks would even be his housekeeper!"

"Maybe a spook take away Harvey, too," observed Cæsar, moving still nearer to the side of the maiden. But a new idea had seized the imagination of the spinster. She thought it not improbable that the prize had been forsaken in the confusion of the retreat; and after deliberating and reasoning for some time with Cæsar, they determined to venture back, and ascertain this important fact, and, if possible, learn what had been the fate of the peddler. Much time was spent in cautiously approaching the dreaded spot; and as the spinster had sagaciously placed herself in the line of the retreat of the Skinners, every stone was examined in the progress in search of abandoned gold. But although the suddenness of the alarm and the cry of Cæsar had impelled the freebooters to so hasty a retreat, they grasped the hoard with a hold that death itself would not have loosened. Perceiving everything to be quiet within, Katy at length mustered resolution to enter the dwelling, where she found the peddler, with a heavy heart, performing the last sad offices for the dead. A few words sufficed to explain to Katy the nature of her mistake; but Cæsar continued to his dying day to astonish the sable inmates of the kitchen with learned disserations on spooks, and to relate how direful was the appearance of that of Johnny Birch.

The danger compelled the peddler to abridge even the short period that American custom leaves the deceased with us; and, aided by the black and Katy, his painful task was soon ended. Cæsar volunteered to walk a couple of miles with orders to a carpenter; and, the body being habited in its ordinary attire, was left, with a sheet thrown decently over it, to await the return of the messenger.

The Skinners had fled precipitately to the wood, which was but a short distance from the house of Birch, and once safely sheltered within its shades, they halted, and mustered their panic-stricken forces.

"What in the name of fury seized your coward hearts?" cried their dissatisfied leader, drawing his breath heavily.

"The same question might be asked of yourself," returned one of the band, sullenly.

"From your fright, I thought a party of De Lancey's men were upon us. Oh! you are brave gentlemen at a race!"

"We follow our captain."

"Then follow me back, and let us secure the scoundrel, and receive the reward."

"Yes; and by the time we reach the house, that black rascal will have the mad Virginian upon us. By my soul I would rather meet fifty Cowboys than that single man."

"Fool," cried the enraged leader, "don't you know Dunwoodie's horse are at the Corners, full two miles from here?"

"I care not where the dragoons are, but I will swear that I saw Captain Lawton enter the house of old Wharton, while I lay watching an opportunity of getting the British colonel's horse from the stable."

"And if he should come, won't a bullet silence a dragoon from the South as well as from old England?"

"Aye, but I don't choose a hornet's nest about my ears; rase the skin of one of that corps, and you will never see another peaceable night's foraging again."

"Well," muttered the leader, as they retired deeper into the wood, "this sottish peddler will stay to see the old devil buried; and though we cannot touch him at the funeral (for that would raise every old woman and priest in America against us), he'll wait to look after the movables, and to-morrow night shall wind up his concerns."

With this threat they withdrew to one of their usual places of resort, until darkness should again give them an opportunity of marauding on the community without danger of detection.

CHAPTER XI

O wo, O woful, woful, woful day!
Most lamentable day; most woful day,
That ever, ever, I did yet behold!
O day! O day! O day! O hateful day!
Never was seen so black a day as this;
O woful day! O woful day!

Shakespeare.

The family at the Locusts had slept, or watched, through all the disturbances at the cottage of Birch, in perfect ignorance of their occurrence. The attacks of the Skinners were always made with so much privacy as to exclude the sufferers, not only from succor, but frequently, through a dread of future depredations, from the commiseration of their neighbors also. Additional duties had drawn the ladies from their pillows at an hour somewhat earlier than usual; and Captain Lawton, notwithstanding the sufferings of his body, had risen in compliance with a rule from which he never departed, of sleeping but six hours at a time. This was one of the few points, in which the care of the human frame was involved, on which the trooper and the surgeon of horse were ever known to agree. The doctor had watched, during the night, by the side of the bed of Captain Singleton, without once closing his eyes. Occasionally he would pay a visit to the wounded Englishman, who, being more hurt in the spirit than in the flesh, tolerated the interruptions with a very ill grace; and once, for an instant, he ventured to steal softly to the bed of his obstinate comrade, and was near succeeding in obtaining a touch of his pulse, when a terrible oath, sworn by the trooper in a dream, startled the prudent surgeon, and warned him of a trite saying in the corps, "that Captain Lawton always slept with one eye open." This group had assembled in one of the parlors as the sun made its appearance over the eastern hill, dispensing the columns of fog which had enveloped the lowland.

Miss Peyton was looking from a window in the direction of the tenement of the peddler, and was expressing a kind anxiety after the welfare of the sick man, when the person of Katy suddenly emerged from the dense covering of an earthly .cloud, whose mists were scattering before the cheering rays of the sun, and was seen making hasty steps towards the Locusts. There was that in the air of the housekeeper which bespoke distress of an unusual nature, and the kind-hearted mistress of the Locusts opened the door of the room, with the benevolent intention of soothing a grief that seemed so overwhelming. A nearer view of the disturbed features of the visitor confirmed Miss Peyton in her belief; and, with the shock that gentle feelings ever experience at a sudden and endless separation from even the meanest of their associates, she said hastily,—

"Katy, is he gone?"

"No, ma'am," replied the disturbed damsel, with great bitterness, "he is not yet gone, but he may go as soon as he pleases now, for the worst is done. I do verily believe, Miss Peyton, they haven't so much as left him money enough to buy him another suit of clothes to cover his nakedness, and those he has on are none of the best, I can tell you."

"How!" exclaimed the other, astonished, "could anyone have the heart to plunder a man in such distress?"

"Hearts," repeated Katy, catching her breath. "Men like them have no bowels at all. Plunder and distress, indeed! Why, ma'am, there were in the iron pot, in plain sight, fifty-four guineas of gold, besides what lay underneath, which I couldn't count without handling; and I didn't like to touch it, for they say that another's gold is apt to stick—so, judging from that in sight, there wasn't less than two hundred guineas, besides what might have been in the deerskin purse. But Harvey is little better now than a beggar; and a beggar, Miss Jeanette, is the most awfully despisable of all earthly creatures."

"Poverty is to be pitied, and not despised," said the lady, still unable to comprehend the extent of the misfortune that had befallen her neighbor during the night. "But how is the old man? And does this loss affect him much?"

The countenance of Katy changed, from the natural expression of concern, to the set form of melancholy, as she answered,—

"He is happily removed from the cares of the world; the chinking of the money made him get out of his bed, and the poor soul found the shock too great for him. He died about two hours and ten minutes before the cock crowed, as near as we can say." She was interrupted by the physician, who, approaching, inquired, with much interest, the nature of the disorder. Glancing her eye over the figure of this new acquaintance, Katy instinctively adjusting her dress, replied,—

" 'Twas the troubles of the times, and the loss of property, that brought him down; he wasted from day to day, and all my care and anxiety were lost; for now Harvey is no better than a beggar, and who is there to pay me for what I have done?"

"God will reward you for all the good you have done," said Miss Peyton , mildly.

"Yes," interrupted the spinster hastily, and with an air of reverence that was instantly succeeded by an expression that denoted more of worldly care; "but then I have left my wages for three years past in the hands of Harvey, and how am I to get them? My brothers told me, again and again, to ask for my money; but I always thought accounts between relations were easily settled."

"Were you related, then, to Birch?" asked Miss Peyton, observing her to pause.

"Why," returned the housekeeper, hesitating a little, "I thought we were as good as so. I wonder if I have no claim on the house and garden; though they say, now it is Harvey's it will surely be confiscated." Turning to Lawton, who had been sitting in one posture, with his piercing eyes lowering at her through his thick brows, in silence, "Perhaps this gentleman knows—he seems to take an interest in my story."

"Madam," said the trooper, bowing very low, "both you and the tale are extremely interesting"—Katy smiled involuntarily—"but my humble knowledge is limited to the setting of a squadron in the field, and using it when there. I beg leave to refer you to Dr. Archibald Sitgreaves, a gentleman of universal attainments and unbounded philanthropy; the very milk of human sympathies, and a mortal foe to all indiscriminate cutting."

The surgeon drew up, and employed himself in whistling a low air, as he looked over some phials on a table; but the housekeeper, turning to him with an inclination of the head, continued,—

"I suppose, sir, a woman has no dower in her husband's property, unless they be actually married."

It was a maxim with Dr. Sitgreaves, that no species of knowledge was to be despised; and, consequently, he was an empiric in everything but his profession. At first, indignation at the irony of his comrade kept him silent; but, suddenly changing his purpose, he answered the applicant with a good-natured smile,—

"I judge not. If death has anticipated your nuptials, I am fearful you have no remedy against his stem decrees."

To Katy this sounded well, although she understood nothing of its meaning, but "death" and "nuptials." To this part of his speech, then, she directed her reply.

"I did think he only waited the death of the old gentleman before he married," said the housekeeper, looking on the carpet. "But now he is nothing more than despisable, or, what's the same thing, a peddler without house, pack, or money. It might be hard for a man to get a wife at all in such a predicary—don't you think it would, Miss Peyton?"

"I seldom trouble myself with such things," said the lady gravely.

During this dialogue Captain Lawton had been studying the countenance and manner of the housekeeper, with a most ludicrous gravity; and, fearful the conversation would cease, he inquired, with an appearance of great interest,—

"You think it was age and debility that removed the old gentleman at last?"

"And the troublesome times. Trouble is heavy pull down to a sick bed; but I. suppose his time had come, and when that happens, it matters but little what doctor's stuff we take."

"Let me set you right in that particular," interrupted the surgeon. "We must all die, it is true, but it is permitted us to use the lights of science, in arresting dangers, as they occur, until—

"We can die secundem artem," cried the trooper.

To this observation the physician did not deign to reply; but, deeming it necessary to his professional dignity that the conversation should continue, he added,—

"Perhaps, in this instance, judicious treatment might have prolonged the life of the patient. Who administered to the case?"

"No one yet," said the housekeeper, with quickness. "I expect he has made his last will and testament."

The surgeon disregarded the smile of the ladies, and pursued his inquiries.

"It is doubtless wise to be prepared for death. But under whose care was the sick man during his indisposition?"

"Under mine," answered Katy, with an air of a little importance. "And care thrown away I may well call it; for Harvey is quite too despisable to be any sort of compensation at present."

The mutual ignorance of each other's meaning made very little interruption to the dialogue, for both took a good deal for granted, and Sitgreaves pursued the subject.

"And how did you treat him?"

"Kindly, you may be certain," said Katy, rather tartly.

"The doctor means medically, madam," observed Captain Lawton, with a face that would have honored the funeral of the deceased.

"I doctored him mostly with yarbs," said the housekeeper, smiling, as if conscious of error.

"With simples," returned the surgeon. "They are safer in the hands of the unlettered than more powerful remedies; but why had you no regular attendant?"

"I'm sure Harvey has suffered enough already from having so much concerns with the rig'lars," replied the housekeeper. "He has lost his all, and made himself a vagabond through the land; and I have reason to rue the day I ever crossed the threshold of his house."

"Dr. Sitgreaves does not mean a rig'lar soldier, but a regular physician, madam," said the trooper.

"Oh!" cried the maiden, again correcting herself, "for the best of all reasons; there was none to be had, so I took care of him myself. If there had been a doctor at hand, I am sure we would gladly have had him; for my part, I am clear for doctoring, though Harvey says I am killing myself with medicines; but I am sure it will make but little difference to him, whether I live or die."

"Therein you show your sense," said the surgeon, approaching the spinster, who sat holding the palms of her hands and the soles of her feet to the genial heat of a fine fire, making the most of comfort amid all her troubles. "You appear to be a sensible, discreet woman, and some who have had opportunities of acquiring more correct views might envy you your respect for knowledge and the lights of science."

Although the housekeeper did not altogether comprehend the other's meaning, she knew he used a compliment, and as such was highly pleased with what he said. With increased animation, therefore, she cried, "It was always said of me, that I wanted nothing but opportunity to make quite a physician myself; so long as before I came to live with Harvey's father, they called me the petticoat doctor."

"More true than civil, I dare say," returned the surgeon, losing sight of the woman's character in his admiration of her respect for the healing art. "In the absence of more enlightened counselors, the experience of a discreet matron is frequently of great efficacy in checking the progress of disease; under such circumstances, madam, it is dreadful to have to contend with ignorance and obstinacy."

"Bad enough, as I well know from experience," cried Katy, in triumph. "Harvey is as obstinate about such things as a dumb beast; one would think the care I took of his. bedridden father might learn him better than to despise good nursing. But some day he may know what it is to want a careful woman in his house, though now I am sure he is too despisable himself to have a house."

"Indeed, I can easily comprehend the mortification you must have felt in having one so self-willed to deal with," returned the surgeon, glancing his eyes reproachfully at his comrade. "But you should rise superior to such opinions, and pity the ignorance by which they are engendered."

The housekeeper hesitated a moment, at a loss to comprehend all that the surgeon expressed, yet she felt it was both complimentary and kind; therefore, suppressing her natural flow of language a little, she replied,—

"I tell Harvey his conduct is often condemnable, and last night he made my words good; but the opinions of such unbelievers is not very consequential; yet it is dreadful to think how he behaves at times: now, when he threw away the needle—"

"What!" said the surgeon, interrupting her, "does he affect to despise the needle? But it is my lot to meet with men, daily, who are equally perverse, and who show a still more culpable disrespect for the information that flows from the lights of science."

The doctor turned his face towards Captain Lawton while

speaking, but the elevation of the head prevented his eyes from resting on the grave countenance maintained by the trooper. Katy listened with admiring attention, and when the other had done, she added,—

"Then Harvey is a disbeliever in the tides."

"Not believe in the tides!" repeated the healer of bodies in astonishment. "Does the man distrust his senses? But perhaps it is the influence of the moon that he doubts."

"That he does!" exclaimed Katy, shaking with delight at meeting with a man of learning, who could support her opinions. "If you was to hear him talk, you would think he didn't believe there was such a thing as a moon at all."

"It is the misfortune of ignorance and incredulity, madam, that they feed themselves. The mind, once rejecting useful information, insensibly leans to superstition and conclusions on the order of nature, that are not less prejudicial to the cause of truth, than they are at variance with the first principles of human knowledge."

The spinster was too much awe-struck to venture an undigested reply to this speech; and the surgeon, after pausing a moment in a kind of philosophical disdain, continued,—

"That any man in his senses can doubt of the flux of the tides is more than I could have thought possible; yet obstinacy is a dangerous inmate to harbor, and may lead us into any error, however gross."

"You think, then, they have an effect on the flux?" said the housekeeper, inquiringly.

Miss Peyton rose and beckoned her nieces to give her their assistance in the adjoining pantry, while for a moment the dark visage of the attentive Lawton was lighted by an animation that vanished by an effort, as powerful and as sudden, as the one that drew it into being.

After reflecting whether he rightly understood the meaning of the other, the surgeon, making due allowance for the love of learning, acting upon a want of education, replied,—

"The moon, you mean; many philosophers have doubted how far it affects the tides; but I think it is willfully rejecting the lights of science not to believe it causes both the flux and reflux."

As reflux was a disorder with which Katy was not acquainted, she thought it prudent to be silent; yet burning with curiosity to know the meaning of certain portentous lights to which the other so often alluded, she ventured to ask,—

"If them lights he spoke of were what was called northern lights in these parts?"

In charity to her ignorance, the surgeon would have entered into an elaborate explanation of his meaning, had he not been interrupted by the mirth of Lawton. The trooper had listened so far with great composure; but now he laughed until his aching bones reminded him of his fall, and the tears rolled over his cheeks in larger drops than had ever been seen there before. At length the offended physician seized an opportunity of a pause to say,—

"To you. Captain Lawton, it may be a source of triumph, that an uneducated woman should make a mistake in a subject on which men of science have long been at variance; but yet you find this respectable matron does not reject the lights—does not reject the use of proper instruments in repairing injuries sustained by the human frame. You may possibly remember, sir, her allusion to the use of the needle."

"Aye," cried the delighted trooper, "to mend the peddler's breeches."

Katy drew up in evident displeasure, and prompt to vindicate her character for more lofty acquirements, she said,—

" 'Twas not a common use that I put that neddle to—but one of much greater virtue."

"Explain yourself, madam," said the surgeon impatiently, "that this gentleman may see how little reason he has for exultation."

Thus solicited, Katy paused to collect sufficient eloquence to garnish her narrative. The substance of her tale was, that a child who had been placed by the guardians of the poor in the keeping of Harvey, had, in the absence of its master, injured itself badly in the foot by a large needle. The offending instrument had been carefully greased, wrapped in woolen, and placed in a certain charmed nook of the chimney; while the foot, from a fear of weakening the incantation, was left in a state of nature. The arrival of the peddler had altered the whole of this admirable treatment; and the consequences were expressed by Katy, as she concluded her narrative, by saying,—

" 'Twas no wonder the boy died of a lockjaw!"

Doctor Sitgreaves looked out of the window in admiration of the brilliant morning, striving all he could to avoid the basilisk eyes of his comrade. He was impelled, by a feeling that he could not conquer, however, to look Captain Lawton in the face. The trooper had arranged every muscle of his countenance to express sympathy for the fate of the poor child; but the exultation of his eyes cut the astounded man of science to the quick; he muttered something concerning the condition of his patients, and retreated with precipitation.

Miss Peyton entered into the situation of things at the house of the peddler, with all the interest of her excellent feelings; she listened patiently while Katy recounted, more particularly, the circumstances of the past night as they had occurred. The spinster did not forget to dwell on the magnitude of the pecuniary loss sustained by Harvey, and in no manner spared her invectives, at his betraying a secret which might so easily have been kept.

"For, Miss Peyton," continued the housekeeper, after a pause to take breath, "I would have given up life before I would have given up that secret. At the most, they could only have killed him, and now a body may say that they have slain both soul and body; or, what's the same thing, they have made him a despisable vagabond. I wonder who he thinks would be his wife, or who would keep his house. For my part, my good name is too precious to be living with a lone man; though, for the matter of that, he is never there. I am resolved to tell him this day, mat stay there a single woman, I will not an hour after the funeral; and marry him I don't think I will, unless he becomes steadier and more of a home body."

The mild mistress of the Locusts suffered the exuberance of the housekeeper's feelings to expend itself, and then, by one or two judicious questions, that denoted a more intimate knowledge of the windings of the human heart in matters of Cupid than might fairly be supposed to belong to a spinster, she extracted enough from Katy to discover the improbability of Harvey's ever presuming to offer himself, with his broken fortunes, to the acceptance of Katharine Haynes. She therefore mentioned her own want of assistance in the present state of her household, and expressed a wish that Katy would change her residence to the Locusts, in case the peddler had no further use for her services. After a few preliminary conditions on the part of the wary housekeeper, the arrangement was concluded; and making a few more piteous lamentations on the weight of her own losses and the stupidity of Harvey, united with some curiosity to know the future fate of the peddler, Katy withdrew to make the necessary preparations for the approaching funeral, which was to take place that day.

During the interview between the two females, Lawton, through delicacy, had withdrawn. Anxiety took him to the room of Captain Singleton. The character of this youth, it has already been shown, endeared him in a peculiar manner to every officer in the corps. The singularly mild deportment of the young dragoon had on so many occasions been proved not to proceed from want of resolution that his almost feminine softness of manner and appearance had failed to bring him into disrepute, even in that band of partisan warriors.

To the major he was as dear as a brother, and his easy submission to the directions of his surgeon had made him a marked favorite with Dr. Sitgreaves. The rough usage the corps often received in its daring attacks had brought each of its officers, in succession, under the temporary keeping of the surgeon. To Captain Singleton the man of science had decreed the palm of docility, on such occasions, and Captain Lawton he had fairly blackballed. He frequently declared, with unconquerable simplicity and earnestness of manner, that it gave him more pleasure to see the former brought in wounded than any officer in the squadron, and that the latter afforded him the least; a compliment and condemnation that were usually received by the first of the parties with a quiet smile of good nature, and by the last with a grave bow of thanks. On the present occasion, the mortified surgeon and exulting trooper met in the room of Captain Singleton, as a place where they could act on common ground: Some time was occupied in joint attentions to the comfort of the wounded officer, and the doctor retired to an apartment prepared for his own accommodation; here, within a few minutes, he was surprised by the entrance of Lawton. The triumph of the trooper had been so complete, that he felt he could afford to be generous, and commencing by voluntarily throwing aside his coat, he cried carelessly,—

"Sitgreaves, administer a little of the aid of the lights of science to my body, if you please."

The surgeon was beginning to feel this was a subject that was intolerable, but venturing a glance towards his comrade, he saw with surprise the preparations he had made, and an air of sincerity about him, that was unusual to his manner when making such a request. Changing his intended burst of resentment to a tone of civil inquiry, he said,—

"Does Captain Lawton want anything at my hands?"

"Look for yourself, my dear sir," said the trooper mildly. "Here seem to be most of the colors of the rainbow, on this shoulder."

"You have reason for saying so," said the other, handling the part with great tenderness and consummate skill. "But happily nothing is broken. It is wonderful how well you escaped!"

"I have been a tumbler from my youth, and I am past minding a few falls from a horse; but, Sitgreaves," he added with affection, and pointing to a scar on his body, "do you remember this bit of work?"

"Perfectly well. Jack; it was bravely obtained, and neatly extracted; but don't you think I had better apply an oil to these bruises?"

"Certainly," said Lawton, with unexpected condescension.

"Now, my dear boy," cried the doctor, exultantly, as he busied himself in applying the remedy to the hurts, "do you not think it would have been better to have done all this last night?"

"Quite probable."

"Yes, Jack, but if you had let me perform the operation of phlebotomy when I first saw you, it would have been of infinite service."

"No phlebotomy," said the other, positively.

"It is now too late; but a dose of oil would carry off the humors famously."

To this the captain made no reply, but grated his teeth, in a way that showed the fortress of his mouth was not to be assailed without a resolute resistance; and the experienced physician changed the subject by saying,—

"It is a pity, John, that you did not catch the rascal, after the danger and trouble you incurred."

The captain of dragoons made no reply; and, while placing

some bandages on the wounded shoulder, the surgeon continued,—

"If I have any wish at all to destroy human life, it is to have the pleasure of seeing that traitor hanged."

"I thought your business was to cure, and not to slay," said the trooper, dryly.

"Aye! but he has caused us such heavy losses by his information, that I sometimes feel a very unsophistical temper towards that spy."

"You should not encourage such feelings of animosity to any of your fellow creatures," returned Lawton, in a tone that caused the operator to drop a pin he was arranging in the bandages from his hand. He looked the patient in the face to remove all doubts of his identity; finding, however, it was his old comrade, Captain John Lawton who had spoken, he rallied his astonished faculties, and proceeded by saying,—

"Your doctrine is just, and in general I subscribe to it. But, John, my dear fellow, is the bandage easy?"

"Quite."

"I agree with you as a whole; but as matter is infinitely devisible, so no case exists without an exception. Lawton, do you feel easy?"

"Very."

"It is not only cruel to the sufferer, but sometimes unjust to others, to take human life where a less punishment would answer the purpose. Now, Jack, if you were only—move your arm a little—if you were only—I hope you feel easier, my dear friend?"

"Much."

"If, my dear John, you would teach your men to cut with more discretion, it would answer you the same purpose—and give me great pleasure."

The doctor drew a heavy sigh, as he was enabled to get rid of what was nearest to the heart; and die dragoon coolly replaced his coat, saying with great deliberation as he retired,—

"I know no troop that cut more judiciously; they generally shave from the crown to the jaw."

The disappointed operator collected his instruments, and with a heavy heart proceeded to pay a visit to the room of Colonel Wellmere.

CHAPTER XII

This fairy form contains a soul as mighty,
As that which lives within a giant's frame;
These slender limbs, that tremble like the aspen
At summer evening's sigh, uphold a spirit,
Which, roused, can tower to the height of heaven,
And light those shining windows of the face
With much of heaven's own radiance.

—Duo

The number and character of her guests had greatly added to the cares of Miss Jeanette Peyton. The morning found them all restored, in some measure, to their former ease of body, with the exception of the youthful captain of dragoons, who had been so deeply regretted by Dunwoodie. The wound of this officer was severe, though the surgeon persevered in saying that it was without danger. His comrade, we have shown, had deserted his couch; and Henry Wharton awoke from a sleep that had been undisturbed by anything but a dream of suffering amputation under the hands of a surgical novice. As it proved, however, to be nothing but a dream, the youth found himself much refreshed by his slumbers; and Dr. Sitgreaves removed all further apprehensions by confidently pronouncing that he would be a well man within a fortnight.

During all this time Colonel Wellmere did not make his appearance; he breakfasted in his own room, and notwithstanding certain significant smiles of the man of science, declared himself too much injured to rise from his bed. Leaving him, therefore, endeavoring to conceal his chagrin in the solitude of his chamber, the surgeon proceeded to the more grateful task of sitting an hour by the bedside of George Singleton. A slight flush was on the face of the patient as the doctor entered the room, and the latter advanced promptly and laid his fingers on the pulse of the youth, beckoning to him to be silent, while he muttered,—

"Growing symptoms of a febrile pulse—no, no, my dear George, you must remain quiet and dumb; though your eyes look better, and your skin has even a moisture."

"Nay, my dear Sitgreaves," said the youth, taking his hand, "you see there is no fever about me; look, is there any of Jack Lawton's hoarfrost on my tongue?"

"No, indeed," said the surgeon, clapping a spoon in the mouth of the other, forcing it open, and looking down his throat as if disposed to visit the interior in person. "The tongue is well, and the pulse begins to lower again. Ah! the bleeding did you good. Phlebotomy is a sovereign specific for southern constitutions. But that madcap Lawton absolutely refused to be blooded for a fall he had from his horse last night. Why, George, your case is becoming singular," continued the doctor, instinctively throwing aside his wig. "Your pulse even and soft, your skin moist, but your eye fiery, and cheek flushed. Oh! I must examine more closely into these symptoms."

"Softly, my good friend, softly," said the youth, falling back on his pillow, and losing some of that color which alarmed his companion. "I believe, in extracting the ball, you did for me all that is required. I am free from pain and only weak, I do assure you."

"Captain Singleton," said the surgeon, with heat, "it is presumptuous in you to pretend to tell your medical attendant when you are free from pain. If it be not to enable us to decide in such matters, of what avail the lights of science? For shame, George, for shame! Even that perverse fellow, John Lawton, could not behave with more obstinacy."

His patient smiled, as he gently repulsed his physician in an attempt to undo the bandages, and with a returning glow to his cheeks, inquired,—

"Do, Archibald,"—a term of endearment that seldom failed to soften the operator's heart,—"tell me what spirit from heaven has been gliding around my apartment, while I lay pretending to sleep?"

"If anyone interferes with my patients," cried the doctor, hastily, "I will teach them, spirit or no spirit, what it is to meddle with another man's concerns."

"Tut—my dear fellow, there was no interference made, nor any intended. See," exhibiting the bandages, "everything is as you left it,—but it glided about the room with the grace of a fairy and the tenderness of an angel."

The surgeon, having satisfied himself that everything was as he had left it, very deliberately resumed his seat and replaced his wig, as he inquired, with a brevity that would have honored Lieutenant Mason,—

"Had it petticoats, George?."

"I saw nothing but its heavenly eyes—its bloom—its majestic step—its grace," replied the young man, with rather more ardor than his surgeon thought consistent with his debilitated condition; and he laid his hand on his mouth to stop him, saying himself,—

"It must have been Miss Jeanette Peyton—a lady of fine accomplishments, with—hem—with something of the kind of step you speak of—a very complacent eye; and as to the bloom, I dare say offices of charity can summon as fine a color to her cheeks, as glows in the faces of her more youthful nieces."

"Nieces? Has she nieces, then? The angel I saw may be a daughter, a sister, or a niece,—but never an aunt."

"Hush, George, hush; your talking has brought your pulse up again. You must observe quiet, and prepare for a meeting with your own sister, who will be here within an hour."

"What, Isabella! And who sent for her?"

"The major."

"Considerate Dunwoodie!" murmured the exhausted youth, sinking again on his pillow, where the commands of his attendant compelled him to remain silent.

Even Captain Lawton had been received with many and courteous inquiries after the state of his health, from all the members of the family, when he made his morning entrance; but an invisible spirit presided over the comforts of the English colonel. Sarah had shrunk with consciousness from entering the room; yet she knew the position of every glass, and had, with her own hands, supplied the contents of every bowl, that stood on his table.

At the time of our tale, we were a divided people, and Sarah thought it was no more than her duty to cherish the institutions of that country to which she yet clung as the land of her forefathers; but there were other and more cogent reasons for the silent preference she was giving to the Englishman. His image had first filled the void in her youthful fancy, and it was an image that was distinguished by many of those attractions that can enchain a female heart. It is true, he wanted the personal excellence of Peyton Dunwoodie, but his pretensions were far from contemptible. Sarah had moved about the house during the morning, casting frequent and longing glances at the door of Wellmere's apartment, anxious to learn the condition of his wounds, and yet ashamed to inquire; conscious interest kept her tongue tied, until her sister, with the frankness of innocence, had put the desired question to Dr. Sitgreaves.

"Colonel Wellmere," said the operator, gravely, "is in what I call a state of free will, madam. He is ill, or he is well, as he pleases. His case, young lady, exceeds my art to heal; and I take it Sir Henry Clinton is the best adviser he can apply to; though Major Dunwoodie has made the communication with his leech rather difficult."

Frances smiled, but averted her face, while Sarah moved, with the grace of an offended Juno, from the apartment. Her own room, however, afforded her but little relief, and in passing through the long gallery that communicated with each of the chambers of the building, she noticed the door of Singleton's room to be open. The wounded youth seemed sleeping, and was alone. She had ventured lightly into the apartment, and busied herself for a few minutes in arranging the tables, and the nourishment provided for the patient, hardly conscious of what she was doing, and possibly dreaming that these little feminine offices were performed for another. Her natural bloom was heightened by the insinuation of the surgeon, nor was the luster of her eye in any degree diminished. The sound of the approaching footsteps of Sitgreaves hastened her retreat down a private stairway, to the side of her sister. The sisters then sought the fresh air on the piazza; and as they pursued their walk, arm in arm, the following dialogue took place:—

"There is something disagreeable about this surgeon of Dunwoodie," said Sarah, "that causes me to wish him away most heartily."

Frances fixed her laughing eyes on her sister; but forbearing to speak, the other readily construed their expression, and hastily added, "But I forget he is one of your renowned corps of Virginians, and must be spoken of reverently."

"As respectfully as you please, my dear sister; there is but little danger of exceeding the truth."

"Not in your opinion," said the elder, with a little warmth. "But I think Mr. Dunwoodie has taken a liberty that exceeds the rights of consanguinity; he has made our father's house a hospital."

"We ought to be grateful that none of the patients it contains are dearer to us."

"Your brother is one."

"True, true," interrupted Frances, blushing to the eyes; "but he leaves his room, and thinks his wound lightly purchased by the pleasure of being with his friends. If," she added, with a tremulous lip, "this dreadful suspicion that is affixed to his visit were removed, I could consider his wound of little moment."

"You now have the fruits of rebellion brought home to you; a brother wounded and a prisoner, and perhaps a victim; your father distressed, his privacy interrupted, and not improbably his estates torn from him, on account of his loyalty to his king."

Frances continued her walk in silence. While facing the northern entrance to the vale, her eyes were uniformly fastened on the point where the road was suddenly lost by the intervention of a hill; and at each turn, as she lost sight of the spot, she lingered until an impatient movement of her sister quickened her pace to an even motion with that of her own. At length, a single horse chaise was seen making its way carefully among the stones which lay scattered over the country road that wound through the valley, and approached the cottage. The color of Frances changed as the vehicle gradually drew nearer; and when she was enabled to see a female form in it by the side of a black in livery, her limbs shook with an agitation that compelled her to. lean on Sarah for support. In a few minutes the travelers approached the gate. It was thrown open by a dragoon who followed the carriage, and who had been the messenger dispatched by Dunwoodie to the father of Captain Singleton. Miss Peyton advanced to receive their guest, and the sisters united in giving her the kindest welcome; still Frances could with difficulty withdraw her truant eyes from the countenance of their visitor. She was young, and of a light and fragile form, but of exquisite proportions. Her eyes were large, full, black, piercing, and at times a little wild. Her hair was luxuriant, and as it was without the powder it was then the fashion to wear, it fell in raven blackness. A few of its locks had fallen on her cheek, giving its chilling whiteness by the contrast a more deadly character. Dr. Sitgreaves supported her from the chaise; and when she gained the floor of the piazza, she turned an expressive look on the face of the practitioner.

"Your brother is out of danger and wishes to see you. Miss Singleton," said the surgeon.

The lady burst into a flood of tears. Frances had stood contemplating the action and face of Isabella with a kind of uneasy admiration, but she now sprang to her side with the ardor of a sister, and kindly drawing her arm within her own, led the way to a retired room. The movement was so ingenuous, so considerate, and so delicate, that even Miss Peyton withheld her interference, following the youthful pair with only her eyes and a smile of complacency. The feeling was communicated to all the spectators, and they dispersed in pursuit of their usual avocations. Isabella yielded to the gentle influence of Frances without resistance; and, having gained the room where the latter conducted her, wept in silence on the shoulder of the observant and soothing girl, until Frances thought her tears exceeded the emotion natural to the occasion. The sobs of Miss Singleton for a time were violent and uncontrollable, until, with an evident exertion, she yielded to a kind observation of her companion, and succeeded in suppressing her tears. Raising her face to the eyes of Frances, she rose, while a smile of beautiful radiance passed over her features; and making a hasty apology for the excess of her emotion, she desired to be conducted to the room of the invalid.

The meeting between the brother and sister was warm, but, by an effort on the part of the lady, more composed than her previous agitation had given reason to expect. Isabella found her brother looking better, and in less danger than her sensitive imagination had led her to suppose. Her spirits rose in proportion; from despondency, she passed to something like gayety; her beautiful eyes sparkled with renovated brilliancy; and her face was lighted with smiles so fascinating, that Frances, who, in compliance with her earnest entreaties, had accompanied her to the sick chamber, sat gazing on a countenance that possessed so wonderful variability, impelled by a charm that was beyond her control. The youth had thrown an earnest look at Frances, as soon as his sister raised herself from his arms, and perhaps it was the first glance at the lovely lineaments of our heroine, when the gazer turned his eyes from the view in disappointment. He seemed bewildered, rubbed his forehead like a man awaking from a dream, and mused.

"Where is Dunwoodie, Isabella?" he said. "The excellent fellow is never weary of kind actions. After a day of such service as that of yesterday, he has spent the night in bringing me a nurse, whose presence alone is able to raise me from my couch."

The expression of the lady's countenance changed; her eye roved around the apartment with a character of wildness in it that repelled the anxious Frances, who studied her movements with unabated interest.

"Dunwoodie! Is he then not here? I thought to have met him by the side of my brother's bed."

"He has duties that require his presence elsewhere; the English are said to be out by the way of the Hudson, and they give us light troops but little rest. Surely nothing else could have kept him so long from a wounded friend. But, Isabella, the meeting has been too much for you; you tremble."

Isabella made no reply; she stretched her hand towards the table which held the nourishment of the captain, and the attentive Frances comprehended her wishes in a moment. A glass of water in some measure revived the sister, who was enabled to say,—

"Doubtless it is his duty. 'Twas said above, a royal party was moving on the river; though I passed the troops but two miles from this spot." The latter part of the sentence was hardly audible, and it was spoken more in the manner of a soliloquy, than as if for the ears of her companions.

"On the march, Isabella?" eagerly inquired her brother.

"No, dismounted, and seemingly at rest," was the reply.

The wondering dragoon turned his gaze on the countenance of his sister, who sat with her eye bent on the carpet in unconscious absence, but found no explanation. His look was changed to the face of Frances, who, startled by the earnestness of his expression, arose, and hastily inquired if he would have any assistance.

"If you can pardon the rudeness," said the wounded officer, making a feeble effort to raise his body, "I would request to have Captain Lawton's company for a moment."

Frances hastened instantly to communicate his wish to that gentleman, and impelled by an interest she could not control, she returned again to her seat by the side of Miss Singleton.

"Lawton," said the youth, impatiently, as the trooper entered, "hear you from the major?"

The eye of the sister was now bent on the face of the trooper, who made his salutations to the lady with ease, blended with the frankness of a soldier.

"His man has been here twice," he said, "to inquire how we fared in the lazaretto."

"And why not himself?"

"That is a question the major can answer best; but you know the redcoats are abroad, and Dunwoodie commands in the county; these English must be looked to."

"True," said Singleton, slowly, as if struck with the other's reasons. "But how is it that you are idle, when there is work to do?"

"My sword arm is not in the best condition, and Roanoke has but a shambling gait this morning; besides, there is another reason I could mention, if it were not that Miss Wharton would never forgive me."

"Speak, I beg, without dread of my displeasure," said Frances, returning the good-humored smile of the trooper, with the archness natural to her own sweet face.

"The odors of your kitchen, then," cried Lawton bluntly, "forbid my quitting the domains, until I qualify myself to speak with more certainty concerning the fatness of the land."

"Oh! Aunt Jeanette is exerting herself to do credit to my father's hospitality," said the laughing girl, "and I am a truant from her labors, as I shall be a stranger to her favor, unless I proffer my assistance."

Frances withdrew to seek her aunt, musing deeply on the character and extreme sensibility of the new acquaintance chance had brought to the cottage.

The wounded officer followed her with his eyes, as she moved, with infantile grace, through the door of his apartment, and as she vanished from his view, he observed,—

"Such an aunt and niece are seldom to be met with, Jack; this seems a fairy, but the aunt is angelic."

"You are doing well, I see; your enthusiasm for the sex holds its own."

"I should be ungrateful as well as insensible, did I not bear testimony to the loveliness of Miss Peyton."

"A good motherly lady, but as to love, that is a matter of taste. A few years younger, with deference to her prudence and experience, would accord better with my fancy."

"She must be under twenty," said the other, quickly.

"It depends on the way you count. If you begin at the heel of life, well; but if you reckon downward, as is most common, I think she is nearer forty."

"You have mistaken an elder sister for the aunt," said Isabella, laying her fair hand on the mouth of the invalid. "You must be silent! Your feelings are beginning to affect your frame."

The entrance of Dr. Sitgreaves, who, in some alarm, noticed the increase of feverish symptoms in his patient, enforced this mandate; and the trooper withdrew to pay a visit of condolence to Roanoke, who had been an equal sufferer with himself in their last night's somersault. To his great joy, the man pronounced the steed to be equally convalescent with the master; and Lawton found that by dint of rubbing the animal's limbs several hours without ceasing, he was enabled to place his feet in what he called systematic motion. Orders were accordingly given to be in readiness to rejoin the troop at the Four Corners, as soon as his master had shared in the bounty of the approaching banquet.

In the meantime, Henry Wharton entered the apartment of Wellmere, and by his sympathy succeeded in restoring the colonel to his own good graces. The latter was consequently enabled to rise, and prepared to meet a rival of whom he had spoken so lightly, and, as the result had proved, with so little reason. Wharton knew that their misfortune, as they both termed their defeat, was owing to the other's rashness; but he forbore to speak of anything except the unfortunate accident which had deprived the English of their leader, and to which he good-naturedly ascribed their subsequent discomfiture.

"In short, Wharton," said the colonel, putting one leg out of bed, "it may be called a combination of untoward events; your own ungovernable horse prevented my orders from being carried to the major, in season to flank the rebels."

"Very true," replied the captain, kicking a slipper towards the bed. "Had we succeeded in getting a few good fires upon them in flank, we should have sent these brave Virginians to the right about."

"Aye, and that in double-quick time," cried the colonel, making the other leg follow its companion. "Then it was necessary to rout the guides, you know, and the movement gave them the best possible opportunity to charge."

"Yes," said the other, sending the second slipper after the first, "and this Major Dunwoodie never overlooks an advantage."

"I think if we had the thing to do over again," continued the colonel, raising himself on his feet, "we might alter the case very materially, though the chief thing the rebels have now to boast of is my capture; they were repulsed, you saw, in their attempt to drive us from the wood."

"At least they would have been, had they made an attack," said the captain, throwing the rest of his clothes within reach of the colonel.

"Why, that is the same thing," returned Wellmere, beginning to dress himself. "To assume such an attitude as to intimidate your enemy, is the chief art of war."

"Doubtless, then, you may remember in one of their charges they were completely routed."

"True—true," cried the colonel, with animation. "Had I been there to have improved that advantage, we might have turned the table on the Yankees"; saying which he displayed still greater animation in completing his toilet; and he was soon prepared to make his appearance, fully restored to his own good opinion, and fairly persuaded that his capture was owing to casualties absolutely beyond the control of man.

The knowledge that Colonel Wellmere was to be a guest at the table in no degree diminished the preparations which were already making for the banquet; and Sarah, after receiving the compliments of the gentleman, and making many kind inquiries after the state of his wounds, proceeded in person to lend her counsel and taste to one of those labored entertainments, which, at that day, were so frequent in country life, and which are not. entirely banished from our domestic economy at the present moment.

CHAPTER XIII

I will stand to and feed,
Although my last.
—Tempest.

The savor of preparation which had been noticed by Captain Lawton began to increase within the walls of the cottage; certain sweet-smelling odors, that arose from the subterranean territories of Cæsar, gave to the trooper the most pleasing assurances that his olfactory nerves, which on such occasions were as acute as his eyes on others, had faithfully performed their duty; and for the benefit of enjoying the passing sweets as they arose, the dragoon so placed himself at a window of the building, that not a vapor charged with the spices of the East could exhale on its passage to the clouds, without first giving its incense to his nose. Lawton, however, by no means indulged himself in this comfortable arrangement, without first making such preparations to do meet honor to the feast, as his scanty wardrobe would allow. The uniform of his corps was always a passport to the best tables, and this, though somewhat tarnished by faithful service and unceremonious usage, was properly brushed and decked out for the occasion. His head, which nature had ornamented with the blackness of a crow, now shone with the whiteness of snow; and his bony hand, that so well became the saber, peered from beneath a ruffle with somthing like maiden coyness. The improvements of the dragoon went no further, excepting that his boots shone with more than holiday splendor, and his spurs glittered in the rays of the sun, as became the pure ore of which they were composed.

Cæsar moved through the apartments with a face charged with an importance exceeding even that which had accompanied him in his melancholy task of the morning. The black had early returned from the errand on which he had been dispatched by the peddler, and, obedient to the commands of his mistress, promptly appeared to give his services where his allegiance was due; so serious, indeed, was his duty now becoming, that it was only at odd moments he was enabled to impart to his sable brother, who had been sent in attendance on Miss Singleton to the Locusts, any portion of the wonderful incidents of the momentous night he had so lately passed. By ingeniously using, however, such occasions as accidentally offered, Cæsar communicated so many of the heads of his tale, as served to open the eyes of his visitor to their fullest width. The gusto for the marvelous was innate in these sable worthies; and Miss Peyton found it necessary to interpose her authority, in order to postpone the residue of the history to a more befitting opportunity.

"Ah! Miss Jinnett," said Cæsar, shaking his head, and looking all that he expressed, " 'twas awful to see Johnny Birch walk on a feet when he lie dead!"

This concluded the conversation; though the black promised himself the satisfaction, and did not fail to enjoy it, of having many a gossip on the subject at a future period.

The ghost thus happily laid, the department of Miss Peyton flourished; and by the time the afternoon's sun had traveled a two hours' journey from the meridian, the formal procession from the kitchen to the parlor commenced, under the auspices of Cæsar, who led the van, supporting a turkey on the palms of his withered hands, with the dexterity of a balance master.

Next followed the servant of Captain Lawton, bearing, as he marched stiffly, and walking wide, as if allowing room for his steed, a ham of true Virginian flavor; a present from the spinster's brother in Accomac. The supporter of this savory dish kept his eye on his trust with military precision; and by the time he reached his destination, it might be difficult to say which contained the most juice, his own mouth or the Accomac bacon.

Third in the line was to be seen the valet of Colonel Wellmere, who carried in either hand chickens fricasseed and oyster patties.

After him marched the attendant of Dr. Sitgreaves, who had instinctively seized an enormous tureen, as most resembling matters he understood, and followed on in place, until the steams of the soup so completely bedimmed the spectacles he wore, as a badge of office, that, on arriving at the scene of action, he was compelled to deposit his freight on the floor, until, by removing the glasses, he could see his way through the piles of reserved china and plate warmers.

Next followed another trooper, whose duty it was to attend on Captain Singleton; and, as if apportioning his appetite to the feeble state of his master, he had contented himself with conveying a pair of ducks, roasted, until their tempting fragrance began to make him repent his having so lately demolished a breakfast that had been provided for his master's sister, with another prepared for himself.

The white boy, who belonged to the house, brought up the rear, groaning under a load of sundry dishes of vegetables, that the cook, by way of climax, had unwittingly heaped on him.

But this was far from all of the preparations for that day's feast;

Cæsar had no sooner deposited his bird, which, but the week before, had been flying amongst the highlands of Dutchess, little dreaming of so soon heading such a goodly assemblage, than he turned mechanically on his heel, and took up his line of march again for the kitchen. In this evolution the black was imitated by his companions in succession, and another procession to the parlor followed in the same order. By this admirable arrangement, whole flocks of pigeons, certain bevies of quails, shoals of flatfish, bass, and sundry woodcock, found their way into the presence of the company.

A third attack brought suitable quantities of potatoes, onions, beets, coldslaw, rice, and all the other minutiae of a goodly dinner.

The board now fairly groaned with American profusion, and Cæsar, glancing his eye over the show with a most approving conscience, after readjusting every dish that had not been placed on the table with his own hands, proceeded to acquaint the mistress of the revels that his task was happily accomplished.

Some half hour before the culinary array just recorded took place, all the ladies disappeared, much in the same unaccountable manner that swallows flee the approach of winter. But the springtime of their return had arrived, and the whole party were collected in an apartment that, in consequence of its containing no side table, and being furnished with a chintz coverlet settee, was termed a withdrawing-room.

The kind-hearted spinster had deemed the occasion worthy, not only of extraordinary preparations in the culinary department, but had seen proper to deck her own person in garments suited to the guests whom it was now her happiness to entertain.

On her head Miss Peyton wore a cap of exquisite lawn, which was ornamented in front with a broad border of lace, that spread from the face in such a manner as to admit of a display of artificial flowers, clustered in a group on the summit of her fine forehead.

The color of her hair was lost in the profusion of powder with which it was covered; but a slight curling of the extremities in some degree relieved the formality of its arrangement, and gave a look of feminine softness to the features.

Her dress was a rich, heavy silk, of violet color, cut low around the bust, with a stomacher of the same material, that fitted close to the figure, and exhibited the form, from the shoulders to the waist in its true proportions. Below, the dress was full, and sufficiently showed that parsimony in attire was not a foible of the day. A small loop displayed the beauty of the fabric to advantage, and aided in giving majesty to the figure.

The tall stature of the lady was heightened by shoes of the same material with the dress, whose heels added more than an inch to the liberality of nature.

The sleeves were short, and close to the limb, until they fell off at the elbows in large ruffles, that hung in rich profusion from the arm when extended; and duplicates and triplicates of lawn, trimmed with Dresden lace, lent their aid in giving delicacy to a hand and arm that yet retained their whiteness and symmetry. A treble row of large pearls closely encircled her throat; and a handkerchief of lace partially concealed that part of the person that the silk had left exposed, but which the experience of forty years had warned Miss Peyton should now be veiled.

Thus attired, and standing erect with the lofty grace that distinguished the manners of that day, the maiden would have looked into nothingness a bevy of modern belles.

The taste of Sarah had kept even pace with the decorations of her aunt; and a dress, differing in no respect from the one just described, but in material and tints, exhibited her imposing form to equal advantage. The satin of her robe was of a pale bluish color. Twenty years did not, however, require the screen that was prudent in forty, and nothing but an envious border-of exquisite lace hid, in some measure, what the satin left exposed to view. The upper part of the bust, and the fine fall of the shoulders, were blazing in all their native beauty, and, like the aunt, the throat was ornamented by a treble row of pearls, to correspond with which were rings of the same quality in the ears. The head was without a cap, and the hair drawn up from the countenance so as to give to the eye all the loveliness of a forehead as polished as marble and as white as snow. A few straggling curls fell gracefully on the neck, and a bouquet of artificial flowers was also placed, like a coronet, over her brow.

Miss Singleton had resigned her brother to the advice of Dr. Sitgreaves, who had succeeded in getting his patient into a deep sleep after quieting certain feverish symptoms that followed the agitation of the interview. The sister was persuaded, by the observant mistress of the mansion, to make one of the party, and she sat by the side of Sarah, differing but little in appearance from that lady, except in refusing the use of powder on her raven locks, and that her unusually high forehead and large, brilliant eyes gave an expression of thoughtfulness to her features, that was possibly heightened by the paleness of her cheek.

Last and least, but not the most unlovely, in this display of female charms, was the youngest daughter of Mr. Wharton. Frances, we have already mentioned, left the city before she had attained to the age of fashionable womanhood. A few adventurous spirits were already beginning to make inroads in those customs which had so long invaded the comforts of the fair sex; and the youthful girl had ventured to trust her beauty to the height which nature had bestowed. This was but little, but that little was a masterpiece. Frances several times had determined, in the course of the morning, to bestow more than usual pains in the decoration of her person. Each time in succession, as she formed this resolution, she spent a few minutes in looking earnestly towards the north, and then she as invariably changed it.

At the appointed hour, our heroine appeared in the drawing-room, clothed in a robe of pale blue silk, of a cut and fashion much like that worn by her sister. Her hair was left to the wild curls of nature, its exuberance being confined to the crown of her head by a long, low comb, made of light tortoise shell; a color barely distinguishable in the golden hue other tresses. Her dress was without a plait or a wrinkle, and fitted the form with an exactitude that might lead one to imagine the arch girl more than suspected the beauties it displayed. A tucker of rich Dresden lace softened the contour of the figure. Her head was without ornament; but around her throat was a necklace of gold clasped in front with a rich cornelian.

Once, and once only, as they moved towards the repast, did Lawton see a foot thrust itself from beneath the folds of her robe, and exhibit its little beauties encased in a slipper of blue silk, clasped close to the shape by a buckle of brilliants. The trooper caught himself sighing as he thought, though it was good for nothing in the stirrup, how enchantingly it would grace a minuet.

As the black appeared on the threshold of the room, making a low reverence, which had been interpreted for some centuries into "dinner waits," Mr. Wharton, clad in a dress of drab, bedecked with enormous buttons, advanced formally to Miss Singleton, and bending his powdered head nearly to the level of the hand he extended, received hers in return.

Dr. Sitgreaves offered the same homage to Miss Peyton, and met with equal favor; the lady first pausing to draw on her gloves.

Colonel Wellmere was honored with a smile from Sarah, while performing a similar duty; and Frances gave the ends of her taper fingers to Captain Lawton with maiden bashfulness.

Much time, and some trouble were expended before the whole party were, to the great joy of Cæsar, comfortably arranged around the table, with proper attention to all points of etiquette and precedence. The black well knew the viands were not improving; and though abundantly able to comprehend the disadvantage of eating a cold dinner, it greatly exceeded his powers of philosophy to weight all the latent consequences to society which depend on social order.

For the first ten minutes all but the captain of dragoons found themselves in a situation much to their liking. Even Lawton would have been perfectly happy, had not excess of civility on the part of his host and Miss Jeanette Peyton kept him from the more agreeable occupation of tasting dishes he did want, in order to decline those he did not. At length, however, the repast was fairly commenced, and a devoted application to the viands was more eloquent than a thousand words in favor of Dinah's skill.

Next came drinking with the ladies; but as the wine was excellent, and the glasses ample, the trooper bore this interruption with consummate good nature. Nay, so fearful was he of giving offense, and of omitting any of the nicer points of punctilio, that having commenced this courtesy with the lady who sat next him, he persevered until not only one of his fair companions could, with justice, reproach him with partiality in this particular.

Long abstemiousness from anything like generous wine might plead the excuse of Captain Lawton, especially when exposed to so strong a temptation as that now before him. Mr. Wharton had been one of a set of politicians in New York, whose principal exploits before the war had been to assemble, and pass sage opinions on the signs of the time, under the inspiration of certain liquor made from a grape that grew on the south side of the island of Madeira, and which found its way into the colonies of North America through the medium of the West Indies, sojourning awhile in the Western Archipelago, by way of proving the virtues of the climate. A large supply of this cordial had been drawn from his storehouse in the city, and some of it now sparkled in a bottle before the captain blushing in the rays of the sun, which were passing obliquely through it, like amber.

Though the meat and vegetables had made their entrance with perfect order and propriety, their exeunt was effected much in the manner of a retreat of militia. The point was to clear the board something after the fabled practice of the harpies, and by dint of scrabling, tossing, breaking, and spilling, the remnants of the overflowing repast disappeared. And now another series of processions commenced, by virtue of which a goodly display of pastry, with its usual accompaniments, garnished the table.

Mr. Wharton poured out a glass of wine for the lady who sat on his right hand, and, pushing the bottle to a guest, said with a low bow,—

"We are to be honored with a toast from Miss Singleton."

Although there was nothing more in this movement than occurred every day on such occasions, yet the lady trembled, colored, and grew pale again, seemingly endcavoring to rally her thoughts, until, by her agitation, she had excited the interest of the whole party; when by an effort, and in a manner as if she had striven in vain to think of another, Isabella said, faintly,—

"Major Dunwoodie."

The health was drunk cheerfully by all but Colonel Wellmere, who wet his lips, and drew figures on the table with some of the liquor he had spilled.

At length Colonel Wellmere broke silence by saying aloud

to Captain Lawton,—

"I suppose, sir, this Mr. Dunwoodie will receive promotion in the rebel army, for the advantage my misfortune gave him over my command."

The trooper had supplied the wants of nature to his perfect satisfaction; and, perhaps, with the exception of Washington and his immediate commander, there was no mortal whose displeasure he regarded a title. First helping himself, therefore, to a little of his favorite bottle, he replied with admirable coolness,—

"Colonel Wellmere, your pardon; Major Dunwoodie owes his allegiance to the confederated states of North America, and where he owes it he pays it. Such a man is no rebel. Promoted I hope he may be, both because he deserves it, and because I am next in rank in the corps; and I know not what you call a misfortune, unless you deem meeting the Virginia horse as such."

"We will not differ about terms, sir," said the colonel, haughtily. "I spoke as duty to my sovereign prompted; but do you not call the loss of a commander a misfortune to a party?"

"It certainly may be so," said the trooper, with emphasis.

"Miss Peyton, will you favor us with a toast?" cried the master of the house, anxious to stop this dialogue.

The lady bowed her head with dignity, as she named "General Montrose"; and the long-absent bloom stole lightly over her features.

"There is no term more doubtful than that word misfortune," said the surgeon, regardless of the nice maneuvers of the host. "Some deem one thing a misfortune, others its opposite; misfortune begets misfortune. Life is a misfortune, for it may be the means of enduring misfortune; and death is a misfortune, as it abridges the enjoyments of life."

"It is a misfortune that our mess has no such wine as this," interrupted the trooper.

"We will pledge you a sentiment in it, sir, as it seems to suit your taste," said Mr. Wharton.

Lawton filled to the brim, and drank, "A speedy peace, or a stirring war."

"I drink your toast. Captain Lawton, though I greatly distrust your construction of activity," said the surgeon. "In my poor judgment, cavalry should be kept in the rear to improve a victory, and not sent in front to gain it. Such may be said to be their natural occupation, if the term can be used in reference to so artificial a body; for all history shows that the horse have done most when held in reserve."

This dissertation, uttered in a sufficiently didactic manner, was a hint that Miss Peyton did not neglect. She arose and retired, followed by her juniors.

Nearly at the same moment, Mr. Wharton and his son made an apology for their absence, which was required on account of the death of a near neighbor, and withdrew.

The retreat of the ladies was the signal for the appearance of the surgeon's cigar, which, being established in a corner of his mouth, in a certain knowing way, caused not the slightest interruption to his discourse.

"If anything can sweeten captivity and wounds, it must be the happiness of suffering in the society of the ladies who have left us," gallantly observed the colonel, as he resumed his seat after closing the door.

"Sympathy and kindness have their influence on the human svstem," returned the surgeon, knocking the ashes from his cigar, with the tip of a little finger, in the manner of an adept. "The connection is intimate between the moral and physical feelings; but still, to accomplish a cure, and restore nature to the healthy tone it has lost from disease or accident, requires more than can flow from unguided sympathies. In such cases, the lights—" the surgeon accidentally caught the eye of the trooper and he paused. Taking two or three hasty puffs, he essayed to finish the sentence, "In such cases, the knowledge that flows from the lights—"

"You were saying, sir," said Colonel Wellmere, sipping his wine,—

"The purport of my remark went to say," continued Sitgreaves, turning his back on Lawton, "that a bread poultice will not set a broken arm."

"More is the pity," cried the trooper, "for next to eating, the nourishment could not be more innocently applied."

"To you, Colonel Wellmere," said the surgeon, "as a man of education, I can with safety appeal." The colonel bowed. "You must have observed the dreadful havoc made in your ranks by the men who were led by this gentleman"; the colonel looked grave, again; "how, when blows lighted on their frames, life was invariably extinguished, beyond all hope of scientific reparation; how certain yawning wounds were inflicted, that must set at defiance the art of the most experienced practitioner; now, sir, to you I triumphantly appeal, therefore, to know whether your detachment would not have been as effectually defeated, if the men had all lost a right arm, for instance, as if they had all lost their heads."

"The triumph of your appeal is somewhat hasty, sir," said Wellmere.

"Is the cause of liberty advanced a step by such injudicious harshness in the field?" continued the surgeon, bent on the favorite principle of his life.

"I am yet to learn that the cause of liberty is in any .manner advanced by the services of any gentleman in the rebel army," rejoined the colonel.

"Not liberty! Good God, for what then are we contending?"

"Slavery, sir; yes, even slavery; you are putting the tyranny of a mob on the throne of a kind and lenient prince. Where is the consistency of your boasted liberty?"

"Consistency!" repeated the surgeon, looking about him a little wildly, at hearing such sweeping charges against a cause he had so long thought holy.

"Aye, sir, your consistency. Your congress of sages have published a manifesto, wherein they set forth the equality of political rights."

" 'Tis true, and it is done most ably."

"I say nothing of its ability; but if true, why not set your slaves at liberty?" This argument, which is thought by most of the colonel's countrymen a triumphant answer to a thousand eloquent facts, lost none of its weight by the manner in which it was uttered.

Every American feels humbled at the necessity of vindicating his country from the apparent inconsistency and injustice of the laws alluded to. His feelings are much like those of an honorable man who is compelled to exonerate himself from a disgraceful charge, although he may know the accusation to be false. At the bottom, Sitgreaves had much good sense, and thus called on, he took up the cudgels of argument in downright earnest.

"We deem it a liberty to have the deciding voice in the

councils by which we are governed. We think it a hardship to be ruled by the king of a people who live at a distance of three thousand miles, and who cannot, and who do not, feel a single political interest in common with ourselves. I say nothing of oppression; the child was of age, and was entitled to the privileges of majority. In such cases, there is but one tribunal to which to appeal for a nation's rights—it is power, and we now make the appeal."

"Such doctrines may suit your present purposes," said Wellmere, with a sneer; "but I apprehend it is opposed to all the opinions and practices of civilized nations."

"It is in conformity with the practices of all nations," said the surgeon, returning the nod and smile of Lawton, who enjoyed the good sense of his comrade as much as he disliked what he called "his medical talk." "Who would be ruled when he can rule? The only rational ground to take is, that every community has a right to govern itself, so that in no manner it violates the laws of God."

"And is holding your fellow creatures in bondage in conformity to those laws?" asked the colonel, impressively.

The surgeon took another glass, and hemming once, returned to the combat.

"Sir," said he, "slavery is of very ancient origin, and it seems to have been confined to no particular religion or form of government: every nation of civilized Europe does, or has held their fellow creatures in this kind of duresse."

"You will except Great Britain," cried the colonel, proudly.

"No, sir," continued the surgeon, confidently, feeling that he was now carrying the war out of his own country, "I cannot except Great Britain. It was her children, her ships, and her laws, that first introduced the practice into these states; and on her institutions the judgment must fall. There is not a foot of ground belonging to England, in which a negro would be useful, that has not its slave. England herself has none, but England is overflowing with physical force, a part of which she is obliged to maintain in the shape of paupers. The same is true of France, and most other European countries. So long as we were content to remain colonies, nothing was said of our system of domestic slavery; but now, when we are resolute to obtain as much freedom as the vicious system of metropolitan rule has left us, that which is England's gift has become our reproach. Will your master liberate the slaves of his subjects should he succeed in subduing the new states, or will he condemn the whites to the same servitude as that in which he has been so long content to see the blacks? It is true, we continue the practice; but we must come gradually to the remedy, or create an evil greater than that which we endure at present. Doubtless, as we advance, the manumission of our slaves will accompany us, until happily these fair regions shall exist, without a single image of the Creator that is held in a state which disqualifies him to judge of that Creator's goodness."

It will be remembered that Doctor Sitgreaves spoke forty years ago, and Wellmere was unable to contradict his prophetic assertion.

Finding the subject getting to be knotty, the Englishman retired to the apartment in which the ladies had assembled; and, seated by the side of Sarah, he found a more pleasing employment in relating the events of fashionable life in the metropolis, and in recalling the thousand little anecdotes of their former associates. Miss Peyton was a pleased listener, as she dispensed the bounties of the tea table, and Sarah frequently bowed her blushing countenance to her needlework, as her face glowed at the flattering remarks of her companion.

The dialogue we have related established a perfect truce between the surgeon and his comrade; and the former having paid a visit to Singleton, they took their leave of the ladies, and mounted; the former to visit the wounded at the encampment, and the latter to rejoin his troop. But their movements were arrested at the gate by an occurrence that we shall relate in the next chapter.

CHAPTER XIV

I see no more those white locks thinly spread
Round the bald polish of that honored head:
No more that meek, that suppliant look in prayer,
Nor that pure faith that gave it force, are there:
But he is blest, and I lament no more,
A wise good man, contented to be poor.

—Crabbe

We have already said that the customs of America leave the dead but a short time in sight of the mourners; and the necessity of providing for his own safety had compelled the peddler to abridge even this brief space. In the confusion and agitation produced by the events we have recorded, the death of the elder Birch had occurred unnoticed; but a sufficient number of the immediate neighbors were hastily collected, and the ordinary rites of sepulture were now about to be paid to the deceased. It was the approach of this humble procession that arrested the movements of the trooper and his comrade. Four men supported the body on a rude bier; and four others walked in advance, ready to relieve their friends from their burden. The peddler walked next the coffin, and by his side moved Katy Haynes, with a most determined aspect of woe, and next to the mourners came Mr. Wharton and the English captain. Two or three old men and women, with a few straggling boys, brought up the rear. Captain Lawton sat in his saddle, in rigid silence, until the bearers came opposite to his position, and then, for the first time, Harvey raised his eyes from the ground, and saw the enemy that he dreaded so near him. The first impulse of the peddler was certainly flight; but recovering his recollection, he fixed his eye on the coffin of his parent, and passed the dragoon with a firm step but swelling heart. The trooper slowly lifted his cap, and continued uncovered until Mr. Wharton and his son had moved by, when, accompanied by the surgeon, he rode leisurely in the rear, maintaining an inflexible silence.

Cæsar emerged from the cellar kitchen of the cottage, and with a face of settled solemnity, added himself to the number of the followers of the funeral, though with a humble mien and at a most respectful distance from the horsemen. The old negro had placed around his arm, a little above the elbow, a napkin of unsullied whiteness, it being the only time since his departure from the city that he had enjoyed an opportunity of exhibiting himself in the garniture of servile mourning. He was a great lover of propriety, and had been a little stimulated to this display by a desire to show his sable friend from Georgia all the decencies of a New York funeral; and the ebullition of his zeal went off very well, producing no other result than a mild lecture from Miss Peyton at his return, on the fitness of things. The attendance of the black was thought well enough in itself; but the napkin was deemed a superfluous exhibition of ceremony, at the funeral of a man who had perfomed all the menial offices in his own person.

The graveyard was an inclosure on the grounds of Mr. Wharton, which had been fenced with stone and set apart for the purpose, by that gentleman, some years before. It was not, however, intended as a burial place for any of his own family. Until the fire, which raged as the British troops took possession of New York, had laid Trinity in ashes, a goodly gilded tablet on its walls proclaimed the virtues of his deceased parents, and beneath a flag of marble, in one of the aisles of the church, their bones left to molder in aristocratical repose. Captain Lawton made a movement as if he was disposed to follow the procession, when it left the highway, to enter the field which contained the graves of the humble dead, but he was recalled to recollection by a hint from his companion that he was taking the wrong road.

"Of all the various methods which have been adopted by man for the disposal of his earthly remains, which do you prefer, Captain Lawton?" said the surgeon, as they separated from the little procession. "In some countries the body is exposed to be devoured by wild beasts; in others it is suspended in the air to exhale its substance in the manner of decomposition; in other regions it is consumed on the funeral pile, and, again, it is inhumed in the bowels of the earth; every people have their own particular fashion, and to which do you give the preference?"

"All are agreeable," said the trooper, following the group they had left with his eyes; "though the speediest interments give the cleanest fields. Of which are you an admirer?"

"The last, as practiced by ourselves, for the other three are destructive of all the opportunities for dissection; whereas, in the last, the coffin can lie in peaceful decency, while the remains are made to subserve the useful purposes of science. Ah! Captain Lawton, I enjoy comparatively but few opportunities of such a nature, to what I expected on entering the army."

"To what may these pleasures numerically amount in a year?" said the captain, withdrawing his gaze from the grave-yard.

"Within a dozen, upon my honor; my best picking is when the corps is detached; for when we are with the main army, there are so many boys to be satisfied, that I seldom get a good subject. Those youngsters are as wasteful as prodigals, and as greedy as vultures."

"A dozen!" echoed the trooper, in surprise. "Why, I furnish you that number with my own hands."

"Ah! Jack," returned the doctor, approaching the subject with great tenderness of manner, "it is seldom I can do anything with your patients; you disfigure them woefully. Believe me, John, when I tell you as a friend that your system is all wrong; you unnecessarily destroy life, and then you injure the body so that it is unfit for the only use that can be made of a dead man.

The trooper maintained a silence, which he thought would be the most probable means of preserving peace between them; and the surgeon, turning his head from taking a last look at the burial, as they rode around the foot of the hill that shut the valley from their sight, continued with a suppressed sigh,—

"One might get a natural death from that graveyard to-night, if there was but time and opportunity! The patient must be the father of the lady we saw this morning."

"The petticoat doctor!—she with the aurora borealis complexion," said the trooper, with a smile, that began to cause uneasiness to his companion. "But the lady was not the gentleman's daughter, only his medico-petticoat attendant; and the Harvey, whose name was made to rime with every word in her song, is the renowned peddler spy."

"What? He who unhorsed you?"

"No man ever unhorsed me. Dr. Sitgreaves," said the dragoon, gravely. "I fell by mischance of Roanoke; rider and beast kissed the earth together."

"A warm embrace, from the love spots it left on your cuticle; 'tis a thousand pities that you cannot find where the tattling rascal lies hid."

"He followed his father's body."

"And you let him pass!" cried the surgeon, checking his horse. "Let us return immediately, and take him; to-morrow you shall have him hanged, Jack, — and, damn him, I'll dissect him!"

"Softly, softly, my dear Archibald. Would you arrest a man while paying the last offices to a dead father? Leave him to me, and I pledge myself he shall have justice."

The doctor muttered his dissatisfaction at any postponement of vengeance; but he was compelled to acquiesce, from a regard to his reputation for propriety; and they continued their ride to the quarters of the corps, engaged in various discussions concerning the welfare of the human body.

Birch supported the grave and collected manner that was thought becoming in a male mourner, on such occasions, and to Katy was left the part of exhibiting the tenderness of the softer sex. There are some people, whose feeling are of such nature that they cannot weep unless it be in proper company, and the spinster was a good deal addicted to this congregation al virtue. After casting her eyes around the small assemblage, the housekeeper found the countenances of the few females, who were present, fixed on her in solemn expectation, and the effect was instantaneous; the maiden really wept, and she gained no inconsiderable sympathy, and some reputation for a tender heart, from the spectators. The muscles of the peddler's face were seen to move, and as the first clod of earth fell on the tenement of his father, sending up that dull, hollow sound that speaks so eloquently the mortality of man, his whole frame was for an instant convulsed. He bent his body down, as if in pain, his fingers worked while the hands hung lifeless by his side, and there was- an expression in his countenance that seemed to announce a writhing of the soul; but it was not unresisted, and it was transient. He stood erect, drew a long breath, and looked around him with an elevated face, that even seemed to smile with a consciousness of having obtained the mastery. The grave was soon filled; a rough stone, placed at either extremity, marked its position, and the turf, whose faded vegetation was adapted to the fortunes of the deceased, covered the little hillock with the last office of seemliness. This office ended, the neighbors, who had officiously pressed forward to offer their services in performing their solemn duty, paused, and lifting their hats, stood looking towards the mourner, who now felt himself to be really alone in the world. Uncovering his head also, the peddler hesitated a moment, to gather energy, and spoke.

"My friends and neighbors," he said, "I thank you for assisting me to bury my dead out of my sight."

A solemn pause succeeded the customary address, and the group dispersed in silence, some few walking with the mourners back to their own habitation, but respectfully leaving them at its entrance. The peddler and Katy were followed into the building by one man, however, who was well known to the surrounding country by the significant term of "a speculator." Katy saw him enter, with a heart that palpitated with dreadful forebodings, but Harvey civilly handed him a chair, and evidently was prepared for the visit.

The peddler went to the door, and, taking a cautious glance about the valley, quickly returned, and commenced the following dialogue: —

"The sun has just left the top of the eastern hill; my time presses me: here is deed for the house and lot; everything is done accordingly to law."

The other took the paper, and conned its contents with a deliberation that proceeded partly from his caution, and partly from the unlucky circumstance of his education having been much neglected when a youth. The time occupied in this tedious examination was employed by Harvey in gathering together certain articles which he intended to include in the stores that were to leave the habitation with himself. Katy had already inquired of the peddler whether the deceased had left a will; and she saw the Bible placed in the bottom of a new pack, which she had made for his accommodation, with a most stoical indifference; but as the six silver spoons were laid carefully by its side, a sudden twinge of her conscience objected to such a palpable waste of property, and she broke silence.

"When you marry, Harvey, you may miss those spoons."

"I shall never marry."

"Well, if you don't there's no occasion to make rash promises, even to yourself. One never knows what one may do, in such a case. I should like to know, of what use so many spoons can be to a single man; for my part, I think it is a duty for every man who is well provided, to have a wife and family to maintain."

At the time when Katy expressed this sentiment, the fortune of women in her class of life consisted of a cow, a bed, the labors of their own hands in the shape of divers pillowcases, blankets, and , sheets, with, where fortune was unusually kind, a half dozen silver spoons. The spinster herself had obtained all the other necessaries by her own industry and prudence, and it can easily be imagined that she saw the articles she had long counted her own vanish in the enormous pack, with a dissatisfaction that was in no degree diminished by the declaration that had preceded the act. Harvey, however, disregarded her opinions and feelings, and continued his employment of filling the pack, which soon grew to something like the ordinary size of the peddler's burden.

"I'm rather timersome about this conveyance;" said the purchaser, having at length waded through the covenants of the deed.

"Why so?"

"I'm afraid it won't stand good in law. I know that two of the neighbors leave home to-morrow morning, to have the place entered for confiscation; and if I should give forty pounds, and lose it all, 'twould be a dead pull back to me."

"They can only take my right," said the peddler. "Pay me two hundred dollars, and the house is yours; you are a well-known Whig, and you at least they won't trouble." As Harvey spoke, there was a strange bitterness of manner, mingled with the shrewd care he expressed concerning the sale of his property.

"Say one hundred, and it is a bargain," returned the man, with a grin that he meant for a good-natured smile.

"A bargain!" echoed the peddler, in surprise. "I thought the bargain already made."

"Nothing is a bargain," said the purchaser, with a chuckle, "until papers are delivered, and the money paid in hand."

"You have the paper."

"Aye, and will keep it, if you will excuse the money. Come, say one hundred and fifty, and I won't be hard; here — here is just the money."

The peddler looked from the window, and saw with dismay that the evening was fast advancing, and knew well that he endangered his life by remaining in the dwelling after dark; yet he could not tolerate the idea of being defrauded in this manner, in a bargain that had already been fairly made; he hesitated.

"Well," said the purchaser, rising, "mayhap you can find another man to trade with between this and morning, but if you don't, your title won't be worth much afterwards."

"Take it, Harvey," said Katy, who felt it impossible to resist a tender like the one before her; for the purchase money was in English guineas. Her voice roused the peddler, and a new idea seemed to strike him.

"I agree to the price," he said; and, turning to the spinster, he placed part of the money in her hand, as he continued, "Had I other means to pay you, I would have lost all, rather than suffer myself to be defrauded of part."

"You may lose all yet," muttered the stranger, with a sneer, as he rose and left the building.

"Yes," said Katy, following him with her eyes, "he knows your failing, Harvey; he thinks with me, now the old gentleman is gone, you will want a careful body to take care of your concerns."

The peddler was busied in making arrangements for his departure, and he took no notice of this insinuation, while the spinster returned again to the attack. She had lived so many years in expectation of a termination to her hopes, so different from that which now seemed likely to occur, that the idea of separation began to give her more uneasiness than she had thought herself capable of feeling, about a man so destitute and friendless.

"Have you another house to go to?" inquired Katy.

"Providence will provide me with a home."

"Yes," said the housekeeper, "but maybe 'twill not be to your liking."

"The poor must not be difficult."

"I'm sure I'm anything but a difficult body," cried the spinster, very hastily; "but I love to see things becoming, and in their places; yet I wouldn't be hard to persuade to leave this place myself. I can't say I altogether like the ways of the people hereabouts."

"The valley is lovely," said the peddler, with fervor, "and the people like all the race of man. But to me it matters nothing; all places are now alike, and all faces equally strange." As he spoke he dropped the article he was packing from his hand, and seated himself on a chest, with a look of vacant misery.

"Not so, not so," said Katy, shoving her chair nearer to the place where the peddler sat. "Not so, Harvey, you must know me at least; my face cannot be strange to you."

Birch turned his eyes slowly on her countenance, which exhibited more of feeling, and less of self, than he had ever seen there before; he took her hand kindly, and his own features lost some of their painful expression as he said,—

"Yes, good woman, you, at least, are not a stranger to me; you may do me partial justice; when others revile me, possibly your feelings may lead you to say something in my defense."

"That I will; that I would!" said Katy, eagerly. "I will defend you, Harvey, to the last drop; let me hear them that dare to revile you! You say true, Harvey, I am partial and just to you; what if you do like the king? I have often heard it said he was at the bottom a good man; but there's no religion in the old country, for everybody allows the ministers are desperate bad!"

The peddler paced the floor in evident distress of mind; his eyes had a look of wildness that Katy had never witnessed before, and his step was measured, with a dignity that appalled the housekeeper.

"While my father lived," murmured Harvey, unable to smother his feelings, "there was one who read my heart, and oh! what a consolation to return from my secret marches of danger, and the insults and wrongs that I suffered, to receive his blessing and his praise; but he is gone," he continued, stopping and gazing wildly towards the corner that used to hold the figure of his parent, "and who is there to do me justice?"

"Why, Harvey! Harvey!"

"Yes, there is one who will, who must know me before I die! Oh! it is dreadful to die, and leave such a name behind me."

"Don't talk of dying, Harvey," said the spinster, glancing her eye around thu room, and pushing the wood in the fire to obtain a light from the blaze.

The ebullition of feeling in the peddler was over. It had been excited by the events of the past day, and a vivid perception of his sufferings. It was not long, however, that passion maintained an ascendency over the reason of this singular man; and perceiving that the night had already thrown an obscurity around objects without doors, he hastily threw his pack over his shoulders, and taking Katy kindly by the hand, in leavetaking,—

"It is painful to part with even you, good woman," he said, "but the hour has come, and I must go. What is left in the house is yours; to me it could be of no use, and it may serve to make you more comfortable. Farewell—we shall meet hereafter."

"In the regions of darkness!" cried a voice that caused the peddler to sink on the chest from which he had risen, in despair.

"What! another pack, Mr. Birch, and so well stuffed so soon!"

"Have you not done evil enough?" cried the peddler, regaining his firmness, and springing on his feet with energy. "Is it not enough to harass the last moments of a dying man—to impoverish me; what more would you have?"

"Your blood!" said the Skinner, with cool malignity.

"And for money," cried Harvey, bitterly. "Like the ancient Judas, you would grow rich with the price of blood!"

"Aye, and a fair price it is, my gentleman; fifty guineas; nearly the weight of that carcass of yours in gold."

"Here," said Katy, promptly, "here are fifteen guineas, and these drawers and this bed are all mine; if you will give Harvey but one hour's start from the door, they shall be yours."

"One hour?" said the Skinner, showing his teeth, and looking with a longing eye at the money.

"But a single hour; here, take the money."

"Hold!" cried Harvey. "Put no faith in the miscreant."

"She may do what she pleases with her faith," said the Skinner, with malignant pleasure, "but I have the money in good keeping; as for you, Mr. Birch, we will bear your insolence, for the fifty guineas that are to pay for your gallows."

"Go on," said the peddler, proudly; "take me to Major Dunwoodie; he, at least, may be kind, although just."

"I can do better than by marching so far in such disgraceful company; this Mr. Dunwoodie has let one or two Tories go at large; but the troop of Captain Lawton is quartered some half mile nearer, and his receipt will get me the reward as soon as his major's. How relish you the idea of supping with Captain Lawton, this evening, Mr. Birch?"

"Give me my money, or set Harvey free," cried the spinster in alarm.

"Your bribe was not enough, good woman, unless there is money in this bed." Thrusting his bayonet through the ticking and ripping it for some distance, he took a malicious satisfaction in scattering its contents about the room.

"If," cried the housekeeper, losing sight of her personal danger in care for her newly-acquired property, "there is law in the land, I will be righted!"

"The law of the neutral ground is the law of the strongest; but your tongue is not as long as my bayonet; you had, therefore, best not set them at loggerheads, or you might be the loser."

A figure stood in the shadow of the door, as if afraid to be seen in the group of Skinners; but a blaze of light, raised by some articles thrown in the fire by his persecutors, showed the peddler the face of the purchaser of his little domain. Occasionally there was some whispering between this man and the Skinner nearest him, that induced Harvey to suspect he had been the dupe of a contrivance in which that wretch had participated. It was, however, too late to repine; and he followed the party from the house with a firm and collected tread, as if marching to a triumph, and not to a gallows. In passing through the yard, the leader of the band fell over a billet of wood, and received a momentary hurt from the fall; exasperated at the incident, the fellow sprang on his feet, filling the air with execrations.

"The curse of heaven light on the log!" he exclaimed. "The night is too dark for us to move in; throw that brand of fire in yon pile of tow, to light up the scene."

"Hold!" roared the speculator; "you'll fire the house."

"And see the farther," said the other, hurling the brand in the midst of the combustibles. In an instant the building was in flames. "Come on; let us move towards the heights while we have light to pick our road."

"Villain!" cried the exasperated purchaser, "is this your friendship—this my reward for kidnapping the peddler?"

" 'Twould be wise to move more from the light, if you mean to entertain us with abuse, or we may see too well to miss our mark," cried the leader of the gang. The next instant he was as good as his threat, but happily missed the terrified speculator and equally appalled spinster, who saw herself again reduced from comparative wealth to poverty, by the blow. Prudence dictated to the pair a speedy retreat; and the next morning, the only remains of the dwelling of the peddler was the huge chimney we have already mentioned.

CHAPTER XV

Trifles, light as air,
Are to the jealous confirmations strong
As proofs of holy writ.

—Othello

The weather, which had been mild and clear since the storm, now changed with the suddenness of the American climate. Towards evening the cold blasts poured down from the mountains, and flurries of snow plainly indicated that the month of November had arrived; a season whose temperature varies from the heats of summer to the cold of winter. Frances had stood at the window of her own apartment, watching the slow progress of the funeral procession, with a melancholy that was too deep to be excited by the spectacle. There was something in the sad office that was in unison with her feelings. As she gazed around, she saw the trees bending to the force of the wind, that swept through the valley with an impetuosity that shook even the buildings; and the forest, that had so lately glittered in the sun with its variegated hues, was fast losing its loveliness, as the leaves were torn from the branches, and were driving irregularly before the eddies of the blast. A few of the Southern dragoons, who were patrolling the passes which led to the encampment of the corps, could be distinguished at a distance on the heights, bending to their pommels as they faced the keen air which had so lately traversed the great fresh-water lakes, and drawing their watch coats about them in tighter folds.

Frances witnessed the disappearance of the wooden tenement of the deceased, as it was slowly lowered from the light of day; and the sight added to the chilling dreariness of the view. Captain Singleton was sleeping under the care of his own man, while his sister had been persuaded to take possession of her room, for the purpose of obtaining the repose of which her last night's journeying had robbed her. The apartment of Miss Singleton communicated with the room occupied by the sisters, through a private door, as well as through the ordinary passage of the house; this door was partly open, and Frances moved towards it, with benevolent intention of ascertaining the situation of her guest, when the surprised girl saw her whom she had thought to be sleeping, not only awake, but employed in a manner that banished all probability of present repose. The black tresses, that during the dinner had been drawn in close folds over the crown of the head, were now loosened, and fell in profusion over her shoulders and bosom, imparting a slight degree of wildness to her countenance; the chilling white of her complexion was strongly contrasted with eyes of the deepest black, that were fixed in rooted attention on a picture she held in her hand. Frances hardly breathed, as she was enabled, by a movement of Isabella, to see that it was the figure of a man in the well-known dress of the Southern horse; but she gasped for breath, and instinctively laid her hand on her heart to quell its throbbings, as she thought she recognized the lineaments that were so deeply seated in her own imagination. Frances felt she was improperly prying into the sacred privacy of another; but her emotions were too powerful to permit her to speak, and she drew back to a chair, where she still retained a view of the stranger, from whose countenance she felt it to be impossible to withdraw her eyes. Isabella was too much engrossed by her own feelings to discover the trembling figure of the witness to her actions, and she pressed the inanimate image to her lips, with an enthusiasm that denoted the most intense passion. The expression of the countenance of the fair stranger was so changeable, and the transitions were so rapid, that Frances had scarcely time to distinguish the character of the emotion, before it was succeeded by another, equally powerful and equally attractive. Admiration and sorrow were however the preponderating passions; the latter was indicated by large drops that fell from her eyes on the picture, and which followed each other over her cheek at such intervals, as seemed to pronounce the grief too heavy to admit of the ordinary demonstrations of sorrow. Every movement of Isabella was marked by an enthusiasm that was peculiar to her nature, and every passion in its turn triumphed in her breast. The fury of the wind, as it whistled round the angles of the building, was in consonance with those feelings, and she rose and moved to a window of her apartment. Her figure was now hid from the view of Frances, who was about to rise and approach her guest, when tones of a thrilling melody chained her in breathless silence to the spot. The notes were wild, and the voice not powerful, but the execution exceeded anything that Frances had ever heard; and she stood, endeavoring to stifle the sounds of her own gentle breathing, until the following song was concluded:—

Cold blow the blasts o'ver the tops of the mountain,
And bare is the oak on the hill;
Slowly the vapors exhale from the fountain,
And bright gleams the ice-bordered rill;
All nature is seeking its annual rest,
But the slumbers of peace have deserted my breast.
Long has the storm poured its weight on my nation,
And long have her braves stood the shock;
Long has her chieftain ennobled his station,
A bulwark on liberty's rock;
Unlicensed ambition relaxes its toil,
Yet blighted affection represses my smile.
Abroad the wild fury of winter is lowering,
And leafless and drear is the tree;
But the vertical sun of the south appears pouring
Its fierce, killing heats upon me:
Without, all the season's chill symptoms begin—
But the fire of passion is raging within.

Frances abandoned her whole soul to the suppressed melody of the music, though the language of the song expressed a meaning, which, united with certain events of that and the preceding day, left a sensation of uneasiness in the bosom of the warm-hearted girl, to which she had hitherto been a stranger. Isabella moved from the window as her last tones melted on the ear of her admiring listener, and, for the first time, her eye rested on the pallid face of the intruder. A glow of fire lighted the countenance of both at the same instant, and the blue eye of Frances met the brilliant black one of her guest for a single moment, and both fell in abashed confusion on the carpet; they advanced, however, until they met, and had taken each other's hand, before either ventured again to look her companion in the face.

"This sudden change in the weather, and perhaps the situation of my brother, have united to make me melancholy, Miss Wharton," said Isabella, in a low tone, and in a voice that trembled as she spoke.

" 'Tis thought you have little to apprehend for your brother," said Frances, in the same embarrassed manner. "Had you seen him when he was brought in by Major Dunwoodie—"

Frances paused, with a feeling of conscious shame, for which she could not account; and, in raising her eyes, she saw Isabella studying her countenance with an earnestness that again drove the blood tumultuously to her temples.

"You were speaking of Major Dunwoodie," said Isabella, faintly.

"He was with Captain Singleton."

"Do you know Dunwoodie? Have you seen him often?"

Once more Frances ventured to look her guest in the face, and again she met the piercing eyes bent on her, as if to search her inmost heart. "Speak, Miss Wharton; is Major Dunwoodie known to you?"

"He is my relative," said Frances, appalled at the manner of the other.

"A relative!" echoed Miss Singleton; "in what degree?—speak, Miss Wharton, I conjure you to speak."

"Our parents were cousins," faintly replied Frances.

"And he is to be your husband?" said the stranger, impetuously.

Frances felt shocked, and all her pride awakened, by this direct attack upon her feeling, and she raised her eyes from the floor to her interrogator a little proudly, when the pale cheek and quivering lip of Isabella removed her resentment in a moment.

"It is true! My conjecture is true! Speak to me, Miss Wharton; I conjure you, in mercy to my feelings, to tell me—do you love Dunwoodie?" There was a plaintive earnestness in the voice of Miss Singleton that disarmed Frances of all resentment, and the only answer she could make was to hide her burning face between her hands, as she sank back in a chair to conceal her confusion.

Isabella paced the floor in silence for several minutes, until she had succeeded in conquering the violence of her feelings, when she approached the place where Frances yet sat, endeavoring to exclude the eyes of companion from reading the shame expressed in her countenance, and, taking the hand of the other, she spoke with an evident effort at composure.

"Pardon me. Miss Wharton, if my ungovernable feelings have led me into impropriety; the powerful motive—the cruel reason"—she hesitated. Frances now raised her face, and their eyes once more met; they fell in each other's arms, and laid their burning cheeks together. The embrace was long—was ardent and sincere—but neither spoke; and on separating, Frances retired to her own room without further explanation.

While this extraordinary scene was acting in the room of Miss Singleton, matters of great importance were agitated in the drawing-room. The disposition of the fragments of such a dinner as the one we have recorded was a task that required no little exertion and calculation. Notwithstanding several of the small game had nestled in the pocket of Captain Lawton's man, and even the assistant of Dr. Sitgreaves had calculated the uncertainty of his remaining long in such good quarters, still there was more left unconsumed than the prudent Miss Peyton knew how to dispose of to advantage. Cæsar and his mistress had, therefore, a long and confidential communication on this important business; and the consequence was, that Colonel Wellmere was left to the hospitality of Sarah Wharton. All the ordinary topics of conversation were exhausted, when the colonel, with a little of the uneasiness that is in some degree inseparable from conscious error, touched lightly on the transactions of the preceding day.

"We little thought, Miss Wharton, when I first saw this Mr. Dunwoodie in your house in Queen Street, that he was to be the renowned warrior he has proved himself," said Wellmere, endeavoring to smile away his chagrin.

"Renowned, when we consider the enemy he overcame," said Sarah, with consideration for her companion's feelings. " 'Twas unfortunate, indeed, in every respect, that you met with the accident, or doubtless the royal arms would have triumphed in their usual manner."

"And yet the pleasure of such society as this accident has introduced me to, would more than repay the pain of a mortified spirit and wounded body," added the colonel, in a manner of peculiar softness.

"I hope the latter is but trifling," said Sarah, stooping to hide her blushes under the pretext of biting a thread from the work on her knee.

"Trifling, indeed, compared to the former," returned the colonel, in the same manner. "Ah! Miss Wharton, it is in such moments that we feel the full value of friendship and sympathy."

Those who have never tried it cannot easily imagine what a rapid progress a warm-hearted female can make in love, in the short space of half an hour, particularly where there is a predisposition to the distemper. Sarah found the conversation, when it began to touch on friendship and sympathy, too interesting to venture her voice with a reply. She, however, turned her eyes on the colonel, and saw him gazing at her fine face with an admiration that was quite as manifest, and much more soothing, than any words could make it.

Their tête-à-tête was uninterrupted for an hour; and although nothing that would be called decided, by an experienced matron, was said by the gentleman, he uttered a thousand things that delighted his companion, who retired to her rest with a lighter heart than she had felt since the arrest of her brother by the Americans.

CHAPTER XVI

And let me the canakin clink, clink
And let me the canakin clink.
A soldier's a man;
A life's but a span;
Why, then, let a soldier drink.
—Othello

The position held by the corps of dragoons, we have already said, was a favorite place of halting with their commander. A cluster of some half dozen small and dilapidated buildings formed what, from the circumstance of two roads intersecting each other at right angles, was called the village of the Four Corners. As usual, one of the most imposing of these edifices had been termed, in the language of the day, "a house of entertainment for man and beast." On a rough board suspended from the gallows-looking post that had supported the ancient sign, was, however, written in red chalk, "Elizabeth Flanagan, her hotel," an ebullition of the wit of some of the idle wags of the corps. The matron, whose name had thus been exalted to an office of such unexpected dignity, ordinarily discharged the duties of a female sutler, washerwoman, and, to use the language of Katy Haynes, petticoat doctor to the troops. She was the widow of a soldier who had been killed in the service, and who, like herself, was a native of a distant island, and had early tried his fortune in the colonies of North America. She constantly migrated with the troops; and it was seldom that they became stationary for two days at a time but the little cart of the bustling woman was seen driving into the encampment loaded with such articles as she conceived would make her presence most welcome. With a celerity that seemed almost supernatural, Betty took up her ground and commenced her occupation. Sometimes the cart itself was her shop; at others the soldiers made her a rude shelter of such materials as offered; but on the present occasion she had seized on a vacant building, and, by dint of stuffing the dirty breeches and half-dried linen of the troopers into the broken windows, to exclude the cold, which had now become severe, she formed what she herself had pronounced to be "most illigant lodgings."

The men were quartered in the adjacent barns, and the officers, collected in the "Hotel Flanagan," as they facetiously called headquarters. Betty was well known to every trooper in the corps, could call each by his Christian or nickname, as best suited her fancy; and, although absolutely intolerable to all whom habit had not made familiar with her virtues, was a general favorite with these partisan warriors. Her faults were, a trifling love of liquor, excessive filthiness, and a total disregard of all the decencies of language; her virtues, an unbounded love for her adopted country, perfect honesty when dealing on certain known principles with the soldiery, and a great good nature. Added to these, Betty had the merit of being the inventor of that beverage which is so well known, at the present hour, to all the patriots who make a winter's march between the commercial and political capitals of this great state, and which is distinguished by the name of "cocktail." Elizabeth Flanagan was peculiarly well qualified, by education and circumstances, to perfect this improvement in liquors, having been literally brought up on its principal ingredient, and having acquired from her Virginian customers the use of mint, from its flavor in a julep to its height of renown in the article in question. Such, then, was the mistress of the mansion, who, reckless of the cold northern blasts, showed her blooming face from the door of the building to welcome the arrival of her favorite, Captain Lawton, and his companion, her master in matters of surgery.

"Ah! by my hopes of promotion, my gentle Elizabeth, but you are welcome!" cried the trooper, as he threw himself from his saddle. "This villainous fresh-water gas* from the Canadas has been whistling among my bones till they ache with the cold, but the sight of your fiery countenance is as cheery as a Christmas fire."

"Now sure, Captain Jack, ye's always full of your complimentaries," replied the sutler, taking the bridle of her customer. "But hurry in for the life of you, darling; the fences hereabouts are not so strong as in the Highlands, and there's that within will warm both sowl and body."

"So you have been laying the rails under contribution, I see. Well, that may do for the body," said the captain coolly; "but I have had a pull at a bottle of cut glass with a silver stand, and I doubt my relish for your whisky for a month to come."

"If it's silver or goold that ye're thinking of, it's but little I have, though I've a trifling bit of the continental," said Betty, with a look of humor; "but there's that within that's fit to be put in vissils of di'monds."

"What can she mean, Archibald?" asked Lawton. "The animal looks as if it meant more than it says!"

" 'Tis probably a wandering of the reasoning powers, created by the frequency of intoxicating drafts," observed the surgeon, as he deliberately threw his left leg over the pommel of the saddle, and slid down on the right side of his horse.

"Faith, my dear jewel of a doctor, but it was this side I was expicting you; the whole corps come down on this side but yeerself," said Betty, winking at the trooper; "but I've been feeding the wounded, in yeer absence, with the fat of the land."

"Barbarous stupidity!" cried the panic-stricken physician, "to feed men laboring under the excitement of fever with powerful nutriment. Woman, woman, you are enough to defeat the skill of Hippocrates!"

"Pooh!" said Betty, with infinite composure, "what a botheration ye make about a little whisky; there was but a gallon betwixt a good dozen of them, and I gave it to the boys to make them sleep asy; sure, jist as slumbering drops."

Lawton and his companion now entered the building, and the first objects which met their eyes explained the hidden meaning of Betty's comfortable declaration. A long table, made of boards torn from the side of an outbuilding, was stretched through the middle of the largest apartment, or the barroom, and on it was a very scanty display of crockery ware. The steams of cookery arose from an adjoining kitchen, but the principal attraction was in a demijohn of fair proportions, which had been ostentatiously placed on high by Betty as the object most worthy of notice. Lawton, soon learned that it was teeming with the real amber-colored juice of the grape, and had been sent from the Locusts, as an offering to Major Dunwoodie, from his friend Captain Wharton of the royal army.

"And a royal gift it is," said the grinning subaltern, who made the explanation. "The major gives us an entertainment in honor of our victory, and you see the principal expense is borne as it should be, by the enemy. Zounds! I am thinking that after we have primed with such stuff, we could charge through Sir

Henry's headquarters, and carry off the knight himself."

The captain of dragoons was in no manner displeased at the prospect of terminating so pleasantly a day that had been so agreeably commenced. He was soon surrounded by his comrades, who made many eager inquiries concerning his adventures, while the surgeon proceeded, with certain quakings of the heart, to examine into the state of his wounded. Enormous fires were snapping in the chimneys of the house, superseding the necessity of candles, by the bright light which was thrown from the blazing piles. The group within were all young men and tried soldiers; in number they were rather more than a dozen, and their manners and conversation were a strange mixture of the bluntness of the partisan with the manners of gentlemen. Their dresses were neat, though plain; and a never-failing topic amongst them was the performance and quality of their horses. Some were endeavoring to sleep on the benches which lined the walls, some were walking the apartments, and others were seated in earnest discussion on subjects connected with the business of their lives. Occasionally, as the door of the kitchen opened, the hissing sounds of the frying pans and the inviting savor of the food created a stagnation in all other employments; even the sleepers, at such moments, would open their eyes, and raise their heads, to reconnoiter the state of the preparations. All this time Dunwoodie sat by himself, gazing at the fire, and lost in reflections which none of his officers presumed to disturb. He had made earnest inquiries of Sitgreaves after the condition of Singleton, during which a profound and respectful silence was maintained in the room; but as soon as he had ended, and resumed his seat, the usual ease and freedom prevailed.

The arrangement of the table was a matter of but little concern to Mrs. Flanagan; and Cæsar would have been sadly scandalized at witnessing the informality with which various dishes, each bearing a wonderful resemblance to the others, were placed before so many gentlemen of consideration. In taking their places at the board, the strictest attention was paid to precedency; for, notwithstanding the freedom of manners which prevailed in the corps, the points of military etiquette were at all times observed, with something approaching to religious veneration. Most of the guests, had been fasting too long to be in any degree fastidious in their appetites; but the case was different with Captain Lawton; he felt an unaccountable loathing at the exhibition of Betty's food, and could not refrain from making a few passing comments on the condition of the knives, and the clouded aspect of the plates. The good nature and the personal affection of Betty for the offender, restrained her, for some time, from answering his innuendoes, until Lawton, having ventured to admit a piece of the black meat into his mouth, inquired, with the affectation of a spoiled child,—

"What kind of animal might this have been when living, Mrs. Flanagan?"

"Sure, captain, and wasn't it the ould cow?" replied the sutler, with a warmth that proceeded partly from dissatisfaction at the complaints of her favorite, and partly from grief at the loss of the deceased.

"What!" roared the trooper, stopping short as he was about to swallow his morsel, "ancient Jenny!"

"The devil!" cried another, dropping his knife and fork, "she who made the campaign of the Jerseys with us?"

"The very same," replied the mistress of the hotel, with a piteous aspect of woe; "a gentle baste, and one that could and did live on less man air, at need. Sure, gentlemen, 'tis awful to have to eat sitch an ould frind."

"And has she sunk to this?" said Lawton, pointing with his knife to the remnants on the table.

"Nay, captain," said Betty, with spirit, "I sould two of her quarters to some of your troop; but divil the word did I tell the boys what an ould frind it was they had bought, for fear it might damage their appetites."

"Fury!" cried the trooper, with affected anger, "I shall have my fellows as limber as supple-jacks on such fare; afraid of an Englishman as a Virginia negro is of his driver."

"Well," said Lieutenant Mason, dropping his knife and fork in a kind of despair, "my jaws have more sympathy than many men's hearts. They absolutely decline making any impression on the relics of their old acquaintance."

"Try a drop of the gift," said Betty, soothingly, pouring a large allowance of the wine into a bowl, and drinking it off as taster to the corps. "Faith, 'tis but a wishy-washy sort of stuff after all!"

The ice once broken, however, a clear glass of wine was

handed to Dunwoodie, who, bowing to his companions, drank the liquor in the midst of a profound silence. For a few glasses there was much formality observed, and sundry patriotic toasts and. sentiments were duly noticed by the company. The liquor, however, performed its wonted office; and before the second sentinel at the door had been relieved, all recollection of the dinner and their cares was lost in the present festivity. Dr. Sitgreaves did not return in season to partake of Jenny, but he was in time to receive his fair proportion of Captain Wharton's present.

"A song, a song from Captain Lawton!" cried two or three of the party in a breath, on observing the failure of some of the points of good-fellowship in the trooper. "Silence, for the song of Captain Lawton."

"Gentlemen," returned Lawton, his dark eyes swimming with the bumpers he had finished, though his head was as impenetrable as a post; "I am not much of a nightingale, but, under the favor of your good wishes, I consent to comply with the demand."

"Now, Jack," said Sitgreaves, nodding on his seat, "remember the air I taught you, and—stop, I have a copy of the words in my pocket."

"Forbear, forbear, good doctor," said the trooper, filling his glass with great deliberation; "I never could wheel round those hard names. Gentlemen, I will give you a humble attempt of my own."

"Silence, for Captain Lawton's song!" roared five or six at once; when the trooper proceeded, in a fine, full tone, to sing the following words to a well-known bacchanalian air, several of his comrades helping him through the chorus with a fervor that shook the crazy edifice they were in:—

Now push the mug, my jolly boys,
    And live, while live we can;
To-morrow's sun may end your joys,
    For briefs the hour of man.
And he who bravely meets the foe
His lease of life can never know.
  Old mother Flanagan
  Come and fill the can again!
  For you can fill, and we can swill,

Good Betty Flanagan.
If love of life pervades your breast,
Or love of ease your frame,
Quit honor's path for peaceful rest,
And bear a coward's name;
For soon and late, we danger know,
And fearless on the saddle go.
Old mother, etc.
When foreign foes invade the land,
And wives and sweethearts call,
In freedom's cause we'll bravely stand
Or will as bravely fall;
In this fair home the fates have given
We'll live as lords, or live in heaven.
Old mother, etc.

At each appeal made to herself, by the united voices of the choir, Betty invariably advanced and complied literally with the request contained in the chorus, to the infinite delight of the singers, and with no small participation in the satisfaction on her account. The hostess was provided with a beverage more suited to the high seasoning to which she had accustomed her palate, than the tasteless present of Captain Wharton; by which means Betty had managed, with tolerable facility, to keep even pace with the exhilaration of her guests. The applause received by Captain Lawton was general, with the exception of the surgeon, who rose from the bench during the first chorus, and paced the floor, in a flow of classical indignation. The bravos and bravissimos drowned all other noises for a short time: but as they gradually ceased, the doctor turned to the musician, and exclaimed with heat,—

"Captain Lawton, I marvel that a gentleman, and a gallant officer, can find no other subject for his muse, in these times of trial, than in such beastly invocations to that notorious follower of the camp, the filthy Elizabeth Flanagan. Methinks the goddess of Liberty could furnish a more noble inspiration, and the sufferings of your country a more befitting theme."

"Heyday!" shouted the hostess, advancing towards him in a threatening attitude; "and who is it that calls me filthy? Master Squirt! Master Popgun—"

"Peace!" said Dunwoodie, in a voice that was exerted but a

little more than common, but which was succeeded by the stillness of death. "Woman, leave the room. Dr. Sitgreaves, I call you to your seat, to wait the order of the revels."

"Proceed, proceed," said the surgeon, drawing himself up in an attitude of dignified composure. "I trust. Major Dunwoodie, I am not unacquainted with the rules of decorum, nor ignorant of the by-laws of good-fellowship." Betty made a hasty but somewhat devious retreat to her own dominions, being unaccustomed to dispute the orders of the commanding officer.

"Major Dunwoodie will honor us with a sentimental song," said Lawton, bowing to his leader, with the collected manner he so well knew how to assume.

The major hesitated a moment, and then sang, with fine execution, the following words:—

Some love the heats of southern suns,
Where's life's warm current maddening runs,
In one quick circling stream;
But dearer far's the mellow light
Which trembling shines, reflected bright
In Luna's milder beam.
Some love the tulip's gaudier dyes,
Where deepening blue with yellow vies,
And gorgeous beauty glows;
But happier he, whose bridal wreath,
By love entwined, is found to breathe
The sweetness of the rose.

The voice of Dunwoodie never lost its authority with his inferiors; and the applause which followed his song, though by no means so riotous as that which succeeded the effort of the captain, was much more flattering.

"If, sir," said die doctor, after joining in the plaudits of his companions, "you would but learn to unite classical allusions with your delicate imagination you would become a pretty amateur poet."

"He who criticizes ought to be able to perform," said Dunwoodie with a smile. "I call on Dr. Sitgreaves for a specimen of the style he admires."

"Dr. Sitgreaves' song! Dr. Sitgreaves' song!" echoed all at the table with delight; "a classical ode from Dr. Sitgreaves!"

The surgeon made a complacent bow, took the remnant of

his glass, and gave a few preliminary hems, that served hugely to delight three or four young comets at the foot of the table. He then commenced singing, in a cracked voice, and to anything but a tune, the following ditty:—

Hast thou ever felt love's dart, dearest,
Or breathed his trembling sigh—
Thought him, afar, was ever nearest,
Before that sparkling eye?
Then hast thou known what 'tis to feel
The pain that Galen could not heal.

"Hurrah!" shouted Lawton. "Archibald eclipses the Muses themselves;* his words flow like the sylvan stream by moonlight, and his melody is a crossbreed of the nightingale and the owl."

"Captain Lawton," cried the exasperated operator, "it is one thing to despise the lights of classical learning, and another to be despised for your own ignorance!"

A loud summons at the door of the building created a dead halt in the uproar, and the dragoons instinctively caught up their arms, to be prepared for the worst. The door was opened, and the Skinners entered, dragging in the peddler, bending beneath the load of his pack.

"Which is Captain Lawton?" said the leader of the gang, gazing around him in some little astonishment.

"He waits your pleasure," said the trooper dryly.

"Then here I deliver to your hands a condemned traitor. This is Harvey Birch, the peddler spy."

Lawton started as he looked his old acquaintance in the face, and, turning to the Skinner with a lowering look, he asked,—

"And who are you, sir, that speak so freely of your neighbors? But," bowing to Dunwoodie, "your pardon, sir; here is the commanding officer; to him you will please address yourself."

"No," said the man, sullenly, "it is to you I deliver the peddler, and from you I claim my reward."

"Are you Harvey Birch?" said Dunwoodie, advancing with an air of authority that instantly drove the Skinner to a corner of the room.

"I am," said Birch, proudly.

"And a traitor to your country," continued the major, with

sternness. "Do you know that I should be justified in ordering your execution this night?"

" 'Tis not the will of God to call a soul so hastily to His presence," said the peddler with solemnity.

"You speak truth," said Dunwoodie; "and a few brief hours shall be added to your life. But as your offense is most odious to a soldier, so it will be sure to meet with the soldier's vengeance. You die to-morrow."

" 'Tis as God wills."

"I have spent many a good hour to entrap the villain," said the Skinner, advancing a little from his corner, "and I hope you will give me a certificate that will entitle us to the reward; 'twas promised to be paid in gold."

"Major Dunwoodie," said the officer of the day, entering the room, "the patrols report a house to be burned near yesterday's battle ground."

" 'Twas the hut of the peddler," muttered the leader of the gang. "We have not left him a shingle for shelter; I should have burned it months ago, but I wanted his shed for a trap to catch the sly fox in."

"You seem a most ingenious patriot," said Lawton. "Major Dunwoodie, I second the request of this worthy gentleman, and crave the office of bestowing the reward on him and his fellows."

"Take it; and you, miserable man, prepare for that fate which will surely befall you before the setting of to-morrow's sun."

"Life offers but little to tempt me with," said Harvey, slowly raising his eyes, and gazing wildly at the strange faces in the apartment.

"Come, worthy children of America!" said Lawton, "follow, and receive your reward."

The gang eagerly accepted the invitation, and followed the captain towards the quarters assigned to his troop. Dunwoodie paused a moment, from reluctance to triumph over a fallen foe, before he proceeded.

"You have already been tried, Harvey Birch; and the truth has proved you to be an enemy too dangerous to the liberties of America to be suffered to live."

"The truth!" echoed the peddler, starting, and raising himself in a manner that disregarded the weight of his pack.

"Aye! the truth; you are charged with loitering near the continental army, to gain intelligence of its movements, and, by communicating them to the enemy, to enable him to frustrate the intentions of Washington."

"Will Washington say so, think you?"

"Doubtless he would; even the justice of Washington condemns you."

"No, no, no," cried the peddler, in a voice and with a manner that startled Dunwoodie. "Washington can see beyond the hollow views of pretended patriots. Has he not risked his all on the cast of a die? If a gallows is ready for me, was there not one for him also? No, no, no, no—Washington would never say, 'Lead him to a gallows.' "

"Have you anything, wretched man, to urge to the commander in chief why you should not die?" said the major, recovering from the surprise created by the manner of the other.

Birch trembled, for violent emotions were contending in his bosom. His face assumed the ghastly paleness of death, and his hand drew a box of tin from the folds of his shirt; he opened it, showing by the act that it contained a small piece of paper. On this document his eye was for an instant fixed—he had already held it towards Dunwoodie, when suddenly withdrawing his hand he exclaimed,—

"No—it dies with me. I know the conditions of my service, and will not purchase life with their forfeiture—it dies with me."

"Deliver that paper, and you may possibly find favor," cried Dunwoodie, expecting a discovery of importance to the cause.

"It dies with me," repeated Birch, a flush passing over his pallid features, and lighting them with extraordinary brilliancy.

"Seize the traitor!" cried the major, "and wrest the secret from his hands."

The order was immediately obeyed; but the movements of the peddler were too quick; in an instant he swallowed the paper. The officers paused in astonishment; but the surgeon cried eagerly,—

"Hold him, while I administer an emetic."

"Forbear!" cried Dunwoodie, beckoning him back with his hand. "If his crime is great, so will his punishment be heavy."

"Lead on," cried the peddler, dropping his pack from his shoulders, and advancing towards the door with a manner of incomprehensible dignity.

"Whither?" asked Dunwoodie, in amazement.

"To the gallows."

"No," said the major, recoiling in horror at his own justice. "My duty requires that I order you to be executed, but surely not so hastily; take until nine to-morrow to prepare for the awful change."

Dunwoodie whispered his orders in the ear of a subaltern, and motioned to the peddler to withdraw. The interruption caused by this scene prevented further enjoyment around the table, and the officers dispersed to their several places of rest. In a short time the only noise to be heard was the heavy tread of the sentinel, as he paced the frozen ground in front of the Hotel Flanagan.

CHAPTER XVII

There are, whose changing lineaments
Express each guileless passion of the breast;
Where Love, and Hope, and tender-hearted Pity
Are seen reflected, as from a mirror's face;
But cold experience can veil these hues
With looks, invented shrewdly to encompass
The cunning purposes of base deceit.

—Duo

The officer to whose keeping Dunwoodie had committed the peddler transferred his charge to the custody of the regular sergeant of the guard. The gift of Captain Wharton had not been lost on the youthful lieutenant; and a certain dancing motion that had taken possession of objects before his eyes, gave him warning of the necessity of recruiting nature by sleep. After admonishing the noncommissioned guardian of Harvey to omit no watchful-ness in securing the prisoner, the youth wrapped himself in his cloak, and, stretched on a bench before a fire, soon found the repose he needed. A rude shed extended the whole length of the rear of the building, and from off one of its ends had been partioned a small apartment, that was intended as a repository for many of the lesser implements of husbandry. The lawless times had, however, occasioned its being stripped of everything of value; and the searching eyes of Betty Flanagan selected this spot, on her arrival, as the storchouse for her movables and a sanctuary for her person. The spare arms and baggage of the corps had also been deposited here; and the united treasures were placed under the eye of the sentinel who paraded the shed as a guardian of the rear of the headquarters. A second soldier, who was stationed near the house to protect the horses of the officers, could command a view of the outside of the apartment; and, as it was without window or outlet of any kind, excepting its door, the considerate sergeant thought this the most befitting place in which to deposit his prisoner until the moment of his execution. Several inducements urged Sergeant Hollister to this determination, among which was the absence of the washerwoman, who lay before the kitchen fire, dreaming that the corps, was attacking a party of the enemy, and mistaking the noise that proceeded from her own nose for the bugles of the Virginians sounding the charge. Another was the peculiar opinions that the veteran entertained of life and death, and by which he was distinguished in the corps as a man of most exemplary piety and holiness of life. The sergeant was more than fifty years of age, and for half that period he had borne arms. The constant recurrence of sudden deaths before his eyes had produced an effect on him differing greatly from that which was the usual moral consequence of such scenes; and he had become not only the most steady, but the most trustworthy soldier in his troop. Captain Lawton had rewarded his fidelity by making him its orderly.

Followed by Birch, the sergeant proceeded in silence to the door of the intended prison, and, throwing it open with one hand, he held a lantern with the other to light the peddler to his prison. Seating himself on a cask, that contained some of Betty's favorite beverage, the sergeant motioned to Birch to occupy another, in the same manner. The lantern was placed on the floor, when the dragoon, after looking his prisoner steadily in the face, observed,—

"You look as if you would meet death like a man; and I have brought you to a spot where you can tranquilly arrange your thoughts, and be quiet and undisturbed."

" 'Tis a fearful place to prepare for the last change in," said Harvey, gazing around his little prison with a vacant eye.

"Why, for the matter of that," returned the veteran, "it can reckon but little in the great account, where a man parades his thoughts for the last review, so that he finds them fit to pass the muster of another world. I have a small book here, which I make it a point to read a little in, whenever we are about to engage, and I find it a great strengthener in time of need." While speaking, he took a Bible from his pocket, and offered it to the peddler. Birch received the volume with habitual reverence; but there was an abstracted air about him, and a wandering of the eye, that induced his companion to think that alarm was getting the mastery of the peddler's feelings; accordingly, he proceeded in what he conceived to be the offices of consolation.

"If anything lies heavy on your mind, now is the best time to get rid of it—if you have done any wrong to anyone, I promise you, on the word of an honest dragoon, to lend you a helping hand to see them righted."

"There are few who have not done so," said the peddler, turning his vacant gaze once more on his companion.

"True—'tis natural to sin; but it sometimes happens that a man does what at other times he may be sorry for. One would not wish to die with any very heavy sin on his conscience, after all."

Harvey had by this time thoroughly examined the place in which he was to pass the night, and saw no means of escape. But as hope is ever the last feeling to desert the human breast, the peddler gave the dragoon more of his attention, fixing on his sunburned features such searching looks, that Sergeant Hollister lowered his eyes before the wild expression which he met in the gaze of his prisoner.

"I have been taught to lay the burden of my sins at the feet of my Savior," replied the peddler.

"Why, yes—all that is well enough, " returned the other. "But justice should be done while there is opportunity. There have been stirring times in this country since the war began, and many have been deprived of their rightful goods. I oftentimes find it hard to reconcile even my lawful plunder to a tender conscience."

"These hands," said the peddler, stretching forth his meager, bony fingers, "have spent years in toil, but not one moment in pilfering."

"It is well that it is so," said the honest-hearted soldier, "and, no doubt, you now feel it a great consolation. There are three great sins, that, if a man can keep his conscience clear of, why, by the mercy of God, he may hope to pass muster with the saints in heaven: they are stealing, murdering, and desertion."

"Thank God!" said Birch, with fervor, "I have never yet taken the life of a fellow creature."

"As to killing a man in lawful battle, that is no more than doing one's duty. If the cause is wrong, the sin of such a deed, you know, falls on the nation, and a man receives his punishment here with the rest of the people; but murdering in cold blood stands next to desertion as a crime in the eye of God."

"I never was a soldier, therefore never could desert," said

the peddler, resting his face on his hand in a melancholy attitude.

"Why, desertion consists of more than quitting your colors, though that is certainly the worst kind; a man may desert his country in the hour of need."

Birch buried his face in both his hands, and his whole frame shook; the sergeant regarded him closely, but good feelings soon got the better of his antipathies, and he continued more mildly,—

"But still that is a sin which I think may be forgiven, if sincerely repented of; and it matters but little when or how a man dies, so that he dies like a Christian and a man. I recommend you to say your prayers, and then to get some rest, in order that you may do both. There is no hope of your being pardoned; for Colonel Singleton has sent down the most positive orders to take your life whenever we met you. No, no—nothing can save you."

"You say the truth," cried Birch. "It is now too late—I have destroyed my only safeguard. But he will do my memory justice at least."

"What safeguard?" asked the sergeant, with awakened curiosity.

'Tis nothing," replied the peddler, recovering his natural manner, and lowering his face to avoid the earnest looks of his companion.

"And who is he?"

"No one," added Harvey, anxious to say no more.

"Nothing and no one can avail but little now," said the sergeant, rising to go. "Lay yourself on the blanket of Mrs. Flanagan, and get a little sleep; I will call you betimes in the morning; and from the bottom of my soul I wish I could be of some service to you, for I dislike greatly to see a man hung up like a dog."

"Then you might save me from this ignominious death," said Birch, springing to his feet, and catching the dragoon by the arm. "And, oh! what will I not give you in reward!"

"In what manner?" asked the sergeant, looking at him in surprise.

"See," said the peddler, producing several guineas from his person; "these are nothing to what I will give you, if you will assist me to escape."

"Were you the man whose picture is on the gold, I would not listen to such a crime," said the trooper, throwing the money on the floor with contempt. "Go—go, poor wretch, and make your peace with God; for it is He only that can be of service to you now."

The sergeant took up the lantern, and, with some indignation in his manner, he left the peddler to sorrowful meditations on his approaching fate. Birch sank, in momentary despair, on the pallet of Betty, while his guardian proceeded to give the necessary instructions to the sentinels for his safe-keeping.

Hollister concluded his injuctions to the man in the shed, by saying, "Your life will depend on his not escaping. Let none enter or quit the room till morning."

"But," said the trooper, "my orders are, to let the washerwoman pass in and out, as she pleases."

"Well, let her then; but be careful that this wily peddler does not get out in the folds of her petticoats." He then continued his walk, giving similar orders to each of the sentinels near the spot.

For some time after the departure of the sergeant, silence prevailed within the solitary prison of the peddler, until the dragoon at his door heard his loud breathings, which soon rose into the regular cadence of one in a deep sleep. The man continued walking his post, musing on an indifference to life which could allow nature its customary rest, even on the threshold of the grave. Harvey Birch had, however, been a name too long held in detestation by every man in the corps, to suffer any feelings of commiseration to mingle with these reflections of the sentinel; for, notwithstanding the consideration and kindness manifested by the sergeant, there probably was not another man of his rank in the whole party who would have discovered equal benevolence to the prisoner, or who would not have imitated the veteran in rejecting the bribe, although probably from a less worthy motive. There was something of disappointed vengeance in the feelings of the man who watched the door of the room on finding his prisoner enjoying a sleep of which he himself was deprived, and at his exhibiting such obvious indifference to the utmost penalty that military rigor could inflict on all his treason to the cause of liberty and America. More than once he felt prompted to disturb the repose of the peddler by taunts and revilings; but the discipline he was under, and a secret sense of shame at the brutality of the act, held him in subjection.

His meditations were, however, soon interrupted by the appearance of the washerwoman, who came staggering through the door that communicated with the kitchen, muttering execrations against the servants of the officers, who, by their waggery, had disturbed her slumbers before the fire. The sentinel understood enough of her maledictions to comprehend the case; but all his efforts to enter into conversation with the enraged woman were useless, and he suffered her to enter her room without explaining that is contained another inmate. The noise of her huge frame falling on the bed was succeeded by a silence that was soon interrupted by the renewed respiration of the peddler, and within a few minutes Harvey continued to breathe aloud, as if no interruption had occurred. The relief arrived at this moment. The sentinel, who felt nettled at the contempt of the peddler, after communicating his orders, while he was retiring, exclaimed to his successor,—

"You may keep yourself warm by dancing, John; the peddler spy has turned his fiddle, you hear, and it will not be long before Betty will strike up, in her turn."

The joke was followed by a general laugh from the party, who marched on in performance of their duty. At this instant the door of the prison was opened, and Betty reappeared, staggering back again toward her former quarters.

"Stop," said the sentinel, catching her by her clothes; "are you sure the spy is not in your pocket?"

"Can't you hear the rascal snoring in my room, you dirty blackguard?" sputtered Betty, her whole frame shaking with rage. "And is it so ye would sarve a dacent female, that a man must be put to sleep in the room wid her, ye rapscallion?"

"Pooh! Do you mind a fellow who's to be hanged in the morning? You see he sleeps already; to-morrow he'll take a longer nap."

"Hands off, ye villain," cried the washerwoman, relinquishing a small bottle that the trooper had succeeded in wresting from her. "But I'll go to Captain Jack, and know if it's orders to put a hang-gallows spy in my room; aye, even in my widowed bed, you tief!"

"Silence, old Jezebel!" said the fellow with a laugh, taking the bottle from his mouth to breath, "or you will wake the gentleman. Would you disturb a man in his last sleep?"

"I'll awake Captain Jack, you reprobate villain, and bring him here to see me righted; he will punish ye all, for imposing on a dacent widowed body, you marauder!"

With these words, which only extorted a laugh from the sentinel Betty staggered round the end of the building, and made the best of her way towards the quarters of her favorite, Captain John Lawton, in search of redress. Neither the officer nor the woman, however, appeared during the night, and nothing further occurred to disturb the repose of the peddler, who, to the astonishment of the different sentinels, continued by his breathing to manifest how little the gallows could affect his slumbers.

CHAPTER XVIII

A Daniel come to judgment; yea, a Daniel!
0 wise young judge, how I do honor thee!
—Merchant of Venice.

The Skinners followed Captain Lawton with alacrity, towards the quarters occupied by the troop of that gentleman. The captain of dragoons had on all occasions manifested so much zeal for the cause in which he was engaged, was so regardless of personal danger when opposed to the enemy, and his stature and stem countenance contributed so much to render him terrific, that these qualities had, in some measure, procured him a reputation distinct from the corps in which he served. His intrepidity was mistaken for ferocity; and his hasty zeal, for the natural love of cruelty. On the other hand, a few acts of clemency, or, more properly speaking, of discriminating justice, had, with one portion of the community, acquired for Dunwoodie the character of undue forbearance. It is seldom that either popular condemnation or popular applause falls, exactly in the quantities earned, where it is merited.

While in the presence of the major the leader of the gang had felt himself under that restraint which vice must ever experience in the company of acknowledged virtue; but having left the house, he at once conceived that he was under the protection of a congenial spirit. There was a gravity in the manner of Lawton that deceived most of those who did not know him intimately; and it was a common saying in his troop, that "when the captain laughed, he was sure to punish." Drawing near his conductor, therefore, the leader commenced a confidential dialogue.

" 'Tis always well for a man to know his friends from his enemies," said the half-licensed freebooter.

To this prefatory observation the captain made no other reply than a sound which the other interpreted into assent.

"I suppose Major Dunwoodie has the good opinion of Washington?" continued the Skinner, in a tone that rather expressed a doubt than asked a question.

"There are some who think so."

"Many of the friends of Congress in this county," the man

proceeded, "wish the horse was led by some other officer. For my part, if I could only be covered by a troop now and then, I could do many an important piece of service to the cause, to which this capture of the peddler would be a trifle."

"Indeed! such as what?"

"For the matter of that, it could be made as profitable to the officer as it would be to us who did it," said the Skinner, with a look of the most significant meaning.

"But how?" asked Lawton, a little impatiently, and quickening his step to get out of the hearing of the rest of the party.

"Why, near the royal lines, even under the very guns of the heights, might be good picking if we had a force to guard us from De Lancey's[8] men, and to cover our retreat from being cut off by the way of King's Bridge."

"I thought the Refugees took all that game to themselves."

"They do a little at it; but they are obliged to be sparing among their own people. I have been down twice, under an agreement with them: the first time they acted with honor; but the second they came upon us and drove us off, and took the plunder to themselves."

"That was a very dishonorable act, indeed; I wonder that an honorable man will associate with such rascals."

"It is necessary to have an understanding with some of them, or we might be taken; but a man without honor is worse than a brute. Do you think Major Dunwoodie is to be trusted?"

"You mean on honorable principles?"

---

[8] The partisan corps called Cowboys in the parlance of the country, was commanded by Colonel De Lancey. This gentleman, for such he was by birth and education, rendered himself very odious to the Americans by his fancied cruelty, though there is no evidence of his being guilty of any acts unusual in this species of warfare.Colonel De Lancey belonged to a family of the highest consequence in the American colonies, his uncle having died in the administration of the government of that of New York. He should not be confounded with other gentlemen of his name and family, many of whom served in the royal army. His cousin, Colonel Oliver De Lancey, was, at the time of our tale, adjutant general of the British forces in America, having succeeded to the unfortunate Andre. The Cowboys were sometimes called Refugees, in consequence of their having taken refuge under the protection of the crown.

"Certainly; you know Arnold was thought well of until the royal major was taken."

"Why, I do not believe Dunwoodie would sell his command as Arnold wished to do; neither do I think him exactly trustworthy in a delicate business like this of yours."

"That's just my notion," rejoined the Skinner, with a self-approving manner that showed how much he was satisfied with his own estimate of character.

By this time they had arrived at a better sort of farm-house, the very extensive outbuildings of which were in tolerable repair, for the times. The barns were occupied by the men of the troop, while the horses were arranged under the long sheds which protected the yard from the cold north wind. The latter were quietly eating, with saddles on their backs and bridles thrown on their necks, ready to be bitted and mounted at the shortest warning. Lawton excused himself for a moment, and entered his quarters. He soon returned, holding in his hand one of the common, stable lanterns, and led the way towards a large orchard that surrounded the buildings on three sides. The gang followed the trooper in silence, believing his object to be facility of communicating further on this interesting topic, without the danger of being overheard.

Approaching the captain, the Skinner renewed the discourse, with a view of establishing further confidence, and of giving his companion a more favorable opinion of his own intellects.

"Do you think the colonies will finally get the better of the king?" he inquired, with a little of the importance of a politician.

"Get the better!" echoed the captain with impetuosity. Then checking himself, he continued, "No doubt they will. If the French will give us arms and money, we will drive out the royal troops in six months."

"Well, so I hope we shall soon; and then we shall have a free government, and we, who fight for it, will get our reward."

"Oh!" cried Lawton, "your claims will be indisputable; while all these vile Tories who live at home peaceably, to take care of their farms, will be held in the contempt they merit. You have no farm, I suppose?"

"Not yet—but it will go hard if I do not find one before the peace is made."

"Right; study your own interests, and you study the interests of your country; press the point of your own services, and rail at the Tories, and I'll bet my spurs against a rusty nail that you get to be a county clerk at least."

"Don't you think Paulding's[9] party were fools in not letting the royal adjutant general escape?" said the man, thrown off his guard by the freedom of the captain's manner.

"Fools!" cried Lawton, with a bitter laugh. "Aye, fools indeed; King George would have paid them better, for he is richer. He would have made them gentlemen for their losses. But, thank God! there is a pervading spirit in the people that seems miraculous. Men who have nothing, act as if the wealth of the Indies depended on their fidelity; all are not villains like yourself, or we should have been slaves to England years ago."

"How!" exclaimed the Skinner, starting back, and dropping his musket to the level of the other's breast; " am I betrayed, and are you my enemy?"

"Miscreant!" shouted Lawton, his saber ringing in its steel scabbard, as he struck the musket of the fellow from his hands, "offer but again to point your gun at me, and I'll cleave you to the .middle."

"And you will not pay us, then, Captain Lawton?" said the Skinner, trembling in every joint, for just then he saw a party of mounted dragoons silently encircling the whole party.

"Oh! pay you—yes, you shall have the full measure of your reward. There is the money that Colonel Singleton sent down for the captors of the spy," throwing a bag of guineas with disdain at the other's feet. "But ground your arms, you rascals, and see that the money is truly gold."

The intimidated band did as they were ordered; and while they were eagerly employed in this pleasing avocation, a few of Lawton's men privately knocked the flints out of their muskets.

"Well," cried the impatient captain, "is it right? Have you the promised reward?"

---

[9] The author must have intended some allusion to an individual, which is too local to be understood by the general reader.Andre, as is well known, was arrested by three countrymen, who were on the lock-out for predatory parties of the enemy; the principal man of this party was named Paulding. The disinterested manner in which they refused the offers of their captive is matter of history.

"There is just the money," said the leader; "and we will now go to our homes, with your permission."

"Hold! so much to redeem our promise—now for justice; we pay you for taking a spy, but we punish you for burning, robbing, and murdering. Seize them, my lads, and give each of them the law of Moses—forty save one."

This command was given to no unwilling listeners; and in the twinkling of an eye the Skinners were stripped and fastened, by the halters of the party, to as many of the apple trees as were necessary to furnish one to each of the gang. Swords were quickly drawn, and fifty branches were cut from the trees, like magic; from these were selected a few of the most supple of the twigs, and a willing dragoon was soon found to wield each of the weapons. Captain Lawton gave the word, humanely cautioning his men not to exceed the discipline prescribed by the Mosaic law, and the uproar of Babel commenced in the orchard. The cries of the leader were easily to be distinguished above those of his men; a circumstance which might be accounted for, by Captain Lawton's reminding his corrector that he had to deal with an officer, and he should remember and pay him unusual honor. The flagellation was executed with great neatness and dispatch, and it was distinguished by no irregularity, excepting that none of the disciplinarians began to count until they had tried their whips by a dozen or more blows, by the way, as they said themselves of finding out the proper places to strike. As soon as this summary operation was satisfactorily completed, Lawton directed his men to leave the Skinners to replace their own clothes and to mount their horses; for they were a party who had been detached for the purpose of patrolling lower down in the county.

"You see, my friend," said the captain to the leader of the Skinners after he had prepared himself to depart, "I can cover you to some purpose, when necessary. If we meet often, you will be covered with scars, which, if not very honorable, will at least be merited."

The fellow made no reply. He was busy with his musket, and hastening his comrades to march; when, everything being ready, they proceeded sullenly towards some rocks at no great distance, which were overhung by a deep wood. The moon was just rising, and the group of dragoons could easily be distinguished where they had been left. Suddenly turning, the whole gang leveled their pieces and drew the triggers. The action was noticed, and the snapping of the locks was heard by the soldiers, who returned their futile attempt with a laugh of derision, the captain crying aloud,—

"Ah! rascals, I knew you, and have taken away your flints."

"You should have taken away that in my pouch, too," shouted the leader, firing his gun in the next instant. The bullet grazed the ear of Lawton, who laughed as he shook his head, saying, "A miss was as good as a mile." One of the dragoons had seen the preparations of the Skinner—who had been left alone by the rest of his gang, as soon as they had made their abortive attempt at revenge—and was in the act of plunging his spurs into his horse as the fellow fired. The distance to the rocks was but small, yet the speed of the horse compelled the leader to abandon both money and musket, to effect his escape. The soldier returned with his prizes, and offered them to the acceptance of his captain; but Lawton rejected them, telling the man to retain them himself, until the rascal appeared in person to claim his property. It would have been a business of no small difficulty for any tribunal then existing in the new states to have enforced a restitution of the money; for it was shortly after most equitably distributed, by the hands of Sergeant Hollister, among a troop of horse. The patrol departed, and the captain slowly returned to his quarters, with an intention of retiring to rest. A figure moving rapidly among the trees, in the direction of the wood whither the Skinners had retired, caught his eye, and, wheeling on his heel, the cautious partisan approached it, and, to his astonishment, saw the washerwoman at that hour of the night, and in such a place.

"What, Betty! Walking in your sleep, or dreaming while awake?" cried the trooper. "Are you not afraid of meeting with the ghost of ancient Jenny in this her favorite pasture?"

"Ah, sure, Captain Jack," returned the sutler in her native accent, and reeling in a manner that made it difficult for her to raise her head, "it's not Jenny, or her ghost, that I'm saaking, but some yarbs for the wounded. And it's the vartue of the rising moon, as it jist touches them, that I want. They grow under yon rocks, and I must hasten, or the charm will lose its power."

"Fool, you are fitter for your pallet than for wandering among those rocks; a fall from one of them would break your bones; besides, the Skinners have fled to those heights, and should you fall in with them, they would revenge on you a sound flogging they have just received from me. Better return, old woman, and finish your nap; we march in the morning."

Betty disregarded his advice, and continued her devious route to the hillside. For an instant, as Lawton mentioned the Skinners, she had paused, but immediately resuming her course, she was soon out of sight, among the trees.

As the captain entered his quarters, the sentinel at the door inquired if he had met Mrs. Flanagan, and added that she had passed there, filling the air with threats against her tormentors at the "Hotel," and inquiring for the captain in search of redress. Lawton heard the man in astonishment—appeared struck with a new idea—walked several yards towards the orchard, and returned again; for several minutes he paced rapidly to and fro before the door of the house, and then hastily entering it, he threw himself on a bed in his clothes, and was soon in a profound sleep.

In the meantime, the gang of marauders had successfully gained the summit of the rocks, and, scattering in every direction, they buried themselves in the depths of the wood. Finding, however, there was no pursuit, which indeed would have been impracticable for horse, the leader ventured to call his band together with a whistle, and in a short time he succeeded in collecting his discomfited party, at a point where they had but little to apprehend from any enemy.

"Well," said one of the fellows, while a fire was lighting to protect them against the air, which was becoming severely cold, "there is an end to our business in Westchester. The Virginia horse will make the county too hot to hold us."

"I'll have his blood," muttered the leader, "if I die for it the next instant."

"Oh, you are very valiant here, in the wood," cried the other, with a savage laugh. "Why did you, who boast so much of your aim, miss your man, at thirty yards?"

" 'Twas the horseman that disturbed me, or I would have ended this Captain Lawton on the spot; besides, the cold had set me a-shivering, and I had no longer a steady hand."

"Say it was fear, and you will tell no lie," said his comrade with a sneer. "For my part, I think I shall never be cold again; my back bums as if a thousand gridirons were laid on it."

"And you would tamely submit to such usage, and kiss the rod that beat you?"

"As for kissing the rod, it would be no easy matter. Mine was broken into so small pieces, on my own shoulders, that it would be difficult to find one big enough to kiss; but I would rather submit to lose half my skin, than to lose the whole of it, with my ears in the bargain. And such will be our fates, if we tempt this mad Virginian again. God willing, I would at any time give him enough of my hide to make a pair of jack boots, to get out his hands with the remainder. If you had known when you were well off, you would have stuck to Major Dunwoodie, who don't know half so much of our evil doings."

"Silence, you talking fool!" shouted the enraged leader; "your prating is sufficient to drive a man mad. Is it not enough to be robbed and beaten, but we must be tormented with your folly? Help to get out the provisions, if any is left in the wallet, and try and stop your mouth with food."

This injunction was obeyed, and the whole party, amidst sundry groans and contortions, excited by the disordered state of their backs, made their arrangements for a scanty meal. A large fire of dry wood was burning in the cleft of a rock, and at length they began to recover from the confusion of their flight, and to collect their scattered senses. Their hunger being appeased, and many of their garments thrown aside for the better opportunity of dressing their wounds, the gang began to plot measures of revenge. An hour was spent in this manner, and various expedients were proposed; but as they all depended on personal prowess for their success, and were attended by great danger, they were of course rejected. There was no possibility of approaching the troops by surprise, their vigilance being ever on the watch; and the hope of meeting Captain Lawton away from his men, was equally forlorn, for the trooper was constantly engaged in his duty, and his movements were so rapid, that any opportunity of meeting with him, at all, must depend greatly on accident. Besides, it was by no means certain that such an interview would result happily for themselves. The cunning of the trooper was notorious; and rough and broken as was Westchester, the fearless partisan was known to take desperate leaps, and stone walls were but slight impediments to the charges of the Southern horse. Gradually, the conversation took another direction, until the gang determined on a plan which should both revenge themselves, and at the same time offer some additional stimulus to their exertions. The whole business was accurately discussed, the time fixed, and the manner adopted; in short, nothing was wanting to the previous arrangement for this deed of villainy, when they were aroused by a voice calling aloud,—

"This way, Captain Jack—here are the rascals 'ating by a fire—this way, and murder the t'ieves where they sit—quick, l'ave your horses and shoot your pistols!"

This terrific summons was enough to disturb all the philosophy of the gang. Springing on their feet, they rushed deeper into the wood, and having already agreed upon a place of rendezvous previously to their intended expedition, they dispersed towards the four quarters of the heavens. Certain sounds and different voices were heard calling on each other, but as the marauders were well trained to speed of foot, they were soon lost in the distance.

It was not long before Betty Flanagan emerged from the darkness, and very coolly took possession of what the Skinners had left behind them; namely, food and divers articles of dress. The washerwoman deliberately seated herself, and made a meal with great apparent satisfaction. For an hour, she sat with her head upon her hand, in deep musing; then she gathered together such articles of the clothes, as seemed to suit her fancy, and retired into the wood, leaving the fire to throw its glimmering light on the adjacent rocks, until its last brand died away, and the place was abandoned to solitude and darkness.

CHAPTER XIX

No longer then perplex the breast—
When thoughts torment, the first are best;
'Tis mad to go, 'tis death to stay!
Away, to Orra, haste away.

— Lapland Love Song.

While his comrades were sleeping, in perfect forgetfulness of their hardships and dangers, the slumbers of Dunwoodie were broken and unquiet. After spending a night of restlessness, he arose, unrefreshed, from the rude bed where he had thrown himself in his clothes, and, without awaking any of the group around him, he wandered into the open air in search of relief. The soft rays of the moon were just passing away in the more distinct light of the morning; the wind had fallen, and the rising mists gave the promise of another of those autumnal days, which, in this unstable climate, succeed a tempest with the rapid transitions of magic. The hour had not yet arrived when he intended moving from his present position; and, willing to allow his warriors all the refreshment that circumstances would permit, he stralled towards the scene of the Skinners' punishment, musing upon the embarrassments of his situation, and uncertain how he should reconcile his sense of duty with his love. Although Dunwoodie himself placed the most implicit reliance on the captain's purity of intention, he was by no means assured that a board of officers would be equally credulous; and, independently of all feelings of private regard, he felt certain that with the execution of Henry would be destroyed all hopes of a union with his sister. He had dispatched an officer, the preceding evening, to Colonel Singleton, who was in command of the advance posts, reporting the capture of the British captain, and, after giving his own opinion of his innocence, requesting orders as to the manner in which he was to dispose of his prisoner. These orders might be expected every hour, and his uneasiness increased, in proportion as the moment approached when his friend might be removed from his protection. In this disturbed state of mind, the major wandered through the orchard, and was stopped in his walk by arriving at the base of those rocks which had protected the Skinners in their flight, before he was conscious whither his steps had carried him. He was about to turn and retrace his path to his quarters, when he was startled by a voice, bidding him,—

"Stand or die!"

Dunwoodie turned in amazement, and beheld the figure of a man placed at a distance above him on a shelving rock, with a musket leveled at himself. The light was not yet sufficiently powerful to reach the recesses of that gloomy spot, and a second look was necessary before he discovered, to his astonishment, that the peddler stood before him. Comprehending, in an instant, the danger of his situation, and disdaining to implore mercy or to retreat, had the latter been possible, the youth cried firmly,—

"If I am to be murdered, fire! I will never become your prisoner."

"No, Major Dunwoodie," said Birch, lowering his musket, "it is neither my intention to capture nor to slay."

"What then would you have, mysterious being?" said Dunwoodie, hardly able to persuade himself that the form he saw was not a creature of the imagination.

"Your good opinion," answered the peddler, with emotion. "I would wish all good men to judge me with lenity."

"To you it must be indifferent what may be the judgment of men; for you seem to be beyond the reach of their sentence."

"God spares the lives of His servants to His own time," said the peddler, solemnly. "A few hours ago I was your prisoner, and threatened with the gallows; now you are mine; but, Major Dunwoodie, you are free. There are men abroad who would treat you less kindly. Of what service would that sword be to you against my weapon and a steady hand? Take the advice of one who has never harmed you, and who never will. Do not trust yourself in the skirts of any wood, unless in company and mounted."

"And have you comrades, who have assisted you to escape, and who are less generous than yourself?"

"No—no, I am alone truly—none know me but my God and *him*."

"And who?" asked the major, with an interest he could not control.

"None," continued the peddler, recovering his composure.

"But such is not your case, Major Dunwoodie; you are young and happy; there are those that are dear to you, and such are not far away—danger is near them you love most—danger within and without—double your watchfulness—strengthen your patrols—and be silent. With your opinion of me, should I tell you more, you would suspect an ambush. But remember and guard them you love best."

The peddler discharged the musket in the air, and threw it at the feet of his astonished auditor. When surprise and the smoke allowed Dunwoodie to look again on the rock where he had stood, the spot was vacant.

The youth was aroused from the stupor, which had been created by this strange scene, by the trampling of horses, and the sound of the bugles. A patrol was drawn to the spot by the report of the musket, and the alarm had been given to the corps. Without entering into any explanation with his men, the major returned quickly to his quarters, where he found the whole squadron under arms, in battle array, impatiently awaiting the appearance of their leader. The officer whose duty it was to superintend such matters, had directed a party to lower the sign of the Hotel Flanagan, and the post was already arranged for the execution of the spy. On hearing from the major that the musket was discharged by himself, and was probably one of those dropped by the Skinners (for by this time Dunwoodie had learned the punishment inflicted by Lawton, but chose to conceal his own interview with Birch), his officers suggested the propriety of executing their prisoner before they marched. Unable to believe that all he had seen was not a dream, Dunwoodie, followed by many of his officers, and preceded by Sergeant Hollister, went to the place which was supposed to contain the peddler.

"Well, sir," said the major to the sentinel who guarded the door. "I trust you have your prisoner in safety."

"He is yet asleep," replied the man, "and he makes such a noise, I could hardly hear the bugles sound the alarm."

"Open the door and bring him forth."

The order was obeyed; but to the utter amazement of the honest veteran who entered the prison, he found the room in no little disorder—the coat of the peddler where his body ought to have been, and part of the wardrobe of Betty scattered in disorder on. the floor. The washerwoman herself occupied the pallet, in profound mental oblivion, clad as when last seen, excepting a little black bonnet, which she so constantly wore, that it was commonly thought she made it perform the double duty of both day and night cap. The noise of their entrance, and the exclamations of their party, awoke the woman.

"Is it the breakfast that's wanting?" said Betty, rubbing her eyes. "Faith, ye look as if ye would ate myself—but patience, a little, darlings, and ye'll see sich a fry as never was."

"Fry!" echoed the sergeant, forgetful of his religious philosophy, and the presence of his officers. "We'll have you roasted, Jezebel!—you've helped that damned peddler to escape."

"Jezebel back ag'in in your own teeth, and damned piddler too, Mr. Sergeant!" cried Betty, who was easily roused. "What have I to do with piddlers, or escapes? I might have been a piddler's lady, and wore my silks, if I'd had Sawny M'Twill, instead of tagging at the heels of a parcel of dragooning rapscallions, who don't know how to trate a lone body with dacency."

"The fellow has left my Bible," said the veteran, taking the book from the floor. "Instead of spending his time in reading it to prepare for his end like a good Christian, he has been busy in laboring to escape."

"And who would stay and be hanged like a dog?" cried Betty, beginning to comprehend the case. " 'Tisn't everyone that's born to meet with sich an ind—like yourself, Mr. Hollister."

"Silence!" said Dunwoodie. "This must be inquired into closely, gentlemen; there is no outlet but the door, and there he could not pass, unless the sentinel connived at his escape, or was asleep at his post. Call up the guard."

As these men were not paraded, curiosity had already drawn them to the place, and they one and all, with the exception of him before mentioned, denied that any person had passed out. The individual in question acknowledged that Betty had gone by him, but pleaded his orders in justification.

"You lie, you fief—you lie!" shouted Betty, who had impatiently listened to his exculpation. "Would ye slanderize a lone woman, by saying she walks a camp at midnight? Here have I been slaping the long night, swaatly as the sucking babe."

"Here, sir," said the sergeant, turning respectfully to Dunwoodie, "is something written in my Bible that was not in it before; for having no family to record, I would not suffer any scribbling in the sacred book."

One of the officers read aloud: "These certify, that if suffered to get free, it is by God's help alone, to whose divine aid I humbly riccommind myself. I'm forced to take the woman's clothes, but in her pocket is a ricompinse. Witness my hand—Harvey Birch."

"What!" roared Betty, "has the fief robbed a lone woman of her all! Hang him—catch him and hang him, major; if there's law of justice in the land."

"Examine your pocket," said one of the youngsters, who was enjoying the scene, careless of the cosequences.

"Ah! faith," cried the washerwoman, producing a guinea, "but he is a jewel of a piddler! Long life and a brisk trade to him, say I; he is wilcome to the duds—and if he is ever hanged, many a bigger rogue will go free."

Dunwoodie turned to leave the apartment, and he saw Captain Lawton standing with folded arms, contemplating the scene with profound silence. His manner, so different -from his usual impetuosity and zeal, struck his commander as singular. Their eyes met, and they walked together for a few minutes in close conversation, when Dunwoodie returned, and dismissed the guard to their place of rendezvous. Sergeant Hollister, however, continued along with Betty, who, having found none of her vestments disturbed but such as the guinea more than paid for, was in high good humor. The washerwoman had for a long time looked on the veteran with the eyes of affection; and she had determined within herself to remove certain delicate objections which had long embarrassed her peculiar situation, as respected the corps, by making the sergeant the successor of her late husband. For some time past the trooper had seemed to flatter this preference; and Betty, conceiving that her violence might have mortified her suitor, was determined to make him all the amends in her power. Besides, rough and uncouth as she was, the washerwoman had still enough of her sex to know that the moments of reconciliation were the moments of power. She therefore poured out a glass of her morning beverage, and handed it to her companion as a peace offering.

"A few warm words between fri'nds are a trifle, ye must be knowing, sargeant," said the washerwoman. "It was Michael

Flanagan that I ever calumn'ated the most when I was loving him the best."

"Michael was a good soldier and a brave man," said the trooper, finishing the glass. "Our troop was covering the flank of his regiment when he fell, and I rode over his body myself during the day. Poor fellow! he lay on his back, and looked as composed as if he had died a natural death after a year's consumption."

"Oh! Michael was a great consumer, and be sartin; two such as us make dreadful inroads in the stock, sargeant. But ye're a sober, discrate man, Mister Hollister, and would be a helpmate indeed."

"Why, Mrs. Flanagan, I've tarriede to speak on a subject that lies heavy at my heart, and I will now open my mind, if you've leisure to listen."

"Is it listen?" cried the impatient woman; "and I'd listen to you, sargeant, if the officers never ate another mouthful. But take a second drop, dear; 'twil encourage you to spake freely."

"I am already bold enough in so good a cause," returned the veteran, rejecting her bounty. "Betty, do you think it was really the peddler spy that I placed in this room the last night?"

"And who should it be else, darling?"

"The evil one."

"What, the divil?"

"Aye, even Beelzebub, disguised as the peddler; and them fellows we thought to be Skinners were his imps."

"Well sure, sargeant dear, ye're but little out this time, anyway; for if the divil's imps go at large in the county Westchester, sure it is the Skinners, themselves."

"Mrs. Flanagan, I mean in their incarnate spirits; the evil one knew there was no one we would arrest sooner than the peddler Birch, and he took on his appearance to gain admission to your room."

"And what should the divil be wanting of me?" cried Betty, tartly. "And isn't there divils enough in the corps already, without one's coming from the bottomless pit to frighten a lone body?"

" 'Twas in mercy to you, Betty, that he was permitted to come. You see he vanished through the door in your form, which is a symbol of your fate, unless you mend your life. Oh! I noticed how he trembled when I gave him the good book. Would any Christian, think you, my dear Betty, write in a Bible in this way; unless it might be the matter of births and deaths, and such lawful chronicles?"

The washerwoman was pleased with the softness of her lover's manner, but dreadfully scandalized at his insinuation. She, however, preserved her temper, and with the quickness of her own country's people, rejoined, "And would the divil have paid for the clothes, think ye?—aye, and overpaid."

"Doubtless the money is base," said the sergeant, a little staggered at such an evidence of honesty in one of whom, as to generals, he thought so meanly. "He tempted me with his glittering coin, but the Lord gave me strength to resist."

"The goold looks well; but I'll change it, anyway, with Captain Jack, the day. He is niver a bit afeard of any divil of them all!"

"Betty, Betty," said her companion, "do riot speak so disreverently of the evil spirit; he is ever at hand, and will owe you a grudge, for your language."

"Pooh! if he has any bowels at all, he won't mind a fillip or two from a poor lone woman; I'm sure no other Christian would."

"But the dark one has no bowels, except to devour the children of men," said the sergeant, looking around him in horror; "and it's best to make friends everywhere, for there is no telling what may happen till it comes. But, Betty, no man could have got out of this place, and passed all the sentinels, without being known. Take awful warning from the visit therefore—"

Here thc dialogue was interrupted by a peremptory summons to the sutler to prepare the morning's repast, and they were obliged to separate; the woman secretly hoping that the interest the sergeant manifested was more earthly than he imagined; and the man, bent on saving a soul from the fangs of the dark spirit that was prowling through their camp in quest of victims.

During the breakfast several expresses arrived, one of which brought intelligence of the actual force and destination of the enemy's expedition that was out on the Hudson; and another, orders to send Captain Wharton to the first post above, under the escort of a body of dragoons. These last instructions, or rather commands, for they admitted of no departure from their letter, completed the sum of Dunwoodie's uneasiness. The despair and misery of Frances were constantly before his eyes, and fifty times he was tempted to throw himself on his horse and gallop to the Locusts; but an uncontrollable feeling prevented. In obedience to the commands of his superior, an officer, with a small party, was sent to the cottage to conduct Henry Wharton to the place directed; and the gentleman who was intrusted with the execution of the order was charged with a letter from Dunwoodie to his friend, containing the most cheering assurances of his safety, as well as the strongest pledges of his own unceasing exertions in his favor. Lawton was left with part of his own troop, in charge of the few wounded; and as soon as the men were refreshed, the encampment broke up, the main body marching towards the Hudson. Dunwoodie repeated his injunctions to Captain Lawton again and again—dwelt on every word that had fallen from the peddler, and canvassed, in every possible manner that his ingenuity could devise, the probable meaning of his mysterious warnings, until no excuse remained for delaying his own departure. Suddenly recollecting, however, that no directions had been given for the disposal of Colonel Wellmere, instead of following the rear of the column, the major yielded to his desires, and turned down the road which led to the Locusts. The horse of Dunwoodie was fleet as the wind, and scarcely a minute seemed to have passed before he gained sight, from an eminence, of the lonely vale, and as he was plunging into the bottom lands that formed its surface, he caught a glimpse of Henry Wharton and his escort, at a distance, defiling through a pass which led to the posts above. This sight added to the speed of the anxious youth, who now turned the angle of the hill that opened to the valley, and came suddenly on the object of his search. Frances had followed the party which .guarded her brother, at a distance; and as they vanished from her sight, she felt deserted by all that she most prized in this world. The unaccountable absence of Dunwoodie, with the shock of parting from Henry under such circumstances, had entirely subdued her fortitude, and she had sunk on a stone by the roadside, sobbing as if her heart would break. Dunwoodie sprang from his charger, threw the reins over the neck of the animal, and in a moment he was by the side of the weeping girl.

"Frances—my own Frances!" he exclaimed, "why this distress? Let not the situation of your brother create any alarm. As soon as the duty I am now on is completed, I will hasten to the feet of Washington, and beg his release. The Father of his Country will never deny such a boon to one of his favorite pupils."

"Major Dunwoodie, for your interest in behalf of my poor brother, I thank you," said the trembling girl, drying her eyes, and rising with dignity; "but such language addressed to me, surely, is improper."

"Improper! are you not mine—by the consent of your father—your aunt—your brother—nay, by your own consent, my sweet Frances?"

"I wish not, Major Dunwoodie, to interfere with the prior claims that any other lady may have to your affections," said Frances, struggling to speak with firmness.

"None other, I swear by Heaven, none other has any claim on me!" cried Dunwoodie, with fervor. "You alone are mistress of my inmost soul."

"You have practiced so much, and so successfully, Major Dunwoodie, that it is no wonder you excel in deceiving the credulity of my sex," returned Frances, attempting a smile, which the tremulousness of her muscles smothered at birth.

"Am I a villain, Miss Wharton, that you receive me with such language? When have I ever deceived you, Frances? Who has practiced in this manner on your purity of heart?"

"Why has not Major Dunwoodie honored the dwelling of his intended father with his presence lately? Did he forget it contained one friend on a bed of sickness, and another in deep distress? Has it escaped his memory that it held his intended wife? Or is he fearful of meeting more than one that can lay a claim to that title? Oh, Peyton—Peyton, how have I been deceived in you! With the foolish credulity of my youth, I thought you all that was brave, noble, generous, and loyal."

"Frances, I see how you have deceived yourself," cried Dunwoodie, his face in a glow of fire. "You do me injustice; I swear by all that is most dear to me that you do me injustice."

"Swear not, Major Dunwoodie," interrupted Frances, her fine countenance lighting with the luster of womanly pride. "The time is gone by for me to credit oaths."

"Miss Wharton, would you have me a coxcomb—make me

contemptible in my own eyes, by boasting with the hope of raising myself in your estimation?"

"Flatter not yourself that the task is so easy, sir," returned Frances, moving towards the cottage. "We converse together in private for the last time; but—possibly—my father would welcome my mother's kinsman."

"No, Miss Wharton, I cannot enter his dwelling now; I should act in a manner unworthy of myself. You drive me from you, Frances, in despair. I am going on desperate service, and may not live to return. Should fortune prove severe, at least do my memory justice; remember that the last breathings of my soul will be for your happiness." So saying, he had already placed his foot in the stirrup, but his youthful mistress, turning on him an eye that pierced his soul, arrested the action.

"Peyton—Major Dunwoodie," she said, "can you ever forget the sacred cause in which you are enlisted? Duty both to your God and to your country forbids your doing anything rashly. The latter has need of your services; besides"—but her voice became choked, and she was unable to proceed.

"Besides what?" echoed the youth, springing to her side, and offering to take her hand in his own. Frances having, however, recovered herself, coldly repulsed him, and continued her walk homeward.

"Is this our parting!" cried Dunwoodie, in agony. "Am I a wretch, that you treat me so cruelly? You have never loved me, and wish to conceal your own fickleness by accusations that you will not explain."

Frances stopped short in her walk, and turned on him a look of so much purity and feeling, that, heart-stricken, Dunwoodie would have knelt at her feet for pardon; but motioning him for silence, she once more spoke:—

"Hear me, Major Dunwoodie, for the last time: it is a bitter knowledge when we first discover our own inferiority; but it is a truth that '1 have lately learned. Against you I bring no charges—make no accusations; no, not willingly in my thoughts. Were my claims to your heart just, I am not worthy of you. It is not a feeble, timid girl, like me, that could make you happy. No, Peyton, you are formed for great and glorious actions, deeds of daring and renown, and should be united to a soul like your own; one that can rise above the weakness of her sex. I should be a weight to drag you to the dust; but with a different spirit in your companion, you might soar to the very pinnacle of earthly glory. To such a one, therefore, I resign you freely, if not cheerfully; and pray, oh, how fervently do I pray! that with such a one you may be happy."

"Lovely enthusiast!" cried Dunwoodie, "you know not yourself, nor me. It is a woman, mild, gentle, and dependent as yourself, that my very nature loves; deceive not yourself with visionary ideas of generosity, which will only make me miserable."

"Farewell, Major Dunwoodie," said the agitated girl, pausing for a moment to gasp for breath; "forget that you ever knew me—remember the claims of your bleeding country; and be happy."

"Happy!" repeated the youthful soldier, bitterly, as he saw her light form gliding through the gate of the lawn, and disappearing behind its shrubbery. "Yes, I am happy, indeed!"

Throwing himself into the saddle, he plunged his spurs into his horse, and soon overtook his squadron, which was marching slowly over the hilly roads of the county, to gain the banks of the Hudson.

But painful as were the feelings of Dunwoodie at this unexpected termination of the interview with his mistress, they were but light compared with those which were experienced by the fond girl herself. Frances had, with the keen eye of jealous love, easily detected the attachment of Isabella Singleton to Dunwoodie. Delicate and retiring herself, it never could present itself to her mind that this love had been unsought. Ardent in her own affections, and artless in their exhibition, she had early caught the eye of the young soldier; but it required all the manly frankness of Dunwoodie to court her favor, and the most pointed devotion to obtain his conquest. This done, his power was durable, entire, and engrossing. But the unusual occurrences of the few preceding days, the altered mien of her lover during those events, his unwonted indifference to herself, and chiefly the romantic idolatry of Isabella, had aroused new sensations in her bosom. With a dread of her lover's integrity had been awakened the never-failing concomitant of the purest affection, a distrust of her own merits. In the moment of enthusiasm, the task of resigning her lover to another, who might be more worthy of him, seemed easy; but it is in vain that the imagination attempts to deceive the heart. Dunwoodie had no sooner disappeared, than our heroine felt all the misery of her situation; and if the youth found some relief in the cares of his command, Frances was less fortunate in the performance of a duty imposed on her by filial piety. The removal of his son had nearly destroyed the little energy of Mr. Wharton, who required all the tenderness of his remaining children to convince him that he was able to perform the ordinary functions of life.

CHAPTER XX

Flatter and praise, commend, extol their graces,
Though ne'er so black, say they have angels' faces,
That man who hath a tongue I say is no man,
If with that tongue he cannot win a woman.
—Two Gentlemen of Verona.

In making the arrangements by which Captain Lawton had been left, with Sergeant Hollister and twelve men, as a guard over the wounded, and heavy baggage of the corps, Dunwoodie had consulted not only the information which had been conveyed in the letter of Colonel Singleton, but the bruises of his comrade's body. In vain Lawton declared himself fit for any duty that man could perform, or plainly intimated that his men would never follow Tom Mason to a charge with the alacrity and confidence with which they followed himself; his commander was firm, and the reluctant captain was compelled to comply with as good a grace a& he could assume. Before parting, Dunwoodie repeated his caution to keep a watchful eye on the inmates of the cottage; and especially enjoined him, if any movements of a particularly suspicious nature were seen in the neighborhood, to break up from his present quarters, and to move down with his party, and take possession of the domains of Mr. Wharton. A vague suspicion of danger to the family had been awakened in the breast of the major, by the language of the peddler, although he was unable to refer it to any particular source, or to understand why it was to be apprehended.

For some time after the departure of the troops, the captain was walking before the door of the "Hotel," inwardly cursing his fate, that condemned him to an inglorious idleness, at a moment when a meeting with the enemy might be expected, and replying to the occasional queries of Betty, who, from the interior of the building, ever and anon demanded, in a high tone of voice, an explanation of various passages in the peddler's escape, which as yet she could not comprehend. At this instant he was joined by the surgeon, who had hitherto been engaged among his patients in a distant building, and was profoundly ignorant of everything that had occurred, even to the departure of the troops.

"Where are all the sentinels, John?" he inquired, as he gazed around with a look of curiosity, "and why are you here alone?"

"Off—all off, with Dunwoodie, to the river. You and I are left to take care of a few sick men and some women."

"I am glad, however," said the surgeon, "that Major Dunwoodie had consideration enough not to move the wounded. Here, you Mrs. Elizabeth Flanagan, hasten with some food, that I may appease my appetite. I have a dead body to dissect and am in haste."

"And here, you Mister Doctor Archibald Sitgreaves," echoed Betty, showing her blooming countenance from a broken window of the kitchen, "you are ever a-coming too late; here is nothing to ate but the skin of Jenny, and the body ye're mentioning."

"Woman!" said the surgeon, in anger, "do you take me for a cannibal, that you address your filthy discourse to me, in this manner? I did you hasten with such food as may be proper to be received into the stomach fasting."

"And I'm sure it's for a popgun that I should be taking you sooner than for a cannon ball," said Betty, winking at the captain; "and I tell ye that it's fasting you must be, unless ye'll let me cook ye a steak from the skin of Jenny. The boys have ate me up intirely."

Lawton now interfered to preserve the peace, and assured the surgeon that he had already dispatched the proper persons in quest of food for the party. A little mollified with this explanation, the operator soon forgot his hunger, and declared his intention of proceeding to business at once.

"And where is your subject?" asked Lawton.

"The peddler," said the other, glancing a look at the signpost. "I made Hollister put a stage so high that the neck would not be dislocated by the fall, and I intend making as handsome a skeleton of him as there is in the states of North America; the fellow has good points, and his bones are well knit. I will make a perfect beauty of him. I have long been wanting something of this sort to send as a present to my old aunt in Virginia, who was so kind to me when a boy."

"The devil!" cried Lawton. "Would you send the old woman a dead man's bones?"

"Why not?" said the surgeon. "What nobler object is there in nature than the figure of a man—and the skeleton may be called his elementary parts. But what has been done with the body?"

"Off too."

"Off! And who has dared to interfere with my perquisites?"

"Sure, jist the divil," said Betty; "and who'll be taking yeerself away some of these times too, without asking yeer lave."

"Silence, you witch!" said Lawton, with difficulty suppressing a laugh. "Is this the manner in which to address an officer?"

"Who called me the filthy Elizabeth Flanagan?" cried the washerwoman, snapping her fingers contemptuously. "I can remimber a frind for a year and don't forgit an inimy for a month."

But the friendship or enmity of Mrs. Flanagan was alike indifferent to the surgeon, who could think of nothing but his loss; and Lawton was obliged to explain to his friend the apparent manner in which it had happened.

"And a lucky escape it was for ye, my jewel of a doctor," cried Betty, as the captain concluded. "Sargeant Hollister, who saw him face to face, as it might be, says it's Beelzeboob, and no piddler, unless it may be in a small matter of lies and thefts, and sich wickedness. Now a pretty figure ye would have been in cutting up Beelzeboob, if the major had hanged him. I don't think it's very 'asy he would have been under yeer knife."

Thus doubly disappointed in his meal and his business, Sitgreaves suddenly declared his intention of visiting the Locusts, and inquiring into the state of Captain Singleton. Lawton was ready for the excursion; and mounting, they were soon on the road, though the surgeon was obliged to submit to a few more jokes from the washerwoman, before he could get out of hearing. For some time the two rode in silence, when Lawton perceiving that his companion's temper was somewhat ruffled by his disappointments and Betty's attack, made an effort to restore the tranquillity of his feelings.

"That was a charming song, Archibald, that you commenced last evening, when we were interrupted by the party that brought in the peddler," he said. "The allusion to Galen was much to the purpose."

"I knew you would like it. Jack, when you had got the fumes of the wine out of your head. Poetry is a respectable art, though it wants the precision of the exact sciences, and the natural beneficence of the physical. Considered in reference to the wants of life, I should define poetry as an emollient, rather than as a succulent."

"And yet your ode was full of the meat of wit."

"Ode is by no means a proper term for the composition; I should term it a classical ballad."

"Very probably," said the trooper. "Hearing only one verse, it was difficult to class the composition."

The surgeon involuntarily hemmed, and began to clear his throat, although scarcely conscious himself to what the preparation tended. But the captain, rolling his dark eyes towards his companion, and observing him to be sitting with great uneasiness on his horse, continued,—

"The air is still, and the road solitary—why not give the remainder? It is never too late to repair a loss."

"My dear John, if I thought it would correct the errors you have imbibed, from habit and indulgence, nothing could give me more pleasure."

"We are fast approaching some rocks on our left; the echo will double my satisfaction."

Thus encouraged, and somewhat impelled by the opinion that he both sang and wrote with taste, the surgeon set about complying with the request in sober earnest. Some little time was lost in clearing his throat, and getting the proper pitch of his voice; but no sooner were these two points achieved, than Lawton had the secret delight of hearing his friend commence—

'Hast thou ever' "—

"Hush!" interrupted the trooper. "What rustling noise is that among the rocks?"

"It must have been the rushing of the melody. A powerful voice is like the breathing of the winds.

" 'Hast thou ever' "—

"Listen!" said Lawton, stopping his horse. He had not done speaking, when a stone fell at his feet, and rolled harmlessly across the path.

"A friendly shot, that," cried the trooper. "Neither the weapon, nor its force, implies much ill will."

"Blows from stones seldom produce more than contusions," said the operator, bending his gaze in every direction in vain, in quest of the hand from which the missile had been hurled. "It must be meteoric; there is no living being in sight, except ourselves."

"It would be easy to hide a regiment behind those rocks," returned the trooper, dismounting, and taking the stone in his hand. "Oh! here is the explanation along with the mystery." So saying, he tore a piece of paper that had been ingeniously fastened to the small fragment of rock which had thus singularly fallen before him; and opening it, the captain read the following words, written in no very legible hand: "A musket bullet will go farther than a stone, and things more dangerous that yarbs for wounded men lie hid in the rocks of Westchester. The horse may be good, but can he mount a precipice?"

"Thou sayest the truth, strange man," said Lawton. "Courage and activity would avail but little against assassination and these rugged passes." Remounting his horse, he cried aloud, "Thanks, unknown friend; your caution will be remembered."

A meager hand was extended for an instant over a rock in the air, and afterwards nothing further was seen, or heard, in that quarter, by the soldiers.

"Quite an extraordinary interruption," said the astonished Sitgreaves, "and a letter of very mysterious meaning."

"Oh! 'tis nothing but the wit of some bumpkin, who thinks to frighten two of the Virginians by an artifice of this kind?" said the trooper, placing the billet in his pocket. "But let me tell you, Mr. Archibald Sitgreaves, you were wanting to dissect, just now, a damned honest fellow."

"It was the peddler—one of the most notorious spies in the enemy's service; and I must say that I think it would be an honor to such a man to be devoted to the uses of science."

"He may be a spy—he must be one," said Lawton, musing; "but he has a heart above enmity, and a soul that would honor a soldier."

The surgeon turned a vacant eye on his companion as he uttered this soliloquy, while the penetrating looks of the trooper had already discovered another pile of rocks, which, jutting forward, nearly obstructed the highway that wound directly around its base.

"What the steed cannot mount, the foot of man can overcome," exclaimed the wary partisan. Throwing himself again from his saddle, and leaping a wall of stone, he began to ascend the hill at a pace which would soon have given him a bird's-eye view of the rocks in question, together with all their crevices. This movement was no sooner made, than Lawton caught a glimpse of the figure of a man stealing rapidly from his approach, and disappearing on the opposite side of the precipice.

"Spur, Sitgreaves—spur," shouted the trooper, dashing over every impediment in pursuit, "and murder the villain as he flies."

The former part of the request was promptly complied with, and a few moments brought the surgeon in full view a man armed with a musket, who was crossing the road, and evidently seeking the protection of the thick wood on its opposite side.

"Stop, my friend—stop until Captain Lawton comes up, if you please," cried the surgeon, observing him to flee with a rapidity that baffled his horsemanship. But as if the invitation contained new terrors, the footman redoubled his efforts, nor paused even to breathe, until he had reached his goal, when, turning on his heel, he discharged his musket towards the surgeon, and was out of sight in an instant. To gain the highway, and throw himself into his saddle, detained Lawton but a moment, and he rode to the side of his comrade just as the figure disappeared.

"Which way has he fled?" cried the trooper.

"John," said the surgeon, "am I not a noncombatant?"

"Whither has the rascal fled?" cried Lawton, impatiently.

"Where you cannot follow—into that wood. But I repeat, John, am I not a noncombatant?"

The disappointed trooper, perceiving that his enemy had escaped him, now turned his eyes, which were flashing with anger, upon his comrade, and gradually his muscles lost their rigid compression, his brow relaxed, and his look changed from its fierce expression, to the covert laughter which so often distinguished his countenance. The surgeon sat in dignified composure on his horse; his thin body erect, and his head elevated with the indignation of one conscious of having been unjustly treated.

"Why did you suffer the villain to escape?" demanded the captain. "Once within reach of my saber, and I would have given you a subject for the dissecting table."

" 'Twas impossible to prevent it," said the surgeon, pointing to the bars, before which he had stopped his horse. "The rogue threw himself on the other side of this fence, and left me where you see; nor would the man in the least attend to my remonstrances, or to an intimation that you wished to hold discourse with him."

"He was truly a discourteous rascal; but why did you not leap the fence, and compel him to a halt? You see but three of the bars are up, and Betty Flanagan could clear them on her cow."

The surgeon, for the first time, withdrew his eyes from the place where the fugitive had disappeared, and turned his look on his comrade. His head, however, was not permitted to lower itself in the least, as he replied,—

"I humbly conceive, Captain Lawton, that neither Mrs. Elizabeth Flanagan, nor her cow, is an example to be emulated by Doctor Archibald Sitgreaves. It would be but a sorry compliment to science, to say that a doctor of medicine had fractured both his legs by injudiciously striking them against a pair of bar-posts." While speaking, the surgeon raised the limbs in question to a nearly horizontal position, an attitude which really appeared to bid defiance to anything like a passage for himself through the defile; but the trooper, disregarding this ocular proof of the impossibility of the movement, cried hastily,—

"Here was nothing to stop you, man; I could leap a platoon through, boot and thigh, without pricking with a single spur. Pshaw! I have often charged upon the bayonets of infantry, over greater difficulties than this."

"You will please to remember. Captain John Lawton, that I am not the riding master of the regiment—nor a drill sergeant—nor a crazy cornet; no, sir—and I speak it with a due respect for the commission of the Continental Congress—nor an inconsiderate captain, who regards his own life as little as that of his enemies. I am only, sir, a poor humble man of letters, a mere doctor of medicine, an unworthy graduate of Edinburgh, and a surgen of dragoons; nothing more, I do assure you, Captain John Lawton." So saying, he turned his horse's head towards the cottage, and recommenced his ride.

"Aye, you speak the truth," muttered the dragoon. "Had I but the meanest rider of my troop with me, I should have taken the scoundrel, and given at least one victim to the laws. But, Archibald, no man can ride well who straddles in this manner like the Colossus of Rhodes. You should depend less on your stirrup, and keep your seat by the power of the knee."

"With proper deference to your experience, Captain Lawton," returned the surgeon, "I conceive myself to be no incompetent judge of muscular action, whether in the knee, or in any other part of the human frame. And although but humbly educated, I am not now to learn that the wider the base, the more firm is the superstructure."

"Would you fill a highway, in this manner, with one pair of legs, when half a dozen might pass together in comfort, stretching them abroad like the scythes of the ancient chariot wheels?"

The allusion to the practice of the ancients somewhat softened the indignation of the surgeon, and he replied, with rather less hauteur,—

"You should speak with reverence of the usages of those who have gone before us, and who, however ignorant they were in matters of science, and particularly that of surgery, yet furnished many brilliant hints to our own improvements. Now, sir, I have no doubt that Galen has operated on wounds occasioned by these very scythes that you mention, although we can find no evidence of the fact in contemporary writers. Ah! they must have given dreadful injuries, and, I doubt not, caused great uneasiness to the medical gentlemen of that day."

"Occasionally a body must have been left in two pieces, to puzzle the ingenuity of those gentry to unite. Yet, venerable and learned as they were, I doubt not they did it."

"What! united two parts of the human body, that have been severed by an edged instrument, to any of the purposes of animal life?"

"That have been rent asunder by a scythe, and are united to do military duty," said Lawton.

" 'Tis impossible—quite impossible," cried the surgeon. "It is in vain, Captain Lawton, that human ingenuity endeavors to baffle the efforts of nature. Think, my dear sir; in this case you separate all the arteries—injure all of the intestines—sever all of the nerves and sinews, and, what is of more consequence, you—"

"You have said enough, Dr. Sitgreaves, to convince a member of a rival school. Nothing shall ever tempt me willingly to submit to be divided in this irretrievable manner."

"Certes, there is little pleasure in a wound which, from its nature, is incurable."

"I should think so," said Lawton, dryly.

"What do you think is the greatest pleasure in life?" asked the operator suddenly.

"That must greatly depend on taste."

"Not at all," cried the surgeon; "it is in witnessing, or rather feeling, the ravages of disease repaired by the lights of science cooperating with nature. I once broke my little finger intentionally, in order that I might reduce the fracture and watch the cure: it was only on a small scale, you know, dear John; still the thrilling sensation excited by the knitting of the bone, aided by the contemplation of the art of man thus acting in unison with nature, exceeded any other enjoyment that I have ever experienced. Now, had it been one of the most important members, such as the leg, or arm, how much greater must the pleasure have been!"

"Or the neck," said the trooper; but their desultory discourse was interrupted by their arrival at the cottage of Mr. Wharton. No one appearing to usher them into an apartment, the captain proceeded to the door of the parlor, where he knew visitors were commonly received. On opening it, he paused for a moment, in admiration at the scene within. The person of Colonel Wellmere first met his eyes, bending towards the figure of the blushing Sarah, with an earnestness of manner that prevented the noise of Lawton's entrance from being heard by either of the parties. Certain significant signs which were embraced at a glance by the prying gaze of the trooper, at once made him a master of their secret; and he was about to retire as silently as he had advanced, when his companion, pushing himself through the passage, abruptly entered the room. Advancing instantly to the chair of Wellmere, the surgeon instinctively laid hold of his arm, and exclaimed,—

"Bless me!—a quick and irregular pulse—flushed cheek and fiery eye—strong febrile symptoms, and such as must be attended to." While speaking, the doctor, who was much addicted to practicing in a summary way,—a weakness of most medical men in military practice,—had already produced his lancet, and was making certain other indications of his intentions to proceed at once to business. But Colonel Wellmere, recovering from the confusion of the surprise, arose from his seat haughtily, and said,—

"Sir, it is the warmth of the room that lends me the color, and I am already too much indebted to your skill to give you any further trouble. Miss Wharton knows that I am quite well, and I do assure you that I never felt better or happier in my life."

There was a peculiar emphasis on the latter part of this speech, that, however it might gratify the feelings of Sarah, brought the color to her cheeks again; and Sitgreaves, as his eye followed the direction of those of his patient, did not fail to observe it.

"Your arm, if you please, madam," said the surgeon, advancing with a bow. "Anxiety and watching have done their work on your delicate frame, and there are symptoms about you that must not be neglected."

"Excuse me, sir," said Sarah, recovering herself with womanly pride; "the heat is oppressive, and I will retire and acquaint Miss Peyton with your presence."

There was but little difficulty in practicing on the abstracted simplicity of the surgeon; but it was necessary for Sarah to raise her eyes to return the salutation of Lawton, as he bowed his head nearly to a level with the hand that held open the door for her passage. One look was sufficient; she was able to control her steps sufficiently to retire with dignity; but no sooner was she relieved from the presence of all observers, than she fell into a chair and abandoned herself to a feeling of mingled shame and pleasure.

A little nettled at the contumacious deportment of the British colonel, Sitgreaves, after once more tendering services that were again rejected, withdrew to the chamber of young Singleton, whither Lawton had already preceded him.

CHAPTER XXI

Oh! Henry, when thou deign'st to sue,
    Can I thy suit withstand?
When thou, loved youth, hast won my heart,
    Can I refuse my hand?
        —Hermit of Warkworth.

The graduate of Edinburgh found his patient rapidly improving in health, and entirely free from fever. His sister, with a cheek that was, if possible, paler than on her arrival, watched around his couch with tender care; and the ladies of the cottage had not, in the midst of their sorrows and varied emotions, forgotten to discharge the duties of hospitality. Frances felt herself impelled towards their disconsolate guest, with an interest for which she could not account, and with a force that she could not control. She had unconsciously connected the fates of Dunwoodie and Isabella in her imagination, and she felt, with the romantic ardor of a generous mind, that she was serving her former lover most by exhibiting kindness to her he loved best. Isabella received her attentions with gratitude, but neither of them indulged in any allusions to the latent source of their uneasiness. The observation of Miss Peyton seldom penetrated beyond things that were visible, and to her the situation of Henry Wharton seemed to furnish an awful excuse for the fading cheeks and tearful eyes of her niece. If Sarah manifested less of care than her sister, still the un-practiced aunt was not at a loss to comprehend the reason. Love is a holy feeling with the virtuous of the female sex, and it hallows all that come within its influence. Although Miss Peyton mourned with sincerity over the danger which threatened her nephew, she well knew that an active campaign was not favorable to love, and the moments that were thus accidentally granted were not to be thrown away.

Several days now passed without any interruption of the usual avocations of the inhabitants of the cottage, or the party at the Four Comers. The former were supporting their fortitude with the certainty of Henry's innocence, and a strong reliance on Dunwoodie's exertions in his behalf, and the latter waiting with impatience the intelligence, that was hourly expected, of a conflict, and their orders to depart. Captain Lawton, however, waited for both these events in vain. Letters from the major announced that the enemy, finding that the party which was to cooperate with them had been defeated, and was withdrawn, had retired also behind the works of Fort Washington, where they continued inactive, threatening constantly to strike a blow in revenge for their disgrace. The trooper was enjoined to vigilance, and the letter concluded with a compliment to his honor, zeal, and undoubted bravery.

"Extremely flattering. Major Dunwoodie," muttered the dragoon, as he threw down this epistle, and stalked across the floor to quiet his impatience. "A proper guard have you selected for this service: let me see—I have to watch over the interests of a crazy, irresolute old man, who does not know whether he belongs to us or to the enemy; four women, three of whom are well enough in themselves, but who are not immensely flattered by my society; and the fourth, who, good as she is, is on the wrong side of forty; some two or three blacks; a talkative housekeeper, that does nothing but chatter about gold and despisables, and signs and omens; and poor George Singleton. Well, a comrade in suffering has a claim on a man,—so I'll make the best of it."

As he concluded this soliloquy, the trooper took a seat and began to whistle, to convince himself how little he cared about the matter, when, by throwing his booted leg carelessly round, he upset the canteen that held his whole stock of brandy. The accident was soon repaired, but in replacing the wooden vessel, he observed a billet lying on the bench, on which the liquor had been placed. It was soon opened, and he read: "The moon will not rise till after midnight—a fit time for deeds of darkness." There was no mistaking the hand; it was clearly the same that had given him the timely warning against assassination, and the trooper continued, for a long time, musing on the nature of these two notices, and the motives that could induce the peddler to favor an implacable enemy in the manner that he had latterly done. That he was a spy of the enemy, Lawton knew; for the fact of his conveying intelligence to the English commander in chief, of a party of Americans that were exposed to the enemy was proved most clearly against him on the trial for his life. The consequences of his treason had been avoided, it is true, by a lucky order from Washington, which withdrew the regiment a short time before the British appeared to cut it off, but still the crime was the same. "Perhaps," thought the partisan, "he wishes. to make a friend of me against the event of another capture; but, at all events, he spared my life on one occasion, and saved it on another. I will endeavor to be as generous as himself, and pray that my duty may never interfere with my feelings."

Whether the danger, intimated in the present note, threatened the cottage or his own party, the captain was uncertain; but he inclined to the latter opinion, and determined to beware how he rode abroad in the dark. To a man in a peaceable country, and in times of quiet and order, the indifference with which the partisan regarded the impending danger would be inconceivable. His reflections on the subject were more directed towards devising means to entrap his enemies, than to escape their machinations. But the arrival of the surgeon, who had been to pay his daily visit to the Locusts, interrupted his meditations. Sitgreaves brought an invitation from the mistress of the mansion to Captain Lawton, desiring that the cottage might be honored with his presence at any early hour on that evening.

"Ha!" cried the trooper; "then they have received a letter also."

"I think nothing more probable," said the surgeon. "There is a chaplain at the cottage from the royal army, who has come out to exchange the British wounded, and who has an order from Colonel Singleton for their delivery. But a more mad project than to remove them now was never adopted."

"A priest, say you!—is he a hard drinker—a real campidler—a fellow to breed a famine in a regiment? Or does he seem a man who is earnest in his trade?"

"'A very respectable and orderly gentleman, and not unreasonably given to intemperance, judging from the outward symptoms," returned the surgeon; "and a man who really says grace in a very regular and appropriate manner."

"And does he stay the night?"

"Certainly, he waits for his cartel; but hasten, John, we have but little time to waste. I will just step up and bleed two or three of the Englishmen who are to move in the morning, in order to anticipate inflammation, and be with you immediately."

The gala suit of Captain Lawton was easily adjusted to his huge frame, and his companion being ready, they once more took their route towards the cottage. Roanoke had been as much benefited by a few days' rest as his master; and Lawton ardently wished, as he curbed his gallant steed, on passing the well-remembered rocks, that his treacherous enemy stood before him, mounted and armed as himself. But no enemy, nor any disturbance whatever, interfered with their progress, and they reached the Locusts just as the sun was throwing his setting rays on the valley, and tingeing the tops of the leafless trees with gold. It never required more than a single look to acquaint the trooper with the particulars of every scene that was not uncommonly veiled, and the first survey that he took on entering the house told him more than the observations of a day had put into the possession of Doctor Sitgreaves. Miss Peyton accosted him with a smiling welcome, that exceeded the bounds of ordinary courtesy and which evidently flowed more from feelings that were connected with the heart, than from manner. Frances glided about, tearful and agitated, while Mr. Wharton stood ready to receive them, decked in a suit of velvet that would have been conspicuous in the gayest drawing-room. Colonel Wellmere was in the uniform of an officer of the household troops of his prince, and Isabella Singleton sat in the parlor, clad in the habiliments of joy, but with a countenance that belied her appearance; while her brother by her side looked, with a cheek of flitting color, and an eye of intense interest, like anything but an invalid. As it was the third day that he had left his room, Dr. Sitgreaves, who began to stare about him in stupid wonder, forgot to reprove his patient for imprudence. Into this scene Captain Lawton moved with all the composure and gravity of a man whose nerves were not easily discomposed by novelties. His compliments were received as graciously as they were offered, and after exchanging a few words with the different individuals present, he approached the surgeon, who had withdrawn, in a kind of confused astonishment, to rally his senses.

"John," whispered the surgeon, with awakened curiosity, "what means this festival?"

"That your wig and my black head would look the better for a little of Betty Flanagan's flour; but it is too late now, and we must fight the battle armed as you see."

"Observe, here comes the army chaplain in his full robes, as a Doctor Divinitatis; what can it mean?"

"An exchange," said the trooper. "The wounded of Cupid are to meet and settle their accounts with the god, in the way of plighting faith to suffer from his archery no more."

The surgeon laid a finger on the side of his nose, and he began to comprehend the case.

"Is it not a crying shame, that a sunshine hero, and an enemy, should thus be suffered to steal away one of the fairest plants that grow in our soil," muttered Lawton; "a flower fit to be placed in the bosom of any man!"

"If he be not more accommodating as-a husband than as a patient, John, I fear me that the lady will lead a troubled life."

"Let her," said the trooper, indignantly; "she has chosen from her country's enemies, and may she meet with a foreigner's virtues in her choice."

Further conversation was interrupted by Miss Peyton, who, advancing, acquainted them that they had been invited to grace the nuptials of her eldest niece and Colonel Wellmere. The gentlemen bowed; and the good aunt, with an inherent love of propriety, went on to add, that the acquaintance was of an old date, and the attachment by no means a sudden thing. To this Lawton merely bowed still more ceremoniously; but the surgeon, who loved to hold converse with the virgin, replied,—

"That the human mind was differently constituted in different individuals. In some, impressions are vivid and transitory; in others, more deep and lasting: indeed, there are some philosophers who pretend to trace a connection between the physical and mental powers of the animal; but, for my part, madam, I believe that the one is much influenced by habit and association, and the other subject altogether to the peculiar laws of matter."

Miss Peyton, in her turn, bowed her silent assent to this remark, and retired with dignity, to usher the intended bride into the presence of the company. The hour had arrived when American custom has decreed that the vows of wedlock must be exchanged; and Sarah, blushing with a variety of emotions, followed her aunt to the drawing-room. Wellmere sprang to receive the hand that, with an averted face, she extended towards him, and, for the first time, the English colonel appeared fully conscious of the important part that he was to act in the approaching ceremony. Hitherto his air had been abstracted, and his manner uneasy; but everything, excepting the certainty of his bliss, seemed to vanish at the blaze of loveliness that now burst on his sight. All arose from their seats, and the reverend gentleman had already opened the sacred volume, when the absence of Frances was noticed! Miss Peyton withdrew in search of her youngest niece, whom she found in her own apartment, and in tears.

"Come, my love, the ceremony waits but for us," said the aunt, affectionately entwining her arm in that of her niece. "Endeavor to compose yourself, that proper honor may be done to the choice of your sister."

"Is he—can he be, worthy of her?"

"Can he be otherwise?" returned Miss Peyton. "Is he not a gentleman?—a gallant soldier, though an unfortunate one? and certainly, my love, one who appears every way qualified to make any woman happy."

Frances had given vent to her feelings, and, with an effort, she collected sufficient resolution to venture to join the party below. But to relieve the embarrassment of this delay, the clergyman had put sundry questions to the bridegroom; one of which was by no means answered to his satisfaction. Wellmere was compelled to acknowledge that he was unprovided with a ring; and to perform the marriage ceremony without one, the divine pronounced to be canonically impossible. His appeal to Mr. Wharton, for the propriety of this decision, was answered affirmatively, as it would have been negatively, had the question been put in a manner to lead to such a result. The owner of the Locusts had lost the little energy he possessed, by the blow recently received through his son, and his assent to the objection of the clergyman was as easily obtained as had been his consent to the premature proposals of Wellmere. In this stage of the dilemma. Miss Peyton and Frances appeared. The surgeon of dragoons approached the former, and as he handed her to a chair, observed,—

"It appears, madam, that untoward circumstances have prevented Colonel Wellmere from providing all of the decorations that custom, antiquity, and the canons of the church have prescribed, as indispensable to enter into the honorable state of wedlock."

Miss Peyton glanced her quiet eye at the uneasy bridegroom, and perceiving him to be adorned with what she thought sufficient splendor, allowing for the time and the suddenness of the occasion, she turned her look on the speaker, as if to demand an explanation.

The surgeon understood her wishes, and proceeded at once to gratify them.

"There is," he observed, "an opinion prevalent, that the heart lies on the left side of the body, and that the connection between the members of that side and what may be called the seat of life is more intimate than that which exists with their opposites. But this is an error which grows out of an ignorance of the organic arrangement of the human frame. In obedience to this opinion, the fourth finger of the left hand is thought to contain a virtue that belongs to no other branch of that digitated member; and it is ordinarily encircled, during the solemnization of wedlock, with a cincture or ring, as if to chain that affection to the marriage state, which is best secured by the graces of the female character." While speaking, the operator laid his hand expressively on his heart, and he bowed nearly to the floor when he had concluded.

"I know not, sir, that I rightly understand your meaning," said Miss Peyton, whose want of comprehension was sufficiently excusable.

"A ring, madam—a ring is wanting for the ceremony."

The instant that the surgeon spoke explicitly, the awkwardness of the situation was understood. She glanced her eyes at her nieces, and in the younger she read a secret exultation that somewhat displeased her; but the countenance of Sarah was suffused with a shame that the considerate aunt well understood. Not for the world would she violate any of the observances of female etiquette. It suggested itself to all the females, at the same moment, that the wedding ring of the late mother and sister was reposing peacefully amid the rest of her jewelry, in a secret receptacle, that had been provided at any early day, to secure the valuables against the predatory inroads of the marauders who roamed through the county. Into this hidden vault, the plate, and whatever was most prized, made a nightly retreat, and there the ring in question had long lain, forgotten until at this moment. But it was the business of the bridegroom, from time immemorial, to furnish this indispensable to wedlock, and on no account would Miss Peyton do anything that transcended the usual reserve of the sex on this solemn occasion; certainly not until sufficient expiation for the offense had been made, by a due portion of trouble and disquiet. This material fact, therefore, was not disclosed by either; the aunt consulting female propriety; the bride yielding to shame; and Frances rejoicing that an embarrassment, proceeding from almost any cause, should delay her sister's vow. It was reserved for Doctor Sitgreaves to interrupt the awkward silence.

"If, madam, a plain ring, that once belonged to a sister of my own—" He paused and hemmed—"If, madam, a ring of that description might be admitted to this honor, I have one that could be easily produced from my quarters at the Corners, and I doubt not it would fit the finger for which it is desired. There is a strong resemblance between—hem—between my late sister and Miss Wharton in stature and anatomical figure; and, in all eligible subjects, the proportions are apt to be observed throughout the whole animal economy."

A glance of Miss Peyton's eye recalled Colonel Wellmere to a sense of his duty, and springing from his chair, he assured the surgeon that in no way could he confer a greater obligation on himself than by sending for that very ring. The operator bowed a little haughtily, and withdrew to fulfill his promise, by dispatching a messenger on the errand. The aunt suffered him to retire; but unwillingness to admit a stranger into the privacy of their domestic arrangements induced her to follow and tender the services of Cæsar, instead of those of Sitgreaves' man, who had volunteered for this duty. Katy Haynes was accordingly directed. to summon the black to the vacant parlor, and thither Miss Peyton and the surgeon repaired, to give their several instructions.

The consent to this sudden union of Sarah and Wellmere, and especially at a time when the life of a member of the family was in such imminent jeopardy, was given from a conviction that the unsettled state of the country would probably prevent another opportunity to the lovers of meeting, and a secret dread on the part of Mr. Wharton, that the death of his son might, by hastening his own, leave his remaining children without a protector. But notwithstanding Miss Peyton had complied with her brother's wish to profit by the accidental visit of a divine, she had not thought it necessary to blazon the intended nuptials of her niece to the neighborhood, had even time been allowed; she thought, therefore, that she was now communicating a profound secret to the negro, and her housekeeper.

"Cæsar," she commenced, with a smile, "you are now to learn that your young mistress, Miss Sarah, is to be united to Colonel Wellmere this evening."

"I t'ink I see him afore," said Caesar, chuckling. "Old black man can tell when a young lady make up he mind."

"Really, Cæsar, I find I have never given you credit for half the observation that you deserve; but as you already know on what emergency your services are required, listen to the directions of this gentleman, and observe them."

The black turned in quiet submission to the surgeon, who commenced as follows:—

"Cæsar, your mistress has already acquainted you with the important event about to be solemnized within this habitation; but a cincture or ring is wanting to encircle the finger of the bride; a custom derived from the ancients, and which has been continued in the marriage forms of several branches of the Christian church, and which is even, by a species of typical wedlock, used in the installation of prelates, as you doubtless understand."

"P'r'aps Massa Doctor will say him over ag'in," interrupted the old negro, whose memory began to fail him, just as the other made so confident an allusion to his powers of comprehension. "I t'ink I get him by heart dis time."

"It is impossible to gather honey from a rock, Cæsar, and therefore I will abridge the little I have to say. Ride to the Four Corners, and present this note to Sergeant Hollister, or to Mrs. Elizabeth Flanagan, either of whom will furnish the necessary pledge of connubial affection; and return forthwith."

The letter which the surgeon put into the hands of his messenger, as he ceased, was conceived in the following terms:—

"If the fever has left Kinder, give him nourishment. Take three ounces more blood from Waston. Have a search made that the woman Flanagan has left none of her jugs of alcohol in the hospital. Renew the dressings of Johnson, and dismiss Smith to duty. Send the ring, which is pendent from the chain of the watch, that I left with you to time the doses, by the bearer.

"Archibald Sitgreaves, M. D.,

"Surgeon of Dragoons."

"Cæsar," said Katy, when she was alone with the black, "put

the ring, when you get it, in your left pocket, for that is nearest your heart; and by no means endeavor to try it on your finger, for it is unlucky."

"Try um on he finger?" interrupted the negro, stretching forth his bony knuckles. "T'ink a Miss Sally's ring go on old Cæsar's finger?"

" 'Tis not consequential whether it goes on or not," said the housekeeper; "but it is an evil omen to place a marrige ring on the finger of another after wedlock, and of course it may be dangerous before."

"I tell you, Katy, I neber t'ink to put um on. a finger."

"Go, then, Cæsar, and do not forget the left pocket; be careful to take off your hat as you pass the graveyard, and be expeditious; for nothing, I am certain, can be more trying to the patience, than thus to be waiting for the ceremony, when a body has fully made up her mind to marry."

With this injunction Cæsar quitted the house, and he was soon firmly fixed in the saddle. From his youth, the black, like all of his race, had been a hard rider; but, bending under the weight of sixty winters, his African blood had lost some of its native heat. The night was dark, and the wind whistled through the vale with the dreariness of November. When Cæsar reached the graveyard, he uncovered his grizzled head with superstitious awe, and threw around him many a fearful glance, in momentary expectation of seeing something superhuman. There was sufficient light to discern a being of earthly mold stealing from among the graves, apparently with a design to enter the highway. It is in vain that philosophy and reason contend with early impressions, and poor Cæsar was even without the support of either of these frail allies. He was, however, well mounted on a coach horse of Mr. Wharton's and, clinging to the back of the animal with instinctive skill, he abandoned the rein to the beast. Hillocks, woods, rocks, fences, and houses flew by him with the rapidity of lightning, and the black had just begun to think whither and on what business he was riding in this headlong manner, when he reached the place where the roads met, and the "Hotel Flanagan" stood before him in its dilapidated simplicity. The sight of a cheerful fire first told the negro that he had reached the habitation of man, and with it came all his dread of the bloody Virginians; his duty must, however, be done, and, dismounting, he fastened the foaming animal to a fence, and approached the window with cautious steps, to reconnoiter.

Before a blazing fire sat Sergeant Hollister and Betty Flanagan, enjoying themselves over a liberal potation.

"I tell ye, sargeant dear," said Betty, removing the mug from her mouth, " 'tis no r'asonable to think it was more than the piddler himself; sure now, where was the smell of sulphur, and the wings, and the tail, and the cloven foot? Besides, sargeant, it's no dacent to tell a lone famale that she had Beelzeboob for a bedfellow."

"It matters but little, Mrs. Flanagan, provided you escape his talons and fangs hereafter," returned the veteran, following the remark by a heavy draft.

Cæsar heard enough to convince him that little danger from this pair was to be apprehended. His teeth already began to chatter, and the cold without and the comfort within stimulated him greatly to enter. He made his approaches with proper caution, and knocked with extreme humility. The appearance of Hollister with a drawn sword, roughly demanding who was without, contributed in no degree to the restoration of his faculties; but fear itself lent him power to explain his errand.

"Advance," said the sergeant, throwing a look of close scrutiny on the black, as he brought him to the light; "advance, and deliver your dispatches. Have you the countersign?"

"I don't t'ink he know what dat be," said the black, shaking in his shoes, "dough massa dat sent me gib me many t'ings to carry, dat he little understand."

"Who ordered you on this duty, did you say?"

"Well, it war he doctor, heself, so he come up on a gallop, as he always do on a doctor's errand."

" 'Twas Doctor Sitgreaves; he never knows the countersign himself. Now, blackey, had it been Captain Lawton he would not have sent you here, close to a sentinel, without' the countersign; for you might get a pistol bullet through your head, and that would be cruel to you; for although you be black, I am none of them who thinks niggers have no souls."

"Sure a nagur has as much sowl as a white," said Betty. "Come hither, ould man, and warm that shivering carcass of yeers by the blaze of this fire. I'm sure a Guinea nagur loves hate as much as a soldier loves his drop."

Cæsar obeyed in silence, and a mulatto boy who was sleeping on a bench in the room, was bidden to convey the note of the surgeon to the building where the wounded were quartered.

"Here," said the washerwoman, tendering to Cæsar a taste of the article that most delighted herself, "try a drop, smooty, 'twill warm the black sowl within your crazy body, and be giving you spirits as you are going homeward."

"I tell you, Elizabeth," said the sergeant, "that the souls of niggers are the same as our own; how often have I heard the good Mr. Whitfield say that there was no distinction of color in heaven. Therefore it is reasonable to believe that the soul of this here black is as white as my own, or even Major Dunwoodie's."

"Be sure he be," cried Cæsar, a little tartly, whose courage had revived by tasting the drop of Mrs. Flanagan.

"It's a good sowl that the major is, anyway," returned the washerwoman; "and a kind of sowl—aye, and a brave sowl too; and ye'll say all that yeerself, sargeant, I'm thinking."

"For the matter of that," returned the veteran, "there is One above even Washington, to judge of souls; but this I will say, that Major Dunwoodie is a gentleman who never says, Go, boys—but always says, Come, boys; and if a poor fellow is in want of a spur or a martingale, and the leatherwhack is gone, there is never wanting the real silver to make up the loss, and that from his own pocket too."

"Why, then, are you here idle when all that he holds most dear are in danger?" cried a voice with startling abruptness. "Mount, mount, and follow your captain; arm and mount, and that instantly, or you will be too late!"

This unexpected interruption produced an instantaneous confusion amongst the tipplers. Cæsar fled instinctively into the fireplace, where he maintained his position in defiance of a heat that would have roasted a white man. Sergeant Hollister turned promptly on his heel, and seizing his saber, the steel was glittering by the firelight, in the twinkling of an eye; but perceiving the intruder to be the peddler, who stood near the open door that led to the lean-to in the rear, he began to fall back towards the position of the black, with a military intuition that taught him to concentrate his forces. Betty alone stood her ground, by the side of the temporary table. Replenishing the mug with a large addition of the article known to the soldiery by the name of "choke-dog," she held it towards the peddler. The eyes of the washerwoman had for some time been swimming with love and liquor, and turning them good-naturedly on Birch, she cried,—

"Faith, but ye're wilcome, Mister Fiddler, or Mister Birch, or Mister Beelzeboob, or what's yeer name. Ye're an honest divil anyway, and I'm hoping that you found the pitticoats convanient. Come forward, dear, and fale the fire; Sargeant Hollister won't be hurting you, for the fear of an ill turn you may be doing him hereafter—will ye, sargeant dear?"

"Depart, ungodly man!" cried the veteran, edging still nearer to Cæsar, but lifting his legs alternately as they scorched with the heat. "Depart in peace! There is none here for thy service, and you seek the woman in vain. There is a tender mercy that will save her from thy talons." The sergeant ceased to utter aloud, but the motion of his lips continued, and a few scattering words of prayer were alone audible.

The brain of the washerwoman was in such a state of confusion that she did not clearly comprehend the meaning of her suitor, but a new idea struck her imagination, and she broke forth,—

"If it's me the man saaks, where's the matter, pray? Am I not a widowed body, and my own property? And you talk of tinderness, sargeant, but it's little I see of it, anyway. Who knows but Mr. Beelzeboob here is free to speak his mind? I'm sure it is willing to hear I am."

"Woman," said the peddler, "be silent; and you, foolish man, mount—arm and mount, and fly to the rescue of your officer, if you are worthy of the cause in which you serve, and would not disgrace the coat you wear." The peddler vanished from the sight of the bewildered trio, with a rapidity that left them uncertain whither he had fled.

On hearing the voice of an old friend, Cæsar emerged from his corner, and fearlessly advanced to the spot where Betty had resolutely maintained her ground, though in a state of utter mental confusion.

"I wish Harvey stop," said the black. "If he ride down a road I should like he company; I don't fink Johnny Birch hurt he own son."

"Poor, ignorant wretch!" exclaimed the veteran, recovering his voice with a long-drawn breath; "think you that figure was made of flesh and blood?"

"Harvey ain't fleshy," replied the black, "but he berry clebber man."

"Pooh! sargeant dear," exclaimed the washerwoman, "talk r'ason for once, and mind what the knowing one tells ye; call out the boys and ride a bit after Captain Jack; remimber, darling, that he told ye, the day, to be in readiness to mount at a moment's warning."

"Aye, but not at a summons from the foul fiend. Let Captain Lawton, or Lieutenant Mason, or Cornet Skipwith, say the word, and who is quicker in the saddle than I?"

"Well, sargeant, how often is it that ye've boasted to myself that the corps wasn't a bit afeard to face the divil?"

"No more are we, in battle array, and by daylight; but it's foolhardy and irreverent to tempt Satan, and on such a night as this. Listen how the wind whistles through the trees; and hark! there is the howling of evil spirits abroad."

"I see him," said Cæsar, opening his eyes to a width that might have embraced more than an ideal form.

"Where?" interrupted the sergeant, instinctively laying his hand on the hilt of his saber.

"No, no," said the black, "I see a Johnny Birch come out of he grave—Johnny walk afore he buried."

"Ah! then he must have led an evil life indeed," said Hollister. "The blessed in spirit lie quiet until the general muster, but wickedness distrubs the soul in this life as well as in that which is to come."

"And what is to come of Captain Jack?" cried Betty, angrily. "Is it yeer orders that ye won't mind , nor a warning given? I'll jist git my cart, and ride down and tell him that ye're afeard of a dead man and Beelzeboob; and it isn't succor he may be expicting from ye. I wonder who'll be the orderly of the troop the morrow, then?—his name won't be Hollister, anyway."

"Nay, Betty, nay," said the sergeant, laying his hand familiarly on her shoulder; "if there must be riding to-night, let it be by him whose duty it is to call out the men and set an example. The Lord have mercy, and send us enemies of flesh and blood!"

Another glass confirmed the veteran in a resolution that was only excited by a dread of his captain's displeasure, and he proceeded to summon the dozen men who had been left under his command. The boy arriving with the ring, Cæsar placed it carefully in the pocket of his waistcoat next his heart, and, mounting, shut his eyes, seized his charger by the mane, and continued in a state of comparative insensibility, until the animal stopped at the door of the warm stable whence he had started.

The movements of the dragoons, being timed to the order of a march, were much slower, for they were made with a watchfulness that was intended to guard against surprise from the evil one himself.

CHAPTER XXII

Be not your tongue thy own shame's orator,
Look sweet, speak fair, become disloyalty,
Apparel vice like virtue's harbinger.
—Comedy of Errors.

The situation of the party in Mr. Wharton's dwelling was sufficiently awkward, during the hour of Cæsar's absence; for such was the astonishing rapidity displayed by his courser, that the four miles of road was gone over, and the events we have recorded had occurred, somewhat within that period of time. Of course, the gentlemen strove to make the irksome moments fly as swiftly as possible; but premeditated happiness is certainly of the least joyous kind. The bride and bridegroom are immemorially privileged to be dull, and but few of their friends seemed disposed, on the present occasion, to dishonor their example. The English colonel exhibited a proper portion of uneasiness at this unexpected interruption of his felicity, and he sat with a varying countenance by the side of Sarah, who seemed to be profiting by the delay to gather fortitude for the solemn ceremony. In the midst of this embarrasing silence. Doctor Sitgreaves addressed himself to Miss Peyton, by whose side he had contrived to procure a chair. "Marriage, madam, is pronounced to be honorable in the sight of God and man; and it may be said to be reduced, in the present age, to the laws of nature and reason. The ancients, in sanctioning polygamy, lost sight of the provisions of nature, and condemned thousands to misery; but with the increase of science have grown the wise ordinances of society, which ordain that man should be the husband of but one woman."

Wellmere glanced a fierce expression of disgust at the surgeon, that indicated his sense of the tediousness of the other's remarks; while Miss Peyton, with a slight hesitation, as if fearful of touching on forbidden subjects, replied,—

"I had thought, sir, that we were indebted to the Christian religion for our morals on this subject."

"True, madam, it is somewhere provided in the prescriptions of the apostles, that the sexes should henceforth be on an equality in this particular. But in what degree could poligamy affect holiness of life? It was probably a wise arrangement of Paul, who was much of a scholar, and probably had frequent conferences, on this important subject, with Luke, whom we all know to have been bred to the practice of medicine—"

There is no telling how far the discursive fancy of Sitgreaves might have led him, on this subject, had he not been interrupted. But Lawton, who had been a close though silent observer of all that passed, profited by the hint to ask abruptly,—

"Pray, Colonel Wellmere, in what manner is bigamy punished in England?"

The bridegroom started, and his lip blanched. Recovering himself, however, on the instant, he answered with a suavity that became so happy a man,—

"Death!—as such an offense merits," he said.

"Death and dissection," continued the operator. "It is seldom that law loses sight of eventual utility in a malefactor. Bigamy, in a man, is a heinous offense!"

"More so than celibacy?" asked Lawton.

"More so," returned the surgeon, with undisturbed simplicity. "One who remains in a single state may devote his life to science and the extension of knowledge, if not of his species; but the wretch who profits by the constitutional tendency of the female sex to credulity and tenderness, incurs the wickedness of a positive sin, heightened by the baseness of deception."

"Really, sir, the ladies are infinitely obliged to you, for attributing folly to them as part of their nature."

"Captain Lawton, in man the animal is more nobly formed than in woman. The nerves are endowed with less sensibility; the whole frame is less pliable and yielding; is it therefore surprising, that a tendency to rely on the faith of her partner is more natural to woman than to the other sex?"

Wellmere, as if unable to listen with any degree of patience to so ill-timed a dialogue, sprang from his seat and paced the floor in disorder. Pitying his situation, the reverend gentleman, who was patiently awaiting the return of Cæsar, changed the discourse, and a few minutes brought the black himself. The billet was handed to Dr. Sitgreaves; for Miss Peyton had expressly enjoined Cæsar not to implicate her, in any manner, in the errand on which he was dispatched. The note contained a summary statement of the several subjects of the surgeon's directions, and referred him to the black for the ring. The latter was instantly demanded, and promptly delivered. A transient look of melancholy clouded the brow of the surgeon, as he stood a moment, and gazed silently on the bauble; nor did he remember the place, or the occasion, while he mournfully soliloquized as follows,—

"Poor Anna! gay as innocence and youth could make thee was thy heart, when this cincture was formed to grace thy nuptials; but ere the hour had come. God had taken thee to Himself. Years have passed, my sister, but never have I forgotten the companion of my infancy!" He advanced to Sarah, and, unconscious of observation, placed the ring on her finger, continued, "She for whom it was intended has long been in her grave, and the youth who bestowed the gift soon followed her sainted spirit; take it, madam, and God grant that it may be an instrument in making you as happy as you deserve!"

Sarah felt a chill at her heart, as this burst of feeling escaped the surgeon; but Wellmere offering his hand, she was led before the divine, and the ceremony began. The first words of this imposing office produced a dead stillness in the apartment; and the minister of God proceeded to the solemn exhortation, and witnessed the plighted troth of the parties, when the investiture was to follow. The ring had been left, from inadvertency and the agitation of the moment, on the finger where Sitgreaves had placed it; the slight interruption occasioned by the circumstances was over, and the clergyman was about to proceed, when a figure gliding into the midst of the party, at once put a stop to the ceremony. It was the peddler. His look was bitter and ironical, while a finger, raised towards the divine, seemed to forbid the ceremony to go any further.

"Can Colonel Wellmere waste the precious moments here, when his wife has crossed the ocean to meet him? The nights are long, and the moon bright; a few hours will take him to the city."

Aghast at the suddenness of this extraordinary address, Wellmere for a moment lost the command of his faculties. To Sarah, the countenance of Birch, expressive as it was, produced no terror; but the instant she recovered from the surprise of his interruption, she turned her anxious gaze on the features of the man to whom she had just pledged her troth. They afforded the most terrible confirmation of all the peddler affirmed; the room whirled round, and she fell lifeless into the arms of her aunt.

There is an instinctive delicacy in woman, that seems to conquer all other emotions; and the insensible bride was immediately conveyed from sight, leaving the room to the sole possession of the other sex.

The confusion enabled the peddler to retreat with a rapidity that would have baffled pursuit, had any been attempted, and Wellmere stood with every eye fixed on him, in ominous silence.

" 'Tis false—'tis false as hell!" he cried striking his forehead. "I have ever denied her claim; nor will the laws of my country compel me to acknowledge it."

"But what will conscience and the laws of God do?" asked Lawton.

" 'Tis well, sir," said Wellmere, haughtily, and retreating towards the door, "my situation protects you now; but a time may come—"

He had reached the entry, when a slight tap on his shoulder caused him to turn his head; it was Captain Lawton, who, with a smile of peculiar meaning, beckoned him to follow. The state of Wellmere's mind was such, that he would gladly have gone anywhere to avoid the gaze of horror and detestation that glared from every eye he met. They reached the stables before the trooper spoke, when he cried aloud,—

"Bring out Roanoke!"

His man appeared with the steed caparisoned for its master. Lawton, coolly throwing the bridle on the neck of the animal, took his pistols from the holsters, and continued, "Here are weapons that have seen good service before to-day—aye, and in honorable hands, sir. These were the pistols of my father, Colonel Wellmere; he used them with credit in the wars with France, and gave them to me to fight the battles of my country with. In what better way can I serve her than in exterminating a wretch who would have blasted one of her fairest daughters?"

"This injurious treatment shall meet with its reward," cried the other, seizing the offered weapon. "The blood lie on the head of him who sought it!"

"Amen! but hold a moment, sir. You are now free, and the passports of Washington are in your pocket; I give you the fire; if I fall, there is a steed that will outstrip pursuit; and I would advise you to retreat without much delay, for even Archibald Sitgreaves would fight in such a cause—nor will the guard above be very apt to give quarter."

"Are you ready?" asked Wellmere, gnashing his teeth with rage.

"Stand forward, Tom, with the lights; fire!"

Wellmere fired, and the bullion flew from the epaulet of the trooper.

"Now the turn is mine," said Lawton, deliberately leveling his pistol.

"And mine!" shouted a voice, as the weapon was struck from his hand. "By all the devils in hell, 'tis the mad Virginian!—fall on, my boys, and take him; this is a prize not hoped for!"

Unarmed, and surprised as he was, Lawton's presence of mind did not desert him; he felt that he was in the hands of those from whom he was to expect no mercy; and, as four of the Skinners fell upon him at once, he used his gigantic strength to the utmost. Three of the band grasped him by the neck and arms, with an intent to clog his efforts, and pinion him with ropes. The first of these he threw from him, with a violence that sent him against the building, where he lay stunned with the blow. But the fourth seized his legs; and, unable to contend with such odds, the trooper came to the earth, bringing with him all of his assailants. The struggle on the ground was short but terrific; curses and the most dreadful imprecations were uttered by the Skinners, who in vain called on more of their band, who were gazing on the combat in nerveless horror, to assist. A difficulty of breathing, from one of the combatants, was heard, accompanied by the stifled meanings of a strangled man; and directly one of the group arose on his feet, shaking himself free from the wild grasp of the others. Both Wellmere and the servent of Lawton had fled: the former to the stables, and the latter to give the alarm, leaving all in darkness. Thc figure that stood erect sprang into the saddle of the unheeded charger; sparks of fire, issuing from the armed feet of the horse, gave a momentary light by which the captain was seen dashing like the wind towards the highway.

"By hell, he's off!" cried the leader, hoarse with rage and exhaustion. "Fire!—bring him down—fire, or you'll be too late."

The order was obeyed, and one moment of suspense followed, in the vain hope of hearing the huge frame of Lawton tumbling from his steed.

"He would not fall if you had killed him," muttered one. "I've known these Virginians sit their horses with two or three balls through them; aye, even after they were dead."

A freshening of the wind wafted the tread of a horse down the valley, which, by its speed, gave assurance of a rider governing its motion.

"These trained horses always stop when the rider falls," observed one of the gang.

"Then," cried the leader, striking his musket on the ground in a rage, "the fellow is safe!—to your business at once. A short half hour will bring down that canting sergeant and the guard upon us. 'Twill be lucky if the guns don't turn them out. Quick, to your posts, and fire the house in the chambers; smoking ruins are good to cover evil deeds."

"What is to be done with this lump of earth?" cried another, pushing the body that yet lay insensible, where it had been hurled by the arm of Lawton; "a little rubbing would bring him to."

"Let him lie," said the leader, fiercely. "Had he been half a man, that dragooning rascal would have been in my power; enter the house, I say, and fire the chambers. We can't go amiss here; there is plate and money enough to make you all gentlemen—and revenge too."

The idea of silver in any way was not to be resisted; and, leaving their companion, who began to show faint signs of life, they rushed tumultuously towards the dwelling. Wellmere availed himself of the opportunity, and, stealing from the stable with his own charger, he was able to gain the highway unnoticed. For an instant he hesitated, whether to ride towards the point where he knew the guard was stationed, and endeavor to rescue the family, or, profiting by his liberty and the exchange that had been effected by the divine, to seek the royal army. Shame, and a consciousness of guilt, determined him to take the latter course, and he rode towards New York, stung with the reflection of his own baseness, and harassed with the apprehension of meeting with an enraged woman, that he had married during his late visit to England, but whose claims, as soon as his passion was sated, he had resolved never willingly to admit. In the tumult and agitation of the moment, the retreat of Lawton and Wellmere was but little noticed; the condition of Mr. Wharton demanding the care and consolation of both the surgeon and the divine. The report of the firearms at first roused the family to the sense of a new danger, and but a moment elapsed before the leader, and one more of the gang, entered the room.

"Surrender! you servants of King George," shouted the leader, presenting his musket to the breast of Sitgreaves, "or I will let a little tory blood from your veins."

"Gently—gently, my friend," said the surgeon. "You are doubtless more expert in inflicting wounds than in healing them; the weapon that you hold so indiscreetly is extremely dangerous to animal life."

"Yield, or take its contents."

"Why and wherefore should I yield?—I am a noncombatant. The articles of capitulation must be arranged with Captain John Lawton; though yielding, I believe, is not a subject on which you will find him particularly complying."

The fellow had by this time taken such a survey of the group, as convinced him that little danger was to be apprehended from resistance, and, eager to seize his share of the plunder, he dropped his musket, and was soon busy with the assistance of his men, in arranging divers articles of plate in bags. The cottage now presented a singular spectacle. The ladies were gathered around Sarah, who yet continued insensible, in one of the rooms that had escaped the notice of the marauders. Mr. Wharton sat in a state of perfect imbecility, listening to, but not profiting by, the meaning words of comfort that fell from the lips of the clergyman. Singleton was lying on a sofa, shaking with debility, and inattentive to surrounding objects; while the surgeon was administering restoratives, and looking at the dressings, with a coolness that mocked the tumult. Cæsar and the attendant of Captain Singleton, had retreated to the wood in the rear of the cottage, and Katy Haynes was flying about the building, busily employed in forming a bundle of valuables, from which, with the most scrupulous honesty, she rejected every article that was not really and truly her own.

But to return to the party at the Four Corners. When the veteran had got his men mounted and under arms, a restless desire to participate in the glory and dangers of the expeditions came over the washerwoman. Whether she was impelled to the undertaking by a dread of remaining alone, or a wish to hasten in person to the relief of her favorite, we will not venture to assert but, as Hollister was giving the orders to wheel and march, the voice of Betty was heard, exclaiming,—

"Stop a bit, sargeant dear, till two of the boys get out the cart, and I'll jist ride wid ye; 'tis like there'll be wounded, and it will be mighty convanient to bring them home in."

Although inwardly much pleased with any cause of delay to a service that he so little relished, Hollister affected some displeasure at the detention.

"Nothing but a cannon ball can take one of my lads from his charger," he said; "and it's not very likely that we shall have as fair fighting as cannon and musketry, in a business of the evil one's inventing; so, Elizabeth, you may go if you will, but the cart will not be wanting."

"Now, sargeant dear, you lie, anyway," said Betty, who was somewhat unduly governed by her potations. "And wasn't Captain Singleton shot off his horse but tin days gone by? Aye, and Captain Jack himself too; and didn't he lie on the ground, face uppermost and back downwards, looking grim? And didn't the boys t'ink him dead, and turn and l'ave the rig'lars the day?"

"You lie back again," cried the sergeant, fiercely; "and so does anyone who says that we didn't gain the day."

"For a bit or so—only I mane for a bit or so," said the washerwoman; "but Major Dunwoodie turned you, and so you licked the rig'lars. But the captain it was that fell, and I'm thinking that there's no better rider going; so, sargeant, it's the cart will be convanient. Here, two of you, jist hitch the mare to the tills, and it's no whisky that ye'll be wanting the morrow; and put the piece of Jenny's hide under the pad; the baste is never the better for the rough ways of the county Westchester." The consent of the sergeant being obtained, the equipage of Mrs. Flanagan was soon in readiness to receive its burden.

"As it is quite uncertain whether we shall be attacked in front, or in rear," said Hollister, "five of you shall march in advance, and the remainder shall cover our retreat towards the barrack, should we be pressed. 'Tis an awful moment to a man of little learning, Elizabeth, to command in such a service; for my part, I wish devoutly that one of the officers were here; but my trust is in the Lord."

"Pooh! man, away wid ye," said the washerwoman, who had

got herself comfortably seated. "The divil a bit of an inimy is there near. March on, hurry-skurry, and let the mare trot, or it's but little that Captain Jack will thank ye for the help."

"Although unlearned in matters of communicating with spirits, or laying the dead, Mrs. Flanagan," said the veteran, "I have not served through the old war, and five years in this, not to know how to guard the baggage. Doesn't Washington always cover the baggage? I am not to be told my duty by a camp follower. Fall in as you are ordered, and dress, men."

"Well, march, anyway," cried the impatient washerwoman. "The black is there already, and it's tardy the captain will think ye."

"Are you sure that it was really a black man that brought the order?" said the sergeant, dropping in between the platoons, where he could converse with Betty, and be at hand, to lead on an emergency, either on an advance or on a retreat.

"Nay—and I'm sure of nothing, dear. But why don't the boys prick their horses and jog a trot? The mare is mighty un'asy, and it's no warm in this cursed valley, riding as much like a funeral party as old rags is to continental."[10]

"Fairly and softly, aye, and prudently, Mrs. Flanagan; it's not rashness that makes the good officer. If we have to encounter a spirit, it's more than likely he'll make his attack by surprise; horses are hot very powerful in the dark, and I have a character to lose, good woman."

"Caractur! and isn't it caractur and life too that Captain Jack has to lose!"

"Halt!" cried the sergeant. "What is that lurking near the root of the rock, on the left?"

"Sure, it's nothing, unless it be a matter of Captain Jack's sowl that's come to haunt ye, for not being brisker on the march."

"Betty, your levity makes you an unfit comrade for such an expedition. Advance, one of you, and reconnoiter the spot; draw swords!—rear rank, close to the front!"

---

[10] The paper money issued by congress was familiarly called continental money. This term "continental" was applied to the army, the congress, the ships of war, and in short, to almost everything of interest which belonged to the new government. It would seem to have been invented as the opposite of the insular position of the mother country.

"Pshaw!" shouted Betty, "is it a big fool or a big coward that ye are? Jist wheel from the road, boys, and I'll shove the mare down upon it in the twinkling of an eye—and it's no ghost that I fear."

By this time one of the men had returned, and declared there was nothing to prevent their advancing, and the party continued their march, but with great deliberation and caution.

"Courage and prudence are the jewels of a soldier, Mrs. Flanagan," said the sergeant; "without the one, the other may be said to be good for nothing."

"Prudence without courage: is it that you mane?—and it's so that I'm thinking myself, sargeant. This baste pulls tight on the reins, any way."

"Be patient, good woman; hark! what is that?" said Hollister, pricking up his ears at the report of Wellmere's pistol. "I'll swear that was a human pistol, and one from our regiment. Rear rank, close to the front!—Mrs. Flanagan, I must leave you." So saying, having recovered all his faculties, by hearing a sound that he understood, he placed himself at the head of his men with an air of military pride, that the darkness prevented the washerwoman from beholding. A volley of musketry now rattled in the night wind, and the sergeant exclaimed,—

"March!—quick time!"

The next instant the trampling of a horse was heard coming up the road, at a rate that announced a matter of life or death; and Hollister again halted his party, riding a short distance in front himself, to meet the rider.

"Stand!—who goes there?" shouted Hollister.

"Ha! Hollister, is it you?" cried Lawton, "ever ready and at your post; but where is the guard?"

"At hand, sir, and ready to follow you through thick and thin," said the veteran, relieved at once from responsibility, and as eager as a boy to be led against his enemy.

" 'Tis well!" said the trooper, riding up to his men; then, speaking a few words of encouragement, he led them down the valley at a rate but little less rapid than his approach. The miserable horse of the sutler was soon distanced, and Betty, thus thrown out in the chase, turned to the side of the road, and observed,—

"There—it's no difficult to tell that Captain Jack is wid 'em, anyway; and away they go like so many nagur boys to a husking-frolic; well, I'll jist hitch the mare to this bit of a fence, and walk down and see the sport afoot—it's no r'asonable to expose the baste to be hurted."

Led on by Lawton, the men followed, destitute alike of fear and reflection. Whether it was a party of the refugees, or a detachment from the royal army, that they were to assail they were profoundly ignorant; but they knew that the officer in advance was distinguished for courage and personal prowess; and these are virtues that are sure to captivate the thoughtless soldiery. On arriving near the gates of the Locusts, the trooper halted his party, and made his arrangements for the assault. Dismounting, he ordered eight of his men to follow his example, and turning to Hollister, said,—

"Stand you here, and guard the horses; if anything attempt to pass, stop it, or cut it down, and—"

The flames at this moment burst through the dormer windows and cedar roof of the cottage, and a bright light glared on the darkness of the night. "Oh!" shouted the trooper, "on!—give quarter when you have done justice!"

There was a startling fierceness in the voice of the trooper that reached to the heart, even amid the horrors of the cottage. The leader of the Skinners dropped his plunder, and, for a moment, he stood in nerveless dread; then rushing to a window, he threw up the sash; at this instant Lawton entered, saber in hand, into the apartment.

"Die, miscreant!" cried the trooper, cleaving a marauder to the jaw; but the leader sprang into the lawn, and escaped his vengeance. The shrieks of the females restored Lawton to his presence of mind, and the earnest entreaty of the divine induced him to attend to the safety of the family. One more of the gang fell in with the dragoons, and met his death; but the remainder had taken the .alarm in season. Occupied with Sarah, neither Miss Singleton, nor the ladies of the house, had discovered the entrance of the Skinners, though the flames were raging around them with a fury that threatened the building with rapid destruction. The shrieks of Katy and the terrified consort of Cæsar, together with the noise and, uproar in the adjacent apartment, first roused Miss Peyton and Isabella to a sense of their danger.

"Merciful Providence!" exclaimed the alarmed aunt; "there

is a dreadful confusion in the house, and there will be blood shed in consequence of this affair."

"There are none to fight," returned Isabella, with a face paler than that of the other. "Dr. Sitgreaves is very peaceable in his disposition, and surely Captain Lawton would not forget himself so far."

"The Southern temper is quick and fiery," continued Miss Peyton; "and your brother, feeble and weak as he is, has looked the whole afternoon flushed and angry."

"Good heaven!" cried Isabella, with difficulty supporting herself on the couch of Sarah; "he is gentle as the lamb by nature, though the lion is not his equal when roused."

"We must interfere: our presence will quell the tumult, and possibly save the life of a fellow creature."

Miss Peyton, excited to attempt what she conceived a duty worthy of her sex and nature, advanced with the dignity of injured female feeling, to the door, followed by Isabella. The apartment to which Sarah had been conveyed was in one of the wings of the building, and it communicated with the principal hall of the cottage by a long and dark passage. This was now light, and across its termination several figures were seen rushing with an impetuosity that prevented an examination of their employment.

"Let us advance," said Miss Peyton, with a firmness her face belied; "they must respect our sex."

"They shall," cried Isabella, taking the lead in the enterprise. Frances was left alone with her sister. A few minutes were passed in silence, when a loud crash, in the upper apartments, was succeeded by a bright light that glared through the open door, and made objects as distinct to the eye as if they were placed under a noonday sun. Sarah raised herself on her bed, and staring wildly around, pressed both her hands on her forehead, endeavoring to recollect herself.

"This, then, is heaven—and you are one of its bright spirits. Oh! how glorious is its radiance! I had thought the happiness I have lately experienced was too much for earth. But we shall meet again; yes—yes—we shall meet again."

"Sarah! Sarah!" cried Frances, in terror; "my sister—my only sister—Oh! do not smile so horridly; know me, or you will break my heart."

"Hush," said Sarah raising her hand for silence; "you may disturb his rest—surely, he will follow me to the grave. Think you there can be two wives in the grave? No—no—no; one—one—one—only one."

Frances dropped her head into the lap of her sister, and wept in agony.

"Do you shed tears, sweet angel?" continued Sarah, soothingly. "Then heaven is not exempt from grief. But where is Henry? He was executed, and he must be here too; perhaps they will come together. Oh! how joyful will be the meeting!"

Frances sprang on her feet, and paced the apartment. The eye of Sarah followed her in childish admiration of her beauty.

"You look like my sister; but all good and lovely spirits are alike. Tell me, were you ever married? Did you ever let a stranger steal your affections from father, and brother, and sister? If not, poor wretch, I pity you, although you may be in heaven."

"Sarah—peace, peace—I implore you to be silent," shrieked Frances, rushing to her bed, "or you will kill me at your feet."

Another dreadful crash shook the building to its center. It was the falling of the roof, and the flames threw their light abroad, so as to make objects visible around the cottage, through the windows of the room. Frances flew to one of them, and saw the confused group that was collected on the lawn. Among them were her aunt and Isabella, pointing with distraction to the fiery edifice, and apparently urging the dragoons to enter it. For the first time she comprehended their danger; and uttering a wild shriek, she flew through the passage without consideration, or object.

A dense and suffocating column of smoke opposed her progress. She paused to breathe, when a man caught her in his arms, and bore her, in a state of insensibility, through the falling embers and darkness, to the open air. The instant that Frances recovered her recollection, she perceived that she owed her life to Lawton, and throwing herself on her knees, she cried,—

"Sarah! Sarah! Sarah! save my sister, and may the blessing of God await you!"

Her strength failed, and she sank on the grass, in insensibility. The trooper pointed to her figure, motioned to Katy for assistance, and advanced once more to the building. The fire had already communicated to the woodwork of the piazzas and windows, and the whole exterior of the cottage was covered with smoke. The only entrance was through these dangers, and even the hardy and impetuous Lawton paused to consider. It was for a moment only, when he dashed into the heat and darkness, where, missing the entrance, he wandered for a minute, and precipitated himself back, again, upon the lawn. Drawing a single breath of pure air, he renewed the effort, and was again unsuccessful. On a third trial, he met a man staggering under the load of a human body. It was neither the place, nor was there time, to question, or to make distinctions; seizing both in his arms, with gigantic strength, he bore them through the smoke. He soon perceived, to his astonishment, that it was the surgeon, and the body of one of the Skinners, that he had saved.

"Archibald!" he exclaimed, "why, in the name of justice, did you bring this miscreant to light again? His deeds are rank to heaven!"

The surgeon, who had been in imminent peril, was too much bewildered to reply instantly, but wiping the moisture from his forehead, and clearing his lungs from the vapor he had inhaled, he said piteously,—

"Ah! it is all over. Had I been in time to have stopped the effusion from the jugular, he might have been saved; but the heat was conducive to hemorrhage; life is extinct indeed. Well, are there any more wounded?"

His question was put to the air, for Frances had been removed to the opposite side of the building, where her friends were collected, and Lawton had once more disappeared in the smoke.

By this time the flames had dispersed much of the suffocating vapor, so that the trooper was able to find the door, and in its very entrance he was met by a man supporting the insensible Sarah. There was but barely time to reach the lawn again, before the fire broke through the windows, and wrapped the whole building in a sheet of flame.

"God be praised!" ejaculated the preserver of Sarah. "It would have been a dreadful death to die."

The trooper turned from gazing at the edifice, to the speaker, and to his astonishment, instead of one of his own men, he beheld the peddler.

"Ha! the spy," he exclaimed; "by heavens, you cross me like a specter."

"Captain Lawton," said Birch, leaning in momentary exhaustion against the fence, to which they had retired from the heat, "I am again in your power, for I can neither flee, nor resist."

"The cause of America is dear to me as life," said the trooper, "but she cannot require her children to forget gratitude and honor. Fly, unhappy man, while yet you are unseen, or it will exceed my power to save you."

"May God prosper you, and make you victorious over your enemies," said Birch, grasping the hand of the dragoon with an iron strength that his meager figure did not indicate.

"Hold!" said Lawton. "But a word—are you what you seem?—can you—are you—"

"A royal spy," interrupted Birch, averting his face, and endeavoring to release his hand.

"Then go, miserable wretch," said the trooper, relinquishing his grasp. "Either avarice or delusion has led a noble heart astray!"

The bright light from the flames reached a great distance around the ruins, but the words were hardly past the lips of Lawton, before the gaunt form of the peddler had glided over the visible space, and plunged into the darkness beyond.

The eye of Lawton rested for a moment on the spot where he had last seen this inexplicable man, and then turning to the yet insensible Sarah, he lifted her in his arms, and bore her, like a sleeping infant, to the care of her friends.

CHAPTER XXIII

And now her charms are fading fast,
Her spirits now no more are gay:
Alas! that beauty cannot last!...
That flowers so sweet so soon decay!
    How sad appears
    The vale of years,
How changed from youth's too flattering scene!
    Where are her fond admirers gone?
    Alas! and shall there then be none
On whom her soul may lean?
—Cynthia's Grave.

The walls of the cottage were all that was left of the building; and these, blackened by smoke, and stripped of their piazzas and ornaments, were but dreary memorials of the content and security that had so lately reigned within. The roof, together with the rest of the woodwork, had tumbled into the cellars, and a pale and flitting light, ascending from their embers, shone faintly through the windows. The early flight of the Skinners left the dragoons at liberty to exert themselves in saving much of the furniture, which lay scattered in heaps on the lawn, giving the finishing touch of desolation to the scene. Whenever a stronger ray of light than common shot upwards, the composed figures of Sergeant Hollister and his associates, sitting on their horses in rigid discipline, were to be seen in the background of the picture, together with the beast of Mrs. Flanagan, which, having slipped its bridle, was quietly grazing by the highway. Betty herself had advanced to the spot where the sergeant was posted, and, with an incredible degree of composure, witnessed the whole of the events as they occurred. More than once she suggested to her companion, that, as the fighting seemed to be over, the proper time for plunder had arrived, but the veteran acquainted her with his orders, and remained inflexible and immovable; until the washerwoman, observing Lawton come round the wing of the building with Sarah, ventured amongst the warriors. The captain, after placing Sarah on a sofa that had been hurled from the building by two of his men, retired, that the ladies might succeed him in his care. Miss Peyton and her niece flew, with a rapture that was blessed with a momentary forgetfullness of all but her preservation, to receive Sarah from the trooper; but the vacant eye and flushed cheek restored them instantly to their recollection.

"Sarah, my child, my beloved niece," said the former, folding the unconscious bride in her arms, "you are saved, and may the blessing of God await him who has been the instrument."

"See," said Sarah, gently pushing her aunt aside, and pointing to the glimmering ruins, "the windows are illuminated in honor of my arrival. They always receive a bride thus—he told me they would do no less. Listen, and you will hear the bells."

"Here is no bride, no rejoicing, nothing but woe!" cried Frances, in a manner but little less frantic than that of her sister. "Oh! may heaven restore you to us—to yourself!"

"Peace, foolish young woman," said Sarah, with a smile of affected pity; "all cannot be happy at the same moment; perhaps you have no brother, or husband, to console you. You look beautiful, and you will yet find one; but," she continued, dropping her voice to a whisper, "see that he has no other wife—'tis dreadful to think what might happen, should he be twice married."

"The shock has destroyed her mind," cried Miss Peyton; "my child, my beauteous Sarah is a maniac!"

"No, no, no," cried Frances, "it is fever; she is lightheaded—she must recover—she shall recover."

The aunt caught joyfully at the hope conveyed in this suggestion, and dispatched Katy to request the immediate aid and advice of Dr. Sitgreaves. The surgeon was found inquiring among the men for professional employment, and inquisitively examining every bruise and scratch that he could induce the sturdy warriors to acknowledge they had received. A summons, of the sort conveyed by Katy, was instantly obeyed, and not a minute elapsed before he was by the side of Miss Peyton.

"This is a melancholy termination to so joyful a commencement of the night, madam," he observed, in a soothing manner. "But war must bring its attendant miseries; though doubtless it often supports the cause of liberty, and improves the knowledge of surgical science."

Miss Peyton could make no reply, but pointed to her niece.

" 'Tis fever," answered Frances; "see how glassy is her eye, and look at her cheek, how flushed."

The surgeon stood for a moment, deeply studying the outward symptoms of his patient, and then he silently took her hand in his own. It was seldom that the hard and abstracted features of Sitgreaves discovered any violent emotion; all his passions seemed schooled, and his countenance did not often betray what, indeed, his heart frequently felt. In the present instance, however, the eager gaze of the aunt and sister quickly detected his emotions. After laying his fingers for a minute on the beautiful arm, which, bared to the elbow and glittering with jewels, Sarah suffered him to retain, he dropped it, and dashing a hand over his eyes, turned sorrowfully away.

"Here is no fever to excite—'tis a case, my dear madam, for time and care only; these, with the blessing of God, may effect a cure."

"And where is the wretch who has caused this ruin?" exclaimed Singleton, rejecting the support of his man, and making an effort to rise from the chair to which he had been driven by debility. "It is in vain that we overcome our enemies, if, conquered, they can inflict such wounds as this."

"Dost think, foolish boy," said Lawton, with a bitter smile, "that hearts can feel in a colony? What is America but a satellite of England—to move as she moves, follow where she wists, and shine, that the mother country may become more splendid by her radiance? Surely you forget that it is honor enough for a colonist to receive ruin from the hand of a child of Britain."

"I forget not that I wear a sword," said Singleton, falling back exhausted; "but was there no willing arm ready to avenge that lovely sufferer—to appease the wrongs of his hoary father?"

"Neither arms nor hearts are wanting, sir, in such a cause," said the trooper, fiercely; "but chance oftentimes helps the wicked. By heavens, I'd give Roanoke himself, for a clear field with the miscreant!"

"Nay! captain dear, no be parting with the horse, anyway," said Betty. "It is no trifle that can be had by jist asking of the right person, if ye're in need of silver; and the baste is sure of foot, and jumps like a squirrel."

"Woman, fifty horses, aye, the best that were ever reared on the banks of the Potomac, would be but a paltry price, for one blow at a villain."

"Come," said the surgeon, "the night air can do no service to George, or these ladies, and it is incumbent on us to remove them where they can find surgical attendance and refreshment. Here is nothing but smoking ruins and the miasma of the swamps."

To this rational proposition no objection could be raised, and the necessary orders were issued by Lawton to remove the whole party to the Four Corners.

America furnished but few and very indifferent carriage-makers at the period of which we write, and every vehicle, that in the least aspired to that dignity, was the manufacture of a London mechanic. When Mr. Wharton left the city, he was one of the very few who maintained the state of a carriage; and, at the time Miss Peyton and his daughters joined him in his retirement, they had been conveyed to the cottage in the heavy chariot that had once so imposingly rolled through the windings of Queen Street, or emerged, with somber dignity, into the more spacious drive of Broadway. This vehicle stood, undisturbed, where it had been placed on its arrival, and the age of the horses alone had protected the favorites of Cæsar from sequestration by the contending forces in their neighborhood. With a heavy heart, the black, assisted by a few of the dragoons, proceeded to prepare it for the reception of the ladies. It was a cumbrous vehicle, whose faded linings and tarnished hammercloth, together with its panels of changing color, denoted the want of that art which had once given it luster and beauty. The "lion couchant" of the Wharton arms was reposing on the riviving splendor of a blazonry that told the armorial bearings of a prince of the church; and the miter, that began to shine through its American mask, was a symbol of the rank of its original owner. The chaise which conveyed Miss Singleton was also safe, for the stable and outbuildings had entirely escaped the flames; it certainly had been no part of the plan of the marauders to leave so well-appointed a stud behind them, but the suddenness of the attack by Lawton, not only disconcerted their arrangements on this point, but on many others also. A guard was left on the ground, under the command of Hollister, who, having discovered that his enemy was of mortal mold, took his position with admirable coolness and no little skill, to guard against surprise. He drew off his small party to such a distance from the ruins, that it was effectually concealed in the darkness, while at the same time the light continued sufficiently powerful to discover anyone who might approach the lawn with an intent to plunder.

Satisfied with this judicious arrangement. Captain Lawton made his dispositions for the march. Miss Peyton, her two nieces, and Isabella were placed in the chariot, while the cart of Mrs. Flanagan, amply supplied with blankets and a bed, was honored with the person of Captain Singleton. Dr. Sitgreaves took charge of the chaise and Mr. Wharton. What became of the rest of the family during that eventful night is unknown, for Caesar alone, of the domestics, was to be found, if we except the housekeeper. Having disposed of the whole party in this manner, Lawton gave the word to march. He remained himself, for a few minutes, alone on the lawn, secreting various pieces of plate and other valuables, that he was fearful might tempt the cupidity of his own men; when, perceiving nothing more that he conceived likely to overcome their honesty, he threw himself into the saddle with the soldierly intention of bringing up the rear.

"Stop, stop," cried a female voice. "Will you leave me alone to be murdered? The spoon is melted. I believe, and I'll have compensation, if there's law or justice in this unhappy land."

Lawton turned an eye in the direction of the sound, and perceived a female emerging from the ruins, loaded with a bundle that vied in size with the renowned pack of the peddler.

"Whom have we here," said the trooper, "rising like a phœnix from the flames? Oh! by the soul of Hippocrates, but it is the identical she-doctor, of famous needle reputation. Well, good woman, what means this outcry?"

"Outcry!" echoed Katy, panting for breath. "Is it not disparagement enough to lose a silver spoon, but I must be left alone in this lonesome place, to be robbed, and perhaps murdered? Harvey would not serve me so; when I lived with Harvey, I was always treated with respect at least, if he was a little close with his secrets, and wasteful of his money."

"Then, madam, you once formed part of the household of Mr. Harvey Birch?"

"You may say I was the whole of his household," returned the other; "there was nobody but I, and he, and the old gentleman. You didn't know the old gentleman, perhaps?"

"That happiness was denied me. How long did you live in the family of Mr. Birch?"

"I disremember the precise time, but it must have been hard on upon nine years; and what better am I for it all?"

"Sure enough; I can see but little benefit that you have derived from the association, truly. But is there not something unusual in the movements and character of this Mr. Birch?"

"Unusual is an easy word for such unaccountables!" replied Katy, lowering her voice and looking around her. "He was a wonderful disregardful man, and minded a guinea no more than I do a kernel of corn. But help me to some way of joining Miss Jinitt, and I will tell you prodigies of what Harvey has done, first and last."

"You will!" exclaimed the trooper, musing. "Here, give me leave to feel your arm above the elbow. There—you are not deficient in bone, let the blood be as it may." So saying, he .gave the spinster a sudden whirl, that effectually confused all her faculties, until she found herself safely, if not comfortably, seated on the crupper of Lawton's steed.

"Now, madam, you have the consolation of knowing that you are as well mounted as Washington. The nag is sure of foot, and will leap like a panther."

"Let me get down," cried Katy, struggling to release herself from his iron grasp, and yet afraid of falling. "This is no way to put a woman on a horse; besides, I can't ride without a pillion."

"Softly, good madam," said Lawton; "for although Roanoke never falls before, he sometimes rises behind. He is far from being accustomed to a pair of heels beating upon his flanks like a drum major on a field day; a single touch of the spur will serve him for a fortnight, and it is by no means wise to be kicking in this manner, for he is a horse that but little likes to be outdone."

"Let me down, I say," screamed Katy; "I shall fall and be killed. Besides, I have nothing to hold on with; my arms are full of valuables."

"True," returned the trooper, observing that he had brought bundle and all from the ground. "I perceive that you belong to the baggage guard; but my sword belt will encircle your little waist, as well as my own."

Katy was too much pleased with this compliment to make any resistance, while he buckled her close to his own herculean frame, and, driving a spur into his charger, they flew from the lawn with a rapidity that defied further denial. After proceeding for some time, at a rate that a good deal discomposed the spinster, they overtook the cart of the washerwoman driving slowly over the stones, with a proper consideration for the wounds of Captain Singleton. The occurrences of that eventful night had produced an excitement in the young soldier, that was followed by the ordinary lassitude of reaction, and he lay carefully enveloped in blankets, and supported by his man, but little able to converse, though deeply brooding over the past. The dialogue between Lawton and his companion ceased with the commencement of their motions, but a footpace being more favorable to speech, the trooter began anew:—

"Then, you have been an inmate in the same house with Harvey Birch?"

"For more than nine years," said Katy, drawing her breath, and rejoicing greatly that their speed was abated.

The deep tones of the trooper's voice were no sooner conveyed to the ears of the washerwoman, than, turning her head, where she sat directing the movements of the mare, she put into the discourse at the first pause.

"Belike, then, good woman, ye're knowing whether or no he's akin to Beelzeboob," said Betty. "It's Sargeant Hollister who's saying the same, and no fool is the sargeant, anyway."

"It's a scandalous disparagement," cried Katy, vehemently, "no kinder soul than Harvey carries a pack; and for a gown or a tidy apron, he will never take a king's farthing from a friend. Beelzcbub, indeed! For what would he read the Bible, if he had dealings with the evil spirit?"

"He's an honest divil, anyway; as I was saying before, the guinea was pure. But then the sargeant thinks him amiss, and it's no want of l'arning that Mister Hollistcr has."

"He's a fool!" said Katy tartly. "Harvey might be a man of substance, were he not so disregardful. How often have I told him, that if he did nothing but peddle, and would put his gains to use, and get married, so that things at home could be kept within doors, and leave off his dealings with the rig'lars, and all incumberments that he would soon become an excellent liver. Sergeant Hollister would be glad to hold a candle to him, indeed!"

"Pooh!" said Betty, in her philosophical way; "ye're no

thinking that Mister Hollister is an officer, and stands next the cornet, in the troop. But this piddler gave warning of the brush the night, and it's no sure that Captain Jack would have got the day, but for the re-enforcement."

"How say you, Betty," cried the trooper, bending forward on his saddle, "had you notice of our danger from Birch?"

"The very same, darling; and it's hurry I was till the boys was in motion; not but I knew ye're enough for the Cowboys any time. But wid the divil on your side, I was sure of the day. I'm only wondering there's so little plunder, in a business of Beelzeboob's contriving."

"I'm obliged to you for the rescue, and equally indebted to the motive."

"Is it the plunder? But little did I t'ink of it till I saw the movables on the ground, some burnt, and some broke, and other some as good as new. It would be convanient to have one feather bed in the corps, anyway."

"By heavens, 'twas timely succor! Had not Roanoke been swifter than their bullets, I must have fallen. The animal is worth his weight in gold."

"It's continental, you mane, darling. Goold weighs heavy, and is no plenty in the states. If the nagur hadn't been staying and frighting the sargeant with his copper-colored looks, and a matter of blarney 'bout ghosts, we should have been in time to have killed all the dogs, and taken the rest prisoners."

"It is very well as it is, Betty," said Lawton. "A day will yet come, I trust, when these miscreants shall be rewarded, if not in judgments upon their persons, at least in the opinions of their fellow citizens. The time must arrive when America will distinguish between a patriot and a robber."

"Speak low," said Katy; "there's some who think much of themselves, that have doings with the Skinners."

"It's more they are thinking of themselves, then, than other people thinks of them," cried Betty. "A t'ief's a t'ief, anyway; whether he stales for King George or for Congress."

"I know'd that evil would soon happen," said Katy. "The sun set tonight behind a black cloud, and the house dog whined, although I gave him his supper with my own hands; besides, it's not a wee sin' I dreamed the dream about the thousand lighted candles, and the cakes burnt in the oven."

"Well," said Betty, "ifs but little I drame, anyway. Jist keep an 'asy conscience and a plenty of the stuff in ye, and ye'll sleep like an infant. The last drame I had was when the boys put the thistle tops in the blankets, and then I was thinking that Captain Jack's man was currying me down, for the matter of Roanoke, but it's no trifle I mind either in skin or stomach."

"I'm sure," said Katy, with a stiff erectness that drew Lawton back in his saddle, "no man shall ever dare to lay hands on bed of mine; it's undecent and despisable conduct."

"Pooh! pooh!" cried Betty; "if you tag after a troop of horse, a small bit of a joke must be born. What would become of the states and liberty, if the boys had never a clane shirt, or a drop to comfort them? Ask Captain Jack, there, if they'd fight, Mrs. Beelzeboob, and they no clane linen to keep the victory in."

"I'm a single woman, and my name is Haynes," said Katy, "and I'd thank you to use no disparaging terms when speaking to me."

"You must tolerate a little license in the tongue of Mrs. Flanagan, madam," said the trooper. "The drop she speaks of is often of an extraordinary size, and then she has acquired the freedom of a soldier's manner."

"Pooh! captain, darling," cried Betty, "why do you bother the woman? Talk like yeerself, dear, and it's no fool of a tongue that ye've got in yeer own head. But jist here-away that sargeant made a halt, thinking there might be more divils than one stirring, the night. The clouds are as black as Arnold's heart and deuce the star is there twinkling among them. Well, the mare is used to a march after nightfall, and is smelling out the road like a pointer slut."

"It wants but little to the rising moon," observed the trooper. He called a dragoon, who was riding in advance, issued a few orders and cautions relative to the comfort and safety of Singleton, and speaking a consoling word to his friend himself, gave Roanoke the spur, and dashed by the car, at a rate that again put to flight all the philosophy of Katharine Haynes.

"Good luck to ye, for a free rider and a bold!"* shouted the washerwoman, as he passed. "If ye're meeting Mister Beelzeboob, jist back the baste up to him, and show him his consort that ye've got on the crupper. I'm thinking it's no long he'd tarry to chat. Well, well, it's his life that we saved, he was saying so himself—though the plunder is nothing to signify."

The cries of Betty Flanagan were too familiar to the ears of Captain Lawton to elicit a reply. Notwithstanding the unusual burden that Roanoke sustained, he got over the ground with great rapidity, and the distance between the cart of Mrs. Flanagan and the chariot of Miss Peyton was passed in a manner that, however it answered the intentions of the trooper, in no degree contributed to the comfort of his companion. The meeting occurred but a short distance from the quarters of Lawton, and at the same instant the moon broke from a mass of clouds, and threw its light on objects.

Compared with the simple elegance and substantial comfort of the Locusts, the "Hotel Flanagan" presented but a dreary spectacle. In the place of carpeted floors and curtained windows, were the yawning cracks of a rudely-constructed dwelling, and board and paper were ingeniously applied to supply the place of the green glass in more than half the lights. The care of Lawton had anticipated every improvement that their situation would allow, and blazing fires were made before the party arrived. The dragoons, who had been charged with this duty, had conveyed a few necessary articles of furniture, and Miss Peyton and her companions, on alighting, found something like habitable apartments prepared for their reception. The mind of Sarah had continued to wander during the ride, and, with the ingenuity of the insane, she accommodated every circumstance to the feelings that were uppermost in her own bosom.

"It is impossible to minister to a mind that has sustained such a blow," said Lawton to Isabella Singleton. "Time and God's mercy can alone cure it, but something more may be done towards the bodily comfort of all. You are a soldier's daughter, and used to scenes like this; help me to exclude some of the cold air from these windows."

Miss Singleton acceded to his request, and while Lawton was endeavoring, from without, to remedy the defect of broken panes, Isabella was arranging a substitute for a curtain within.

"I hear the cart," said the trooper, in reply to one of her interrogatories. "Betty is tender-hearted in the main; believe me, poor George will not only be safe, but comfortable."

"God bless her, for her care, and bless you all," said Isabella, fervently. "Dr. Sitgreaves has gone down the road to meet him, I know. What is that glittering in the moon?"

Directly opposite the window where they stood, were the outbuildings of the farm, and the quick eye of Lawton caught at a glance the object to which she alluded.

" 'Tis the glare of firearms," said the trooper, springing from the window towards his charger, which yet remained caparisoned at the door. His movement was quick as thought, but a flash of fire was followed by the whistling of a bullet, before he had proceeded a step. A loud shriek burst from the dwelling, and the captain sprang into his saddle; the whole was the business of but a moment.

"Mount—mount, and follow!" shouted the trooper; and before his astonished men could understand the cause of alarm, Roanoke had carried him in safety over the fence which lay between him and his foe. The chase was for life or death, but the distance to the rocks was again too short, and the disappointed trooper saw his intended victim vanish in their clefts, where he could not follow.

"By the life of Washington," muttered Lawton, as he sheathed his saber, "I would have made two halves of him, had he not been so nimble on the foot—but a time will come!" So saying, he returned to his quarters, with the indifference of a man who knew his life was at any moment to be offered a sacrifice to his country. An extraordinary tumult in the house induced him to quicken his speed, and on arriving at the door, the panic-stricken Katy informed him that the bullet aimed at his own life had taken effect in the bosom of Miss Singleton.

CHAPTER XXIV

Hushed were his Gertrude's lips; hut still their bland
And beautiful expression seemed to melt
With love that could not die! and still his hand
She presses to the heart no more that felt.
—Gertrude of Wyoming.

The brief arrangements of the dragoons had prepared two apartments for the reception of the ladies, the one being intended as a sleeping room, and situated within the other. Into the latter Isabella was immediately conveyed, at her own request, and placed on a rude bed by the side of the unconscious Sarah. When Miss Peyton and Frances flew to her assistance, they found her with a smile on her pallid lip, and a composure in her countenance, that induced them to think her uninjured.

"God be praised!" exclaimed the trembling aunt. "The report of firearms, and your fall, had led me into error. Surely, surely, there was enough horror before; but this has been spared us."

Isabella pressed her hand upon her bosom, still smiling, but with a ghastliness that curdled the blood of Frances.

"Is George far distant?" she asked. "Let him know—hasten him, that I may see my brother once again."

"It is as I apprehended!" shrieked Miss Peyton. "But you smile—surely you are not hurt!"

"Quite well—quite happy," murmured Isabella: "here is a remedy for every pain."

Sarah arose from the reclining posture she had taken, and gazed wildly at her companion. She stretched forth her own hand, and raised that of Isabella from her bosom. It was dyed in blood.

"See," said Sarah, "but will it not wash away love? Marry, young woman, and then no one can expel him from your heart, unless," she added, whispering, and bending over the other,—"you find another there before you; then die, and go to heaven—there are no wives in heaven."

The lovely maniac hid her face under the clothes, and continued silent during the remainder of the night. At this moment Lawton entered. Inured as he was to danger in all its forms, and accustomed to the horrors of a partisan war, the trooper could not behold the ruin before him unmoved. He bent over the fragile form of Isabella, and his gloomy eye betrayed the workings of his soul.

"Isabella," he at length uttered, "I know you to possess a courage beyond the strength of women."

"Speak," she said, earnestly; "if you have anythingto say, speak fearlessly."

The trooper averted his face as he replied, "None ever receive a ball there, and survive."

"I have no dread of death, Lawton," returned Isabella. "I thank you for not doubting me; I felt it from the first."

"These are not scenes for a form like yours," added the trooper. " 'Tis enough that Britain calls our youth to the field; but when such loveliness becomes the victim of war, I sicken of my trade."

"Hear me, Captain Lawton," said Isabella, raising herself with difficulty, but rejecting aid. "From early womanhood to the present hour have I been an inmate of camps and garrisons. I have lived to cheer the leisure of an aged father, and think you I would change those days of danger and privation for any ease? No! I have the consolation of knowing, in my dying moments, that what woman could do in such a cause, I have done."

"Who could prove a recreant, and witness such a spirit! Hundreds of warriors have I witnessed in their blood, but never a firmer soul among them all."

" 'Tis the soul only," said Isabella. "My sex and strength have denied me the dearest of privileges. But to you, Captain Lawton, nature has been more bountiful; you have an arm and a heart to devote to the cause; and I know they are an arm and a heart that will prove true to the last. And George—and—" she paused, her lip quivered, and her eye sank to the floor.

"And Dunwoodie!" added the trooper. "Would you speak of Dunwoodie?"

"Name him not," said Isabella, sinking back, and concealing her face in her garments, "Leave me, Lawton—prepare poor George for this unexpected blow."

The trooper continued for a little while gazing, in melancholy interest, at the convulsive shudderings of her frame, which the scanty covering could not conceal, and withdrew to meet his comrade. The interview between Singleton and his sister was painful, and, for a moment, Isabella yielded to a burst of tenderness; but, as if aware that her hours were numbered, she was the first to rouse herself to exertion. At her earnest request, the room was left to herself, the captain, and Frances. The repeated applications of the surgeon, to be permitted to use professional aid, were steadily rejected, and, at length, he was obliged unwillingly to retire.

"Raise me," said the dying young woman, "and let me look on a face that I love, once more." Frances silently complied, and Isabella turned her eyes in sisterly affection upon George. "It matters but little, my brother—a few hours must close the scene."

"Live, Isabella, my sister, my only sister!" cried the youth, with a burst of sorrow that he could not control. "My father! my poor father—"

"There is the sting of death; but he is a soldier and a Christian. Miss Wharton, I would speak of what interests you, while yet I have strength for the task."

"Nay," said Frances, tenderly, "compose yourself; let no desire to oblige me endanger a life that is precious to—to—so many." The words were nearly stifled by her emotions, for the other had touched a chord that thrilled to her heart.

"Poor, sensitive girl!" said Isabella, regarding her with tender interest; "But the world is still before you, and why should I disturb the little happiness it may afford! Dream on, lovely innocent! and may God keep the evil day of knowledge far distant!"

"Oh, there is even now little left for me to enjoy," said Frances, burying her face in the clothes. "I am heart-stricken, in all that I most loved."

"No!" interrupted Isabella; "you have one inducement to wish for life, that pleads strongly in a woman's breast. It is a delusion that nothing but death can destroy—" Exhaustion compelled her to pause, and her auditors continued in breathless suspense, until, recovering her strength, she laid her hand on that of Frances, and continued more mildly, "Miss Wharton, if there breathes a spirit congenial to Dunwoodie's, and worthy of his love, it is your own."

A flush of fire passed over the face of the listener, and she raised her eyes, flashing with an ungovernable look of delight, to the countenance of Isabella; but the ruin she beheld recalled better feelings, and again her head dropped upon the covering of the bed. Isabella watched her emotion with a look that partook both of pity and admiration.

"Such have been the feelings that I have escaped," she continued. "Yes, Miss Wharton, Dunwoodie is wholly yours."

"Be just to yourself, my sister," exclaimed the youth; "let no romantic generosity cause you to forget your own character."

She heard him, and fixed a gaze of tender interest on his face, but slowly shook her head as she replied,—

"It is not romance, but truth, that bids me speak. Oh! how much have I lived within an hour! Miss Wharton, I was born under a burning sun, and my feelings seem to have imbibed its warmth; I have existed for passion only."

"Say not so—say not so, I implore you," cried the agitated brother. "Think how devoted has been your love to our aged father; how disinterested, how tender, your affection to me!"

"Yes," said Isabella, a smile of mild pleasure beaming on her countenance, "that, at least, is a reflection which may be taken to the grave."

Neither Frances nor her brother interrupted her meditations, which continued for several minutes; when, suddenly recollecting herself, she continued,—

"I remain selfish even to the last; with me. Miss Wharton, America and her liberties were my earliest passion, and—" Again she paused, and Frances thought it was the struggle of death that followed; but reviving, she proceeded, "Why should I hesitate, on the brink of the grave! Dunwoodie was my next and my last. But," burying her face in her hands, "it was a love that was unsought."

"Isabella!" exclaimed her brother, springing from the bed, and pacing the floor in disorder.

"See how dependent we become under the dominion of worldly pride; it is painful to George to learn that one he loves had not feelings superior to her nature and education."

"Say no more," whispered Frances; "you distress us both—say no more, I entreat you."

"In justice to Dunwoodie I must speak; and for the same reason, my brother, you must listen. By no act or word has Dunwoodie ever induced me to believe he wished me more than a friend; nay, latterly, I have had the burning shame of thinking that he avoided my presence."

"Would he dare?" said Singleton, fiercely.

"Peace, my brother, and listen," continued Isabella, rousing herself with an effort that was final. "Here is the innocent, the justifiable cause. We are both motherless; but that aunt—that mild, plain-hearted, observing aunt, has given you the victory. Oh! how much she loses, who loses a female guardian to her youth. I have exhibited those feelings which you have been taught to repress. After this, can I wish to live?"

"Isabella! my poor Isabella! you wander in your mind."

"But one word more—for I feel that blood, which ever flowed too swiftly, rushing where nature never intended it to go. Woman must be sought to be prized; her life is one of concealed emotions; blessed are they whose early impressions make the task free from hypocrisy, for such only can be happy with men like—like Dunwoodie." Her voice failed, and she sank back on her pillow in silence. The cry of Singleton brought the rest of the party to her bedside; but death was already upon her countenance; her remaining strength just sufficed to reach the hand of George, and pressing it to her bosom for a moment, she relinquished her grasp, and, with a slight convulsion, expired.

Frances Wharton had thought that fate had done its worst, in endangering the life of her brother, and destroying the reason of her sister; but the relief conveyed by the dying declaration of Isabella taught her that another sorrow had aided in loading her heart with grief. She saw the whole truth at glance; nor was the manly delicacy of Dunwoodie lost upon her—everything tended to raise him in her estimation; and, for mourning that duty and pride had induced her to strive to think less of him, she was compelled to substitute regret that her own act had driven him from her in sorrow, if not in desperation. It is not in the nature of youth, however, to despair; and Frances now knew a secret joy that gave a new spring to her existence.

The sun broke forth, on the morning that succeeded this night of desolation, in unclouded luster, and seemed to mock the petty sorrows of those who received his rays. Lawton had early ordered his steed, and was ready to mount as the first burst of light broke over the hills. His orders were already given, and the trooper threw his leg across the saddle, in silence; and, casting a glance of fierce chagrin at the narrow space that had favored the flight of the Skinner, he gave Roanoke the rein, and moved slowly towards the valley.

The stillness of death pervaded the road, nor was there a single vestige of the scenes of the night, to tarnish the loveliness of a glorious morn. Struck with the contrast between man and nature, the fearless trooper rode by each pass of danger, regardless of what might happen; nor did he rouse himself from his musing, until the noble charger, snuffing the morning air, greeted the steeds of the guard under Sergeant Hollister.

Here, indeed, was to be seen sad evidence of the midnight fray, but the trooper glanced his eye over it with the coolness of one accustomed to such sights. Without wasting the moments in useless regrets, he proceeded, at once, to business.

"Have you seen anything?" he demanded of the orderly.

"Nothing, sir, that we dared to charge upon," returned Hollister; "but we mounted once, at the report of distant firearms."

"'Tis well," said Lawton, gloomily. "Ah! Hollister, I would give the animal I ride, to have had your single arm between the wretch who drew that trigger and these useless rocks, which overhang every bit of ground, as if they grudged pasture to a single hoof."

"Under the light of day, and charging man to man, I am as good as another; but I can't say that I'm overfond of fighting with those that neither steel nor lead can bring down."

"What silly crochet is uppermost, now, in that mystified brain of thine, Deacon Hollister?"

"I like not the dark object that has been maneuvering in the skirt of the wood since the first dawn of day; and twice, during the night, it was seen marching across the firelight, no doubt with evil intent."

"Is it yon ball of black, at the foot of the rock maple, that you mean? In truth it moves."

"But without mortal motion," said the sergeant, regarding it with awful reverence. "It glides along, but no feet have been seen by any who watch here."

"Had it wings," cried Lawton, "it is mine; stand fast, until I join." The words were hardly uttered before Roanoke was flying across the plain, and apparently verifying the boast of his master.

"Those cursed rocks!" ejaculated the trooper, as he saw the

object of his pursuit approaching the hillside; but, either from want of practice or from terror, it passed the obvious shelter they offered, and fled into the open plain.

"I have you, man or devil!" shouted Lawton, whirling his saber from its scabbard. "Halt, and take quarter!"

His proposition was apparently acceded to; for, at the sound of his powerful voice, the figure sank upon the ground, exhibiting a shapeless ball of black, without life or motion.

"What have we here?" cried Lawton, drawing up by its side. "A gala suit of the good maiden, Jeanette Peyton, wandering around its birthplace—or searching in vain for its discomfited mistress?" He leaned forward in his stirrups, and placing the point of his sword under the silken garment, by throwing aside the covering, discovered part of the form of the reverend gentleman who had fled from the Locusts, the evening before, in his robes of office.

"In truth, Hollister had some ground for his alarm; an army chaplain is, at any time, a terror to a troop of horse."

The clergyman had collected enough of his disturbed faculties, to discover that it was a face he knew, and somewhat disconcerated at the terror he had manifested, and the indecent attitude in which he had been found, he endeavored to rise and offer some explanation. Lawton received his apologies good-humoredly, of not with much faith in their truth; and, after a short communication upon the state of the valley, the trooper courteously alighted, and they proceeded towards the guard.

"I am so little acquainted, sir, with the rebel uniform, that I really was unable to distinguish, whether those men, whom you say are your own, did or did not belong to the gang of marauders."

"Apology, sir, is unnecessary," replied the trooper, curling his lip. "It is not your task, as a minister of God, to take note of the facings of a coat. The standard under which you serve is acknowledged by us all."

"I serve under the standard of his gracious Majesty, George III," returned the priest, wiping the cold sweat from his brow. "But really the idea of being scalped has a strong tendency to unman a new-beginner, like myself."

"Scalped!" echoed Lawton, stopping short in his walk. Then recollecting himself, he added, with composure, "If it is to Dunwoodie's squadron of Virginia light dragoons that you allude, it may be well to inform you that they generally take a bit of the skull with the skin."

"Oh! I can have no apprehensions of gentlemen of your appearance," said the divine, with a smirk. "It is the natives that I apprehend."

"Natives! I have the honor to be one, I assure you, sir."

"Nay, I beg that I may be understood—I mean the Indians; they who do nothing but rob, and murder, and destroy."

"And scalp!"

"Yes, sir, and scalp too," continued the clergyman, eying his companion a little suspiciously; "the copper-colored, savage Indians."

"And did you expect to meet those nose-jeweled gentry in the neutral ground?"

"Certainly; we understand in England that the interior swarms with them."

"And call you this the interior of America?" cried Lawton, again halting, and staring the other in the face, with a surprise too naturally expressed to be counterfeited.

"Surely, sir, I conceive myself to be in the interior."

"Attend," said Lawton, pointing towards the east, "See you not that broad sheet of water which the eye cannot compass? Thither lies the England you deem worthy to hold dominion over half the world. See you the land of your nativity?"

" 'Tis impossible to behold objects at a distance of three thousand miles!" exclaimed the wondering priest, a little suspicious of his companion's sanity.

"No! what a pity it is that the powers of man are not equal to his ambition. Now turn your eyes westward; observe that vast expanse of water which rolls between the shores of America and China."

"I see nothing but land," said the trembling priest; "there is no water to be seen."

" 'Tis impossible to behold objects at a distance of three thousand miles!" repeated Lawton, pursuing his walk. "If you apprehend the savages, seek them in the ranks of your prince. Rum and gold have preserved their loyalty."

"Nothing is more probable than my being deceived," said the man of peace, casting furtive glances at the colossal stature and whiskered front of his companion; "but the rumors we have at home, and the uncertainty of meeting with such an enemy as yourself, induced me to fly at your approach."

" 'Twas not judiciously determined," said the trooper, "as Roanoke has the heels of you greatly; and flying from Scylla, you were liable to encounter Charybdis. Those woods and rocks cover the very enemies you dread."

"The savages!" exclaimed the divine, instinctively placing the trooper in the rear.

"More than savages; men who, under the guise of patriotism, prowl through the community, with a thirst for plunder that is unsatiable, and a love of cruelty that mocks the ingenuity of the Indian—fellows whose mouths are filled with liberty and equality, and whose hearts are overflowing with cupidity and gall—gentlemen that are ycleped Skinners."

"I have heard them mentioned in our army," said the frightened divine, "and had thought them to be the aborigines."

"You did the savages injustice."

They now approached the spot occupied by Hollister, who witnessed with surprise the character of the prisoner made by his captain. Lawton gave his orders, and the men immediately commenced securing and removing such articles of furniture as were thought worthy of the trouble; and the captain, with his reverend associate, who was mounted on a mettled horse, returned to the quarters of the troop.

It was the wish of Singleton that the remains of his sister should be conveyed to the post commanded by his father, and preparations were early made to this effect. The wounded British were placed under the control of the chaplain; and towards the middle of the day Lawton saw all the arrangements so far completed, as to render it probable that in a few hours he would he left with his small party, in undisturbed possession of the Corners.

While leaning in the doorway, gazing in moody silence at the ground which had been the scene of the last night's chase, his ear caught the sound of a horse, and the next moment a dragoon of his own troop appeared dashing up the road, as if on business of the last importance. The steed was foaming, and the rider had the appearance of having done a day's service. Without speaking, he placed a letter in the hand of Lawton, and led his charger to the stable. The trooper knew the hand of the major, and ran his eye over the following:—

"I rejoice it is the order of Washington, that the family of the Locusts are to be removed above the Highlands. They are to be admitted to the society of Captain Wharton, who waits only for their testimony to be tried. You will communicate this order, and with proper delicacy I do not doubt. The English are moving up the river; and the moment you see the Whartons in safety, break up and join your troop. There will be good service to be done when we meet, as Sir Henry is reported to have sent out a real soldier in command. Reports must be made to the commandant at Peekskill, for Colonel Singleton is withdrawn to headquarters, to preside over the inquiry upon poor Wharton. Fresh orders have been sent to hang the peddler if we can take him, but they are not from the commander in chief. Detail a small guard with the ladies, and get into the saddle as soon as possible.

"Yours sincerely,

"Peyton Dunwoodie."

This communication entirely changed the whole arrangement. There was no longer any motive for removing the body of Isabella, since her father was no longer with his command, and Singleton reluctantly acquiesced in an immediate interment. A retired and lovely spot was selected, near the foot of the adjacent rocks, and such rude preparations were made as the time and the situation of the country permitted. A few of the neighboring inhabitants collected from curiosity and interest, and Miss Peyton and Frances wept in sincerity over her grave. The solemn offices of the church were performed by the minister, who had so lately stood forth to officiate in another and very different duty; and Lawton bent his head, and passed his hand across his brow, while the words that accompanied the first clod were uttered.

A new stimulus was given to the Whartons by the intelligence conveyed in the letter of Dunwoodie; and Cæsar with his horses, was once more put in requisition. The relics of the property were intrusted to a neighbor, in whom they had confidence; and, accompanied by the unconscious Sarah, and attended by four dragoons and all of the American wounded, Mr. Wharton's party took their departure. They were speedily followed by the English chaplain, with his countrymen, who were conveyed to the waterside, where a vessel was in waiting to receive them.

Lawton joyfully witnessed these movements; and as soon as the latter were out of sight, he ordered his own bugle to sound. Everything was instantly in motion. The mare of Mrs. Flanagan was again fastened to the cart; Dr. Sitgreaves exhibited his shapeless form once more on horseback; and the trooper appeared in the saddle, rejoicing in his emancipation.

The word to march was given; and Lawton, throwing a look of sullen ferocity at the place of the Skinner's concealment, and another of melancholy regret towards the grave of Isabella, led the way accompanied by the surgeon in a brown study; while Sergeant Hollister and Betty brought up the rear, leaving a fresh southerly wind to whistle through the open doors and broken windows of the "Hotel Flanagan," where the laugh of hilarity, the joke of the hardy partisan, and the lamentations of the sorrowing, had so lately echoed.

CHAPTER XXV

No vernal blooms their torpid rocks array,
But winter, lingering, chills the lap of May;
No zephyr fondly sues the mountain's breast,
But meteors glare, and stormy glooms invest.

—Goldsmith.

The roads of Westchester are, at this hour, below the improvements of the country. Their condition at the time of the tale has already been alluded to in these pages; and the reader will, therefore, easily imagine the task assumed by Cæsar, when he undertook to guide the translated chariot of the English prelate through their windings, into one of the less frequented passes of the Highlands of the Hudson.

While Cæsar and his steeds were contending with these difficulties, the inmates of the carriage were too much engrossed with their own cares to attend to those who served them. The mind of Sarah had ceased to wander so wildly as at first; but at every advance that she made towards reason, she seemed to retire a step from animation; from being excited and flighty, she was gradually becoming moody and melancholy. There were moments, indeed, when her anxious companions thought that they could discern marks of recollection; but the expression of exquisite woe that accompanied these transient gleams of reason, forced them to the dreadful alternative of wishing that she might forever be spared the agony of thought. The day's march was performed chiefly in silence, and the party found shelter for the night in different farmhouses.

The following morning the cavalcade dispersed. The wounded diverged towards the river, with the intention of taking water at Peekskill, in order to be transported to the hospitals of the American army above. The litter of Singleton was conveyed to a part of the Highlands where his father held his quarters, and where it was intended that the youth should complete his cure; the carriage of Mr. Wharton, accompanied by a wagon conveying the housekeeper and what baggage had been saved, and could be transported, resumed its route towards the place where

Henry Wharton was held in duress, and where he only waited their arrival to be put on trial for his life.

The country which lies between the waters of the Hudson and Long Island Sound, is, for the first forty miles, from their junction, a succession of hills and dales. The land bordering on the latter then becomes less abrupt, and gradually assumes a milder appearance, until it finally melts into the lovely plains and meadows of the Connecticut. But as you approach the Hudson, the rugged aspect increases, until you at length meet with the formidable barrier of the Highlands. Here the neutral ground ceased. The royal army held the two points of land that commanded the southern entrance of the river into the mountains; but all the remaining passes were guarded by the Americans.

We have already stated that the pickets of the continental army were sometimes pushed low into the country, and that the hamlet of the White Plains was occasionally maintained by parties of its troops. At other times, the advanced guards were withdrawn to the northern extremity of the country, and, as has been shown, the intermediate country was abandoned to the ravages of the miscreants who plundered between both armies, serving neither.

The road taken by our party was not the one that communicates between the two principal cities of the states, but was a retired and unfrequented pass, that to this hour is but little known, and which, entering the hills near the eastern boundary, emerges into the plain above, many miles from the Hudson.

It would have been impossible for the tired steeds of Mr. Wharton to drag the heavy chariot up the lengthened and steep ascents which now lay before them; and a pair of country horses were procured, with but little regard to their owner's wishes, by the two dragoons who still continued to accompany the party. With their assistance, Cæsar was enabled to advance, by slow and toilsome steps, into the bosom of the hills. Willing to relieve her own melancholy by breathing a fresher air, and also to lessen the weight, Frances alighted as they reached the foot of the mountain. She found that Katy had made similar preparations, with the like intention of walking to the summit. It was near the setting of the sun, and, from the top of the mountain, their guard had declared that the end of their journey might be discerned. Frances moved forward with the elastic step of youth; and, followed by the housekeeper at a little distance, she soon lost sight of the sluggish carriage, that was slowly toiling up the hill, occasionally halting to allow the cattle to breathe.

"Oh, Miss Fanny, what dreadful times these be!" said Katy, when they paused for breath themselves. "I know'd that calamity was about to befall, ever sin' the streak of blood was seen in the clouds."

"There has been blood upon earth, Katy, though but little is ever seen in the clouds."

"Not blood in the clouds!" echoed the housekeeper. "Yes, that there has, often, and comets with fiery, smoking tails. Didn't people see armed men in the heavens, the year the war began? And, the night before the battle of the Plains, wasn't there thunder, like the cannon themselves? Ah! Miss Fanny, I'm fearful that no good can follow rebellion against the Lord's anointed!"

"These events are certainly dreadful," returned Frances, "and enough to sicken the stoutest heart. But what can be done, Katy? Gallant and independent men are unwilling to submit to oppression; and I am fearful that such scenes are but too common in war.

"If I could but see anything to fight about," said Katy, renewing her walk as the young lady proceeded, "I shouldn't mind it so much. 'Twas said the king wanted all the tea for his own family, at one time; and then again, that he meant the colonies should pay over to him all their earnings. Now this is matter enough to fight about—for I'm sure that no one, however he may be lord or king, has a right to the hard earnings of another. Then it was all contradicted, and some said Washington wanted to be king himself; so that, between the two, one doesn't know which to believe."

"Believe neither—for neither is true. I do not pretend to understand, myself, all the merits of this war, Katy; but to me it seems unnatural, that a country like this should be ruled by another so distant as England."

"So I have heard Harvey say to his father, that is dead and in his grave," returned Katy, approaching nearer to the young lady, and lowering her voice. "Many is the good time that I've listened to them talking, when all the neighborhood was asleep; and such conversations. Miss Fanny, that you can have no idea on! Well, to say the truth, Harvey was a mystified body, and he was like the winds in the good book; no one could tell whence he came, or whither he went."

Frances glanced her eye at her companion with an apparent desire to hear more.

"There are rumors abroad relative to the character of Harvey," she said, "that I should be sorry were true."

" 'Tis a desparagement, every word on't," cried Katy, vehemently. "Harvey had no more dealings with Beelzebub than you or I had. I'm sure if Harvey had sold himself, he would take care to be better paid; though, to speak the truth, he was always a wasteful and disregardful man."

"Nay, nay," returned the smiling Frances, "I have no such injurious suspicion of him; but has he not sold himself to an earthly prince—one too much attached to the interests of his native island to be always just to this country?"

"To the king's majesty!" replied Katy. "Why, Miss Fanny, your own brother that's in jail serves King George."

"True," said Frances, "but not in secret—openly, manfully, and bravely."

" 'Tis said he is a spy, and why ain't one spy as bad as another?"

" 'Tis untrue; no act of deception is worthy of my brother; nor of any would he be guilty, for so base a purpose as gain or promotion."

"Well, I'm sure," said Katy, a little appalled at the manner of the young lady, "if a body does the work, he should be paid for it. Harvey is by no means partic'lar about getting his lawful dues; and I dar'st to say, if the truth were forthcoming, King George owes him money this very minute."

"Then you acknowledge his connection with the British army," said Frances. "I confess there have been moments when I have thought differently."

"Lord, Miss Fanny, Harvey is a man that no calculation can be made on. Though I lived in his house for a long concourse of years, I have never known whether he belonged above or below.[11] The time that Burg'yne was taken he came home, and

[11] The American party was called the party belonging "above," and the British that of "below." The terms had reference to the course of the Hudson.

there was great doings between him and the old gentleman, but for my life I couldn't tell if 'twas joy or grief. Then, here, the other day, when the great British general—I'm sure I have been so flurried with losses and troubles, that I forget his name—"

"André," said Frances.

"Yes, Ondree; when he was hanged, acrost the Tappan, the old gentleman was near hand to going crazy about it, and didn't sleep for night nor day, till Harvey got back; and then his money was mostly golden guineas; but the Skinners took it all, and now he is a beggar, or, what's the same thing, despisable for poverty and want."

To this speech Frances made no reply, but continued her walk up the hill, deeply engaged in her own reflections. The allusion to André had recalled her thoughts to the situation of her own brother.

They soon reached the highest point in their toilsome progress to the summit, and Frances seated herself on a rock to rest and to admire. Immediately at her feet lay a deep dell, but little altered by cultivation, and dark with the gloom of a November sunset. Another hill rose opposite to the place where she sat, at no great distance, along whose rugged sides nothing was to be seen but shapeless rocks, and oaks whose stunted growth showed a meager soil.

To be seen in their perfection, the Highlands must be passed immediately after the fall of the leaf. The scene is then the finest, for neither the scanty foliage which the summer lends the trees, nor the snows of winter, are present to conceal the minutest objects from. the eye. Chilling solitude is the characteristic of the scenery; nor is the mind at liberty, as in March, to look forward to a renewed vegetation that is soon to check, without improving, the view.

The day had been cloudy and cool, and thin fleecy clouds hung around the horizon, often promising to disperse, but as frequently disappointing Frances in the hope of catching a parting beam from the setting sun. At length a solitary gleam struck on the base of the mountain on which she was gazing, and moved gracefully up its side, until reaching the summit, it stood for a minute, forming a crown of glory to the somber pile. So strong were the rays, that what was before indistinct now clearly opened to the view. With a feeling of awe at being thus unexpectedly admitted, as it were, into the secrets of that desert place, Frances gazed intently, until, among the scattered trees and fantastic rocks, something like a rude structure was seen. It was low, and so obscured by the color of its materials, that but for its roof, and the glittering of a window, it must have escaped her notice. While yet lost in the astonishment created by discovering a habitation in such a spot, on moving her eyes she perceived another object that increased her wonder. It apparently was a human figure, but of singular mold and unusual deformity. It stood on the edge of a rock, a little above the hut, and it was no difficult task for our heroine to fancy it was gazing at the vehicles that were ascending the side of the mountain beneath her. The distance, however, was too great to distinguish with precision. After looking at it a moment in breathless wonder, Frances had just come to the conclusion that it was ideal, and that what she saw was a part of the rock itself, when the object moved swiftly from its position, and glided into the hut, at once removing every doubt as to the nature of either. Whether it was owing to the recent conversation that she had been holding with Katy, or to some fancied resemblance that she discerned, Frances thought, as the figure vanished from her view, that it bore a marked likeness to Birch, moving under the weight of his pack. She continued to gaze towards the mysterious residence, when the gleam of light passed away, and at the same instant the tones of a bugle rang through the glens and hollows, and were re-echoed in every direction. Springing on her feet, the alarmed girl heard the trampling of horses, and directly a party in the well-known uniform of the Virginians came sweeping round the point of a rock near her, and drew up at a short distance. Again the bugle sounded a lively strain, and before the agitated Frances had time to rally her thoughts, Dunwoodie dashed by the party of dragoons, threw himself from his charger, and advanced to her side.

His manner was earnest and interested, but in a slight degree constrained. In a few words he explained that he had been ordered up, with a party of Lawton's men, in the absence of the captain himself, to attend the trial of Henry, which was fixed for the morrow; and that, anxious for their safety in the rude passes of the mountain, he had ridden a mile or two in quest of the travelers. Frances explained, with trembling voice, the reason of her being in advance, and taught, him momentarily to expect the arrival of her father. The constraint of his manner had, however, unwillingly on her part, communicated itself to her own deportment, and the approach of the chariot was a relief to both. The major handed her in, spoke a few words of encouragement to Mr. Wharton and Miss Peyton, and, again mounting, led the way towards the plains of Fishkill, which broke on their sight, on turning the rock, with the effect of enchantment. A short half hour brought them to the door of the farmhouse which the care of Dunwoodie had already prepared for their reception, and where Captain Wharton was anxiously expecting their arrival.

CHAPTER XXVI

These limbs are strengthened with a soldier's toil,
Nor has this cheek been ever blanched with fear—
But this sad tale of thine enervates all
Within me that I once could boast as man;
Chill trembling agues seize upon my frame,
And tears of childish sorrow pour, apace,
Through scarred channels that were marked by wounds.

—Duo

The friends of Henry Wharton had placed so much reliance on his innocence, that they were unable to see the full danger of his situation. As the moment of trial, however, approached, the uneasiness of the youth himself increased; and after spending most of the night with his afflicted family, he awoke, on the following morning, from a short and disturbed slumber, to a clearer sense of his condition, and a survey of the means that were to extricate him from it with life. The rank of André, and the importance of the measures he was plotting, together with the powerful intercessions that had been made in his behalf, occasioned his execution to be stamped with greater notoriety than the ordinary events of the war. But spies were frequently arrested; and the instances that occurred of summary punishment for this crime were numerous. These were facts that were well known to both Dunwoodie and the prisoner; and to their experienced judgments the preparations for the trial were indeed alarming. Notwithstanding their apprehensions, they succeeded so far in concealing them, that neither Miss Peyton nor Frances was aware of their extent. A strong guard was stationed in the outbuilding of the farmhouse where the prisoner was quartered, and several sentinels watched the avenues that approached the dwelling. Another was constantly near the room of the British officer. A court was already detailed to examine into the circumstances; and upon their decision the fate of Henry rested.

The moment at length arrived, and the different actors in the approaching investigation assembled. Frances experienced a feeling like suffocation, as, after taking her seat in the midst of her family, her eyes wandered over the group who were thus collected. The judges, three in number, sat by themselves, clad in the vestments of their profession, and maintained a gravity worthy of the occasion, and becoming in their rank. In the center was a man of advanced years, and whose whole exterior bore the stamp of early and long-tried military habits. This was the president of the court; and Frances, after taking a hasty and unsatisfactory view of his associates, turned to his benevolent countenance as to the harbinger of mercy to her brother. There was a melting and subdued expression in the features of the veteran, that, contrasted with the rigid decency and composure of the others, could not fail to attract her notice. His attire was strictly in conformity to the prescribed rules of the service to which he belonged; but while his air was erect and military, his fingers trifled with a kind of convulsive and unconscious motion, with a bit of crape that entwined the hilt of the sword on which his body partly reclined, and which, like himself, seemed a relic of older times. There were the workings of an unquiet soul within; but his military front blended awe with the pity that its exhibition excited. His associates were officers selected from the eastern troops, who held the fortresses of West Point and the adjacent passes; they were men who had attained the meridian of life, and the eye sought in vain the expression of any passion or emotion on which it might seize as an indication of human infirmity. In their demeanor there was a mild, but grave, intellectual reserve. If there was no ferocity nor harshness to chill, neither was there compassion nor interest to attract. They were men who had long acted under the dominion of a prudent reason, and whose feelings seemed trained to a perfect submission to their judgments.

Before these arbiters of his fate Henry Wharton was ushered under the custody of armed men. A profound and awful silence succeeded his entrance, and the blood of Frances chilled as she noted the grave character of the whole proceedings. There was but little of pomp in the preparations, to impress her imagination; but the reserved, businesslike air of the whole scene made it seem, indeed, as if the destinies of life awaited the result. Two of the judges sat in grave reserve, fixing their inquiring eyes on the object of their investigation; but the president continued gazing around with uneasy, convulsive motions of the muscles of the face, that indicated a restlessness foreign to his years and duty. It was Colonel Singleton, who, but the day before, had learned the fate of Isabella, but who stood forth in the discharge of a duty that his country required at his hand. The silence, and the expectation in every eye, at length struck him, and making an effort to collect himself, he spoke, in the tones of one used to authority.

"Bring forth the prisoner," he said, with a wave of the hand.

The sentinels dropped the points of their bayonets towards the judges, and Henry Wharton advanced, with a firm step, into the center of the apartment. All was now anxiety and eager curiosity. Frances turned for a moment in grateful emotion, as the deep and perturbed breathing of Dunwoodie reached her ears; but her brother again concentrated all her interest in one feeling of intense care. In the background were arranged the inmates of the family who owned the dwelling, and behind them, again, was a row of shining faces of ebony, glistening with pleased wonder. Amongst these was the faded luster of Cæsar Thompson's countenance.

"You are said," continued the president, "to be Henry Wharton, a captain in his Britannic Majesty's 60th regiment of foot."

"I am."

"I like your candor, sir; it partakes of the honorable feelings of a soldier, and cannot fail to impress your judges favorably."

"It would be prudent," said one of his companions, "to advise the prisoner that he is bound to answer no more than he deems necessary; although we are a court of martial law, yet, in this respect, we own the principles of all free governments."

A nod of approbation from the silent member was bestowed on this remark, and the president proceeded with caution, referring to the minutes he held in his hand.

"It is an accusation against you, that, being an officer of the enemy, you passed the pickets of the American army at the White Plains, in disguise, on the 29th of October last, whereby you are suspected of views hostile to the interests of America, and have subjected yourself to the punishment of a spy."

The mild but steady tones of the speaker, as he slowly repeated the substance of this charge, were full of authority. The accusation was so plain, the facts so limited, the proof so obvious, and the penalty so well established, that escape seemed impossible. But Henry replied, with earnest grace,—

"That I passed your pickets in disguise, is true; but—"

"Peace!" interrupted the president. "The usages of war are stern enough in themselves; you need not aid them to your own condemnation."

"The prisoner can retract that declaration, if he please," remarked another judge. "His confession, if taken, goes fully to prove the charge."

"I retract nothing that is true," said Henry proudly.

The two nameless judges heard him in silent composure, yet there was no exultation mingled with their gravity. The president now appeared, however, to take new interest in the scene.

"Your sentiment is noble, sir," he said. "I only regret that a youthful soldier should so far be misled by loyalty as to lend himself to the purposes of deceit."

"Deceit!" echoed Wharton. "I thought it prudent to guard against capture from my enemies."

"A soldier, Captain Wharton, should never meet his enemy but openly, and with arms in his hands. I have served two kings of England, as I now serve my native land; but never did I approach a foe, unless under the light of the sun, and with honest notice that an enemy was nigh."

"You are at liberty to explain what your motives were in entering the ground held by our army in disguise," said the other judge, with a slight movement of the muscles of his mouth.

"I am the son of this aged man before you," continued Henry. "It was to visit him that I encountered the danger. Besides, the country below is seldom held by your troops, and its very name implies a right to either party to move at pleasure over its territory."

"Its name, as a neutral ground, is unauthorized by law; it is an appellation that originates with the condition of the country. But wherever an army goes, it carries its rights along, and the first is the ability to protect itself."

"I am no casuist, sir," returned the youth; "but I feel that my father is entitled to my affection, and I would encounter greater risks to prove it to him in his old age."

"A very commendable spirit," cried the veteran. "Come, gentlemen, this business brightens. I confess, at first, it was very bad, but no man can censure him for desiring to see his parents."

"And have you proof that such only was your intention?"

"Yes—here," said Henry, admitting a ray of hope. "Here is proof—my father, my sister, Major Dunwoodie, all know it."

"Then, indeed," returned his immovable judge, "we may be able to save you. It would be well, sir, to examine further into this business."

"Certainly," said the president, with alacrity. "Let the elder Mr. Wharton approach and take the oath."

The father made an effort at composure, and, advancing with a feeble step, he complied with the necessary forms of the court.

"You are the father of the prisoner?" said Colonel Singleton, in a subdued voice, after pausing a moment in respect for the agitation of the witness.

"He is my only son."

"And what do you know of his visit to your house, on the 29th day of October last?"

"He came, as he told you, to see me and his sisters."

"Was he in disguise?" asked the other judge.

"He did not wear the uniform of the 60th."

"To see his sisters, too!" said the president with great emotion. "Have you daughters, sir?"

"I have two—both are in this house."

"Had he a wig?" interrupted the officer.

"There was some such thing I do believe, upon his head."

"And how long had you been separated?" asked the president.

"One year and two months."

"Did he wear a loose greatcoat of coarse materials?" inquired the officer, referring to the paper that contained the charges.

"There was an overcoat."

"And you think that it was to see you, only, that he came out?"

"Me, and my daughters."

"A boy of spirit," whispered the president to his silent comrade. "I see but little harm in such a freak; 'twas imprudent, but then it was kind."

"Do you know that your son was intrusted with no commission from Sir Henry Clinton, and that the visit to you was not merely a cloak to other designs?"

"How can I know it?" said Mr. Wharton, in alarm. "Would Sir Henry intrust me with such a business?"

"Know you anything of this pass?" exhibiting the paper that Dunwoodie had retained when Wharton was taken.

"Nothing—upon my honor, nothing," cried the father, shrinking from the paper as from contagion.

"On your oath?"

"Nothing."

"Have you other testimony? This does not avail you, Captain Wharton. You have been taken in a situation where your life is forfeited; the labor of proving your innocence rests with yourself. Take time to reflect, and be cool."

There was a frightful calmness in the manner of this judge that appalled the prisoner. In the sympathy of Colonel Singleton, he could easily lose sight of his danger; but the obdurate and collected air of the others was ominous of his fate. He continued silent, casting imploring glances towards his friend. Dunwoodie understood the appeal, and offered himself as a witness. He was sworn, and desired to relate what he knew. His statement did not materially alter the case, and Dunwoodie felt that it could not. To him personally but little was known, and that little rather militated against the safety of Henry than otherwise. His account was listened to in silence, and the significant shake of the head that was made by the silent member spoke too plainly what effect it had produced.

"Still you think that the prisoner had no other object than what he has avowed?" said the president, when he had ended.

"None other, I will pledge my life," cried the major, with fervor.

"Will you swear it?" asked the immovable judge;

"How can I? God alone can tell the heart; but I have known this gentleman from a boy; deceit never formed part of his character. He is above it."

"You say that he escaped, and was retaken in open arms?" said the president.

"He was; nay, he received a wound in the combat. You see he yet moves his arm with difficulty. Would he, think you, sir, have trusted himself where he could fall again into our hands, unless conscious of innocence?"

"Would André have deserted a field of battle, Major Dunwoodie, had he encountered such an event, near Tarry-town?" asked his deliberate examiner. "Is it not natural to youth to seek glory?"

"Do you call this glory?" exclaimed the major: "an ignominious death and a tarnished name."

"Major Dunwoodie," returned the other, still with inveterate gravity, "you have acted nobly; your duty has been arduous and severe, but it has been faithfully and honorably discharged; ours must not be less so."

During the examination, the most intense interest prevailed among the hearers. With that kind of feeling which could not separate the principle from the cause, most of the auditors thought that if Dunwoodie failed to move the hearts of Henry's judges, no other possessed the power. Cæsar thrust his misshapen form forward and his features, so expressive of the concern he felt, and so different from the vacant curiosity pictured in the countenance of the other blacks, caught the attention of the silent judge. For the first time he spoke:—

"Let that black be brought forward."

It was too late to retreat, and Cæsar found himself confronted with a row of rebel officers, before he knew what was uppermost in his thoughts. The others yielded the examination to the one who suggested it, and using all due deliberation, he proceeded accordingly.

"You know the prisoner?"

"I t'ink he ought," returned the black, in a manner as sententious as that of his examiner.

"Did he give you the wig when he threw it aside?"

"I don't want 'em," grumbled Cæsar; "got a berry good hair heself."

"Were you employed in carrying any letters or messages of any kind while Captain Wharton was in your master's house?"

"I do what a tell me," returned the black.

"But what did they tell you to do?"

"Sometime a one ting—sometime another."

"Enough," said Colonel Singleton, with dignity. "You have the noble acknowledgment of a gentleman, what more can you obtain from this slave?—Captain Wharton, you perceive the unfortunate impression against you. Have you other testimony to adduce?"

To Henry there now remained but little hope; his confidence in his security was fast ebbing, but with an indefinite expectation of assistance from the loveliness of his sister, he fixed an earnest gaze on the pallid features of Frances. She arose, and with a tottering step moved towards the judges; the paleness of her cheek continued but for a moment, and gave place to a flush of fire, and with a light but firm tread, she stood before them. Raising her hand to -her polished forehead, Frances threw aside her exuberant locks and displayed a picture of beauty and innocence to their view that might have moved even sterner natures. The president shrouded his eyes for a moment, as if the wild eye and speaking countenance recalled the image of another. The movement was transient, and recovering himself, with an earnestness that betrayed his secret wishes,—

"To you, then, your brother previously communicated his intention of paying your family a secret visit?"

"No!—no!" said Frances, pressing her hand on her brain, as if to collect her thoughts; "he told me nothing—we knew not of the visit until he arrived; but can it be necessary to explain to gallant men, that a child would incur hazard to meet his only parent, and that in times like these, and in a situation like ours?"

"But was this the first time? Did he never even talk of doing so before?" inquired the colonel, leaning towards her with paternal interest.

"Certain—certainly," cried Frances, catching the expression of his own benevolent countenance. "This is but the fourth of his visits."

"I knew it!" exclaimed the veteran, rubbing his hands with delight. "An adventurous, warm-hearted son—I warrant me, gentlemen, a fiery soldier in the field! In what disguises did he come?"

"In none, for none were then necessary; the royal troops covered the country, and gave him safe passage."

"And was this the first of his visits out of the uniform of his regiment?" asked the colonel, in a suppressed voice, avoiding the penetrating looks of his companions.

"Oh! the very first," exclaimed the eager girl. "His first offense, I do assure you, if offense it be."

"But you wrote him—you urged the visit; surely, young lady, you wished to see your brother?" added the impatient colonel.

"That we wished it, and prayed for it,—oh, how fervently we prayed for it!—is true; but to have held communion with the royal army would have endangered our father, and we dared not."

"Did he leave the house until taken, or had he intercourse with any out of your own dwelling?"

"With none—no one, excepting our neighbor, the peddler Birch."

"With whom!" exclaimed the colonel, turning pale, and shrinking as from the sting of an adder.

Dunwoodie groaned aloud, and striking his head with his hand, cried in piercing tones, "He is lost!" and rushed from the apartment.

"But Harvey Birch," repeated Frances, gazing wildly at the door through which her lover had disappeared.

"Harvey Birch!" echoed all the judges. The two immovable members of the court exchanged looks, and threw an inquisitive glance at the prisoner.

"To you, gentlemen, it can be no new intelligence to hear that Harvey Birch is suspected of favoring the royal cause," said Henry, again advancing before the judges; "for he has already been condemned by your tribunals to the fate that I now see awaits myself. I will therefore explain, that it was by his assistance I procured the disguise, and passed your pickets; but to my dying moments, and with my dying breath, I will avow, that my intentions were as pure as the innocent being before you."

"Captain Wharton," said the president, solemnly, "the enemies of American liberty have made mighty and subtle efforts to overthrow our power. A more dangerous man, for his means and education, is not ranked among our foes than this peddler of Westchester. He is a spy—artful, delusive, arid penetrating, beyond the abilities of any of his class. Sir Henry could not do better than to associate him with the officer in his next attempt. He would have saved André. Indeed, young man, this is a connection that may prove fatal to you!"

The honest indignation that beamed on the countenance of the aged warrior was met by a look of perfect conviction on the part of his comrades.

"I have ruined him!" cried Frances, clasping her hands in terror. "Do you desert us? then he is lost, indeed!"

"Forbear! lovely innocent, forbear!" said the colonel, with strong emotion; "you injure none, but distress us all."

"Is it then such a crime to possess natural affection?" said Frances wildly. "Would Washington—the noble, upright, impartial Washington, judge so harshly? Delay, till Washington can hear his tale."

"It is impossible," said the president, covering his eyes, as if to hide her beauty from his view.

"Impossible! oh! but for a week suspend your judgment. On my knees I entreat you, as will expect mercy yourself, when no human power can avail you, give him but a day."

"It is impossible," repeated the colonel, in a voice that was nearly choked. "Our orders are peremptory, and too long delay has been given already."

He turned from the kneeling suppliant, but could not, or would not, extricate that hand that she grasped with frenzied fervor.

"Remand your prisoner," said one of the judges to the officer who had charge of Henry. "Colonel Singleton, shall we withdraw?"

"Singleton! Singleton!" echoed Frances. "Then you are a father, and know how to pity a father's woes; you cannot, will not, wound a heart that is now nearly crushed. Hear me, Colonel Singleton; as God will listen to your dying prayers, hear me, and spare my brother!"

"Remove her," said the colonel, gently endeavoring to extricate his hand; but none appeared disposed to obey. Frances eagerly strove to read the expression of his averted face, and resisted all his efforts to retire.

"Colonel Singleton! how lately was your own son in suffering and in danger! Under the roof of my father he was cherished—under my father's roof he found shelter and protection. Oh! suppose that son the pride of your age, the solace and protection of your infant children, and then pronounce my brother guilty, if you dare!"

"What right has Heath* to make an executioner of me!" exclaimed the veteran fiercely, rising with a face flushed like fire, and every vein and artery swollen with suppressed emotion. "But I forget myself; come, gentlemen, let us mount, our painful duty must be done."

"Mount not! go not!" shrieked Frances. "Can you tear a son from his parent—a brother from his sister, so coldly? Is this the cause I have so ardently loved? Are these the men that I have been taught to reverence? But you relent, you do hear me, you will pity and forgive."

"Lead on, gentlemen," said the colonel, motioning towards the door, and erecting himself into an air of military grandeur, in the vain hope of quieting his feelings.

"Lead not on, but hear me," cried Frances, grasping his hand convulsively. "Colonel Singleton, you are a father!—pity—mercy—mercy for the son! mercy for the daughter! Yes—you had a daughter. On this bosom she poured out her last breath; these hands closed her eyes; these very hands, that are now clasped in prayer, did those offices for her that you condemn my poor, poor brother, to require."

One mighty emotion the veteran struggled with, and quelled; but with a groan that shook his whole frame. He even looked around in conscious pride at his victory; but a second burst of feeling conquered. His head, white with the frost of seventy winters, sank upon the shoulder of the frantic suppliant. The sword that had been his companion in so many fields of blood dropped from his nerveless hand, and as he cried, "May God bless you for the deed!" he wept aloud.

Long and violent was the indulgence that Colonel Singleton yielded to his feelings. On recovering, he gave the senseless Frances into the arms of her aunt, and, turning with an air of fortitude to his comrades, he said,—

"Still, gentlemen, we have our duty as officers to discharge; our feelings as men may be indulged hereafter. What is your pleasure with the prisoner?"

One of the judges placed in his hand a written sentence, that he had prepared while the colonel was engaged with Frances, and declared it to be the opinion of himself and his companion.

It briefly stated that Henry Wharton had been detected in passing the lines of the American army as a spy, and in disguise. That thereby, according to the laws of war, he was liable to suffer death, and that this court adjudged him to the penalty; recommending him to be executed by hanging, before nine o'clock on the following morning.

It was not usual to inflict capital punishments, even on the enemy, without referring the case to the commander in chief, for his approbation; or, in his absence, to the officer commanding for the time being. But, as Washington held his headquarters at New Windsor, on the western bank of the Hudson, there was sufficient time to receive his answer.

"This is short notice," said the veteran, holding the pen in his hand, in a suspense that had no object; "not a day to fit one so young for heaven?"

"The royal officers gave Hale[12] but an hour," returned his comrade; "we have granted the usual time. But Washington has the power to extend it, or to pardon."

"Then to Washington will I go," cried the colonel, returning the paper with his signature; "and if the services of an old man like me, or that brave boy of mine, entitle me to his ear, I will yet save the youth."

So saying, he departed, full of his generous intentions in favor of Henry Wharton.

The sentence of the court was communicated, with proper tenderness, to the -prisoner; and after giving a few necessary instructions to the officer in command, and dispatching a courier to headquarters with their report, the remaining judges mounted, and rode to their own quarters, with the same unmoved exterior, but with the consciousness of the same dispassionate integrity, that they had maintained throughout the trial.

---

[12] An American officer of this name wax detected within the British lines, in disguise, in search of military information. He was tried and executed, as stated in the text, as soon as the preparations could be made. It is said that he was reproached under the gallows with dishonoring the rank he held by his fate. "What a death for an officer to die!" said one of his captors. "Gentlemen, any death is honorable when a man dies in a cause like that of America," was his answer.Andre was executed amid the tears of his enemies; Hale died unpitied and with reproaches in his ears; and yet one was the victim of ambition, and the other of devotion to his country. Posterity will do justice between them.

CHAPTER XXVII

Have you no countermand for Claudio yet,
But he must die to-morrow?
—Measure for Measure.

A few hours were passed by the prisoner, after his sentence was received, in the bosom of his family. Mr. Wharton wept in hopeless despondency over the untimely fate of his son; and Frances, after recovering from her insensibility, experienced an anguish of feeling to which the bitterness of death itself would have been comparatively light. Miss Peyton alone retained a vestige of hope, or presence of mind to suggest what might be proper to be done under their circumstances. The comparative composure of the good aunt arose in no degree from any want of interest in the welfare of her nephew, but it was founded in a kind of instinctive dependence on the character of Washington. He was a native of the same colony with herself; and although his early military services, and her frequent visits to the family of her sister, and subsequent establishment at its head, had prevented their ever meeting, still she was familiar with his domestic virtues, and well knew that the rigid inflexibility for which his public acts were distinguished formed no part of his reputation in private life. He was known in Virginia as a consistent but just and lenient master; and she felt a kind of pride in associating in her mind her countryman with the man who led the armies, and in a great measure controlled the destinies, of America. She knew that Henry was innocent of the crime for which he was condemned to suffer, and, with that kind of simple faith that is ever to be found in the most ingenuous characters, could not conceive of those constructions and interpretations of law that inflicted punishment without the actual existence of crime. But even her confiding hopes were doomed to meet with a speedy termination. Towards noon, a regiment of militia, that were quartered on the banks of the river, moved to the ground in front of the house that held our heroine and family, and deliberately pitched their tents, with the avowed intention of remaining until the following morning, to give solemnity and effect to the execution of a British spy.

Dunwoodie had performed all that was required of him by his orders, and was at liberty to retrace his steps to his expectant squadron, which was impatiently waiting his return to be led against a detachment of the enemy that was known to be slowly moving up the banks of the river, in order to cover a party of foragers in its rear. He was accompanied by a small party of Lawton's troop, under the expectation that their testimony might be required to convict the prisoner; and Mason, the lieutenant, was in command. But the confession of Captain Wharton had removed the necessity of examining any witnesses on behalf of the people.[13] The major, from an unwillingness to encounter the distress of Henry's friends, and a dread of trusting himself within its influence, had spent the time we have mentioned in walking by himself, in keen anxiety, at a short distance from the dwelling. Like Miss Peyton, he had some reliance on the mercy of Washington, although moments of terrific doubt and despondency were continually crossing his mind. To him the rules of service were familiar, and he was more accustomed to consider his general in the capacity of a ruler, than as exhibiting the characteristics of the individual. A dreadful instance had too recently occurred, which fully proved that Washington was above the weakness of sparing another in mercy to himself. While pacing, with hurried steps, through the orchard, laboring under these constantly recurring doubts, enlivened by transient rays of hope, Mason approached, accoutered completely for the saddle.

"Thinking you might have forgotten the news brought this morning from below, sir, I have taken the liberty to order the detachment under arms," said the lieutenant, very coolly, cutting down with his sheathed saber the mullein tops that grew within his reach.

"What news?" cried the major, starting.

"Only that John Bull is out in Westchester, with a train of wagons, which, if he fills, will compel us to retire through these cursed hills, in search of provender. These greedy Englishmen are so shut up on York Island, that when they do venture out, they seldom leave straw enough to furnish the bed of a Yankee heiress."

---

[13] In America justice is administered in the name of "the good people," etc., etc., the sovereignty residing with them.

"Where did the express leave them, did you say? The intelligence has entirely ecsaped my memory."

"On the heights above Sing Sing," returned the lieutenant, with no little amazement. "The road below looks like a hay market, and all the swine are sighing forth their lamentations, as the corn passes them towards King's Bridge. George Singleton's orderly, who brought up the tidings, say that our horses were holding consultation if they should not go down without their riders, and eat another meal, for it is questionable with them whether they can get a full stomach again. If they are suffered to get back with their plunder, we shall not be able to find a piece of pork at Christmas fat enough to fry itself."

"Peace, with all this nonsense of Singleton's orderly, Mr. Mason," cried Dunwoodie, impatiently; "let him learn to wait the orders of his superiors."

"I beg pardon in his name. Major Dunwoodie," said the subaltern; "but, like myself, he was in error. We both thought it was the order of General Heath, to attack and molest the enemy whenever he ventured out of his nest."

"Recollect yourself, Lieutenant Mason," said the major, "or I may have to teach you that your orders pass through me."

"I know it, Major Dunwoodie—I know it; and I am sorry that your memory is so bad as to forget that I never have yet hesitated to obey them."

"Forgive me, Mason," cried Dunwoodie, taking both his hands. "I do know you for a brave and obedient soldier; forget any humor. But this business—had you ever a friend?"

"Nay, nay," interrupted the lieutenant, "forgive me and my honest zeal. I knew of the orders, and was fearful that censure might fall on my officer. But remain, and let a man breathe a syllable against the corps, and every sword will start from the scabbard of itself; besides, they are still moving up, and it is a long road from Croton to King's Bridge. Happen what may, I see plainly that we shall be on their heels before they are housed again."

"Oh! that the courier was returned from headquarters!" exclaimed Dunwoodie. "This suspense is insupportable."

"You have your wish," cried Mason. "Here he is at the moment, and riding like the bearer of good news. God send it may be so; for I can't say that I particularly like myself to see a brave young fellow dancing upon nothing."

Dunwoodie heard but very little of this feeling declaration; for, ere half of it was uttered, he had leaped the fence and stood before the messenger.

"What news?" cried the major, the moment that the soldier stopped his horse.

"Good!" exclaimed the man; and feeling no hesitation to intrust an officer so well known as Major Dunwoodie, he placed the paper in his hands, as he added, "but you can read it, sir, for yourself."

Dunwoodie paused not to read; but flew, with the elastic spring of joy, to the chamber of the prisoner. The sentinel knew him, and he was suffered to pass without question.

"Oh! Peyton," cried Frances, as he entered the apartment, "you look like a messenger from heaven; bring you tidings of mercy?"

"Here, Frances—here, Henry—here, dear cousin Jeanette," cried the youth, as with trembling hands he broke the seal; "here is the letter itself, directed to the captain of the guard. But listen—"

All did listen with intense anxiety; and the pang of blasted hope was added to their misery, as they saw the glow of delight which had beamed on the countenance of the major give place to a look of horror. The paper contained the sentence of the court, and underneath was written these simple words,—

"Approved—GEO. WASHINGTON."

"He's lost, he's lost!" cried Frances, sinking into the arms of her aunt.

"My son! my son!" sobbed the father, "there is mercy in heaven, if there is none on earth. May Washington never want that mercy he thus denies to my innocent child!"

"Washington!" echoed Dunwoodie, gazing around him in vacant horror. "Yes, 'tis the act of Washington himself; these are his characters; his very name is here, to sanction the dreadful deed."

"Cruel, cruel Washington!" cried Miss Peyton. "How has familiarity with blood changed his nature!"

"Blame him not," said Dunwoodie; "it is the general, and not the man; my life on it, he feels the blow he is compelled to inflict."

"I have been deceived in him," cried Frances. "He is not the savior of his country; but a cold and merciless tyrant. Oh! Peyton, Peyton! how have you misled me in his character!"

"Peace, dear Frances; peace, for God's sake; use not such language. He is but the guardian of the law."

"You speak the truth, Major Dunwoodie," said Henry, recovering from the shock of having his last ray of hope extinguished, and advancing from his seat by the side of his father. "I, who am to suffer, blame him not. Every indulgence has been granted me that I can ask. On the verge of the grave I cannot continue unjust. At such a moment, with so recent an instance of danger to your cause from treason, I wonder not a Washington's unbending justice. Nothing now remains but to prepare for that fate which so speedily awaits me. To you, Major Dunwoodie, I make my first request."

"Name it," said the major, giving utterance with difficulty.

Henry turned, and pointing to the group of weeping mourners near him, he continued,—

"Be a son to this aged man; help his weakness, and defend him from any usage to which the stigma thrown upon me may subject him. He has not many friends amongst the rulers of this country; let your powerful name be found among them."

"It shall."

"And this helpless innocent," continued Henry, pointing to where Sarah sat, unconscious of what was passing. "I had hoped for an opportunity to revenge her wrongs;" a flush of excitement passed over his features; "but such thoughts are evil—I feel them to be wrong. Under your care, Peyton, she will find sympathy and refuge."

"She shall," whispered Dunwoodie.

"This good aunt has claims upon you already; of her I will not speak; but here," taking the hand of Frances, and dwelling upon her countenance with an expression of fraternal affection, "here is the choicest gift of all. Take her to your bosom, and cherish her as you would cultivate innocence and virtue."

The major could not repress the eagerness with which he extended his hand to receive the precious boon; but Frances, shrinking from his touch, hid her face in the bosom of her aunt.

"No, no, no!" she murmured. "None can ever be anything to me who aid in my brother's destruction."

Henry continued gazing at her in tender pity for several moments, before he again resumed a discourse that all felt was most peculiarly his own.

"I have been mistaken, then. I did think, Peyton, that your worth, your noble devotion to a cause that you have been taught to revere, that your kindness to our father when in imprisonment, your friendship for me,— in short, that your character was understood and valued by my sister."

"It is—it is," whispered Frances, burying her face still deeper in the bosom of her aunt.

"I believe, dear Henry," said Dunwoodie, "this is a subject that had better not be dwelt upon now."

"You forget," returned the prisoner, with a faint smile, "how much I have to do, and how little time is left to do it in."

"I apprehend," continued the major, with a face of fire, "that Miss Wharton has imbibed some opinions of me that would make a compliance with your request irksome to her—opinions that it is now too late to alter."

"No, no, no," cried Frances, quickly, "you are exonerated, Peyton—with her dying breath she removed my doubts."

"Generous Isabella!" murmured Dunwoodie; "but, still, Henry, spare your sister now; nay, spare even me."

"I speak in pity to' myself," returned the brother, gently removing Frances from the arms of her aunt. "What a time is this to leave two such lovely females without a protector! Their abode is destroyed, and misery will speedily deprive them of their last male friend," looking at his father; "can I die in peace with the knowledge of the danger to which they will be exposed?"

"You forget me," said Miss Peyton, shrinking at the idea of celebrating nuptials at such a moment.

"No, my dear aunt, I forget you not, nor shall I, until I cease to remember; but you forget the times and the danger. The good woman who lives in this house has already dispatched a messenger for a man of God, to smooth my passage to another world. Frances, if you wish me to die in peace, to feel a security that will allow me to turn my whole thoughts to heaven, you will let this clergyman unite you to Dunwoodie."

Frances shook her head, but remained silent.

"I ask for no joy—no demonstration of a felicity that you

will not, cannot feel, for months to come; but obtain a right to his powerful name—give him an undisputed title to protect you—"

Again the maid made an impressive gesture of denial.

"For the sake of that unconscious sufferer"—pointing to Sarah, "for your sake—for my sake—my sister—"

"Peace, Henry, or you will break my heart," cried the agitated girl. "Not for worlds would I at such a moment engage in the solemn vows that you wish. It would render me miserable for life."

"You love him not," said Henry, reproachfully. "I cease to importune you to do what is against your inclinations."

Frances raised one hand to conceal her countenance, as she extended the other towards Dunwoodie, and said earnestly,—

"Now you are unjust to me—before, you were unjust to yourself."

"Promise me, then," said Wharton, musing awhile in silence, "that as soon as the recollection of my fate is softened, you will give my friend that hand for life, and I am satisfied."

"I do promise," said Frances, withdrawing the hand that Dunwoodie delicately relinquished, without even presuming to press it to his lips.

"Well, then, my good aunt," continued Henry, "will you leave me for a short time alone with my friend? I have a few melancholy commissions with which to intrust him, and would spare you and my sister the pain of hearing them."

"There is yet time to see Washington again," said Miss Peyton, moving towards the door; and then, speaking with extreme dignity, she continued, "I will go myself; surely he must listen to a woman from his own colony!—and we are in some degree connected with his family."

"Why not apply to Mr. Harper?" said Frances, recollecting the parting words of their guest for the first time.

"Harper!" echoed Dunwoodie, turning towards her with the swiftness of lightning; "what of him? Do you know him?"

"It is in vain," said Henry, drawing him aside; "Frances clings to hope with the fondness of a sister. Retire, my love, and leave me with my friend."

But Frances read an expression in the eye of Dunwoodie that chained her to the spot. After struggling to command her feelings, she continued,—

"He stayed with us for two days—he was with us when Henry was arrested."

"And—and—did you know him?"

"Nay," continued Frances, catching her breath as she witnessed the intense interest of her lover, "we knew him not; he came to us in the night, a stranger, and remained with us during the severe storm; but he seemed to take an interest in Henry, and promised him his friendship."

"What!" exclaimed the youth in astonishment. "Did he know your brother?"

"Certainly; it was at his request that Henry threw aside his disguise."

"But," said Dunwoodie, turning pale with suspense, "he knew him not as an officer of the royal army?"

"Indeed he did," cried Miss Peyton; "and he cautioned us against this very danger."

Dunwoodie caught up the fatal paper, that still lay where it had fallen from his own hands, and studied its characters intently. Something seemed to bewilder his brain. He passed his hand over his forehead, while each eye was fixed on him in dreadful suspense—all feeling afraid to admit those hopes anew that had been so sadly destroyed.

"What said he? What promised he?" at length Dunwoodie asked, with feverish impatience.

"He bid Henry apply to him when in danger, and promised to requite the son for the hospitality of the father."

"Said he this, knowing him to be a British officer?"

"Most certainly; and with a view to this very danger."

"Then," cried the youth aloud, and yielding to his rapture, "then you are safe—then will I save him; yes, Harper will never forget his word."

"But has he the power to?" said Frances. "Can he move the stubborn purpose of Washington?"

"Can he? If he cannot," shouted the youth, "if he cannot, who can? Greene, and Heath, and young Hamilton are nothing compared to this Harper. But," rushing to his mistress, and pressing her hands convulsively, "repeat to me—you say you have his promise?"

"Surely, surely, Peyton; his solemn, deliberate promise, knowing all the circumstances."

"Rest easy," cried Dunwoodie, holding her to his bosom for a moment, "rest easy, for Henry is safe."

He waited not to explain, but darting from the room, he left the family in amazement. They continued in silent wonder until they heard the feet of his charger, as he dashed from the door with the speed of an arrow.

A long time was spent after this abrupt departure of the youth, by the anxious friends he had left, in discussing the probability of his success. The confidence of his manner had, however, communicated to his auditors something of his own spirit. Each felt that the prospects of Henry were again brightening, and with their reviving hopes they experienced a renewal of spirits, which in all but Henry himself amounted to pleasure; with him, indeed, his state was too awful to admit of trifling, and for a few hours he was condemned to feel how much more intolerable was suspense than even the certainty of calamity. Not so with Frances. She, with all the reliance of affection, reposed in security on the assurance of Dunwoodie, without harassing herself with doubts that she possessed not the means of satisfying; but believing her lover able to accomplish everything that man could do, and retaining a vivid recollection of the manner and benevolent appearance of Harper, she abandoned herself to all the felicity of renovated hope.

The joy of Miss Peyton was more sobered, and she took frequent occasions to reprove her niece for the exuberance of her spirits, before there was a certainty that their expectations were to be realized. But the slight smile that hovered around the lips of the virgin contradicted the very sobriety of feeling that she inculcated.

"Why, dearest aunt," said Frances, playfully, in reply to one of her frequent reprimands, "would you have me repress the pleasure that I feel at Henry's deliverance, when you yourself have so often declared it to be impossible that such men as ruled in our country could sacrifice an innocent man?"

"Nay, I did believe it impossible, my child, and yet think so; but still there is a discretion to be shown in joy as well as in sorrow."

Frances recollected the declaration of Isabella, and turned an eye filled with tears of gratitude on her excellent aunt, as she replied,—

"True; but there are feelings that will not yield to reason. Ah! here are those monsters, who have come to witness the death of a fellow creature, moving around yon field, as if life was, to them, nothing but a military show."

"It is but little more to the hireling soldier," said Henry, endeavoring to forget his uneasiness.

"You gaze, my love, as if you thought a military show of some importance," said Miss Peyton, observing her niece to be looking from the window with a fixed and abstracted attention. But Frances answered not.

From the window where she stood, the pass that they had traveled through the Highlands was easily to be seen; and the mountain which held on its summit the mysterious hut was directly before her. Its side was rugged and barren; huge and apparently impassable barriers of rocks presenting themselves through the stunted oaks, which, stripped of their foliage, were scattered over its surface. The base of the hill was not half a mile from the house, and the object which attracted the notice of Frances was the figure of a man emerging from behind a rock of remarkable formation, and as suddenly disappearing. The maneuver was several times repeated, as if it were the intention of the fugitive (for such by his air he seemed to be) to reconnoiter the proceedings of the soldiery, and assure himself of the position of things on the plain. Notwithstanding the distance, Frances instantly imbibed the opinion that it was Birch. Perhaps this impression was partly owing to the air and figure of the man, but in a great measure to the idea that presented itself on formerly beholding the object at the summit of the mountain. That they were the same figure she was confident, although this wanted the appearance which, in the other, she had taken for the pack of the peddler. Harvey had so connected himself with mysterious deportment of Harper, within her imagination, that under circumstances of less agitation than those in which she had labored since her arrival, she would have kept her suspicions to herself. Frances, therefore, sat ruminating on this second appearance in silence, and endeavoring to trace what possible connection this extraordinary man could have with the fortunes of her own family. He had certainly saved Sarah in some degree, from the blow that had partially alighted on her, and in no instance had be proved himself to be hostile to their interests.

After gazing for a long time at the point where she had last seen the figure, in the vain expectation of its reappearance, she turned to her friends in the apartment. Miss Peyton was sitting by Sarah, who gave some slight additional signs of observing what passed, but who still continued insensible either to joy or grief.

"I suppose, by this time, my love, that you are well acquainted with the maneuvers of a regiment," said Miss Peyton. "It is no bad quality in a soldier's wife, at all events."

"I am not a wife yet," said Frances, coloring to the eyes; "and we have little reason to wish for another wedding in our family."

"Frances!" exclaimed her brother, starting from his seat, and pacing the floor in violent agitation. "Touch not the chord again, I entreat you. While my fate is uncertain, I would wish to be at peace with all men."

"Then let the uncertainty cease," cried Frances, springing to the door, "for here comes Peyton with the joyful intelligence of your release."

The words were hardly uttered, before the door opened, and the major entered. In his air there was the appearance of neither success nor defeat, but there was a marked display of vexation. He took the hand that Frances, in the fullness of her heart, extended towards him, but instantly relinquishing it, threw himself into a chair, in evident fatigue.

"You have failed," said Wharton, with a bound of his heart, but an appearance of composure.

"Have you seen Harper?" cried Frances, turning pale.

"I have not. I crossed the river in one boat as he must have been coming to this side, in another. I returned without delay, and traced him for several miles into the Highlands, by the western pass, but there I unaccountably lost him. I have returned here to relieve your uneasiness, but see him I will this night, and bring a respite for Henry."

"But you saw Washington?" asked Miss Peyton.

Dunwoodie gazed at her a moment in abstracted musing, and the question was repeated. He answered ravely, and with some reserve,—

"The commander in chief had left his quarters."

"But, Peyton," cried Frances, in returning terror, "if they should not see each other, it will be too late. Harper alone will not be sufficient."

Her lover turned his eyes slowly on her anxious countenance, and dwelling a moment on her features, said, still musing,—

"You say that he promised to assist Henry."

"Certainly, of his own accord and in requital for the hospitality he had received."

Dunwoodie shook his head, and began to look grave.

"I like not that word hospitality—it has an empty sound; there must be something more reasonable to tie Harper. I dread some mistake; repeat to me all that passed."

Frances, in a hurried and earnest voice, complied with his request. She related particularly the manner of his arrival at the Locusts, the reception that he received, and the events that passed as minutely as her memory could supply her with the means. As she alluded to the conversation that occurred between her father and his guest, the major smiled but remained silent. She then gave a detail of Henry's arrival and the events of the following day. She dwelt upon the part where Harper had desired her brother to throw aside his disguise, and recounted, with wonderful accuracy, his remarks upon the hazard of the step that the youth had taken. She even remembered a remarkable expression of his to her brother, "that he was safer from Harper's knowledge of his person, than he would be without it." Frances mentioned, with the warmth of youthful admiration, the benevolent character of his deportment to herself, and gave a minute relation of his adieus to the whole family.

Dunwoodie at first listened with grave attention; evident satisfaction followed as she proceeded. When she spoke of herself in connection with their guest, he smiled with pleasure, and as she concluded, he exclaimed, with delight,—

"We are safe!—we are safe!"

But he was interrupted, as will be seen in the following chapter.

CHAPTER XXVIII

The owlet loves the gloom of night,
The lark salutes the day,
The timid dove will coo at hand—
But falcons soar away.
—Song in Duo.

In a country settled, like these states, by a people who fled their native land and much-loved firesides, victims of consciences and religious zeal, none of the decencies and solemnities of a Christian death are dispensed with, when circumstances will admit of their exercise. The good woman of the house was a strict adherent to the forms of the church to which she belonged; and having herself been awakened to a sense of her depravity, by the ministry of the divine who harangued the people of the adjoining parish, she thought it was from his exhortations only that salvation could be meted out to the short-lived hopes of Henry Wharton. Not that the kind-hearted matron was so ignorant of the doctrines of the religion which she professed, as to depend, theoretically, on mortal aid for protection; but she had, to use her own phrase, "sat so long under the preaching of good Mr.—," that she had unconsciously imbibed a practical reliance on his assistance, for that which her faith should have taught her could come from Deity alone. With her, the consideration of death was at all times awful; and the instant that the sentence of the prisoner was promulgated, she dispatched Cæsar, mounted on one of her husband's best horses, in quest of her clerical monitor. This step had been taken without consulting either Henry or his friends; and it was only when the services of Cæsar were required on some domestic emergency, that she explained the nature of his absence. The youth heard her, at first, with an unconquerable reluctance to admit of-such a spiritual guide; but as our view of the things of this life becomes less vivid, our prejudices and habits cease to retain their influence; and a civil bow of thanks was finally given, in requital for the considerate care of the well-meaning woman.

The black returned early from his expedition, and, as well as could be gathered from his somewhat incoherent narrative, a minister of God might be expected to arrive in the course of the day. The interruption that we mentioned in our preceding chapter was occasioned by the entrance of the landlady. At the intercession of Dunwoodie, orders had been given to the sentinel who guarded the door of Henry's room, that the members of the prisoner's family should, at all times, have free access to his apartment. Cæsar was included in this arrangement, as a matter of convenience, by the officer in command; but strict inquiry and examination was made into the errand of every other applicant for admission. The major had, however, included himself among the relatives of the British officer; and one pledge, that no rescue should be attempted, was given in his name, for them all. A short conversation was passing between the woman of the house and the corporal of the guard, before the door that the sentinel had already opened in anticipation of the decision of his noncommissioned commandant.

"Would you refuse the consolations of religion to a fellow creature about to suffer death?" said the matron, with earnest zeal. "Would you plunge a soul into the fiery furnace, and a minister at hand to point out the straight and narrow path?"

"I'll tell you what, good woman," returned the corporal, gently pushing her away; "I've no notion of my back being a highway for any man to walk to heaven upon. A pretty figure I should make at the pickets, for disobeying orders. Just step down and ask Lieutenant Mason, and you may bring in a whole congregation. We have not taken the guard from the foot soldiers, but an hour, and I shouldn't like to have it said that we know less than the militia."

"Admit the woman," said Dunwoodie, sternly, observing, for the first time, that one of his own corps was on post.

The corporal raised his hand to his cap, and fell back in silence; the soldier stood to his arms, and the matron entered.

"Here is a reverend gentleman below, come to soothe the parting soul, in the place of our own divine, who is engaged with an appointment that could not be put aside; 'tis to bury old Mr.—"

"Show him in at once," said Henry, with feverish impatience.

"But will the sentinel let him pass? I would not wish a friend of Mr.— to be rudely stopped on the threshold, and he a stranger."

All eyes were now turned on Dunwoodie, who, looking at his watch, spoke a few words with Henry, in an undertone, and hastened from the apartment, followed by Frances. The subject of their conversation was a wish expressed by the prisoner for a clergyman of his own persuasion, and a promise from the major, that one should be sent from Fishkill town, through which he was about to pass, on his way to the ferry to intercept the expected return of Harper. Mason soon made his bow at the door, and willingly complied with the wishes of the landlady; and the divine was invited to make his appearance accordingly.

The person who was ushered into the apartment, preceded by Cæsar, and followed by the matron, was a man beyond the middle age, or who might rather be said to approach the downhill of life. In stature he was above the size of ordinary men, though his excessive leanness might contribute in deceiving as to his height; his countenance was sharp and unbending, and every muscle seemed set in rigid compression. No joy or relaxation appeared ever to have dwelt on features that frowned habitually, as if in detestation of the vices of mankind. The brows were beetling, dark, and forbidding, giving the promise of eyes of no less repelling expression; but the organs were concealed beneath a pair of enormous green goggles, through which they glared around with a fierceness that denounced the coming day of wrath. All was fanaticism, uncharitableness, and denunciation. Long, lank hair, a mixture of gray and black, fell down his neck, and in some degree obscured the sides of his face, and, parting on his forehead, fell in either direction in straight and formal screens. On the top of this ungraceful exhibition was laid impending forward, so as to overhang in some measure the whole fabric, a large hat of three equal cocks. His coat was of a rusty black, and his breeches and stockings were of the same color; his shoes without luster, and half-concealed beneath huge plated buckles.

He stalked into the. room, and giving a stiff nod with his head, took the chair offered him by the black, in dignified silence. For several minutes no one broke this ominous pause in the conversation; Henry feeling a repugnance to his guest, that he was vainly endeavoring to conquer, and the stranger himself drawing forth occasional sighs and groans, that threatened a dissolution of the unequal connection between his sublimated soul and its ungainly tenement. During this deathlike preparation, Mr. Wharton, with a feeling nearly allied to that of his son, led Sarah from the apartment. His retreat was noticed by the divine, in a kind of scornful disdain, who began to hum the air of a popular psalm tune, giving it the full richness of the twang that distinguishes the Eastern[14] psalmody.

"Cæsar," said Miss Peyton, "hand the gentleman some refreshment; he must need it after his ride."

"My strength is not in the things of this life," said the divine, speaking in a hollow, sepulchral voice. "Thrice have I this day held forth in my Master's service, and fainted not; still it is prudent to help this frail tenement of clay, for, surely, 'the laborer is worthy of his hire.' "

Opening a pair of enormous jaws, he took a good measure of the proffered brandy, and suffered it to glide downwards, with that sort of facility with which man is prone to sin.

"I apprehend, then, sir, that fatigue will disable you from performing the duties which kindness has induced you to attempt."

"Woman!" exclaimed the stranger, with energy, "when was I ever known to shrink from a duty? But 'judge not lest ye be judged,' and fancy not that it is given to mortal eyes to fathom the intentions of the Deity."

"Nay," returned the maiden, meekly, and slightly disgusted with his jargon, "I pretend not to judge of either events, or the intentions of my fellow creatures, much less of those of Omnipotence."

" 'Tis well, woman,—'tis well," cried the minister, moving his head with supercilious disdain; "humility becometh thy sex and lost condition; thy weakness driveth thee on headlong like 'unto the bosom of destruction.' "

Surprised at this extraordinary deportment, but yielding to that habit which urges us to speak reverently on sacred subjects, even when perhaps we had better continue silent. Miss Peyton replied,—

---

[14] By "Eastern" is meant the states of New England, which being originally settled by Puritans, still retain many distinct shades of character.

"There is a Power above, that can and will sustain us all in well-doing, if we seek its support in humility and truth."

The stranger turned a lowering look at the speaker, and then composing himself into an air of self-abasement, he continued in the same repelling tones,—

"It is not everyone that crieth out for mercy, that will be heard. The ways of Providence are not to be judged by men—'Many are called, but few are chosen.' It is easier to talk of humility than to feel it. Are you so humble, vile worm, as to wish to glorify God by your own damnation? If not, away with you for a publican and a Pharisee!"

Such gross fanaticism was uncommon in America, and Miss Peyton began to imbibe the impression that her guest was deranged; but remembering that he had been sent by a well-known divine, and one of reputation, she discarded the idea, and, with some forbearance, observed,—

"I may deceive myself, in believing that mercy is proffered to all, but it is so soothing a doctrine, that I would not willingly be undeceived."

"Mercy is only for the elect," cried the stranger, with an unaccountable energy; "and you are in the 'valley of the shadow of death.' Are you not a follower of idle ceremonies, which belong to the vain church that our tyrants would gladly establish here, along with their stamp acts and tea laws? Answer me that, woman; and remember, that Heaven hears your answer; are you not of that idolatrous communion?"

"I worship at the altars of my fathers," said Miss Peyton, motioning to Henry for silence; "but bow to no other idol than my own infirmities."

"Yes, yes, I know ye, self-righteous and papal as ye are—followers of forms, and listeners to bookish preaching; think you, woman, that holy Paul* had notes in his hand to propound the Word to the believers?"

"My presence disturbs you," said Miss Peyton, rising. "I will leave you with my nephew, and offer those prayers in private that I did wish to mingle with his."

So saying, she withdrew, followed by the landlady, who was not a little shocked, and somewhat surprised, by the intemperate zeal of her new acquaintance; for, although the good woman believed that Miss Peyton and her whole church were on the high-road to destruction, she was by no means accustomed to hear such offensive and open avowals of their fate.

Henry had with difficulty repressed the indignation excited by this unprovoked attack on his meek and unresisting aunt; but as the door closed on her retiring figure, he gave way to his feelings.

"I must confess, sir," he exclaimed with heat, "that in receiving a minister of God, I thought I was admitting a Christian; and one who, by feeling his own weaknesses, knew how to pity the frailties of. others. You have wounded the meek spirit of an excellent woman, and I acknowledge but little inclination to mingle in prayer with so intolerant a spirit."

The minister stood erect, with grave composure, following with his eyes, in a kind of scornful pity, the retiring females, and suffered the expostulation of the youth to be given, as if unworthy of his notice. A third voice, however, spoke,—

"Such a denunciation would have driven many women into fits; but it has answered the purpose well enough, as it is."

"Who's that?" cried the prisoner, in amazement, gazing around the room in quest of the speaker.

"It is I, Captain Wharton," said Harvey Birch, removing the spectacles, and exhibiting his piercing eyes, shining under a pair of false eyebrows.

"Good heavens—Harvey!"

"Silence!" said the peddler, solemnly. " 'Tis a name not to be mentioned, and least of all here, within the heart of the American army." Birch paused and gazed around him for a moment, with an emotion exceeding the base passion of fear, and then continued in a gloomy tone, "There are a thousand halters in that very name, and little hope would there be left me of another escape, should I be again taken. This is a fearful venture that I am making; but I could not sleep in quiet, and know that an innocent man was about to die the death of a dog, when I might save him."

"No," said Henry, with a glow of generous feeling on his cheek, "if the risk to yourself be so heavy, retire as you came, and leave me to my fate. Dunwoodie is making, even now, powerful exertions in my behalf; and if he meets with Mr. Harper in the course of the night, my liberation is certain."

"Harper!" echoed the peddler, remaining with his hands

raised, in the act of replacing the spectacles. "What do you know of Harper? And why do you think he will do you service?"

"I have his promise; you remember our recent meeting in my father's dwelling, and he then gave an unasked promise to assist me."

"Yes—but do you know him? That is—why do you think he has the power? Or what reason have you for believing he will remember his word?"

"If ever there was the stamp of truth, or simple, honest benevolence, in the countenance of man, it shone in his," said Henry. "Besides, Dunwoodie has powerful friends in the rebel army, and it would be better that I take the chance where I am, than thus to expose you to certain death, if detected."

"Captain Wharton," said Birch, looking guardedly around and speaking with impressive seriousness of manner, "if I fail you, all fail you. No Harper nor Dunwoodie can save your life; unless you get out with me, and that within the hour, you die to-morrow on the gallows of a murderer. Yes, such are their laws; the man who fights, and kills, and plunders, is honored; but he who serves his country as a spy, no matter how faithfully, no matter how honestly, lives to be reviled, or dies like the vilest criminal!"

"You forget, Mr. Birch," said the youth, a little indignantly, "that I am not a treacherous, lurking spy, who deceives to betray; but innocent of the charge imputed to me."

The blood rushed over the pale, meager features of the peddler, until his face was one glow of fire; but it passed quickly away, as he replied,—

"I have told you truth. Cæsar met me, as he was going on his errand this morning, and with him I have laid the plan which, if executed as I wish, will save you—otherwise you are lost; and I again tell you, that no other power on earth, not even Washington, can save you."

"I submit," said the prisoner, yielding to his earnest manner, and goaded by the fears that were thus awakened anew.

The peddler beckoned to him to be silent, and walking to the door, opened it, with the stiff, formal air with which he had entered the apartment.

"Friend, let no one enter," he said to the sentinel. "We are about to go to prayer, and would wish to be alone."

"I don't know that any will wish to interrupt you," returned the soldier, with a waggish leer of his eye; "but, should they be so disposed, I have no power to stop them, if they be of prisoner's friends. I have my orders, and must mind them; whether the Englishman goes to heaven, or not."

"Audacious sinner!" said the pretended priest, "have you not the fear of God before your eyes? I tell you, as you will dread punishment at the last day, to let none of the idolatrous communion enter, to mingle in the prayers of the righteous."

"Whew-ew-ew—what a noble commander you'd make for Sergeant Hollister! You'd preach him dumb in a roll call. Harkee, I'll thank you not to make such a noise when you hold forth, as to drown our bugles, or you may get a poor fellow a short horn at his grog, for not turning out to the evening parade. If you want to be alone, have you no knife to stick over the door latch, that you must have a troop of horse to guard your meetinghouse?"

The peddler took the hint, and closed the door immediately, using the precaution suggested by the dragoon.

"You overact your part," said young Wharton, in constant apprehension of discovery; "your zeal is too intemperate."

"For a foot soldier and them Eastern militia, it might be," said Harvey, turning a bag upside down, that Cæsar now handed him; "but these dragoons are fellows that you must drag down. A faint heart. Captain Wharton, would do but little here; but come, here is a black shroud for your good-looking countenance," taking, at the same time, a parchment mask, and fitting it to the face of Henry. "The master and the man must change places for a season."

"I don't t'ink he look a bit like me," said Cæsar, with disgust, as he surveyed his young master with his new complexion.

"Stop a minute, Cæsar," said the peddler, with the lurking drollery that at times formed part of his manner, "till we get on the wool."

"He worse than ebber now," cried the discontended African. "A t'ink colored man like a sheep! I nebber see sich a lip, Harvey; he most as big as a suasage!"

Great pains had been taken in forming the different articles used in the disguise of Captain Wharton, and when arranged, under the skillful superintendence of the peddler, they formed together a transformation that would easily escape detection, from any but an extraordinary observer.

The mask was stuffed and shaped in such a manner as to preserve the peculiarities, as well as the color, of the African visage; and the wig was so artfully formed of black and white wool, as to imitate the pepper-and-salt color of Cæsar's own head, and to exact plaudits from the black himself, who thought it an excellent counterfeit in everything but quality.

"There is but one man in the American army who could detect you, Captain Wharton," said the peddler, surveying his work with satisfaction, "and he is just now out of our way."

"And who is he?"

"The man who made you prisoner. He would see your white skin through a plank. But strip, both of you; your clothes must be exchanged from head to foot."

Cæsar, who had received minute instructions from the peddler in their morning interview, immediately commenced throwing aside his coarse garments, which the youth took up and prepared to invest himself with; unable, however, to repress a few signs of loathing.

In the manner of the peddler there was an odd mixture of care and humor; the former was the result of a perfect knowledge of their danger, and the means necessary to be used in avoiding it; and the latter proceeded from the unavoidably ludicrous circumstances before him, acting on an indifference which sprang from habit, and long familiarity with such scenes as the present.

"Here, captain," he said, taking up some loose wool, and beginning to stuff the stockings of Cæsar, which were already on the leg of the prisoner; "some judgment is necessary in shaping this limb. You will have to display it on horseback; and the Southern dragoons are so used to the brittleshins', that should they nonce your well-turned calf, they'd know at once it never belonged TO a black."

"Golly!" said Cæsar, with a chuckle, that exhibited a mouth open from ear to ear, "Massa Harry breeches fit."

"Anything but your leg," said the peddler, coolly pursuing the toilet of Henry. "Slip on the coat, captain, overall. Upon my word, you'd pass well at a punkster frolic; and here, Cæsar, place this powdered wig over your curls, and be careful and look out of the window, whenever the door is open, and on no account speak, or you will betray all."

"I s'pose Harvey fink a colored man ain't got a tongue like oder folk," grumbled the black, as he took the station assigned to him.

Everything now was arranged for action, and the peddler very deliberately went over the whole of his injunctions to the two actors in the scene. The captain he conjured to despense with his erect military carriage, and for a season to adopt the humble paces of his father's negro; and Cæsar he enjoined to silence and disguise, so long as he could possibly maintain them. Thus prepared, he opened the door, and called aloud to the sentinel, who had retired to the farthest end of the passage, in order to avoid receiving any of that spiritual comfort, which he felt was the sole property of another.

"Let the woman of the house be called," said Harvey, in the solemn key of his assumed character; "and let her come alone. The prisoner is in a happy train of meditation, and must not be led from his devotions."

Cæsar sank his face between his hands; and when the soldier looked into the apartment, he thought he saw his charge in deep abstraction. Casting a glance of huge contempt at the divine, he called aloud for the good woman of the house. She hastened at the summons, with earnest zeal, entertaining a secret hope that she was to be admitted to the gossip of a death-bed repentance.

"Sister," said the minister, in the authoritative tones of a master, "have you in the house 'The Christian Criminal's last Moments, or Thoughts on Eternity, for them who die a violent Death'?"

"I never heard of the book!" said the matron in astonishment.

" 'Tis not unlikely; there are many books you have never heard of: it is impossible for this poor penitent to pass in peace, without the consolations of that volume. One hour's reading in it is worth an age of man's preaching."

"Bless me, what a treasure to possess! When was it put out?"

"It was first put out at Geneva in the Greek language, and then translated at Boston. It is a book, woman, that should be in the hands of every Christian, especially such as die upon the gallows. Have a horse prepared instantly for this black, who shall accompany me to my brother—, and I will send down the volume yet in season. Brother, compose thy mind; you are now in the narrow path to glory."

Cæsar wriggled a little in his chair, but he had sufficient recollection to conceal his face with hands that were, in their turn. concealed by gloves. The landlady departed, to comply with this very reasonable request, and the group of conspirators were again left to themselves.

"This is well," said the peddler; "but the difficult task is to deceive the officer who commands the guard—he is lieutenant to Lawton, and has learned some of the captain's own cunning in these things. Remember, Captain Wharton," continued he with an air of pride, "that now is the moment when everything depends on our coolness."

"My fate can be made but little worse than it is at present, my worthy fellow," said Henry; "but for your sake I will do all that in me lies."

"And wherein can I be more forlorn and persecuted than I now am?" asked the peddler, with that wild incoherence which often crossed his manner. "But I have promised one to save you, and to him I have never yet broken my word."

"And who is he?" said Henry, with awakened interest.

"No one."

The man soon returned, and announced that the horses were at the door. Harvey gave the captain a glance, and led the way down the stairs, first desiring the woman to leave the prisoner to himself, in order that he might digest the wholesome mental food that he had so lately received.

A rumor of the odd character of the priest had spread from the sentinel at the door to his comrades; so that when Harvey and Wharton reached the open space before the building, they found a dozen idle dragoons loitering about with the waggish intention of quizzing the fanatic, and employed in affected admiration of the steeds.

"A fine horse!" said the leader in this plan of mischief; "but a little low in flesh. I suppose from hard labor in your calling."

"My calling may be laborsome to both myself and this faithful beast, but then a day of settling is at hand, that will reward me for all my outgoings and incomings," said Birch, putting his foot in the stirrup, and preparing to mount.

"You work for pay, then, as we fight for't? cried another of the party.

"Even so—is not the laborer worthy of his hire?"

"Come, suppose you give us a little preaching; we have a leisure moment just now, and there's no telling how much good you might do a set of reprobates like us, in a few words. Here, mount this horseblock, and take your text where you please."

The men now gathered in eager delight around the peddler, who, glancing his eye expressively towards the captain, who had been suffered to mount, replied,—

"Doubtless, for such is my duty. But, Cæsar, you can ride up the road and deliver the note—the unhappy prisoner will be wanting the book, for his hours are numbered."

"Aye, aye, go along, Cæsar, and get the book," shouted half a dozen voices, all crowding eagerly around the ideal priest, in anticipation of a frolic.

The peddler inwardly dreaded, that, in their unceremonious handling of himself and garments, his hat and wig might be displaced, when detection would be certain: he was therefore fain to comply with their request. Ascending the horseblock, after hemming once or twice, and casting several glances at the captain, who continued immovable, he commenced as follows:—

"I shall call your attention, my brethren, to that portion of Scripture which you will find in the second book of Samuel, and which is written in the following words:—'And the king lamented over Abner, and said. Died Abner as a fool dieth? Thy hands were not bound, nor thy feet put into fetters: as a man falleth before wicked men, so fellest thou. And all the people wept again over him.' Cæsar, ride forward, I say, and obtain the book as directed; thy master is groaning in spirit even now for the want of it."

"An excellent text!" cried the dragoons. "Go on—go on—let the snowball stay; he wants to be edified as well as another."

"What are you at there, scoundrels?" cried Lieutenant Mason, as he came in sight from a walk he had taken to sneer at the evening parade of the regiment of militia. "Away with every man of you to your quarters, and let me find that each horse is cleaned and littered, when I come round." The sound of the officer's voice operated like a charm, and no priest could desire a more silent congregation, although he might possibly have wished for one that was more numerous. Mason had not done speaking, when it was reduced to the image of Cæsar only. The peddler took that opportunity to mount, but he had to preserve the gravity of his movements, for the remark of the troopers upon the condition of their beasts was but too just, and a dozen dragoon horses stood saddled and bridled at hand, ready to receive their riders at a moment's warning.

"Well, have you bitted the poor fellow within," said Mason, "that he can take his last ride under the curb of divinity, old gentleman?"

"There is evil in thy conversation, profane man," cried the priest, raising his hands and casting his eyes upwards in holy horror; "so I will depart from thee unhurt, as Daniel was liberated from the lions' den."

"Off with you, for a hypocritical, psalm-singing, canting rogue in disguise," said Mason scornfully. "By the life of Washington! it worries an honest fellow to see such voracious beast of prey ravaging a country for which he sheds his blood. If I had you on a Virginia plantation for a quarter of an hour, I'd teach you to worm the tobacco with the turkeys."

"I leave you, and shake the dust off my shoes, that no remnant of this wicked hole may tarnish the vestments of the godly."

"Start, or I will shake the dust from your jacket, designing knave! A fellow to be preaching to my men! There's Hollister put the devil in them by his exhorting; the rascals were getting too conscientious to strike a blow that would raze the skin. But hold! Whither do you travel. Master Blackey, in such godly company?"

"He goes," said the minister, hastily speaking for his companion, "to return with a book of much condolence and virtue to the sinful youth above, whose soul will speedily become white, even as his outwards are black and unseemly. Would you deprive a dying man of the consolation of religion?"

"No, no, poor fellow, his fate is bad enough; a famous good breakfast his prim body of an aunt gave us. But harkee, Mr. Revelation, if the youth must die secundum artem, let it be under a gentleman's directions, and my advice is, that you never trust that skeleton of yours among us again, or I will take the skin off and leave you naked."

"Out upon thee for a reviler and scoffer of goodness!" said

Birch, moving slowly, and with a due observance of clerical dignity, down the road, followed by the imaginary Cæsar. "But I leave thee, and that behind me that will prove thy condemnation, and take from thee a hearty and joyful deliverance."

"Damn him," muttered the trooper. "The fellow rides like a stake, and his legs stick out like the cocks of his hat. I wish I had him below these hills, where the law is not over-particular I'd—"

"Corporal of the guard!—corporal of the guard!" shouted the sentinel in the passage to the chambers, "corporal of the guard!—corporal of the guard!"

The subaltern flew up the narrow stairway that led to the room of the prisoner, and demanded the meaning of the outcry.

The soldier was standing at the open door of the apartment, looking in with a suspicious eye on the supposed British officer. On observing his lieutenant, he fell back with habitual respect, and replied, with an air of puzzled thought,—

"I don't know, sir; but just now the prisoner looked queer. Ever since the preacher left him, he don't look as he used to do —but," gazing intently over his shoulder of his officer, "it must be him, too! There is the same powdered head, and the dam in the coat, where he was hit the day we had the last brush with the enemy."

"And then all this noise is occasioned by your doubting whether that poor gentleman is your prisoner, or not, is it, sirrah? Who the devil do you think it can be else?"

"I don't know who else it can be," returned the fellow, sullenly; "but he has grown thicker and shorter, if it is he; and see for yourself, sir, he shakes all over, like a man in an ague."

This was but too true. Cæsar was an alarmed auditor of this short conversation, and, from congratulating himself upon the dexterous escape of his young master, his thoughts were very naturally beginning to dwell upon the probable consequences to his own person. The pause that succeeded the last remark of the sentinel, in no degree contributed to the restoration of his faculties. Lieutenant Mason was busied in examining with his own eyes the suspected person of the black, and Cæsar was aware of the fact, by stealing a look through a passage under one of his arms, that he had left expressly for the purpose of reconnoitering. Captain Lawton would have discovered the fraud immediately. but Mason was by no means so quick-sighted as his commander.

He therefore turned rather contemptuously to the soldier. and, speaking in an undertone, observed,—

"That anabaptist, methodistical, quaker, psalm-singing rascal has frightened the boy, with his farrago about flames and brimstone. I'll step in and cheer him with a little rational conversation."

"I have heard of fear making a man white," said the soldier. drawing back, and staring as if his eyes would start from their sockets, "but it has changed the royal captain to a black!"

The truth was, that Cæsar, unable to hear what Mason uttered in a low voice, and having every fear aroused in him by what had already passed, incautiously removed the wig a little from one of his ears, in order to hear the better, without in the least remembering that its color might prove fatal to his disguise. The sentinel had kept his eyes fastened on his prisoner, and noticed the action. The attention of Mason was instantly drawn to the same object: and, forgetting all delicacy for a brother officer in distress, or, in short, forgetting everything but the censure that might alight on his corps, the lieutenant sprang forward and seized the terrified African by the throat; for no sooner had Cæsar heard his color named, than he knew his discovery was certain; and at the first sound of Mason's heavy boot on the floor, he arose from his seat, and retreated precipitately to a corner of the room.

"Who are you?" cried Mason, dashing the head of the old man against the angle of the wall at each interrogatory. "Who the devil are you, and where is the Englishman? Speak, thou thundercloud! Answer me, you jackdaw, or I'll hang you on the gallows of the spy!"

Cæsar continued firm. Neither the threats nor the blows could extract any reply, until the lieutenant, by a very natural transition in the attack, sent his heavy boot forward in a direction that brought it in direct contact with the most sensitive part of the negro—his shin. The most obdurate heart could not have exacted further patience, and Cæsar instantly gave in. The first words he spoke were—

"Golly! massa, you fink I got no feelin'?"

"By heavens!" shouted the lieutenant, "it is the negro himself! Scoundrel! where is your master, and who was the priest?" While speaking, he made a movement as if about to renew the attack; but Cæsar cried aloud for mercy, promising to tell all that he knew.

"Who was the priest?" repeated the dragoon, drawing back his formidable leg, and holding it in threatening suspense.

"Harvey, Harvey!" cried Cæsar, dancing from one leg to the other, as he thought each member in turn might be assailed.

"Harvey who, you black villain?" cried the impatient lieutenant, as he executed a full measure of vengeance by letting his leg fly.

"Birch!" shrieked Cæsar, falling on his knees, the tears rolling in large drops over his shining face.

"Harvey Birch!" echoed the trooper, hurling the black from him, and rushing from the room. "To arms! to arms! Fifty guineas for the life of the peddler spy—give no quarter to either. Mount, mount! to arms! to horse!"

During the uproar occasioned by the assembling of the dragoons, who all rushed tumultuously to their horses, Cæsar rose from the floor, where he had been thrown by Mason, and began to examine into his injuries. Happily for himself, he had alighted on his head, and consequently sustained no material damage.

CHAPTER XXIX

A way went Gilpin, neck or nought,
A way went hat and wig;
He little dreamt, when he set out,
Of running such a rig.
—Cowper.

The road which it was necessary for the peddler and the English captain to travel, in order to reach the shelter of the hills, lay, for a half mile, in full view from the door of the building that had so recently been the prison of the latter; running for the whole distance over the rich plain, that spreads to the very foot of the mountains, which here rise in a nearly perpendicular ascent from their bases; it then turned short to the right, and was obliged to follow the windings of nature, as it won its way into the bosom of the Highlands.

To preserve the supposed difference in their stations, Harvey rode a short distance ahead of his companion, and maintained the sober, dignified pace, that was suited to his assumed character. On their right, the regiment of foot, that we have already mentioned, lay, in tents; and the sentinels who guarded their encampment were to be seen moving with measured tread under the hills themselves.

The first impulse of Henry was, certainly, to urge the beast he rode to his greatest speed at once, and by a coup de main not only accomplish his escape, but relieve himself from the torturing suspense of his situation. But the forward movement that the youth made for this purpose was instantly checked by the peddler.

"Hold up!" he cried, dexterously reining his own horse across the path of the other. "Would you ruin us both? Fall into the place of a black, following his master. Did you not see their blooded chargers, all saddled and bridled, standing in the sun before the house? How long do you think that miserable Dutch horse you are on would hold his speed, if pursued by the Virginians? Every foot that we can gain, without giving the alarm, counts a day in our lives. Ride steadily after me, and on no account look back. They are as subtle as foxes, aye, and as ravenous for blood as wolves!"

Henry reluctantly restrained his impatience, and followed the direction of the peddler. His imagination, however, continually alarmed him with the fancied sounds of pursuit, though Birch, who occasionally looked back under the pretense of addressing his companion, assured him that all continued quiet and peaceful.

"But," said Henry, "it will not be possible for Cæsar to remain long undiscovered. Had we not better put our horses to the gallop, and by the time they can reflect on the cause of our flight, we can reach the corner of the woods?"

"Ah! you little know them, Captain Wharton," returned the peddler. "There is a sergeant at this moment looking after us, as if he thought all was not right; the keen-eyed fellow watches me like a tiger lying in wait for his leap. When I stood on the horse-block, he half suspected that something was wrong. Nay, check your beast—we must let the animals walk a little, for he is laying his hand on the pommel of his saddle. If he mounts, we are gone. The foot-soldiers could reach us with their muskets."

"What does he now?" asked Henry, reining his horse to a walk, but at the same time pressing his heels into the animal's sides, to be in readiness for a spring.

"He turns from his charger, and looks the other way, now trot on gently—not so fast—no so fast. Observe the sentinel in the field, a little ahead of us—he eyes us keenly."

"Never mind the footman," said Henry, impatiently, "he can do nothing but shoot us—whereas these dragoons may make me a captive again. Surely, Harvey, there are horse moving down the road behind us. Do you see nothing particular?"

"Humph!" ejaculated the peddler. "There is something particular, indeed, to be seen behind the thicket on our left. Turn your head a little, and you may see and profit by it too."

Henry eagerly seized this permission to look aside, and the blood curdled to his heart as he observed that they were passing a gallows, which unquestionably had been erected for his own execution. He turned his face from the sight, in undisguised horror.

"There is a warning to be prudent," said the peddler, in the sententious manner that he often adopted.

"It is a terrific sight, indeed!" cried Henry, for a moment

veiling his eyes with his hand, as if to drive a vision from before him.

The peddler moved his body partly around, and spoke with energetic but gloomy bitterness, "And yet. Captain Wharton, you see it where the setting sun shines full upon you; the air you breathe is clear, and fresh from the hills before you. Every step that you take leaves that hated gallows behind; and every dark hollow, and every shapeless rock in the mountains, offers you a hiding place from the vengeance of your enemies. But I have seen the gibbet raised, when no place of refuge offered. Twice have I been buried in dungeons, where, fettered and in chains, I have passed nights in torture, looking forward to the morning's dawn that was to light me to a death of infamy. The sweat has started from limbs that seemed already drained of their moisture; and if I ventured to the hole that admitted air through grates of iron to look out upon the smiles of nature, which God has bestowed for the meanest of His creatures, the gibbet has glared before my eyes, like an evil conscience harrowing the soul of a dying man. Four times have I been in their power, besides this last; but— twice—did I think my hour had come. It is hard to die at the best, Captain Wharton; but to spend your last moments alone and unpitied, to know that none near you so much as think of the fate that is to you the closing of all that is earthly; to think that, in a few hours, you are to be led from the gloom, which, as you dwell on what follows, becomes dear to you, to the face of day, and there to meet all eyes fixed upon you, as if you were a wild beast; and to lose sight of everything amidst the jeers and scoffs of your fellow creatures—that, Captain Wharton, that indeed is to die!"

Henry listened in amazement, as his companion uttered this speech with a vehemence altogether new to him; both seemed to have forgotten their danger and their disguises.

"What! were you ever so near death as that?"

"Have I not been the hunted beast of these hills for three years past?" resumed Harvey; "and once they even led me to the foot of the gallows itself, and I escaped only by an alarm from the royal troops. Had they been a quarter of an hour later, I must have died. There was I placed in the midst of unfeeling men, and gaping women and children, as a monster to be cursed. When I would pray to God, my ears were insulted with the history of my crimes: and when, in all that multitude, I looked around for a single face that showed me any pity, I could find none—no, not even one; all cursed me as a wretch who would sell his country for gold. The sun was brighter to my eyes than common—but it was the last time I should see it. The fields were gay and pleasant, and everything seemed as if this world was a kind of heaven. Oh, how sweet life was to me at that moment! 'Twas a dreadful hour, Captain Wharton, and such as you have never known. You have friends to feel for you, but I had none but a father to mourn my loss, when he might hear of it; but there was no pity, no consolation near, to soothe my anguish. Everything seemed to have deserted me. I even thought that HE had forgotten that I lived."

"What! did you feel that God Himself had forgotten you, Harvey?"

"God never forsakes His servants," returned Birch, with reverence, and exhibiting naturally a devotion that hitherto he had only assumed.

"And whom did you mean by HE?"

The peddler raised himself in his saddle to the stiff and upright posture that was suited to his outward appearance. The look of fire, that for a short time glowed on his countenance, disappeared in the solemn lines of unbending self-abasement, and, speaking as if addressing a negro, he replied,—

"In heaven there is no distinction of color, my brother, therefore you have a precious charge within you, that you must hereafter render an account of;" dropping his voice—"this is the last sentinel near the road; look not back, as you value your life."

Henry remembered his situation, and instantly assumed the humble demeanor of his adopted character. The unaccountable energy of the peddler's manner was soon forgotten in the sense of his own immediate danger; and with the recollection of his critical situation, returned all the uneasiness that he had momentarily forgotten.

"What see you, Harvey?" he cried, observing the peddler to gaze towards the building they had left, with ominous interest. "What see you at the house?"

"That which bodes no good to us," returned the pretended priest. "Throw aside the mask and wig; you will need all your senses without much delay; throw them in the road. There are none before us that I dread, but there are those behind who will give us a fearful race!"

"Nay, then," cried the captain, casting the implements of his disguise into the highway, "let us improve our time to the utmost. We want a full quarter to the turn; why not push for it, at once?"

"Be cool; they are in alarm, but they will not mount without an officer, unless they see us fly—now he comes, he moves to the stables; trots briskly; a dozen are in their saddles, but the officer stops to tighten his girths; they hope to steal a march upon us; he is mounted; now ride. Captain Wharton, for your life, and keep at my heels. If you quit me, you will be lost!"

A second request was unnecessary. The instant that Harvey put his horse to his speed Captain Wharton was at his heels, urging the miserable animal he rode to the utmost. Birch had selected his own beast; and although vastly inferior to the high-fed and blooded chargers of the dragoons, still it was much superior to the little pony that had been thought good enough to carry Cæsar Thompson on an errand. A very few jumps convinced the captain that his companion was fast leaving him, and a fearful glance thrown behind informed the fugitive that his enemies were as speedily approaching. With that abandonment that makes misery doubly grievous, when it is to be supported alone, Henry cried aloud to the peddler not to desert him. Harvey instantly drew up, and suffered his companion to run alongside of his own horse. The cocked hat and wig of the peddler fell from his head the moment that his steed began to move briskly, and this development of their disguise, as it might be termed, was witnessed by the dragoons, who announced their observation by a boisterous shout, that seemed to be uttered in the very ears of the fugitives; so loud was the cry, and so short the distance between them.

"Had we not better leave our horses," said Henry, "and make for the hills across the fields, on our left? The fence will stop our pursuers."

"That way lies the gallows," returned the peddler. "These fellows go three feet to our two, and would mind the fences no more than we do these ruts; but it is a short quarter to the turn, and there are two roads behind the wood. They may stand to choose until they can take the track, and we shall gain a little upon them there."

"But this miserable horse is blown already," cried Henry, urging his beast with the end of his bridle, at the same time that Harvey aided his efforts by applying the lash of a heavy riding whip he carried. "He will never stand it for half a mile farther."

"A quarter will do; a quarter will do," said the peddler, "a single quarter will save us, if you follow my directions."

Somewhat cheered by the cool and confident manner of his companion, Henry continued silently urging his horse forward. A few moments brought them to the desired turn, and as they doubled round a point of low underbrush, the fugitives caught a glimpse of their pursuers scattered along the highway. Mason and the sergeant, being better mounted than the rest of the party, were much nearer to their heels than even the peddler thought could be possible.

At the foot of the hills, and for some distance up the dark valley that wound among the mountains, a thick underwood of saplings had been suffered to shoot up, where the heavier growth was felled for the sake of the fuel. At the sight of this cover. Henry again urged the peddler to dismount, and to plunge into the woods; but his request was promtly refused. The two roads, before mentioned, met at very sharp angles at a short distance from the turn, and both were circuitous, so that but little of either could be seen at a time. The peddler took the one which led to the left, but held it only a moment, for, on reaching a partial opening in the thicket, he darted across into the right-hand path and led the way up a steep ascent, which lay directly before them. This maneuver saved them. On reaching the fork, the dragoons followed the track and passed the spot where the fugitives had crossed to the other road, before they missed the marks of the footsteps. Their loud cries were heard by Henry and the peddler, as their wearied and breathless animals toiled up the hill, ordering their comrades in the rear to ride in the right direction. The captain again proposed to leave their horses and dash into the thicket.

"Not yet, not yet," said Birch, in a low voice. "The road falls from the top of this hill as steep as it rises; first let us gain the top." While speaking, they reached the desired summit, and both threw themselves from their horses. Henry plunging into the thick underwood, which covered the side of the mountain for some distance above them. Harvey stopped to give each of their beasts a few severe blows of his whip, that drove them headlong down the path on the other side of the eminence, and then followed his example.

The peddler entered the thicket with a little caution, and avoided, as much as possible, rustling or breaking the branches in his way. There was but time only to shelter his person from view when a dragoon led up the ascent, and on reaching the height, he cried aloud,—

"I saw one of their horses turning the hill this minute."

"Drive on; spur forward, my lads," shouted Mason; "give the Englishman quarter, but cut down the peddler, and make an end of him."

Henry felt his companion grip his arm hard, as he listened in a great tremor to this cry, which was followed by the passage of a dozen horsemen, with a vigor and speed that showed too plainly how little security overtired steeds could have afforded them.

"Now," said the peddler, rising from the cover to reconnoiter, and standing for a moment in suspense, "all that we gain is clear gain; for, as we go up, they go down. Let us be stirring."

"But will they not follow us, and surround this mountain?" said Henry, rising, and imitating the labored but rapid progress of his companion. "Remember, they have foot as well as horse, and, at any rate, we shall starve in the hills."

"Fear nothing, Captain Wharton," returned the peddler, with confidence; "this is not the mountain that I would be on, but necessity has made me a dexterous pilot among these hills. I will lead you where no man will dare to follow. See, the sun is already setting behind the tops of the western mountains, and it will be two hours to the rising of the moon. Who, think you, will follow us far, on a November night, among these rocks and precipices?"

"Listen!" exclaimed Henry; "the dragoons are shouting to each other; they miss us already."

"Come to the point of this rock, and you may see them," said Harvey, composedly setting himself down to rest. "Nay, they can see us—observe, they are pointing up with their fingers. There! one has fired his pistol, but the distance is too great even for a musket."

"They will pursue us," cried the impatient Henry, "let us be moving."

"They will not think of such a thing," returned the peddler, picking the checkerberries that grew on the thin soil where he sat, and very deliberately chewing them, leaves and all, to refresh his mouth. "What progress could they make here, in their heavy boots and spurs, and long swords? No, no—they may go back and turn out the foot, but the horse pass through these defiles, when they can keep the saddle, with fear and trembling. Come, follow me. Captain Wharton; we have a troublesome march before us, but I will bring you where none will think of venturing this night."

So saying, they both arose, and were soon hid from view amongst the rocks and caverns of the mountain.

The conjecture of the peddler was true. Mason and his men dashed down the hill, in pursuit, as they supposed, of their victims, but, on reaching the bottom lands, they found only the deserted horses of the fugitives. Some little time was spent in examining the woods near them, and in endeavoring to take the trail on such ground as might enable to horse to pursue, when one of the party descried the peddler and Henry seated on the rock already mentioned.

"He's off," muttered Mason, eying Harvey, with fury; "he's off, and we are disgraced. By heavens, Washington will not trust us with the keeping of a suspected Tory, if we let the rascal trifle in this manner with the corps; and there sits the Englishman, too, looking down upon us with a smile of benevolence! I fancy that I can see it. Well, well, my lad, you are comfortably seated, I will confess, and that is something better than dancing upon nothing; but you are not to the west of the Harlem River yet, and I'll try your wind before you tell Sir Henry what you have seen."

"Shall I fire and frighten the peddler?" asked one of the men, drawing his pistol from the holster.

"Aye, startle the birds from their perch—let us see how they can use the wing." The man fired the pistol, and Mason continued— " 'Fore George, I believe the scoundrels laugh at us. But homeward, or we shall have them rolling stones upon our heads, and the royal gazettes teeming with an account of a rebel regiment routed by two loyalists. They have told bigger lies than that, before now."

The dragoons moved sullenly after their officer, who rode

towards their quarters, musing on the course it behooved him to pursue in the present dilemma. It was twilight when Mason's party reached the dwelling, before the door of which were collected a great number of the officers and men, busily employed in giving and listening to the most exaggerated accounts of the escape of the spy. The mortified dragoons gave their ungrateful tidings with the sullen air of disappointed men; and most of the officers gathered round Mason, to consult of the steps that ought to be taken. Miss Peyton and Frances were breathless and unobserved listeners to all that passed between them, from the window of the chamber immediately above their heads.

"Something must be done, and that speedily," observed the commanding officer of the regiment, which lay encamped before the house. "This English officer is doubtless an instrument in the great blow aimed at us by the enemy lately; besides, our honor is involved in his escape."

"Let us beat the woods!" cried several at once. "By morning we shall have them both again."

"Softly, softly, gentlemen," returned the colonel. "No man can travel these hills after dark, unless used to the passes. Nothing but horse can do service in this business, and I presume Lieutenant Mason hesitates to move without the ciders of his major."

"I certainly dare not," replied the subaltern, gravely shaking his head, "unless you will take the responsibility of an order; but Major Dunwoodie will be back again in two hours, and we can carry the tidings through the hills before daylight; so that by spreading patrols across, from one river to the other, and offering a reward to the country people, their escape will yet be impossible, unless they can join the party that is said to be out on the Hudson."

"A very plausible plan," cried the colonel, "and one that must succeed; but let a messenger be dispatched to Dunwoodie, or he may continue at the ferry until it proves too late; though doubtless the runaways will lie in the mountains to-night."

To this suggestion Mason acquiesced, and a courier was sent to the major with the important intelligence of the escape of Henry, and an intimation of the necessity of his presence to conduct the pursuit. After this arrangement, the officers separated.

When Miss Peyton and her niece first learned the escape of

Captain Wharton, it was with difficulty they could credit their senses. They both relied so implicitly on the success of Dunwoodie's exertions, that they thought the act, on the part of their relative, extremely imprudent; but it was now too late to mend it. While listening to the conversation of the officers, both were struck with the increased danger of Henry's situation, if recaptured, and they trembled to think of the great exertions that would be made to accomplish this object. Miss Peyton consoled herself, and endeavored to cheer her niece, with the probability that the fugitives would pursue their course with unremitting diligence, so that they might reach the neutral ground before the horse would carry down the tidings of their flight. The absence of Dunwoodie seemed to her all-important, and the artless lady was anxiously devising some project that might detain her kinsman, and thus give her nephew the longest possible time. But very different were the reflections of Frances. She could no longer doubt that the figure she had seen on the hill was Birch, and she felt certain that, instead of flying to the friendly forces below, her brother would be taken to the mysterious hut to pass the night.

Frances and her aunt held a long and animated discussion by themselves, when the good spinster reluctantly yielded to the representation of her niece, and folding her in her arm, she kissed her cold cheek, and, fervently blessing her, allowed her to depart on an errand of fraternal love.

CHAPTER XXX

And here, forlorn and lost, I tread,
With fainting steps, and slow;
Where wilds, immeasurably spread,
Seem length'ning as I go.
—Goldsmith.

The night had set in dark and chilling, as Frances Wharton, with a beating heart but light step, moved through the little garden that lay behind the farmhouse which had been her brother's prison, and took her way to the foot of the mountain, where she had seen the figure of him she supposed to be the peddler. It was still early, but the darkness and the dreary nature of a November evening would, at any other moment, or with less inducement to exertion, have driven her back in terror to the circle she had left. Without pausing to reflect, however, she flew over the ground with a rapidity that seemed to bid defiance to all impediments, nor stopped even to breathe, until she had gone half the distance to the rock that she had-marked as the spot where Birch made his appearance on that very morning.

The good treatment of their women is the surest evidence that a people can give of their civilization; and there is no nation which has more to boast of, in this respect, than the Americans. Frances felt but little apprehension from the orderly and quiet troops who were taking their evening's repast on the side of the highway, opposite to the field through which she was flying. They were countrymen, and she knew that her sex would be respected by the Eastern militia, who composed this body; but in the volatile and reckless character of the Southern horse she had less confidence. Outrages of any description were seldom committed by the really American soldiery; but she recoiled, with exquisite delicacy, from even the appearance of humiliation. When, therefore, she heard the footsteps of a horse moving slowly up the road, she shrank, timidly, into a little thicket of wood which grew around the spring that bubbled from the side of a hillock near her. The vidette, for such it proved to be, passed her without noticing her form, which was enveloped as to be as little conspicuous as possible, humming a low air to himself, and probably thinking of some other fair that he had left on the banks of the Potomac.

Frances listened anxiously to the retreating footsteps of his horse, and, as they died upon her ear, she ventured from her place of secrecy, and advanced a short distance into the field, where, startled at the gloom, and appalled with dreariness of the prospect, she paused to reflect on what she had undertaken. Throwing back the hood of her cardinal, she sought the support of a tree, and gazed towards the summit of the mountain that was to be the goal of her enterprise. It rose from the plain like a huge pyramid, giving nothing to the eye but its outlines. The pinnacle could be faintly discerned in front of a lighter background of clouds, between which a few glimmering stars occasionally twinkled in momentary brightness, and then gradually became obscured by the passing vapor that was moving before the wind, at a vast distance below the clouds themselves. Should she return. Henry and the peddler would most probably pass the night in fancied security upon that very hill towards which she was straining her eyes, in the vain hope of observing some light that might encourage her to proceed. The deliberate, and what to her seemed cold-blooded, project of the officer for the recapture of the fugitives, still rang in her ears, and stimulated her to go on; but the solitude into which she must venture, the time, the actual danger of the ascent, and the uncertainty of her finding the hut, or what was still more disheartening, the chance that it might be occupied by unknown tenants, and those of the worst description—urged her to retreat.

The increasing darkness was each moment rendering objects less and less distinct, and the clouds were gathering more gloomily in the rear of the hill, until its form could no longer be discerned. Frances threw back her rich curls with both hands on her temples, in order to possess her senses in their utmost keenness; but the towering hill was entirely lost to the eye. At length she discovered a faint and twinkling blaze in the direction in which she thought the building stood, that, by its reviving and receding luster, might be taken for the glimmering of a fire. But the delusion vanished, as the horizon again cleared, and the star of evening shone forth from a cloud, after struggling hard, as if for existence. She now saw the mountain to the left of the place where the planet was shining, and suddenly a streak of mellow light burst upon the fantastic oaks that were thinly scattered over its summit, and gradually moved down its side, until the whole pile became distinct under the rays of the rising moon. Although it would have been physically impossible for our heroine to advance without the aid of the friendly light, which now gleamed on the long line of level land before her, yet she was not encouraged to proceed. If she could see the goal of her wishes, she could also perceive the difficulties that must attend her reaching it.

While deliberating in distressing incertitude, now shrinking with the timidity of her sex and years from the enterprise, and now resolving to rescue her brother at every hazard, Frances turned her looks towards the east, in earnest gaze at the clouds which constantly threatened to involve her again in comparative darkness. Had an adder stung her, she could not have sprung with greater celerity than she recoiled from the object against which she was leaning, and which she for the first time noticed. The two upright posts, with a crossbeam on their tops, and a rude platform beneath, told but too plainly the nature of the structure; even the cord was suspended from an iron staple, and was swinging to and fro, in the night air. Frances hesitated no longer, but rather flew than ran across the meadow, and was soon at the base of the rock, where she hoped to find something like a path to the summit of the mountain. Here she was compelled to pause for breath, and she improved the leisure by surveying the ground about her. The ascent was quite abrupt, but she soon found a sheep path that wound among the shelving rocks and through the trees, so as to render her labor much less tiresome than it otherwise would have been. Throwing a fearful glance behind, the determined girl commenced her journey upwards. Young, active, and impelled by her generous motive, she moved up the hill with elastic steps, and very soon emerged from the cover of the woods, into an open space of more level ground, that had evidently been cleared of its timber, for the purpose of cultivation. But either the war or the sterility of the soil had compelled the adventurer to abandon the advantages that he had obtained over the wilderness, and already the bushes and briers were springing up afresh, as if the plow had never traced furrows through the mold which nourished them.

Frances felt her spirits invigorated by these faint vestiges of the labor of man, and she walked up the gentle acclivity with renewed hopes of success. The path now diverged in so many different directions, that she soon saw it would be useless to follow their windings, and abandoning it, at the first turn, she labored forward towards what she thought was the nearest point of the summit. The cleared ground was soon past, and woods and rocks, clinging to the precipitous sides of the mountain, again opposed themselves to her progress. Occasionally, the path was to be seen running along the verge of the clearing, and then striking off into the scattering patches of grass and herbage, but in no instance could she trace it upward. Tufts of wool, hanging to the briers, sufficiently denoted the origin of these tracks, and Frances rightly conjectured that whoever descended the mountain, would avail himself of their existence, to lighten the labor. Seating herself on a stone, the wearied girl again paused to rest and to reflect; the clouds were rising before the moon, and the whole scene at her feet lay pictured in softest colors.

The white tents of the militia were stretched in regular lines immediately beneath her. The light was shining in the window of her aunt, who, Frances easily fancied, was watching the mountain, racked with all the anxiety she might be supposed to feel for her niece. Lanterns were playing about in the stable yard, where she knew the horses of the dragoons were kept, and believing them to be preparing for their night march, she again sprang upon her feet, and renewed her toil.

Our heroine had to ascend more than a quarter of a mile farther, although she had already conquered two thirds of the height of the mountain. But she was now without a path or any guide to direct her in her course. Fortunately, the hill was conical, like most of the mountains in that range, and, by advancing upwards, she was certain of at length reaching the desired hut, which hung, as it were, on the very pinnacle. Nearly an hour did she struggle with the numerous difficulties that she was obliged to overcome, when, having been repeatedly exhausted with her efforts, and, in several instances, in great danger from falls, she succeeded in gaining the small piece of tableland on the summit.

Faint with her exertions, which had been unusually severe for so slight a frame, she sank on a rock, to recover her strength and fortitude for the approaching interview. A few moments sufficed for this purpose, when she proceeded in quest of the hut.

All of the neighboring hills were distinctly visible by the aid of the moon, and Frances was able, where she stood, to trace the route of the highway, from the plains into the mountains. By following this line with her eyes, she soon discovered the point whence she had seen the mysterious dwelling, and directly opposite to that point she well knew the hut must stand.

The chilling air sighed through the leafless branches of the gnarled and crooked oaks, as with a step so light as hardly to rustle the dry leaves on which she trod, Frances moved forward to that part of the hill where she expected to find this secluded habitation; but nothing could she discern that in the least resembled a dwelling of any sort. In vain she examined every recess of the rocks, or inquisitively explored every part of the summit that she thought could hold the tenement of the peddler. No hut, nor any vestige of a human being could she tract. The idea of her solitude struck on the terrified mind of the affrighted girl, and approaching to the edge of a shelving rock, she bent forward to gaze on the signs of life in the vale, when a ray of keen light dazzled her eyes, and a warm ray diffused itself over her whole frame. Recovering from her surprise, Frances looked on the ledge beneath her, and at once perceived that she stood directly over the object of her search. A hole through its roof afforded a passage to the smoke, which, as it blew aside, showed her a clear and cheerful fire crackling and snapping on a rude hearth of stone. The approach to the front of the hut was by a winding path around the point of the rock on which she stood, and by this, she advanced to its door.

Three sides of this singular edifice, if such it could be called, were composed of logs laid alternately on each other, to a little more than the height of a man; and the fourth was formed by the rock against which it leaned. The roof was made of the bark of trees, laid in long strips from the rock to its eaves; the fissures between the logs had been stuffed with clay, which in many places had fallen out, and dried leaves were made use of as a substitute, to keep out the wind. A single window of four panes of glass was in front, but a board carefully closed it, in such a manner as to emit no light from the fire within. After pausing some time to view this singularly constructed hiding place, for such Frances well knew it to be, she applied her eye to a crevice to examine the inside. There was no lamp or candle, but the blazing fire of dry wood made the interior of the hut light enough to read by. In one corner lay a bed of straw, with a pair of blankets thrown carelessly over it, as if left where they had last been used. Against the walls and rock were suspended, from pegs forced into the crevices, various garments, and such as were apparently fitted for all ages and conditions, and for either sex. British and American uniforms hung peaceably by the side of each other; and on the peg that supported a gown of striped calico, such as was the usual country wear, was also depending a well-powdered wig: in short, the attire was numerous and as various as if a whole parish were to be equipped from this one wardrobe.

In the angle against the rock, and opposite to the fire which was burning in the other corner, was an open cupboard, that held a plate or two, a mug, and the remains of some broken meat. Before the fire was a table, with one of its legs fractured, and made of rough boards; these, with a single stool, composed the furniture, if we except a few articles of cooking. A book, that by its size and shape, appeared to be a Bible, was lying on the table, unopened. But it was the occupant of the hut in whom Frances was chiefly interested. This was a man, sitting on the stool, with his head leaning on his hand, in such a manner as to conceal his features, and deeply occupied in examining some open papers. On the table lay a pair of curiously and richly mounted horseman's pistols, and the handle of a sheathed rapier, of exquisite workmanship, protruded from between the legs of the gentleman, one of whose hands carelessly rested on its guard. The tall stature of this unexpected tenant of the hut, and his form, much more athletic than that of either Harvey or her brother, told Frances, without the aid of his dress, that it was neither of those she sought. A close surtout was buttoned high in the throat of the stranger, and parting at his knees, showed breeches of buff, with military boots and spurs. His hair was dressed so as to expose the whole face; and, after the fashion of that day, it was profusely powdered. A round hat was laid on the stones that formed a paved floor to the hut, as if to make room for a large map, which, among the other papers, occupied the table.

This was an unexpected event to our adventurer. She had been so confident that the figure twice seen was the peddler, that on learning his agency in her brother's escape, she did not in the least doubt of finding them both in the place, which, she now discovered, was occupied by another and a stranger. She stood, earnestly looking through the crevice, hesitating whether to retire, or to wait with the expectation of yet meeting Henry, as the stranger moved his hand from before his eyes, and raised his face, apparently in deep musing, when Frances instantly recognized the benevolent and strongly marked, but composed features of Harper.

All that Dunwoodie had said of his power and disposition, all that he had himself promised her brother, and all the confidence that had been created by his dignified and paternal manner, rushed across the mind of Frances, who threw open the door of the hut, and falling at his feet, clasped his knees with her arms, as she cried,—

"Save him—save him—save my brother; remember your promise, and save him!"

Harper had risen as the door opened, and there was a slight movement of one hand towards his pistols; but it was cool and instantly checked. He raised the hood of the cardinal, which had fallen over her features, and exclaimed, with some uneasiness,—

"Miss Wharton! But you cannot be alone?"

"There is none here but my God and you; and by His sacred name, I conjure you to remember your promise, and save my brother!"

Harper gently raised her from her knees, and placed her on the stool, begging her at the same time to be composed, and to acquaint him with the nature of her errand. This Frances instantly did, ingenuously admitting him to a knowledge of all her views in visiting that lone spot at such an hour, and by herself.

It was at all times difficult to probe the thoughts of one who held his passions in such disciplined subjection as Harper, but still there was a lighting of his thoughtful eye, and a slight unbending of his muscles, as the hurried and anxious girl proceeded in her narrative. His interest, as she dwelt upon the manner of Henry's escape, and the flight to the woods, was deep and manifest, and he listened to the remainder of her tale with a marked expression of benevolent indulgence. Her apprehensions, that her brother might still be too late through the mountains, seemed to have much weight with him, for, as she concluded, he walked a turn or two across the hut, in silent musing.

Frances hesitated, and unconsciously played with the handle of one of the pistols, and the paleness that her fears had spread over her fine features began to give place to a rich tint, as, after a short pause, she added,—

"We can depend much on the friendship of Major Dunwoodie, but his sense of honor is so pure, that—that—notwithstanding his—his—feelings—his desire to serve us—he will conceive it to be his duty to apprehend my brother again. Besides, he thinks there will be no danger in so doing, as he relies greatly on your interference."

"On mine," said Harper, raising his eyes in surprise.

"Yes, on yours. When we told him of your kind language, he at once assured us all that you had the power, and, if you had promised, would have the inclination, to procure Henry's pardon."

"Said he more?" asked Harper, who appeared slightly uneasy.

"Nothing but reiterated assurances of Henry's safety; even now he is in quest of you."

"Miss Wharton, that I bear no mean part, in the unhappy struggle between England and America, it might now be useless to deny. You owe your brother's escape, this night, to my knowledge of his innocence, and the remembrance of my word. Major Dunwoodie is mistaken when he says that I might openly have procured his pardon. I now, indeed, can control his fate, and I pledge to you a word which has some influence with Washington, that means shall be taken to prevent his recapture. But from you, also, I exact a promise, that this interview, and all that has passed between us, remain confined to your own bosom, until you have my permission to speak upon the subject."

Frances gave the desired assurance, and he continued,—

"The peddler and your brother will soon be here, but I must not be seen by the royal officer, or the life of Birch might be the forfeiture."

"Never!" cried Frances, ardently. "Henry could never be so base as to betray the man who saved him."

"It is no childish game that we are now playing, Miss Wharton. Men's lives and fortunes hang upon slender threads, and nothing must be left to accident that can be guarded against. Did Sir Henry Clinton know that the peddler had communion with me, and under such circumstances, the life of the miserable man would be taken instantly; therefore, as you value human blood, or remember the rescue of your brother, be prudent, and be silent. Communicate what you know to them both, and urge them to instant departure. If they can reach the last pickets of our army before morning, it shall be my care that there are none to intercept them. There is better work for Major Dunwoodie than to be exposing the life of his friend."

While Harper was speaking, he carefully rolled up the map he had been studying, and placed it, together with sundry papers that were also open, into his pocket. He was still occupied in this manner, when the voice of the peddler, talking in unusually loud tones, was heard directly over their heads.

"Stand farther this way, Captain Wharton, and you can see the tents in the moonshine. But let them mount and ride; I have a nest here, that will hold us both, and we will go in at our leisure."

"And where is this nest? I confess that I have eaten but little the last two days, and I crave some of the cheer you mention."

"Hem!" said the peddler, exerting his voice still more. "Hem—this fog has given me a cold; but move slow—and be careful not to slip, or you may land on the bayonet of the sentinel on the flats; 'tis a steep hill to rise, but one can go down it with ease."

Harper pressed his finger on his lip, to remind Frances of her promise, and, taking his pistols and hat, so that no vestige of his visit remained, he retired deliberately to a far corner of the hut, where, lifting several articles of dress, he entered a recess in the rock, and, letting them fall again, was hid from view. Frances noticed, by the strong firelight, as he entered, that it was a natural cavity, and contained nothing but a few more articles of domestic use.

The surprise of Henry and the peddler, on entering and finding Frances in possession of the hut, may be easily imagined. Without waiting for explanations or questions, the warm-hearted girl flew into the arms of her brother, and gave a vent to her emotions in tears. But the peddler seemed struck with very different feelings. His first look was at the fire, which had been recently supplied with fuel; he then drew open a small drawer of the table, and looked a little alarmed at finding it empty.

"Are you alone, Miss Fanny?" he asked, in a quick voice.

"You did not come here alone?"

"As you see me, Mr. Birch," said Frances, raising herself from her brother's arms, and turning an expressive glance towards the secret cavern, that the quick eye of the peddler instantly understood.

"But why and wherefore are you here?" exclaimed her astonished brother; "and how knew you of this place at all?"

Frances entered at once into a brief detail of what had occurred at the house since their departure, and the motives which induced her to seek them.

"But," said Birch, "why follow us here, when we were left on the opposite hill?"

Frances related the glimpse that she had caught of the hut and peddler, in her passage through the Highlands, as well as her view of him on that day, and her immediate conjecture that the fugitives would seek the shelter of this habitation for the night. Birch examined her features as, with open ingenuousness, she related the simple incidents that had made her mistress of his secret; and, as she ended, he sprang upon his feet, and, striking the window with the stick in his hand, demolished it at a blow.

" 'Tis but little luxury or comfort that I know," he said, "but even that little cannot be enjoyed in safety! Miss Wharton," he added, advancing before Frances, and speaking with the bitter melancholy that was common to him, "I am hunted through these hills like a beast of the forest; but whenever, tired with my toils, I can reach this spot, poor and dreary as it is, I can spend my solitary nights in safety. Will you aid to make the life of a wretch still more miserable?"

"Never!" cried Frances, with fevor; "your secret is safe with me."

"Major Dunwoodie"—said the peddler, slowly, turning an eye upon her that read her soul.

Frances lowered her head upon her bosom, for a moment, in shame; then, elevating her fine and glowing face, she added, with enthusiasm,—

"Never, never, Harvey, as God may hear my prayers!"

The peddler seemed satisfied; for he drew back, and watching his opportunity, unseen by Henry, slipped behind the screen, and entered the cavern.

Frances and her brother, who thought his companion had

passed through the door, continued conversing on the latter's situation for several minutes, when the former urged the necessity of expedition on his part, in order to precede Dunwoodie, from whose sense of duty they knew they had no escape. The captain took out his pocketbook, and wrote a few lines with his pencil; then folding the paper, he handed it to his sister.

"Frances," he said, "you have this night proved yourself to be an incomparable woman. As you love me, give that unopened to Dunwoodie, and remember that two hours may save my life."

"I will—I will; but why delay? Why not fly, and improve these precio'us moments?"

"Your sister says well. Captain Wharton," exclaimed Harvey, who had re-entered unseen; "we must go at once. Here is food to eat, as we travel."

"But who is to see this fair creature in safety?" cried the captain. "I can never desert my sister in such a place as this."

"Leave me! leave me!" said Frances. "I can descend as I came up. Do not doubt me; you know not my courage nor my strength."

"I have not known you, dear girl, it is true; but now, as I learn your value, can I quit you here? Never, never!"

"Captain Wharton," said Birch, throwing open the door, "you can trifle with your own lives, if you have many to spare; I have but one, and must nurse it. Do I go alone, or not?"

"Go, go, dear Henry," said Frances embracing him; "go; remember our father; remember Sarah." She waited not for his answer, but gently forced him through the door, and closed it with her own hands.

For a short time there was a warm debate between Henry and the peddler; but the latter finally prevailed, and the breathless girl heard the successive plunges, as they went down the sides of the mountain at a rapid rate.

Immediately after the noise of their departure had ceased, Harper reappeared. He took the arm of Frances in silence, and led her from the hut. The way seemed familiar to him; for, ascending to the ledge above them, he led his companion across the tableland tenderly, pointing out the little difficulties in their route, and cautioning her against injury.

Frances felt, as she walked by the side of this extraordinary man, that she was supported by one of no common stamp. The firmness of his step, and the composure of his manner, seemed to indicate a mind settled and resolved. By taking a route over the back of the hill, they descended with great expedition, and but little danger. The distance it had taken Frances an hour to conquer, was passed by Harper and his companion in ten minutes, and they entered the open space already mentioned. He struck into one of the sheep paths, and, crossing the clearing with rapid steps, they came suddenly upon a horse, caparisoned for a rider of no mean rank. The noble beast snorted and pawed the earth, as his master approached and replaced the pistols in the holsters.

Harper then turned, and, taking the hand of Frances, spoke as follows:—

"You have this night saved your brother. Miss Wharton. It would not be proper for me to explain why there are limits to my ability to serve him; but if you can detain the horse for two hours, he is assuredly safe. After what you have already done, I can believe you equal to any duty. God has denied to me children, young lady; but if it had been His blessed will that my marriage should not have been childless, such a treasure as yourself would I have asked from His mercy. But you are my child: all who dwell in this broad land are my children, and my care; and take the blessing of one who hopes yet to meet you in happier days."

As he spoke, with a solemnity that touched Frances to the heart, he laid his hand impressively upon her head. The guileless girl turned her face towards him, and the hood again falling back, exposed her lovely features to the moonbeams. A tear was glistening on either cheek, and her mild blue eyes were gazing upon him in reverence. Harper bent and pressed a paternal kiss upon her forehead, and continued: "Any of these sheep paths will take you to the plain; but here we must part—I have much to do and far to ride; forget me in all but your prayers."

He then mounted his horse, and lifting his hat, rode towards the back of the mountain, descending at the same time, and was soon hid by the trees. Frances sprang forward with a lightened heart, and taking the first path that led downwards, in a few minutes she reached the plain in safety. While busied in stealing through the meadows towards the house, the noise of horse approaching startled her, and she felt how much more was to be apprehended from man, in some situations, than from solitude.

Hiding her form in the angle of a fence near the road, she remained quiet for a moment, and watched their passage. A small party of dragoons, whose dress was different from the Virginians, passed at a brisk trot. They were followed by a gentleman, enveloped in a large cloak, whom she at once knew to be Harper. Behind him rode a black in livery, and two youths in uniform brought up the rear. Instead of taking the road that led by the encampment, they turned short to the left* and entered the hills.

Wondering who this unknown but powerful friend of her brother could be, Frances glided across the fields, and using due precautions in approaching the dwelling, regained her residence undiscovered and in safety.

CHAPTER XXXI

Hence, bashful cunning!
And prompt me plain and holy innocence;
I am your wife, if you will marry me.
—Tempest

On joining Miss Peyton, Frances learned that Dunwoodie was not yet returned; although, with a view to relieve Henry from the importunities of the supposed fanatic, he had desired a very respectably divine of their own church to ride up from the river and offer his services. This gentleman was already arrived, and had been passing the half hour he had been there, in a sensible and well-bred conversation with the spinster, that in no degree touched upon their domestic affairs.

To the eager inquiries of Miss Peyton, relative to her success in her romantic excursion, Frances could say no more than that she was bound to be silent, and to recommend the same precaution to the good maiden also. There was a smile playing around the beautiful mouth of Frances, while she uttered this injunction, which satisfied her aunt that all was as it should be. She was urging her niece to take some refreshment after her fatiguing expedition, when the noise of a horseman riding to the door, announced the return of-the major. He had been found by the courier who was dispatched by Mason,, impatiently waiting the return of Harper to the ferry, and immediately flew to the place where his friend had been confined, tormented by a thousand conflicting fears. The heart of Frances bounded as she listened to his approaching footsteps. It wanted yet an hour to the termination of the shortest period that the peddler had fixed as the time necessary to effect his escape. Even Harper, powerful and well-disposed as he acknowledged himself to be, had laid great stress upon the importance of detaining the Virginians during that hour. She, however, had not time to rally her thoughts, before Dunwoodie entered one door, as Miss Peyton, with the readiness of female instinct, retired through another.

The countenance of Peyton was flushed, and an air of vexation and disappointment pervaded his manner.

" 'Twas imprudent, Frances; nay, it was unkind," he cried,

throwing himself in a chair, "to fly at the very moment that I had assured him of safety! I can almost persuade myself that you delight in creating points of difference in our feelings and duties."

"In our duties there may very possibly be a difference," returned his mistress, approaching, and leaning her slender form against the wall; "but not in our feelings, Peyton. You must certainly rejoice in the escape of Henry!"

"There was no danger impending. He had the promise of Harper; and it is a word never to be doubted. 0 Frances! Frances! had you known the man, you would never have distrusted his assurance; nor would you have again reduced me to this distressing alternative."

"What alternative?" asked Frances, pitying his emotions deeply, but eagerly seizing upon every circumstance to prolong the interview.

"What alternative! Am I not compelled to spend this night in the saddle to recapture your brother, when I had thought to lay my head on its pillow, with the happy consciousness of having contributed to his release? You make me seem your enemy; I, who would cheerfully shed the last drop of blood in your service. I repeat, Frances, it was rash; it was unkind; it was a sad, sad mistake."

She bent towards him and timidly took one of his hands, while with the other she gently removed the curls from his burning brow.

"Why go at all, dear Peyton?" she asked. "You have done much for your country, and she cannot exact such a sacrifice as this at your hand."

"Frances! Miss Wharton!" exclaimed the youth, springing on his feet, and pacing the floor with a cheek that burned through its brown covering, and an eye that sparkled with wounded integrity. "It is not my country, but my honor, that requires the sacrifice. Has he not fled from a guard of my own corps? But for this, I might have been spared the blow! But if the eyes of the Virginians are blinded to deception and artifice, their horses are swift of foot, and their sabers keen. We shall see, before to-morrow's sun, who will presume to hint that the beauty of the sister furnished a mask to conceal the brother! Yes, yes, I should like, even now," he continued, laughing bitterly, "to hear the villain who would dare to surmise that such treachery existed!"

"Peyton, dear Peyton," said Frances, recoiling from his angry eye, "you curdle my blood—would you kill my brother?"

"Would I not die for him!" exclaimed Dunwoodie, as he turned to her more mildly. "You know I would; but I am distracted with the cruel surmise to which this step of Henry's subjects me. What will Washington think of me, should he learn that I ever became your husband?"

"If that alone impels you to act so harshly towards my brother," returned Frances, with a slight tremor in her voice, "let it never happen for him to learn."

"And this is consolation, Frances!"

"Nay, dear Dunwoodie, I meant nothing harsh or unkind; but are you not making us both of more consequence with Washington than the truth will justify?"

"I trust that my name is not entirely unknown to the commander in chief," said the major, a little proudly; "nor are you as obscure as your modesty would make you. I believe you, Frances, when you say that you pity me, and it must be my task to continue worthy of such feelings. But I waste the precious moments; we must go through the hills to-night, that we may be refreshed in time for the duty of to-morrow. Mason is already waiting my orders to mount. Frances, I leave you with a heavy heart; pity me, but feel no concern for your brother; he must again become a prisoner, but every hair of his head is sacred."

"Stop! Dunwoodie, I conjure you," cried Frances, gasping for breath, as she noticed that the hand of the clock still wanted many minutes to the desired hour. "Before you go on your errand of fastidious duty, read this note that Henry has left for you, and which, doubtless, he thought he was writing to the friend of his youth."

"Frances, I excuse your feelings; but the time will come when you will do me justice."

"That time is now," she answered, extending her hand, unable any longer to feign a displeasure that she did not feel.

"Where got you this note?" exclaimed the youth, glancing his eyes over its contents. "Poor Henry, you are indeed my friend! If anyone wishes me happiness, it is you!"

"He does, he does," cried Frances, eagerly; "he wishes you every happiness; believe what he tells you; every word is true."

"I do believe him, lovely girl, and he refers me to you for its confirmation. Would that I could trust equally to your affections!"

"You may, Peyton," said Frances, looking up with innocent confidence towards her lover.

"Then read for yourself, and verify your words," interrupted Dunwoodie, holding the note towards her.

Frances received it in astonishment, and read the following:

"Life is too precious to be trusted to uncertainties. I leave you, Peyton, unknown to all but Cæsar, and I recommend him to your mercy. But there is a care that weighs me to the earth. Look at my aged and infirm parent. He will be reproached for the supposed crime of his son. Look at those helpless sisters that I leave behind me without a protector. Prove to me that you love us all. Let the clergyman whom you will bring with you, unite you this night to Frances, and become at once, brother, son, and husband."

The paper fell from the hands of Frances, and she endeavored to raise her eyes to the face of Dunwoodie, but they sank abashed to the floor.

"Am I worthy of this confidence? Will you send me out this night, to meet my own brother? or will it be the officer of Congress in quest of the officer of Britain?"

"And would you do less of your duty because I am your wife, Major Dunwoodie? In what degree would it better the condition of Henry?"

"Henry, I repeat, is safe. The word of Harper is his guarantee; but I will show the world a bridegroom," continued the youth, perhaps deceiving himself a little, "who is equal to the duty of arresting the brother of his bride."

"And will the world comprehend this refinement?" said Frances, with a musing air, that lighted a thousand hopes in the bosom of her lover. In fact, the temptation was mighty. Indeed, there seemed no other way to detain Dunwoodie until the fatal hour had elapsed. The words of Harper himself, who had so lately told her that openly he could do but little for Henry, and that everything depended upon gaining time, were deeply engraved upon her memory. Perhaps there was also a fleeting thought of the possibility of an eternal separation from her lover, should he proceed and bring back her brother to punishment. It is difficult at all times to analyze human emotions, and they pass through the sensitive heart of a woman with the rapidity and nearly with the vividness of lightning.

"Why do you hesitate, dear Frances?" cried Dunwoodie, who was studying her varying countenance. "A few minutes might give me a husband's claim to protect you." .

Frances grew giddy. She turned an anxious eye to the clock, and the hand seemed to linger over its face, as if with intent to torture her.

"Speak, Frances," murmured Dunwoodie; "may I summon my good kinswoman? Determine, for time presses."

She endeavored to reply, but could only whisper something that was inaudible, but which her lover, with the privilege of immemorial custom, construed into assent. He turned and flew to the door, when his mistress recovered her voice:—

"Stop, Peyton! I cannot enter into such a solemn engagement with a fraud upon my conscience. I have seen Henry since his escape, and time is all-important to him. Here is my hand; if, with this knowledge of the consequences of delay, you will not reject, it is freely yours."

"Reject it!" cried the delighted youth. "I take it as the richest gift of heaven. There is time enough for us all. Two hours will take me through the hills; and by noon to-morrow I will return with Washington's pardon for your brother, and Henry will help to enliven our nuptials."

"Then meet me here, in ten minutes," said Frances, greatly relieved by unburdening her mind, and filled with the hope of securing Henry's safety, "and I will return and take those vows which will bind me to you forever."

Dunwoodie paused only to press her once to his bosom, and flew to communicate his wishes to the priest.

Miss Peyton received the avowal of her niece with infinite astonishment, and a little displeasure. It was violating all the order and decorum of a wedding to get it up so hastily, and with so little ceremony. But Frances, with modest firmness, declared that her resolution was taken; she had long possessed the consent of her friends, and their nuptials, for months, had only waited her pleasure. She had now promised Dunwoodie; and it was her wish to comply; more she dare not say without committing herself, by entering into explanations that might endanger Birch, or Harper, or both. Unused to contention, and really much attached to her kinsman, the feeble objections of Miss Peyton gave way to the firmness of her niece. Mr. Wharton was too completely a convert to the doctrine of passive obedience and nonresistance, to withstand any solicitation from an officer of Dunwoodie's influence in the rebel armies; and the maid returned to the apartment, accompanied by her father and aunt, at the expiration of the time that she had fixed. Dunwoodie and the clergyman were already there. Frances, silently, and without the affectation of reserve, placed in his hand, the wedding ring of her own mother, and after some little time spent in arranging Mr. Wharton and herself, Miss Peyton suffered the ceremony to proceed.

The clock stood directly before the eyes of Frances, and she turned many an anxious glance at the dial; but the solemn language of the priest soon caught her attention, and her mind became intent upon the vows she was uttering. The ceremony was quickly over, and as the clergyman closed the words of benediction, the clock told the hour of nine. This was the time that Harper had deemed so important, and Frances felt as if a mighty load was at once removed from her heart.

Dunwoodie folded her in his arms, saluted the mild aunt again and again, and shook Mr. Wharton and the divine repeatedly by the hands. In the midst of the felicitation, a tap was heard at the door. It was opened, and Mason appeared.

"We are in the saddle," said the lieutenant, "and, with your permission, I will lead on; as you are so well mounted, you can overtake us at your leisure."

"Yes, yes, my good fellow; march," cried Dunwoodie, gladly seizing an excuse to linger. "I will reach you at the first halt."

The subaltern retired to execute these orders; he was followed by Mr. Wharton and the divine.

"Now, Peyton," said Frances, "it is indeed a brother that you seek; I am sure I need not caution you in his behalf, should you unfortunately find him."

"Say fortunately," cried the youth, "for I am determined he shall yet dance at my wedding. Would that I could win him to our cause. It is the cause of his country; and I could fight with more pleasure, Frances, with your brother by my side."

"Oh! mention it not! You awaken terrible reflections."

"I will not mention it," returned her husband; "but I must

now leave you. But the sooner I go, Frances, the sooner I shall return."

The noise of a horseman was heard approaching the house, and Dunwoodie was yet taking leave of his bride and her aunt, when an officer was shown into the room by his own man.

The gentleman wore the dress of an aid-de-camp, and the major at once knew him to be one of the military family of Washington.

"Major Dunwoodie," he said, after bowing to the ladies, "the commander in chief has directed me to give you these orders."

He executed his mission, and, pleading duty, took his leave immediately.

"Here, indeed!" cried the major, "is an unexpected turn in the whole affair; but I understand it: Harper has got my letter, and already we feel his influence."

"Have you news affecting Henry?" cried Frances, springing to his side.

"Listen, and you shall judge."

"Sir,—Upon receipt of this, you will concentrate your squadron, so as to be in front of a covering party which the enemy has sent up in front of his foragers, by ten o'clock tomorrow, on the heights of Croton, where you will find a body of foot to support you. The escape of the English spy has been reported to me, but his arrest is unimportant, compared with the duty I now assign you. You will, therefore, recall your men, if any are in pursuit, and endeavor to defeat the enemy forthwith.

"Your obedient servant,

"GEO. WASHINGTON."

"Thank God!" cried Dunwoodie, "my hands are washed of Henry's recapture; I can now move to my duty with honor."

"And with prudence, too, dear Peyton," said Frances, with a face as pale as death. "Remember, Dunwoodie, you leave behind you new claims on your life."

The youth dwelt on her lovely but pallid features with rapture; and, as he folded her to his heart, exclaimed,—

"For your sake, I will, lovely innocent!" Frances sobbed a moment on his bosom, and he tore himself from her presence.

Miss Peyton retired with her niece, to whom she conceived it necessary, before they separated for the night, to give an admonitory lecture on the subject of matrimonial duty. Her instruction was modestly received, if not properly digested. We regret that history has not handed down to us this precious dissertation; but the result of all our investigation has been to learn that it partook largely of those peculiarities which are said to tincture the rules prescribed to govern bachelors' children. We shall now leave the ladies of the Wharton family, and return to Captain Wharton and Harvey Birch.

CHAPTER XXXII

Allow him not a parting word;
Short be the shrift, and sure the cord!
—Rokeby

The peddler and his companion soon reached the valley, and after pausing to listen, and hearing no sounds which announced that pursuers were abroad, they entered the highway. Acquainted with every step that led through the mountains, and possessed of sinews inured to toil, Birch led the way, with the lengthened strides that were peculiar to the man and his profession; his pack alone was wanting to finish the appearance of his ordinary business air. At times, when they approached one of those little posts held by the American troops, with which the Highlands abounded, he would take a circuit to avoid the sentinels, and plunge fearlessly into a thicket, or ascend a rugged hill, that to the eye seemed impassable. But the peddler was familiar with every turn in their difficult route, knew where the ravines might be penetrated, or where the streams were fordable. In one or two instances. Henry thought that their further progress was absolutely at an end, but the ingenuity, or knowledge, of his guide, conquered every difficulty. After walking at a great rate for three hours, they suddenly diverged from the road, which inclined to the east, and held their course directly across the hills, in a due south direction. This movement was made, the peddler informed his companion, in order to avoid the parties who constantly patrolled in the southern entrance of the Highlands, as well as to shorten the distance, by traveling in a straight line. After reaching the summit of a hill, Harvey seated himself by the side of a little run, and opening a wallet, that he had slung where his pack was commonly suspended, he invited his comrade to partake of the coarse fare it contained. Henry had kept pace with the peddler, more by the excitement natural to his situation, than by the equality of his physical powers. The idea of a halt was unpleasant, so long as there existed a possibility of. the horse getting below him in time to intercept their retreat through the neutral ground. He therefore stated his apprehensions to his companion, and urged a wish to proceed.

"Follow my example, Captain Wharton," said the peddler, commencing his frugal meal. "If the horse have started, it will be more than man can do to head them; and if they have not, work is cut out for them, that will drive all thoughts of you and me from their brains."

"You said yourself, that two hours' detention was all-important to us, if we loiter here, of what use will be the advantage that we may have already obtained?"

"The time is past, and Major Dunwoodie thinks little of following two men, when hundreds are waiting for him on the banks of the river."

"Listen!" interrupted Henry, "there are horse at this moment passing the foot of the hill. I hear them even laughing and talking to each other. Hist! there is the voice of Dunwoodie himself; he calls to his comrade in a manner that shows but little uneasiness. One would think that the situation of his friend would lower his spirits; surely Frances could not have given him the letter."

On hearing the first exclamation of the captain, Birch arose from his seat, and approached cautiously to the brow of the hill, taking care to keep his body in the shadow of the rocks, so as to be unseen at any distance, and earnestly reconnoitered the group of passing horsemen. He continued listening, until their quick footsteps were no longer audible, and then quietly returned to his seat, and with incomparable coolness resumed his meal.

"You have a long walk, and a tiresome one, before you, Captain Wharton; you had better do as I do—you were eager for food at the hut above Fishkill, but traveling seems to have worn down your appetite."

"I thought myself safe, then, but the information of my sister fills me with uneasiness, and I cannot eat."

"You have less reason to be troubled now than at any time since the night before you were taken, when you refused my advice, and an offer to see you in safety," returned the peddler. "Major Dunwoodie is not a man to laugh and be gay when his friend is in difficulty. Come, then, and eat, for no horse will be in our way, if we can hold our legs for four hours longer, and the sun keeps behind the hills as long as common."

There was a composure in the peddler's manner that encouraged his companion; and having once determined to submit to Harvey's government, he suffered himself to be persuaded into a tolerable supper, if quantity be considered without any reference to the quality. After completing their repast, the peddler resumed his journey.

Henry followed in blind submission to his will. For two hours more they struggled with the difficult and dangerous passes of the Highlands, without road, or any other guide than the moon, which was traveling the heavens, now wading through flying clouds, and now shining brightly. At length they arrived at a point where the mountains sank into rough and unequal hillocks, and passed at once from the barren sterility of the precipices, to the imperfect culture of the neutral ground.

The peddler now became more guarded in the manner in which they proceeded, and took divers precautions to prevent meeting any moving parts of the Americans. With the stationary posts he was too familiar to render it probable he might fall upon any of them unawares. He wound among the hills and vales, now keeping the highways and now avoiding them, with a precision that seemed instinctive. There was nothing elastic in his tread, but he glided over the ground with enormous strides, and a body bent forward, without appearing to use exertion, or know weariness.

The moon had set, and a faint streak of light was beginning to show itself in the east. Captain Wharton ventured to express a sense of fatigue, and to inquire if they were not yet arrived at a part of the country where it might be safe to apply at some of the farmhouses for admission.

"See here," said the peddler, pointing to a hill, at a short distance in the rear, "do you not see a man walking on the point of that rock? Turn, so as to bring the daylight in the range—now, see, he moves, and seems to be looking earnestly at something to the eastward. That ?s a royal sentinel; two hundred of the rig'lar troops lay on that hill, no doubt sleeping on their arms."

"Then," cried Henry, "let us join them, and our danger is ended."

"Softly, softly, Captain Wharton," said the peddler, dryly, "you've once been in the midst of three hundred of them, but there was a man who could take you out; see you not yon dark body, on the side of the opposite hill, just above the cornstalks? There are the—the rebels (since that is the word for us loyal subjects), waiting only for day, to see who will be master of the ground."

"Nay, then," exclaimed the fiery youth, "I will join the troops of my prince, and share their fortune, be it good or be it bad."

"You forget that you fight with a halter round your neck; no, no—I have promised one whom I must not disappoint, to carry you safe in; and unless you forget what I have already done, and what I have risked for you, Captain Wharton, you will turn and follow me to Harlem."

To this appeal the youth felt unwillingly obliged to submit; and they continued their course towards the city. It was not long before they gained the banks of the Hudson. After searching for a short time under the shore, the peddler discovered a skiff, that appeared to be an old acquaintance; and entering it with his companion he landed him on the south side of the Croton. Here Birch declared they were in safety; for the royal troops held the continentals at bay, and the former were out in too great strength for the light parties of the latter to trust themselves below that river, on the immediate banks of the Hudson.

Throughout the whole of this arduous flight, the peddler had manifested a coolness and presence of mind that nothing appeared to disturb. All his faculties seemed to be of more than usual perfection, and the infirmities of nature to have no dominion over him. Henry had followed him like a child in leading strings, and he now reaped his reward, as he felt a bound of pleasure at his heart, on hearing, that he was relieved from apprehension, and permitted to banish every doubt of security.

A steep and laborious ascent brought them from the level of the tidewaters to the high lands that form, in this part of the river, the eastern banks of the Hudson. Retiring a little from the highway, under the shelter of a thicket of cedars, the peddler threw his form on a flat rock, and announced to his companion that the hour for rest and refreshment was at length arrived. The day was now opened, and objects could be seen in the distance, with distinctness. Beneath them lay the Hudson, stretching to the south in a straight line, as far as the eye could reach. To the north, the broken fragments of the Highlands threw upwards their lofty heads, above masses of fog that hung over the water, and by which the course of the river could be traced into the bosom of hills whose conical summits were grouping together, one behind another, in that disorder which might be supposed to have succeeded their gigantic, but fruitless, efforts to stop the progress of the flood. Emerging from these confused piles, the river, as if rejoicing at its release from the struggle, expanded into a wide bay, which was ornamented by a few fertile and low points that jutted humbly into its broad basin. On the opposite, or western shore, the rocks of Jersey were gathered into an array that has obtained for them the name of the "Palisades," elevating themselves for many hundred feet, as if to protect the rich country in their rear from the inroads of the conqueror; but, disdaining such an enemy, the river swept proudly by their feet, and held its undeviating way to the ocean. A ray of the rising sun darted upon the slight cloud that hung over the placid river, and at once the whole scene was in motion, changing and assuming new forms, and exhibiting fresh objects in each successive moment. At the daily rising of this great curtain of nature, at the present time, scores of white sails and sluggish vessels are seen thickening on the water, with that air of life which denotes the neighborhood to the metropolis of a great and flourishing empire; but to Henry and the peddler it displayed only the square yards and lofty masts of a vessel of war, riding a few miles below them. Before the fog had begun to move, the tall spars were seen above it, and from one of them a long pennant was feebly borne abroad in the current of night air, that still quivered along the river; but as the smoke arose, the black hull, the crowded and complicated mass of rigging, and the heavy yards and booms, spreading their arms afar, were successively brought into view.

"There, Captain Wharton," said the peddler, "there is a safe resting place for you; America has no arm that can reach you, if you gain the deck of that ship. She is sent up to cover the foragers, and support the troops; the rig'lar officers are fond of the sound of cannon from their shipping."

Without condescending to reply to the sarcasm conveyed in this speech, or perhaps not noticing it, Henry joyfully acquiesced in the proposal, and it was accordingly arranged between them, that, as soon as they were refreshed, he should endeavor to get on board the vessel.

While busily occupied in the very indispensable operation of breaking their fast, our adventurers were startled with the sound of distant firearms. At first a few scattering shots were fired, which were succeeded by a long and animated roll of musketry, and then quick and heavy volleys followed each other.

"Your prophecy is made good," cried the English officer, springing upon his feet. "Our troops and the rebels are at it! I would give six months' pay to see the charge."

"Umph!" returned his companion, without ceasing his meal, "they do very well to look at from a distance; I can't say but the company of this bacon, cold as it is, is more to my taste, just now, than a hot fire from the continentals."

"The discharges are heavy for so small a force; but the fire seems irregular."

"The scattering guns are from the Connecticut militia," said Harvey, raising his head to listen; "they rattle it off finely, and are no fools at a mark. The volleys are the rig'lars, who, you know, fire by word—as long as they can."

"I like not the warmth of what you call a scattering fire," exclaimed the captain, moving about with uneasiness; "it is more like the roll of a drum than skirmishers' shooting."

"No, no; I said not skrimmagers," returned the other, raising himself upon a knee, and ceasing to eat; "so long as they stand, they are too good for the best troops in the royal army. Each man does his work as if fighting by the job; and then, they think while they fight, and don't send bullets to the clouds, that were meant to kill men on earth."

"You talk and look, sir, as if you wished them success," said Henry, sternly.

"I wish success to the good cause only, Captain Wharton. I thought you knew me too well, to be uncertain which party I favored."

"Oh! you are reputed loyal, Mr. Birch. But the volleys have ceased!"

Both now listened intently for a little while, during which the irregular reports became less brisk, and suddenly heavy and repeated volleys followed.

"They've been at the bayonet," said the peddler; "the rig'lars have tried the bayonet, and the rebels are driven."

"Aye, Mr. Birch, the bayonet is the thing for the British soldier, after all. They delight in the bayonet!"

"Well, to my notion," said the peddler, "there's but little delight to be taken in any such fearful weapon. I dare say the militia are of my mind, for half of them don't carry the ugly things. Lord! Lord! captain, I wish you'd go with me once into the rebel camp, and hear what lies the men will tell about Bunker Hill and Burg'yne; you'd think they loved the bayonet as much as they do their dinners."

There was a chuckle, and an air of affected innocence about his companion, that rather annoyed Henry, and he did not deign to reply.

The firing now became desultory, occasionally intermingled with heavy volleys. Both of the fugitives were standing, listening with anxiety, when a man, armed with a musket, was seen stealing towards them, under the shelter of the cedar bushes, that partially covered the hill. Henry first observed this suspicious-looking stranger, and instantly pointed him out to his companion. Birch started, and certainly made an indication of sudden flight; but recollecting himself, he stood, in .sullen silence, until the stranger was within a few yards of them.

" 'Tis friends," said the fellow, clubbing his gun, but apparently afraid to venture nearer.

"You had better retire," said Birch; "here are rig'lars at hand. We are not near Dunwoodie's horse now, and you will not find me an easy prize to-day."

"Damn Major Dunwoodie and his horse!" cried the leader of the Skinners (for it was he); "God bless King George! and a speedy end to the rebellion, say I. If you would show me the safe way in to the refugees, Mr. Birch, I'll pay you well, and ever after stand your friend, in the bargain."

"The road is as open to you as to me," said Birch, turning from him in ill-concealed disgust. "If you want to find the refugees, you know well where they lay."

"Aye, but I'm a little doubtful of going in upon them by myself; now, you are well known to them all, and it will be no detriment to you just to let me go in with you."

Henry here interfered, and after holding a short dialogue with the fellow, he entered into a compact with him, that, on condition of surrendering his arms, he might join the party. The man complied instantly, and Birch received his gun with eagerness; nor did he lay it upon his shoulder to renew their march, before he had carefully examined the priming, and ascertained, to his satisfaction, that it contained a good, dry, ball cartridge.

As soon as this engagement was completed, they commenced their journey anew. By following the bank of the river, Birch led the way free from observation, until they reached the point opposite to the frigate, when, by making a signal, a boat was induced to approach. Some time was spent, and much precaution used, before the seamen would trust themselves ashore; but Henry having finally succeeded in making the officer who commanded the party credit his assertions, he was able to rejoin his companions in arms in safety. Before taking leave of Birch, the captain handed him his purse, which was tolerably well supplied for the times; the peddler received it, and, watching an opportunity, he conveyed it, unnoticed by the Skinner, to a part of his dress that was ingeniously contrived to hold such treasures.

The boat pulled from the shore, and Birch turned on his heel, drawing his breath, like one relieved, and shot up the hills with the strides for which he was famous. The Skinner followed, and each party pursued the common course, casting frequent and suspicious glances at the other, and both maintaining a most impenetrable silence.

Wagons were moving along the river road, and occasional parties of horse were seen escorting the fruits of the inroad towards the city. As the peddler had views of his own, he rather avoided falling in with any of these patrols, than sought their protection. But, after traveling a few miles on the immediate banks of the river, during which, notwithstanding the repeated efforts of the Skinner to establish something like sociability, he maintained a most determined silence, keeping a firm hold of the gun, and always maintaining a jealous watchfulness of his associate, the peddler suddenly struck into the highway, with an intention of crossing the hills towards Harlem. At the moment he gained the path, a body of horse came over a little eminence, and was upon him before he perceived them. It was too late to retreat, and after taking a view of the materials that composed this party, Birch rejoiced in the rencounter, as a probable means of relieving him from his unwelcome companion. There were some eighteen or twenty men, mounted and equipped as dragoons, though neither their appearance nor manners denoted much discipline. At their head rode a heavy, middle-aged man, whose features expressed as much of animal courage, and as little of reason, as could be desired for such an occupation. He wore the dress of an officer, but there was none of that neatness in his attire, nor grace in his movements, that was usually found about the gentlemen who bore the royal commission. His limbs were firm, and not pliable, and he sat his horse with strength and confidence, but his bridle hand would have been ridiculed by the meanest rider amongst the Virginians. As he expected, this leader instantly hailed the peddler, in a voice by no means more conciliating than his appearance.

"Hey! my gentlemen, which way so fast?" he cried. "Has Washington sent you down as spies?"

"I am an innocent peddler," returned Harvey meekly, "and am going below, to lay in a fresh stock of goods."

"And how do you expect to get below, my innocent peddler? Do you think we hold the forts at King's Bridge to cover such peddling rascals as you, in your goings in and comings out?"

"I believe I hold a pass that will carry me through," said the peddler, handing him a paper, with an air of indifference.

The officer, for such he was, read it, and cast a look of surprise and curiosity at Harvey, when he had done.

Then turning to one or two of his men, who had officiously stopped the way, he cried,—

"Why do you detain the man? Give way, and let him pass in peace. But whom have we here? Your name is not mentioned in the pass!"

"No, sir," said the Skinner, lifting his hat with humility. "I have been a poor, deluded man, who has been serving in the rebel army; but, thank God, I've lived to see the error of my ways, and am now come to make reparation, by enlisting under the Lord's anointed."

"Umph! a deserter—a Skinner, I'll swear, wanting to turn Cowboy! In the last brush I had with the scoundrels, I could hardly tell my own men from the enemy. We are not over well supplied with coats, and as for countenances, the rascals change sides so often, that you may as well count their faces for nothing; but trudge on, we will contrive to make use of you, sooner or later."

Ungracious as was this reception, if you could judge of the Skinner's feelings from his manner, it nevertheless delighted him. He moved with alacrity towards the city, and really was so happy to escape the brutal looks and frightful manner of his interrogator, as to lose sight of all other considerations. But the man who performed the functions of orderly in the irregular troop, rode up to the side of his commander, and commenced a close and apparently a confidential discourse with his principal. They spoke in whispers, and cast frequent and searching glances at the Skinner, until the fellow began to think himself an object of more than common attention. His satisfaction at this distinction was somewhat heightened, at observing a smile on the face of the captain, which, although it might be thought grim, certainly denoted satisfaction. This pantomime occupied the time they were passing a hollow, and concluded as they rose another hill. Here the captain and his sergeant both dismounted, and ordered the party to halt. The two partisans each took a pistol from his holster, a movement that excited no suspicion or alarm, as it was a precaution always observed, and beckoned to the peddler and the Skinner to follow. A short walk brought them to a spot where the hill overhung the river, the ground falling nearly perpendicularly to the shore. On the brow of the eminence stood a deserted and dilapidated barn. Many boards of its covering were torn from their places, and its wide doors were lying, the one in front of the building, and the other halfway down the precipice, whither the wind had cast it. Entering this desolate spot, the refugee officer very coolly took from his pocket a short pipe, which, from long use, had acquired not only the hue but the gloss of ebony, a tobacco box, and a small roll of leather, that contained steel, flint, and tinder. With this apparatus, he soon furnished his mouth with a companion that habit had long rendered necessary to reflection. So soon as a large column of smoke arose from this arrangement, the captain significantly held forth a hand towards his assistant. A small cord was produced from the pocket of the sergeant, and handed to the other. The refugee threw out vast puffs of smoke, until nearly all of his head was obscured, and looked around the building with an inquisitive eye. At length he removed the pipe, and inhaling a draft of pure air, returned it to its domicile, and proceeded at once to business. A heavy piece of timber lay across the girths of the barn, but a little way from the southern door, which opened directly upon a full view of the river, as it stretched far away towards the bay of New York. Over this beam the refugee threw one end of the rope, and, regaining it, joined the two parts in his hand. A small and weak barrel, that wanted a head, the staves of which were loose, and at one end standing apart, was left on the floor, probably as useless. The sergeant, in obedience to a look from his officer, placed it beneath the beam. All of these arrangements were made with composure, and they now seemed completed to the officer's perfect satisfaction.

"Come," he said coolly to the Skinner, who, admiring the preparations, had stood a silent spectator of their progress. He obeyed; and it was not until he found his neckcloth removed, and hat thrown aside, that he took the alarm. But he had so often resorted to a similar expedient to extort information, or plunder, that he by no means felt the terror an unpracticed man would have suffered, at these ominous movements. The rope was adjusted to his neck with the same coolness that formed the characteristic of the whole movement, and a fragment of board being laid upon the barrel, he was ordered to mount.

"But it may fall," said the Skinner, for the first time beginning to tremble. "I will tell you anything—even how to surprise our party at the Pond, without all this trouble, and it is commanded by my own brother."

"I want no information," returned his executioner (for such he now seemed really to be), throwing the rope repeatedly over the beam, first drawing it tight so as to annoy the Skinner a little, and then casting the end from him, beyond the reach of anyone.

"This is joking too far," cried the Skinner, in a tone of remonstrance, and raising himself on his toes, with the vain hope of releasing himself from the cord, by slipping his head through the noose. But the caution and experience of the refugee officer had guarded against this escape.

"What have you done with the horse you stole from me, rascal?" muttered the officer of the Cowboys, throwing out columns of smoke while he waited for a reply.

"He broke down in the chase," replied the Skinner quickly; "but I can tell you where one is to be found that is worth him and his sire."

"Liar! I will help myself when I am in need; you had better call upon God for aid, as your hour is short." On concluding this consoling advice, he struck the barrel a violent blow with his heavy foot, and the slender staves flew in every direction, leaving the Skinner whirling in the air. As his hands were unconfined, he threw them upwards, and held himself suspended by main strength.

"Come, captain," he said, coaxingly, a little huskiness creeping into his voice, and his knees beginning to shake with tremor, "and the joke; 'tis enough to make a laugh, and my arms begin to tire—I can't hold on much longer."

"Harkee, Mr. Peddler," said the refugee, in a voice that would not be denied, "I want not your company. Through that door lies your road—march! offer to touch that dog, and you'll swing in his place, though twenty Sir Henrys wanted your services." So saying, he retired to the road with the sergeant, as the peddler precipitately retreated down the bank.

Birch went no farther than a bush that opportunely offered itself as a screen to his person, while he yielded to an unconquerable desire to witness the termination of this extraordinary scene.

Left alone, the Skinner began to throw fearful glances around, to espy the hiding places of his tormentors. For the first time the horrid idea seemed to shoot through his brain that something serious was intended by the Cowboy. He called entreatingly to be released, and made rapid and incoherent promises of important information, mingled with affected pleasantry at their conceit, which he would hardly admit to himself could mean anything so dreadful as it seemed. But as he heard the tread of the horses moving on their course, and in vain looked around for human aid, violent trembling seized his limbs, and his eyes began to start from his head with terror. He made a desperate effort to reach the beam; but, too much exhausted with his previous exertions, he caught the rope in his teeth, in a vain effort to sever the cord, and fell to the whole length of his arms. Here his cries were turned into shrieks.

"Help! cut the rope! captain!—Birch! good peddler! Down with the Congress!—sergeant! for God's sake, help! Hurrah for the king!—0 God! 0 God!—mercy, mercy—mercy!"

As his voice became suppressed, one of his hands endeavored to make its way between the rope and his neck, and partially succeeded; but the other fell quivering by his side. A convulsive shuddering passed over his whole frame, and he hung a hideous corpse.

Birch continued gazing on this scene with a kind of infatuation. At its close he placed his hands to his ears, and rushed towards the highway. Still the cries for mercy rang through his brain, and it was many weeks before his memory ceased to dwell on the horrid event. The Cowboys rode steadily on their route, as if nothing had occurred; and the body was left swinging in the wind, until chance directed the wandering footsteps of some lonely straggler to the place.

CHAPTER XXXIII

Green be the turf above thee,
Friend of my better days;
None knew thee but to love thee,
None named thee but to praise.
—Halleck.

While the scenes and events that we have recorded were occurring, Captain Lawton led his small party, by slow and wary marches, from the Four Corners to the front of a body of the enemy; where he so successfully maneuvered, for a short time, as completely to elude all their efforts to entrap him, and yet so disguised his own force as to excite the constant apprehension of an attack from the Americans. This forbearing policy, on the side of the partisan, was owing to positive orders received from his commander. When Dunwoodie left his detachment, the enemy were known to be slowly advancing, and he directed Lawton to hover around them, until his own return, and the arrival of a body of foot, might enable him to intercept their retreat.

The trooper discharged his duty to the latter but with no little of the impatience that made part of his character when restrained from the attack.

During these movements, Betty Flanagan guided her little card with indefatigable zeal among the rocks of Westchester, now discussing with the sergeant the nature of evil spirits, and now combating with the surgeon sundry points of practice that were hourly arising between them. But the moment arrived that was to decide the temporary mastery of the field. A detachment of the eastern militia moved out from their fastnesses, and approached the enemy.

The junction between Lawton and his auxiliaries was made at midnight, and an immediate consultation was held between him and the leader of the foot soldiers. After listening to the statements of the partisan, who rather despised the prowess of his enemy, the commandant of the party determined to attack the British, the moment daylight enabled him to reconnoiter their position, without waiting for the aid of Dunwoodie and his horse. So soon as this decision was made, Lawton retired from the building where the consultation was held, and rejoined his own small command.

The few troopers who were with the captain had fastened their horses in a spot adjacent to a haystack, and laid their own frames under its shelter, to catch a few hours' sleep. But Dr. Sitgreaves, Sergeant Hollister, and Betty Flanagan were congregated at a short distance by themselves, having spread a few blankets upon. the dry surface of a rock. Lawton threw his huge frame by the side of the surgeon, and folding his cloak about him, leaned his head upon one hand, and appeared deeply engaged in contemplating the moon as it waded through the heavens. The sergeant was sitting upright, in respectful deference to the surgeon, and the washerwoman was now raising her head, in order to vindicate some of her favorite maxims, and now composing it to sleep.

"So, sergeant," continued Sitgreaves, following up a previous position, "if you cut upwards, the blow, by losing the additional momentum of your weight, will be less destructive, and at the same time effect the true purpose of war, that of disabling your enemy."

"Pooh! Pooh! sergeant dear," said the washerwoman, raising her head from the blanket, "where's the harm of taking a life, jist in the way of battle? Is it the rig'lars who'll show favor, and they fighting? Ask Captain Jack there, if the country could get free, and the boys no strike their might. I wouldn't have them disparage the whisky so much."

"It is not to be expected that an ignorant female like yourself, Mrs. Flanagan," returned the surgeon, with a calmness that only rendered his contempt more stinging to Betty, "can comprehend the distinctions of surgical science; neither are you accomplished in the sword exercise; so that dissertations upon the judicious use of that weapon could avail you nothing either in theory or in practice."

"It's but little I care, anyway, for such botherment; but fighting is no play, and a body shouldn't be partic'lar how they strike, or who they hit, so it's the inimy."

"Are we likely to have a warm day. Captain Lawton?"

'Tis more than probable," replied the trooper; "these militia seldom fail of making a bloody field, either by their cowardice or their ignorance, and the real soldier is made to suffer for their bad conduct."

"Are you ill, John?" said the surgeon, passing his hand along the arm of the captain, until it instinctively settled on his pulse; but the steady, even beat announced neither bodily nor mental malady.

"Sick at heart, Archibald, at the folly of our rulers, in believing that battles are to be fought and victories won, by fellows who handle a musket as they would a flail; lads who wink when they pull a trigger, and form a line like a hoop pole. The dependence we place on these men spills the best blood of the country."

The surgeon listened with amazement. It was not the matter, but the manner that surprised him. The trooper had uniformly exhibited, on the eve of battle, an animation, and an eagerness to engage, that was directly at variance with the admirable coolness of his manner at other times. But now there was a despondency in the tones of his voice, and a listlessness in his air, that was entirely different. The operator hesitated a moment, to reflect in what manner he could render this change of service in furthering his favorite system, and then continued,—

"It would be wise, John, to advise the colonel to keep at long shot; a spent ball will disable—"

"No!" exclaimed the trooper, impatiently, "let the rascals singe their whiskers at the muzzles of the British muskets, if they can be driven there. But, enough of them. Archibald, do you deem that moon to be a world like this, containing creatures like ourselves?"

"Nothing more probable, dear John; we know its size, and, reasoning from analogy, may easily conjecture its use. Whether or not its inhabitants have attained to that perfection in the sciences which we have acquired, must depend greatly on the state of its society, and in some measure upon its physical influences."

"I care nothing about their learning, Archibald; but 'tis a wonderful power that can create such worlds, and control them in their wanderings. I know not why, but there is a feeling of melancholy excited within me as I gaze on that body of light, shaded as it is by your fancied sea and land. It seems to be the resting place of departed spirits!"

"Take a drop, darling," said Betty, raising her head once more, and proffering her own bottle. " 'Tis the night damp that chills the blood—and then the talk with the cursed militia is no good for a fiery temper. Take a drop, darling, and ye'll sleep till the morning. I fed Roanoke myself, for I thought ye might need hard riding the morrow."

" ' Tis a glorious heaven to look upon," continued the trooper, in the same tone, disregarding the offer of Betty, "and 'tis a thousand pities that such worms as men should let their vile passions deface such goodly work."

"You speak the truth, dear John; there is room for all to live and enjoy themselves in peace, if each could be satisfied with his own. Still, war has its advantages; it particularly promotes the knowledge of surgery; and—"

"There is a star," continued Lawton, still bent on his own ideas, "struggling to glitter through a few driving clouds; perhaps that too is a world, and contains its creatures endowed with reason like ourselves. Think you that they know of war and bloodshed?"

"If I might be so bold," said Sergeant Hollister, mechanically raising his hand to his cap, " 'tis mentioned in the good book, that the Lord made the sun to stand still while Joshua was charging the enemy, in order, sir, as I suppose, that they might have daylight to turn their flank, or perhaps make a feint in the rear, or some such maneuver. Now, if the Lord would lend them a hand, fighting cannot be sinful. I have often been nonplused, though, to find that they used them chariots instead of heavy dragoons, who are, in all comparison, better to break a line of infantry, and who, for the matter of that, could turn such wheel carriages, and getting into the rear, play the very devil with them, horse and all."

"It is because you do not understand the construction of those ancient vehicles, Sergeant Hollister, that you judge of them so erroneously," said the surgeon. "They were armed with sharp weapons that protruded from their wheels, and which broke up the columns of foot, like dismembered particles of matter. I doubt not, if similar instruments were affixed to the cart of Mrs. Flanagan, that great confusion might be carried info the ranks of the enemy thereby, this very day."

"It's but little that the mare would go, and the rig'lars firing at her," grumbled Betty, from under her blanket. "When we got the plunder, the time we drove them through the Jarseys it was, I had to back the baste up to the dead; for the divil the foot would she move, foment the firing, wid her eyes open. Roanoke and Captain Jack are good enough for the redcoats, letting alone myself and the mare."

A long roll of the drums, from the hill occupied by the British, announced that they were on the alert; and a corresponding signal was immediately heard from the Americans. The bugle of the Virginians struck up its martial tones; and in a few moments both the hills, the one held by the royal troops and the other by their enemies, were alive with armed men. Day had begun to dawn, and preparations were making by both parties, to give and to receive the attack. In numbers the Americans had greatly the advantage; but in discipline and equipment the superiority was entirely with their enemies. The arrangements for the battle were brief, and by the time the sun rose the militia moved forward.

The ground did not admit of the movements of horse; and the only duty that could be assigned to the dragoons was to watch the moment of victory, and endeavor to improve the success to the utmost. Lawton soon got his warriors into the saddle; and leaving them to the charge of Hollister, he rode himself along the line of foot, who, in varied dresses, and imperfectly armed, were formed in a shape that in some degree resembled a martial array. A scornful smile lowered about the lip of the trooper as he guided Roanoke with a skillful hand through the windings of their ranks; and when the word was given to march, he turned the flank of the regiment, and followed close in the rear. The Americans had to descend into a little hollow, and rise a hill on its opposite side, to approach the enemy.

The descent was made with tolerable steadiness, until near the foot of the hill, when the royal troops advanced in a beautiful line, with their flanks protected by the formation of the ground. The appearance of the British drew a fire from the militia, which was given with good effect, and for a moment staggered the regulars. But they were rallied by their officers, and threw in volley after volley with great steadiness. For a short time the fire was warm and destructive, until the English advanced with the bayonet. This assault the militia had not sufficient discipline to withstand. Their line wavered, then paused, and finally broke into companies and fragments of companies, keeping up at the same time a scattering and desultory fire.

Lawton witnessed these operations in silence, nor did he

open his mouth until the field was covered with parties of the flying Americans. Then, indeed, he seemcd strung with the disgrace thus heaped upon the arms of his country.

Spurring Roanoke along the side of the hill, he called to the fugitives in all the strength of his powerful voice. He pointed to the enemy, and assured his countrymen that they had mistaken the way. There was such a mixture of indifference and irony in his exhortations that a few paused in surprise—more joined them, until, roused by the example of the trooper, and stimulated by their own spirit, they demanded to be led against their foe once more.

"Come on, then, my brave friends!" shouted the trooper, turning his horse's head toward the British line, one flank of which was very near him; "come on, and hold your fire until it will scorch their eyebrows."

The men sprang forward, and followed his example, neither giving nor receiving a fire until they had come within a very short distance of the enemy. An English sergeant, who had been concealed by a rock, enraged with the audacity of the officer who thus dared their arms, stepped from behind his cover, and leveled his musket.

"Fire and you die!" cried Lawton, spurring his charger, which leaped forward at the instant. The action and the tone of his voice shook the nerve of the Englishman, who drew his trigger with an uncertain aim. Roanoke sprang with all his feet from the earth, and, plunging, fell headlong and lifeless at the feet of his destroyer. Lawton kept his feet, standing face to face with his enemy. The latter presented his bayonet, and made a desperate thrust at the trooper's heart. The steel of their weapons emitted sparks of fire, and the bayonet flew fifty feet in the air. At the next moment its owner lay a quivering corpse.

"Come on!" shouted the trooper, as a body of English appeared on the rock, and threw in a close fire. "Come on!" he repeated, and brandished his saber fiercely. Then his gigantic form fell backward, like a majestic pine yielding to the axe; but still, as he slowly fell, he continued to wield his saber, and once more the deep tones of his voice were heard uttering, "Come on!"

The advancing Americans paused aghast, and, turning, they abandoned the field to the royal troops.

It was neither the intention nor the policy of the English

commander to pursue his success, for he well knew that strong parties of the Americans would soon arrive; accordingly he only tarried to collect his wounded, and forming in a square, he commenced his retreat towards the shipping. Within twenty minutes of the fall of Lawton, the ground was deserted by both English and Americans. When the inhabitants of the country were called upon to enter the field, they were necessarily attended by such surgical advisers as were furnished by the low state of the profession in the interior at that day. Dr. Sitgreaves entertained quite as profound a contempt for the medical attendants of the militia as the captain did of the troops themselves. He wandered, therefore, around the field, casting many a glance of disapprobation at the slight operations that came under his eye; but when, among the flying troops, he found that his comrade and friend was nowhere to be seen, he hastened back to the spot at which Hollister was posted, to inquire if the trooper had returned. Of course, the answer was in the negative. Filled with a thousand uneasy conjectures, the surgeon, without regarding, or indeed without at all reflecting upon any dangers that might lie in his way, strode over the ground at an enormous rate, to the point where he knew the final struggle had been. Once before, the surgeon had rescued his friend from death in a similar situation; and he felt a secret joy in his own conscious skill, as he perceived Betty Flanagan seated on the ground, holding in her lap the head of a man whose size and dress he knew could belong only to the trooper. As he approached the spot, the surgeon became alarmed at the aspect of the washerwoman. Her little black bonnet was thrown aside, and her hair, which was already streaked with gray, hung around her face in disorder.

"John! dear John!" said the doctor, tenderly, as he bent and laid his hand upon the senseless wrist of the trooper, from which it recoiled with an intuitive knowledge of his fate. "John! where are you hurt?—can I help you?"

"Ye talk to the senseless clay," said Betty, rocking her body, and unconsciously playing with the raven ringlets of the trooper's hair, "it's no more will he hear, and it's but little will he mind yeer probes and yeer med'cines. Och hone, och hone!—and where will be the liberty now? or who will there be to fight the battle, or gain the day?"

"John!" repeated the surgeon, still unwilling to believe the evidence of his unerring senses. "Dear John, speak to me; say that you will, that you do but speak. Oh, God! he is dead; would that I had died with him!"

"There is but little use in living and fighting now," said Betty. "Both him and the baste! see, there is the poor cratur, and here is the master! I fed the horse with my own hands, the day; and the last male that he ate was of my own cooking. Och hone! och hone!—that Captain Jack should live to be killed by the rig'lars!"

"John! my dear John!" said the surgeon, with convulsive sobs, "thy hour has come, and many a more prudent man survives thee; but none better, nor braver. Oh John, thou wert to me a kind friend, and very dear; it is unphilosophical to grieve; but for thee I must weep, in bitterness of heart."

The doctor buried his face in his hands, and for several minutes sat yielding to an ungovernable burst of sorrow; while the washerwoman gave vent to her grief in words, moving her body in a kind of writhing, and playing with different parts of her favorite's dress with her fingers.

"And who'll there be to encourage the boys now?" she said. "0 Captain Jack! ye was the sowl of the troop, and it was but little we knowed of the danger, and ye fighting. Och! he was no maly-mouthed, that quarreled wid widowed a woman for the matter of a burn in the mate, or the want of a breakfast. Taste a drop, darling, and it may be, 'twill revive ye. Och! and he'll niver taste ag'in; here's the doctor, honey, him ye used to blarney wid, waping as if the poor sowl would die for ye. Och! he's gone, he's gone; and the liberty is gone with him."

A thundering sound of horses' feet came rolling along the road which led near the place where Lawton lay, and directly the whole body of Virginians appeared, with Dunwoodie at their head. The news of the captain's fate had reached him, for the instant that he saw the body he halted the squadron, and, dismounting, approached the spot. The countenance of Lawton was not in the least distorted, but the angry frown which had lowered over his brow during the battle was fixed even in death. His frame was composed, and stretched as in sleep. Dunwoodie took hold of his hand, and gazed a moment in silence; his own dark eye kindled, and the paleness which had overspread his features was succeeded by a spot of deep red in either cheek.

"With his own sword will I avenge him!" he cried, endeavoring to take the weapon from the hand of Lawton; but the grasp resisted his utmost strength. "It shall be buried with him. Sitgreaves, take care of our friend, while I revenge his death."

The major hastened back to his charger, and led the way in pursuit of the enemy.

While Dunwoodie had been thus engaged, the body of Lawton lay in open view of the whole squadron. He was a universal favorite, and the sight inflamed the men to the utmost: neither officer or soldiers possessed that coolness which is necessary to insure success in military operations; they spurred after their enemies, burning for vengeance.

The English were formed in a hollow square, which contained their wounded, who were far from numerous, and were marching steadily across a very uneven country as the dragoons approached. The horse charged in column, and were led by Dunwoodie, who, burning with revenge, thought to ride through their ranks, and scatter them at a blow. But the enemy knew their own strength too well, and, standing firm, they received the charge on the points of their bayonets. The horses of the Virginians recoiled, and the rear rank of the foot throwing in a close fire, the major, with a few men, fell. The English continued their retreat the moment they were extricated from their assailants; and Dunwoodie, who was severely, but not dangerously wounded, recalled his men from further attempts, which must be fruitless.

A sad duty remained to be fulfilled. The dragoons retired slowly through the hills, conveying their wounded commander, and the body of Lawton. The latter they interred under the ramparts of one of the Highland forts, and the former they consigned to the tender care of his afflicted bride.

Many weeks were gone before the major was restored to sufficient strength to be removed. During those weeks, how often did he bless the moment that gave him a right to the services of his beautiful nurse! She hung around his couch with fond attention, administered with her own hands every prescription of the indefatigable Sitgreaves, and grew each hour in the affections and esteem of her husband. An order from Washington soon sent the troops into winter quarters, and permission was given to Dunwoodie to repair to his own plantation, with the rank of lieutenant colonel, in order to complete the restoration of his health. Captain Singleton made one of the party; and the whole family retired from the active scenes of the war, to the ease and plenty of the major's own estate. Before leaving Fishkill, however, letters were conveyed to them, through an unknown hand, acquainting them with Henry's safety and good health; and also that Colonel Wellmere had left the continent for his native island, lowered in the estimation of every honest man in the royal army.

It was a happy winter for Dunwoodie, and smiles once more began to play around the lovely mouth of Frances.

CHAPTER XXXIV

'Midst furs, and silks, and jewels' sheen,
He stood, in simple Lincoln green,
The center of the glittering ring;
And Snowdon's knight is Scotland's king!
—Lady of the Lake.

The commencement of the following year was passed, on the part of the Americans, in making great preparations, in conjunction with their allies, to bring the war to a close. In the South, Greene and Rawdon made a bloody campaign, that was highly honorable to the troops of the latter, but which, by terminating entirely to the advantage of the former, proved him to be the better general of the two.

New York was the point that was threatened by the allied armies; and Washington, by exciting a constant apprehension for the safety of that city, prevented such re-enforcements from being sent to Cornwallis as would have enabled him to improve his success.

At length, as autumn approached, every indication was given that the final moment had arrived.

The French forces drew near to the royal lines, passing through the neutral ground, and threatened an attack in the direction of King's Bridge, while large bodies of Americans were acting in concert. By hovering around the British posts, and drawing nigh in the Jerseys, they seemed to threaten the royal forces from that quarter also. The preparations partook of the nature of both a siege and a storm. But Sir Henry Clinton, in the possession of intercepted letters from Washington, rested within his lines, and cautiously disregarded the solicitations of Cornwallis for succor.

It was at the close of a storm day in the month of September, that a large assemblage of officers was collected near the door of a building that was situated in the heart of the Americans troops, who held the Jerseys. The age, the dress, and the dignity of deportment of most of these warriors, indicated them to be of high rank; but to one in particular was paid a deference and obedience that announced him to be of the highest. His dress was plain, but it bore the usual military distinctions of command. He was mounted on a noble animal, of a deep bay; and a group of young men, in gayer attire, evidently awaited his pleasure and did his bidding. Many a hat was lifted as its owner addressed this officer; and when he spoke, a profound attention, exceeding the respect of mere professional etiquette, was exhibited on very countenance. At length the general raised his own hat, and bowed gravely to all around him. The salute was returned, and the party dispersed, leaving the officer without a single attendant, except his body servants and one aid-de-camp. Dismounting, he stepped back a few paces, and for a moment viewed the condition of his horse with the eye of one who well understood the animal, and then, casting a brief but expressive glance at his aid, he retired into the building, followed by that gentleman.

On entering an apartment that was apparently fitted for his reception, he took a seat, and continued for a long time in a thoughtful attitude, like one in the habit of communing much with himself. During this silence, the aid-de-camp stood in expectation of his orders. At length the general raised his eyes, and spoke in those low, placid tones that seemed natural to him.

"Has the man whom I wished to see arrived, sir?"

"He waits the pleasure of your excellency."

"I will receive him here, and alone, if you please."

The aid bowed and withdrew. In a few minutes the door again opened, and a figure, gliding into the apartment, stood modestly at a distance from the general, without speaking. His entrance was unheard by the officer, who sat gazing at the fire, still absorbed in his own meditations. Several minutes passed, when he spoke to himself in an undertone,—

"To-morrow we must raise the curtain, and expose our plans. May Heaven prosper them!"

A slight movement made by the stranger caught his ear, and he turned his head, and saw that he was not alone. He pointed silently to the fire, toward which the figure advanced, although the multitude of his garments, which seemed more calculated for disguise than comfort, rendered its warmth unnecessary. A second mild and courteous gesture motioned to a vacant chair, but the stranger refused it with a modest acknowledgment. Another pause followed, and continued for some time. At length the officer arose, and opening a desk that was laid upon the table near which he sat, took from it a small, but apparently heavy bag.

"Harvey Birch," he said, turning to the stranger, "the time has arrived when our connection must cease; henceforth and forever we must be strangers."

The peddler dropped the folds of the greatcoat that concealed his features, and gazed for a moment earnestly at the face of the speaker; then dropping his head upon his bosom, he said, meekly,—

"If it be your excellency's pleasure."

"It is necessary. Since I have filled the station which I now hold, it has become my duty to know many men, who, like yourself, have been my instruments in procuring intelligence. You have I trusted more than all; I early saw in you a regard to truth and principle, that, I am pleased to say, has never deceived me—you alone know my secret agents in the city, and on your fidelity depend, not only their fortunes, but their lives."

He paused, as if to reflect in order that full justice might be done to the peddler, and then continued,—

"I believe you are one of the very few that I have employed who have acted faithfully to our cause; and, while you have passed as a spy of the enemy, have never given intelligence that you were not permitted to divulge. To me, and to me only of all the world, you seem to have acted with a strong attachment to the liberties of America."

During this address, Harvey gradually raised his head from his bosom, until it reached the highest point of elevation; a faint tinge gathered in his cheeks, and, as the officer concluded, it was diffused over his whole countenance in a deep glow, while he stood proudly swelling with his emotions, but with eyes that sought the feet of the speaker.

"It is now my duty to pay you for these services; hitherto you have postponed receiving your reward, and the debt has become a heavy one—I wish not to undervalue your dangers; here are a hundred doubloons; remember the poverty of our country, and attribute to it the smallness of your pay."

The peddler raised his eyes to the countenance of the speaker; but, as the other held forth the money, he moved back, as if refusing the bag.

"It is not much for your services and risks, I acknowledge," continued the general, "but it is all that I have to offer; hereafter, it may be in my power to increase it."

"Does your excellency think that I have exposed my life, and blasted my character, for money?"

"If not for money, what then?"

"What has brought your excellency into the field? For what do you daily and hourly expose your precious life to battle and the halter? What is there about me to mourn, when such men as you risk their all for our country? No, no, no—not a dollar of your gold will I touch; poor America has need of it all!"

The bag dropped from the hand of the officer, and fell at the feet of the peddler, where it lay neglected during the remainder of the interview. The officer looked steadily at the face of his companion, and continued,—

"There are many motives which might govern me, that to you are unknown. Our situations are different; I am known as the leader of armies—but you must descend into the grave with the reputation of a foe to your native land. Remember, that the veil which conceals your true character cannot be raised in years—perhaps never."

Birch again lowered his face, but there was no yielding of the soul in the movement.

"You will soon be old; the prime of your days is already past; what have you to subsist on?"

"These!" said the peddler, stretching forth his hands, that were already embrowned with toil.

"But those may fail you; take enough to secure a support to your age. Remember your risks and cares. I have told you that the characters of men who are much esteemed in life depend on your secrecy; what pledge can I give them of your fidelity?"

"Tell them," said Birch, advancing and unconsciously resting one foot on the bag, "tell them that I would not take the gold!"

The composed features of the officer relaxed into a smile of benevolence, and he grasped the hand of the peddler firmly.

"Now, indeed, I know you; and although the same reasons which have hitherto compelled me to expose your valuable life will still exist, and prevent my openly asserting your character, in private I can always be your friend; fail not to apply to me when in want or suffering, and so long as God giveth to me, so long will I freely share with a man who feels so nobly and acts so well. If sickness or want should ever assail you and peace once more smile upon our efforts, seek the gate of him whom you have so often met as Harper, and he will not blush to acknowledge you."

"It is little that I need in this life," said Harvey; "so long as God gives me health and honest industry, I can never want in this country; but to know that your excellency is my friend is a blessing that I prize more than all the gold of England's treasury."

The officer stood for a few moments in the attitude of intense thought. He then drew to him the desk, and wrote a few lines on a piece of paper, and gave it to the peddler.

"That Providence destines this country to some great and glorious fate I must believe, while I witness the patriotism that pervades the bosoms of her lowest citizens," he said. "It must be dreadful to a mind like yours to descend into the grave, branded as a foe to liberty; but you already know the lives that would be sacrificed, should your real character be revealed. It is impossible to do you justice now, but I fearlessly intrust you with this certificate; should we never meet again, it may be serviceable to your children."

"Children!" exclaimed the peddler, "can I give to a family the infamy of my name?"

The officer gazed at the strong emotion he exhibited with pain, and he made a slight movement towards the gold; but it was arrested by the expression of his companion's face. Harvey saw the intention, and shook his head, as he continued more mildly,—

"It is, indeed, a treasure that your excellency gives me: it is safe, too. There are men living who could say that my life was nothing to me, compared to your secrets. The paper that I told you was lost I swallowed when taken last by the Virginians. It was the only time I ever deceived your excellency, and it shall be the last; yes, this is, indeed, a treasure to me; perhaps," he continued, with a melancholy smile, "it may be known after my death who was my friend; but if it should not, there are none to grieve for me."

"Remember," said the officer, with strong emotion, "that in me you will always have a secret friend; but openly I cannot know you."

"I know it, I know it," said Birch; "I knew it when I took the service. 'Tis probably the last time that I shall ever see your excellency. May God pour down His choicest blessings on your head!" He paused, and moved towards the door. The officer followed him with eyes that expressed deep interest. Once more the peddler turned, and seemed to gaze on the placid, but commanding features of the general with regret and reverence, and, bowing low, he withdrew.

The armies of America and France were led by their illustrious commander against the enemy under Cornwallis, and terminated a campaign in triumph that had commenced in difficulties. Great Britain soon after became disgusted with the war; and the States' independence was acknowledged.

As years rolled by, it became a subject of pride among the different actors in the war, and their descendants, to boast of their efforts in the cause which had confessedly heaped so many blessings upon their country; but the name of Harvey Birch died away among the multitude of agents who were thought to have labored in secret against the rights of their countrymen. His image, however, was often present to the mind of the powerful chief, who alone knew his true character; and several times did he cause secret inquiries to be made into the other's fate, one of which only resulted in any success. By this he learned that a peddler of a different name, but similar appearance, was toiling through the new settlements that were springing up in every direction, and that he was struggling with the advance of years and apparent poverty. Death prevented further inquiries on the part of the officer, and a long period passed before he was again heard of.

CHAPTER XXXV

Some village Hampden, that with dauntless breast
The village tyrant of his fields withstood—
Some mute, inglorious Milton here may rest;
Some Cromwell, guiltless of his country's blood.

—Gray.

It was thirty-three years after the interview which we have just related that an American army was once more arrayed against the troops of England; but the scene was transferred from Hudson's banks to those of the Niagara.

The body of Washington had long lain moldering in the tomb; but as time was fast obliterating the slight impressions of political enmity or personal envy, his name was hourly receiving new luster, and his worth and integrity each moment became more visible, not only to his countrymen, but to the world. He was already the acknowledged hero of an age of reason and truth; and many a young heart, amongst those who formed the pride of our army in 1814, was glowing with the recollection of the one great name of America, and inwardly beating with the sanguine expectation of emulating, in some degree, its renown. In no one were these virtuous hopes more vivid than in the bosom of a young officer who stood on the table rock, contemplating the great cataract, on the evening of the 25th of July of that bloody year. The person of this youth was tall and finely molded, indicating a just proportion between strength and activity; his deep black eyes were of a searching and dazzling brightness. At times, as they gazed upon the flood of waters that rushed tumultuously at his feet, there was a stern and daring look that flashed from them, which denoted the ardor of an enthusiast. But this proud expression was softened by the lines of a mouth around which there played a suppressed archness, that partook of feminine beauty. His hair shone in the setting sun like ringlets of gold, as the air from the falls gently moved the rich curls from a forehead whose whiteness showed that exposure and heat alone had given their darker hue to a face glowing with health. There was another officer standing by the side of this favored youth;

and both seemed, by the interest they betrayed, to be gazing, for the first time, at the wonder of the western world. A profound silence was observed by each, until the companion of the officer that we have described suddenly started, and pointing eagerly with his sword into the abyss beneath, exclaimed,—

"See! Wharton, there is a man crossing in the very eddies of the cataract, and in a skiff no bigger than an eggshell."

"He has a knapsack—it is probably a soldier," returned the other. "Let us meet him at the ladder, Mason, and learn his tidings."

Some time was expended in reaching the spot where the adventurer was intercepted. Contrary to the expectations of the young soldiers, he proved to be a man far advanced in life, and evidently no follower of the camp. His years might be seventy, and they were indicated more by the thin hairs of silver that lay scattered over his wrinkled brow, than by any apparent failure of his system. His frame was meager and bent; but it was the attitude of habit, for his sinews were strung with the toil of half a century. His dress was mean, and manifested the economy of its owner, by the number and nature of its repairs. On his back was a scantily furnished pack, that had led to the mistake in his profession. A few words of salutation, and, on the part of the young men, of surprise, that one so aged should venture so near the whirlpools of the cataract, were exchanged; when the old man inquired, with a voice that began to manifest the tremor of age, the news from the contending armies.

"We whipped the redcoats here the other day, among the grass on the Chippewa plains," said the one who was called Mason; "since when, we have been playing hide and go seek with the ships: but we are now marching back from where we started, shaking our heads, and as surly as the devil."

"Perhaps you have a son among the soldiers," said his companion, with a mild demeanor, and an air of kindness; "if so, tell me his name and regiment, and I will take you to him."

The old man shook his head, and, passing his hand over his silver locks, with an air of meek resignation, he answered,—

"No; I am alone in the world!"

"You should have added. Captain Dunwoodie," cried his careless comrade, "if you could find either; for nearly half our army has marched down the road, and may be, by this time, under the walls of Fort George, for anything that we know to the contrary."

The old man stopped suddenly, and looked earnestly from one of his companions to the other; the action being observed by the soldiers, they paused also.

"Did I hear right?" the stranger uttered, raising his hand to screen his eyes from the rays of the setting sun. "What did he call you?"

"My name is Wharton Dunwoodie," replied the youth, smiling.

The stranger motioned silently for him to remove his hat, which the youth did accordingly, and his fair hair blew aside like curls of silk, and opened the whole of his ingenuous countenance to the inspection of the other.

" 'Tis like our native land!" exclaimed the old man with vehemence, "improving with time; God has blessed both."

"Why do you stare thus, Lieutenant Mason?" cried Captain Dunwoodie, laughing a little. "You show more astonishment than when you saw the falls."

"Oh, the falls!—they are a thing to be looked at on a moonshiny night, by your Aunt Sarah and that gay old bachelor. Colonel Singleton; but a fellow like myself never shows surprise, unless it may be at such a touch as this."

The extraordinary vehemence of the stranger's manner had passed away as suddenly as it was exhibited, but he listened to this speech with deep interest, while Dunwoodie replied, a little gravely,—

"Come, come, Tom, no jokes about my good aunt, I beg; she is kindness itself, and I have heard it whispered that her youth was not altogether happy."

"Why, as to rumor," said Mason, "there goes one in Accomac, that Colonel Singleton offers himself to her regularly every Valentine's day; and there are some who add that your old great-aunt helps his suit."

"Aunt Jeanette!" said Dunwoodie, laughing. "Dear, good soul, she thinks but little of marriage in any shape, I believe, since the death of Dr. Sitgreaves. There were some whispers of a courtship between them formerly, but it ended in nothing but civilities, and I suspect that the whole story arises from the intimacy of Colonel Singleton and my father. You know they were comrades in the horse, as indeed was your own father."

"I know all that, of course; but you must not tell me that the particular, prim bachelor goes so often to General Dunwoodie's plantation merely for the sake of talking old soldier with your father. The last time I was there, that yellow, sharp-nosed housekeeper of your mother's took me into the pantry, and said that the colonel was no despicable match, as she called it, and how the sale of his plantation in Georgia had brought him—oh, Lord! I don't know how much."

"Quite likely," returned the captain, "Katy Haynes is no bad calculator."

They had stopped during this conversation, in uncertainty whether their new companion was to be left or not.

The old man listened to each word as it was uttered, with the most intense interest; but, towards the conclusion of the dialogue, the earnest attention of his countenance changed to a kind of inward smile. He shook his head, and, passing his hands over his forehead, seemed to be thinking of other times. Mason paid but little attention to the expression of his features, and continued,—

"To me, she is selfishness embodied!"

"Her selfishness does but little harm," returned Dunwoodie. "One of her greatest difficulties is her aversion to the blacks. She says that she never saw but one she liked."

"And who was he?"

"His name was Cæsar; he was a house servant of my late grandfather Wharton. You don't remember him, I believe; he died the same year with his master, while we were children. Katy yearly sings his requiem, and, upon my word, I believe he deserved it. I have heard something of his helping my English uncle, as we call General Wharton, in some difficulty that occurred in the old war. My mother always speaks of him with great affection. Both Cæsar and Katy came to Virginia with my mother when she married. My mother was—"

"An angel!" interrupted the old man, in a voice that startled the young soldier by its abruptness and energy.

"Did you know her?" cried the son, with a glow of pleasure on his cheek.

The reply of the stranger was interrupted by sudden and heavy explosions of artillery, which were immediately followed by continued volleys of small arms, and in a few minutes the air was filled with the tumult of a warm and well-contested battle.

The two soldiers hastened with precipitation towards the camp, accompanied by their new acquaintance. The excitement and anxiety created by the approaching fight prevented a continuance of the conversation, and the three held their way to the army, making occasional conjectures on the cause of the fire, and the probability of a general engagement. During their short and hurried walk, Captain Dunwoodie, however, threw several friendly glances at the old man, who moved over the ground with astonishing energy for his years, for the heart of the youth was warmed by an eulogium on a mother that he adored. In a short time they joined the regiment to which the officers belonged, when the captain, squeezing the stranger's hand, earnestly begged that he would make inquiries after him on the following morning, and that he might see him in his own tent. Here they separated.

Everything in the American camp announced an approaching struggle. At a distance of a few miles, the sound of cannon and musketry was heard above the roar of the cataract. The troops were soon in motion, and a movement made to support the division of the army which was already engaged. Night had set in before the reserve and irregulars reached the foot of Lundy's Lane, a road that diverged from the river and crossed a conical eminence, at no great distance from the Niagara highway. The summit of this hill was crowned with the cannon of the British, and in the flat beneath was the remnant of Scott's gallant brigade, which for a long time had held an unequal contest with distinguished bravery. A new line was interposed, and one column of the Americans directed to charge up the hill, parallel to the road. This column took the English in flank, and, bayoneting their artillerists, gained possession of the cannon. They were immediately joined by their comrades, and the enemy was swept from the hill. But large re-enforcements were joining the English general momentarily, and their troops were too brave to rest easy under the defeat. Repeated and bloody charges were made to recover the guns, but in all they were repulsed with slaughter. During the last of these struggles, the ardor of the youthful captain whom we have mentioned urged him to lead his men some distance in advance, to scatter a daring party of the enemy. He succeeded, but in returning to the line missed his lieutenant from the station that he ought to have occupied. Soon after this repulse, which was the last, orders were given to the shattered troops to return to the camp. The British were nowhere to be seen, and preparations were made to take in such of the wounded as could be moved. At this moment Wharton Dunwoodie, impelled by affection for his friend, seized a lighted fusee, and taking two of his men went himself in quest of his body, where he was supposed to have fallen. Mason was found on the side of the hill, seated with great composure, but unable to walk from a fractured leg. Dunwoodie saw and flew to the side of his comrade, saying,—

"Ah! dear Tom, I knew I should find you the nearest man to the enemy."

"Softly, softly; handle me tenderly," replied the lieutenant. "No, there is a brave fellow still nearer than myself, and who he can be I know not. He rushed out of our smoke, near my platoon, to make a prisoner or some such thing, but, poor fellow, he never came back; there he lies just over the hillock. I have spoken to him several times, but I fancy he is past answering."

Dunwoodie went to the spot, and to his astonishment beheld the aged stranger.

"It is the old man who knew my mother!" cried the youth. "For her sake he shall have honorable burial; lift him, and let him be carried in; his bones shall rest on native soil."

The men approached to obey. He was lying on his back, with his face exposed to the glaring light of the fusee; his eyes were closed, as if in slumber; his lips, sunken with years, were slightly moved from their natural position, but it seemed more like a smile than a convulsion which had caused the change. A soldier's musket lay near him; his hands were pressed upon his breast, and one of them contained a substance that glittered like silver. Dunwoodie stooped, and removing the limbs, perceived the place where the bullet had found a passage to his heart. The subject of his last care was a tin box, through which the fatal lead had gone; and the dying moments of the old man must have passed in drawing it from his bosom. Dunwoodie opened it, and found a paper in which, to his astonishment, he read the following:—

"Circumstances of political importance, which involve the

lives and fortunes of many, have hitherto kept secret what this paper now reveals. Harvey Birch has for years been a faithful and unrequited servant of his country. Though man does not, may God reward him for his conduct!

"GEO. WASHINGTON."

It was the SPY OF THE NEUTRAL GROUND, who died as he had lived, devoted to his country, and a martyr to her liberties.

1964222R00220

Printed in Great Britain
by Amazon.co.uk, Ltd.,
Marston Gate.